W9-ADW-609

HALFWAY
HOME

Also by Paul Monette

NOVELS

Taking Care of Mrs. Carroll
The Gold Diggers
The Long Shot
Lightfall
Afterlife

POEMS

The Carpenter at the Asylum
No Witnesses
Love Alone: 18 Elegies for Rog

NONFICTION

Borrowed Time: An AIDS Memoir

HALFWAY HOME

PAUL MONETTE

CROWN PUBLISHERS, INC.
NEW YORK

A portion of this book previously appeared in *Men on Men 3*.

Copyright © 1991 by Paul Monette

All rights reserved. No part of this book may be reproduced or transmitted in any form or by any means, electronic or mechanical, including photocopying, recording, or by any information storage and retrieval system, without permission in writing from the publisher.

Published by Crown Publishers, Inc., 201 East 50th Street, New York, New York 10022. Member of the Crown Publishing Group.

CROWN is a trademark of Crown Publishers, Inc.

Manufactured in the United States of America

Library of Congress Cataloging-in-Publication Data
Monette, Paul.
    Halfway home / Paul Monette.
    I. Title.
    PS3563.0523H35 1991   90-22933
    813'.54—dc20   CIP

ISBN 0-517-58329-1

10 9 8 7 6 5 4 3 2 1

First Edition

Stephen Kolzak
my guerrilla, my love
1953–1990

There are no words anymore.

HALFWAY
HOME

O N E

M Y BROTHER USED TO TELL ME I WAS THE DEVIL. THIS would be while he was torturing me—not beating me up exactly, since he didn't want to hurt his knuckles and maybe miss a game. But he'd pounce and drag me to the floor and pin my shoulders with his knees. Then he'd snap his fingers against my nose, or drool spit in my face while I bucked and jerked my head, or singe my hair with matches. He was ten, I was seven. Already he had enormous strength. I never thought of Brian as a kid. He'd loom above me with that flame-red Irish hair, his blue eyes dancing wickedly, and he was brute and cruel as any man. There are boys in Ireland now throwing pipe bombs and torching cars. That was Brian, a terrorist before his time. And I was his mortal enemy.

"Is Tommy gonna cry now?" he'd taunt me, rubbing those knuckles across my scalp. "You big fuckin' baby."

And I would, I'd cry, not from pain but sorrow. I'd blubber and bite my lip till Brian would release me in disgust, full of immense disdain because I couldn't take it. He'd lumber away and grab his glove, off to find one of his buddies from Saint Augustine's, tough like him. I'd stare in the mirror above the dresser in the room we shared, still gasping the sobs away, hating my sallow skin and my blue-black crewcut.

That's why I was so diabolical to him, because I didn't look anything like Brian or Dad, both of them fair and freckled, lobster-red in the summer sun, big in the shoulders like stevedores. I got all the Italian blood instead from Mom's side, so that I was the only Sicilian in a mick neighborhood. Hell, it seemed the whole county was Irish, from Hartford all the way to New Haven. And the Irish hated everybody, especially wops. So I never stood a chance, lean and olive and alien as I was. But the reason I cried had nothing to do with my differentness, not then. It was because I wasn't good enough to play with my big brother. This boy who never ceased to make me suffer, beating me down and plucking my wings like a hapless fly, and all I ever seemed to feel was that I'd failed him.

I haven't thought about any of that in twenty years. Well, nine anyway: since the day my father was buried in the blue-collar graveyard behind Saint Augustine's. Brian and I had our last words then, raw and rabid, finishing one another off. He was twenty-eight, I was twenty-five, though in fact we hadn't really spoken for at least ten years before that. As soon as Brian understood I was queer—and I swear he knew it before I did—he iced me out for good. No more roughhouse, no more nugies and body checks. I didn't exist anymore. By then of course Brian had become a delirious high school hero, the darling of the Brothers as he glided from season to effortless season, football and hockey and baseball. Me, I was so screwed up I missed being tormented by him. I played no games myself.

It doesn't matter anymore. I sit out here on this terrace, three thousand miles from the past, and stare down the bluff to the weed-choked ocean, and the last thing I think of is Chester, Connecticut. Once a day, toward sunset, I walk down the blasted wooden stairs jerry-built into the fold of the cliff, eighty steps to the beach below. At the bottom I sit at the lip of the shallow cave that opens behind the steps, the winter tide churning before me, the foam almost reaching my toes.

I brood about all the missed chances, the failures of nerve, but I never go back as far as being a kid. I put all that behind me when I came out, Brian and Dad and their conspiracy of silence. I never look in the mirror if I can help it. My real life stretches from coming out to here, fifteen years. *That's* what I'm greedy for more of. Sometimes out of nowhere perfect strangers will ask: "You got any brothers and sisters?" No, I say, I was an only child. I never had any time for that family porn, even when I had all the time in the world.

Which I don't have now. I know it as clear as anything when I turn and climb the eighty steps up. I take it very slow, gripping the rotting banister as I puff my way. This is my daily encounter with what I've lost in stamina. The neuropathy in my left leg throbs with every step. I wheeze and gulp for air. But I also love the challenge, climbing the mountain because it's there, proving every day that the nightmare hasn't won yet.

The cliff cascades with ice plant, a blanket of gaudy crimson that nearly blinds in the setting sun. The gray terns wheel above me, cheering me on. I feel like I'm claiming a desert island, the first man ever to scale this height. As I reach the top, where a row of century cactus guards the bluff with a hundred swords, I can look back and see a quarter mile down Trancas Beach, empty and all mine, the rotting sandstone cliffs clean as the end of the world.

Not that the Baldwins own all of it anymore. The beach house on the bluff sits in the middle of five acres, shaded by old trees, shaggy eucalyptus and sycamores eight feet thick, no neighbors in sight on either side. To the north is a pop singer's compound, a great white whale of a house that's visible from the coast road, all its new-planted trees still puny and struggling for purchase. To the south an aerospace mogul has gussied himself a Norman pile complete with drawbridge and watchtower, which the surfers in the Trancas Wash call Camelot.

The Baldwin place is like none of these—a lazy, overgrown bungalow with red-tile roof, balconies off the bedrooms, and a drizzling Moorish fountain in the courtyard. Built in 1912, when the Baldwins *did* own as far as the eye can see, twenty-two miles of coastline all the way south through Malibu to the edge of Santa Monica. Till the thirties this was the only house on the water, with a bare dirt road that snaked up into the mountains where the big ranch house stood, seat of a vast Spanish land grant. Gray remembers his Baldwin aunts saying the only way to the beach house was half a day's ride on horseback from the ranch.

That's how it feels to me still after two months here, remote and inaccessible. I've only had to leave twice, to go see my doctor in Hollywood, about an hour away—who had the gall to tell me I was fine, without a trace of irony. "He's right," insisted Gray, who drove me there and back, "you look terrific."

I'll say this much: considering I'm on Medi-Cal, living on six-hundred-bucks-a-month disability, I'm doing very well to be in a house in a eucalyptus grove, with a view that seems to go all the way to Hawaii. No hit record, no Pentagon kickbacks, and I live like a fucking rock star. You get very used to being lord of all you survey.

But even here reality intrudes. Yesterday was full of portents, now I see that. I didn't go down to the beach till almost five, because I woke up late from my nap. The sun was already dancing on the ocean when I started, and gone below by the time I reached the sand. Immediately it was colder, even with the gold and purple rockets trailing in the afterglow. I saw right away there was junk in the mouth of the cave, beer cans and an empty bag of chips. I was furious. I snatched up the litter, grumbling at the trespass. The property line goes to mid-tide. In theory nobody ought to walk on my three hundred yards of beach at all.

I started back up the stairs sour as a Republican. No one had ever violated my grotto before. Maybe a sign was in order: QUARANTINE—INFECTIOUS WASTE. NO LOITERING. THIS MEANS YOU. Then about step sixty I got this terrible stab in my heart—doubled me over. I dropped the trash and sagged against the crimson ice. Oh shit, I was going to die of a heart attack. Even in my bone-zero panic I could feel a sort of black laughter welling up inside. Leave it to Tom Shaheen not to die of AIDS, after all that drama and street theater.

It passed as quick as it came but left me heaving, clammy with cold sweat. For a minute I was scared to breathe too deep, and kept kneading my chest in a fruitless amateur version of CPR. But the pain was gone. If anything, there was a queer feeling of utter emptiness at the center of the chest, the way you feel when someone walks out on you.

I took the last twenty steps most gingerly. It was folly to think my little coronary event wasn't AIDS-related. I was probably heading for a massive stroke, the virus in my spinal column swirling like eels in a sunken ship, and I'd end up mute and paralyzed. Generally I don't waste a minute, especially out here in Trancas, figuring how short my time is. I've been at this thing for a year and a half, three if you count all the fevers and rashes. I operate on the casual assumption that I've still got a couple of years, give or take a galloping lymphoma. Day to day I'm not a dying man, honestly.

But I reached the top pretty winded and shaken, gazing down the bluff with a melancholy dread that things could change any minute. I've given up everything else but this, I thought; don't let me lose this too, my desert island. I couldn't have said exactly whom I was addressing, some local god of the bluff. Not big-G God. I've been on Her hit list now for a long time. If She's really out there, I'm douched.

Then I saw Mona. She lay on one of the white chaises, her back to me and the view, smoking a cigarette. From the top of the beach stairs it's maybe twenty paces across the lawn to the terrace. I flinched and tried to think if I could sneak around her, but no way.

Mona's like my sister, she doesn't have to call first. But after my *crise de coeur* I wanted to collapse. And Mona doesn't indulge me like Gray. She wants me *up*. For a renegade dyke committed to anarchy, in fact, she is remarkably Donna Reed in her dealings with me, cutting the crusts off sandwiches.

I started across the lawn, emitting a tentative whimper. Mona turned in startled delight. "Pumpkin! I've just come from the workshop!" She leaped off the chaise and darted toward me. Her tortoise-rim glasses covered half her face, her platinum hair beveled and moussed. "They were appalling, all of them," she said, reaching a hand with black-painted nails and scratching the hair on my chest. "Dumb little stand-up routines, clubfoot dances, thrift-shop chic. The usual. But oh, there was this girl from Torrance, squeaky clean—"

She stopped and peered more closely at my face. "*Cara mia,* are you all right? You're looking more than usual like the French leftenant's woman."

"I just had a heart attack."

"Come on, I'll make you hot chocolate." See? Very Mom-is-it-lunch-yet. "I brought you a tin of shortbread. Twenty-two bucks at Neiman's. Now this *girl.* Rosy as a cheerleader, practically carrying pompoms. I was wet all day."

She steered me across the terra-cotta terrace, through the peeling colonnade and into the musty cool of the house. I tried on a pouting scowl, but Mona was off, full of raptures about her little bimbette from Torrance. In the kitchen I sat at the zinc-top table, a palimpsest of dents and scratches, while Mona free-floated about, putting the milk to boil.

The workshop she speaks of is Introduction to Performance, a grab-bag of mime and movement and "auto-exploration," thirty dollars for three Saturday sessions, a veritable magnet for the egregiously untalented. But it keeps the wolf from the door of AGORA—our feisty open space in Venice that we reclaimed from a ball-point pen factory, famous throughout the netherworld of Performance, with its own FBI file to boot. Except "our" is not exactly right. It's Mona's. I am no longer an impresario.

"Someone was looking for you today," says Mona, mixing the cocoa.

"A rabid fan, perhaps."

"Some guy. Looked like he sold insurance. He came by during

the break—said nobody'd seen you around your apartment since Christmas."

"Probably sent to cancel my disability. I've been getting these 'Aren't you dead yet' letters from Sacramento."

We took the tray of chocolate and biscuits into the parlor. Through the arched gallery windows the sunset had turned to dusty rose. Mona went to the woodbox, knelt, and laid a fire, more butch than I. I cozied up in an afghan as old as the shedding velvet that covered the swayback sofa. No one has bothered to upgrade anything at the beach house, not for decades. When Gray dies this last piece of the Baldwin vastness will be disposed of, and then some starlet can swath it in white upholstery, so it looks like everyone else's house. Meanwhile the tattiness and furred edges are just my cup of tea.

Once the fire is crackling, Mona snuggles in under the afghan with me. "You know," she says conspiratorially, "we don't have anything set for tomorrow night. Queen Isabella canceled—the piece isn't ready. If you just did forty-five minutes, you'd save our ass." I begin to shake my head slowly, as if I have a slight crick in my neck. "Oh, Tommy, why not?" says Mona, more pettish now. "It'd do you good. You're stronger than you realize."

I turn and give her a withering look. Mona is of the persuasion, diametrically opposed to the "Aren't you dead yet" theory, that I am not really *sick* sick, and thus should push my limits. "My life on the stage is like a dream to me now," I reply in a dusky Garbo voice. "I have put away childish things."

"People still call and ask, 'When are you having Miss Jesus?' I swear, we could fill the place three months running."

Mona sighs. She knows I am not convinceable. Not that I'm unsympathetic. I understand the longing for a breakthrough gig that sets the whole town buzzing. In the first two years of AGORA, before I retired, Miss Jesus was a sensation whenever I did it. Bomb threats would pour in, and church groups from Pacoima would picket back and forth in the parking lot, practically speaking in tongues. Mona and I were devastated to have only ninety-nine seats, with ten standees additional permitted by the fire laws, because at the height of the outrage we could have packed two-fifty in.

I lay my head on her shoulder and offer her the plate of shortbread. She shakes her head no thanks. We sit there slumped against each other, watching the fire, not needing to talk. I love the smoky elusiveness of Mona's perfume, a scent she swears is the very same Dietrich wears, a beauty tip passed in whispers through the shadowy dyke underground. She seems more pensive than I today, unusual for her, an action girl. I think she's about to ask me something about my illness, like how do I stand it, but she says, "Do you ever think about your brother?"

I shoot her the most baleful look I can summon. "In a word, no."

"But don't you ever wonder? He's prob'ly got kids—" She waves her hands in a circular motion, flailing with possibilities. "I mean he could be *dead*, and you wouldn't even know."

If anything I grow more icily impassive. "I believe I'm the one who's passing away around here."

"Don't be defensive. I just wondered."

"Mona, how is it you are the only person in the world who knows this person exists, and yet you forget the punch line. He *loathes* me. I make his skin crawl. I have not imagined these things. He said them, over and over for years, knuckles white with passion. Get it?"

She pulls her head slightly in under the afghan, rather like a blond turtle. Cautiously she observes, "People change."

I scramble out of my side of the blanket. Kneeling almost on top of her, I push my face close and hiss: "Girl, what's your problem today? I did not request an Ann Landers consultation. I *hope* he's dead, frankly, may he rot in hell. And I hope his orphan children are begging with bowls in the street—"

"Sorry I brought it up."

"Well, it's a little late for that now, isn't it?"

I'm actually feeling rather juiced, more energy than I've had in days. Mona knows I'm not going to actually pummel her. I'm a total wimp, abuse-wise. She may even think it's good for me to blow off steam. I am speechless though as I pant with rage, my head reeling with images of Brian. Midfield, running for daylight. Serving Mass with Father Donegan. Riding away laughing in his first new car, surrounded by his mick buddies, leaving me in the driveway eating their exhaust. Not even the really painful stuff, the punishment and the hatred, and still I want to let out a primal scream, as if I know I have to die before all of this is really put to rest.

Then we hear a knocking on the screen door in the kitchen. And the really strange thing is this: suddenly Mona looks terrified. As I clamber off the sofa to go and answer, her face is ashen, the hand on my arm beseeching, as if I am about to let a monster in.

I *know* who it is. I zap Mona with a perplexed frown—what's *she* on—as I amble into the kitchen. "Coming!"

Gray stands resolutely on the back stoop, a bag of groceries in either arm, which was why he couldn't let himself in. The beach house is never locked, unlike the compounds on either side, which have laser rays and aerial surveillance. "Did I say I needed anything?" I ask as I bang the door wide.

"Just a few staples," he says, trooping by me to set the bags on the zinc table. Then turns and searches my face. "How you feeling?"

Earnest Gray, in drab and rumpled Brooks Brothers mufti, his wispy vanishing hair somehow making him look younger than his fifty-one years. But then WASPs on the high end age in an absentminded fashion, like the old shoes they never throw away. In addition to which, Gray has been effectively retired his whole life. He is also the least vain man I have ever known.

"I had heart failure coming up from the beach, but otherwise I'm dandy. How much was all this?" I grab my jacket from behind the door to pull out my wallet, but Gray, who is already unloading muffins and ginger ale, waves vaguely, as if money is something vulgar that gentlemen don't discuss. "Gray, you can't keep buying me groceries."

And I wave twenty dollars by his shoulder, but he has that maddening WASP habit of pretending things aren't happening. "I thought I'd barbecue tonight," he says with boyish enthusiasm, and I lay the twenty on the table, in no-man's-land.

The irony is, Gray doesn't have a lot to spare, despite being the last of one of the nine families that owned California. There's a trust, of course, and coupons to clip, and the beach house is his for life, as well as the gardener's cottage on the ranch where he's lived for twenty-five years. But none of this amounts to very much actual cash, because the old man poured almost everything into his wacko foundation, funding white supremacist day camps and fag-bash seminars, that sort of thing. Still, with all those connections no one ever expected Gray to grow up to be a loser, unable to make his own harvest in the Reagan fields of money. On the contrary, he's spent most of his life giving away his share, as a sort of patron saint of the avant-garde.

"That one he injected looks smaller to me," observes Gray, slapping a couple of steaks on the counter. He's talking about the eggplant-purple lesion on my right cheek, the size of a dime. This is the only public sign of my leprous state, and on my last visit the doctor gave it a direct hit of chemo. It doesn't look any different to me. Gray is the only one who ever mentions my lesion. Everyone else steps around it, like a turd on the carpet. "And look, we'll make some guacamole," he says, triumphantly producing three dented avocadoes.

Then Mona is standing in the doorway, giving a hopeless impersonation of demure. Gray spots her and instantly wilts. "Oh I'm sorry," he murmurs fretfully, unable to meet our eyes, gazing with dismay at all the groceries he's unpacked, as if he's come to the wrong place.

"Listen, I was just leaving, you guys go ahead," declares Mona magnanimously.

"Don't be silly, there's plenty," I say, perversely enjoying their twin discomfort. They don't exactly dislike each other, but they're like in-laws from different marriages, unrelated except by bad shit. "*You* make the margaritas," I command Mona with a bony finger.

And because I am the sick boy, what can they do? Guilt has gotten more dinners on the table than hunger ever dreamed of. Mona goes right to the liquor cabinet, and Gray is already peeling the avocadoes. Like a veritable matchmaker I decide to give them some time alone and run up to my room for a sweater.

First thing I do, I check my cheek in the mirror. Maybe he's right, one edge is faintly lighter, but nothing to write home about. It's not like I could cruise a boy at the Malibu Safeway. I move to shut the balcony doors, catching a glimpse of the gibbous moon as it flings its pearls on the water. Then I grab my red-checked crew-neck from the dresser and shrug it on.

Though I only brought a single duffel bag with me here when I came just after New Year's, right away this place felt more like home than my own place ever did. My bleak one-bedroom in West Hollywood, with a view out over four dumpsters, looks like a garage sale driven indoors by rain. Nothing nice or comfortable, not a nesting person's space by any stretch. Whereas here I have a lovely overstuffed chaise across from the bed, swathed in a faded Arcadian chintz, and a blue-painted wicker table by the window with shelves underneath for books. The ancient curtains are swagged and fringed and look like they would crumble at the touch. If it sounds a bit Miss Havisham, don't forget the sea breeze blowing through clean as sunlight every day.

Above the mahogany bed is a poster of Miss Jesus. The cross is propped against the wall at AGORA, and I'm leaning against it in full drag, pulling up my caftan to show a little leg. The expression on my face can only be called abandoned. My crown of thorns is cocked at a rakish angle. In the lower right-hand corner, in Gothic script, it says *"Oh Mary!"*

This is only the third time I've managed to put Mona and Gray together, and I find myself excited by the prospect of spending an evening, just us three. The two of them have come to be my most immediate family, somewhat by elimination, my friends all having died, but I couldn't have chosen better. I realize I want them to know each other as well as I know them, for when it gets bad. When I'm curled in a ball and can't play anymore, sucking on a respirator, and then of course when it's over. They'll be good for each other, so opposite in every way.

I've forgiven Mona already for bringing up Brian. It clearly won't happen again; she's not *that* dumb. The memory overload has passed, and once again my brother has faded into the septic murk of the past. What surprises me is this: as I trot down the spiral stair and hear my two friends laughing in the kitchen, I am so happy that some part of my heart kicks in and takes back the curse. *I hope you're not dead and your kids are great.* That's all. Good-bye. Fini.

Gray is regaling Mona with the tale of his three Baldwin aunts—Cora, Nonny, and Foo. Mona is riveted. These three estimable ladies, maiden sisters of Gray's grandfather, the old rancher tycoon himself, had the beach house built for themselves and resided here every summer for sixty years. I who have heard this all before never tire of the least detail.

We bear the steaks and our margaritas out the kitchen door to the side terrace, where Gray lights the gas barbecue. At the other end of the arbor we can hear the fountain playing. The moon is all the light we need. It's too cold to actually eat outside, but for now there's something delicious about being together around the fire, knocking down tequila and imagining the aunts.

"They used to put on plays and musicales, right here," says Gray, gesturing down the arbor, then to the gentle slope of lawn beside it. "We'd all sit out there. I don't remember the plays, except Foo wrote them. They were very peculiar."

"And none of these women ever married?" Mona stares over the rim of her drink into the shadows of the arbor, willfully trying to conjure them. "Were they ugly?"

"Oh no, they were all very striking. Wonderful masses of hair, even when they were old ladies. And they wore these flowing gowns like Greek statues."

"They sound like Isadora Duncan," I say.

"They sound like dykes," Mona declares emphatically, then turns to Gray. "Weren't they?"

I feel this sudden protective urge toward Gray, as he lays the steaks sizzling on the grill. He has barely ever admitted to me that he's gay himself. There's not a whole lot to admit, I gather. He seems to carry on his rounded shoulders centuries of repression. But now he shrugs easily as he slathers on the barbecue sauce. "You'd have to ask them," he declares. "I never really gave it a thought. Something tells me they never really did either."

Mona is very quiet, but the answer seems to satisfy her. I have a bit of a brood myself, thinking how much the history of my tribe lies behind veils of ambiguity. Ever since I've been at the beach I've had this romantic longing, wishing I'd lived here during the aunts' heyday. But now I wonder, were they happy? Or were they trapped, making the best of it, away from the rigid straightness of the ranch? They seem more real to me tonight than half the people I know in L.A., who can't take my illness and talk to me funny, as if I'm a ghost.

"Isn't it curious, Tom," Mona says softly. "They ran a little art space, just like us."

Gray laughs. "Not quite. You guys are much more over the edge." He says this proudly. "Their stuff was more like a *school* play. Historical pageants, that kind of thing."

He bends and studies the meat, poking it with a finger. And yet, amateur though the aunts may have been, they were obviously the core influence on their oddball great-nephew. Gray Baldwin was subsidizing beat poets and jazz players in Venice—a hundred here, a hundred there, covering rents and bad habits—when he was still in high school. If you were way-out enough, dancing barefoot on broken glass, painting the sand by the Venice pier, Gray was your biggest fan. All the while, of course, he was having a sort of extended breakdown, growing more and more dysfunctional, estranged from the Baldwin throne. And no one pretends that Gray put his money on names that lasted or broke through to greatness. Marginal they stayed, like Gray himself.

"Still," Mona says puckishly, "I wish I'd had women like that around. In my house the drift was very home ec."

"I don't want to overcook it," Gray murmurs gravely, "but I can't really see."

"I'll go get the flashlight," pipes in Mona, darting for the kitchen.

"And I'll set the table." I hurry in after her. We are both laughing, at nothing really. Not drunk at all, just glad to be here together. Mona doesn't have to say she finally gets Gray Baldwin; I know it already. She grabs the flashlight from the shelf above the stove, while I fetch plates and three not-too-bent forks. We will have to share the steak knife. Minimal, everything's minimal here—that's the way the beach house works.

Mona is lurching toward the screen door, I am making for the dining room, when suddenly she turns. "I love you, Tom," she says, blinking behind her tortoise rims, half blushing at the overdose of sentiment.

"Yeah," I reply laconically, but she knows what I mean.

In the dining room I set us up at the big round pedestal table, the base of which is as thick as the mast of a schooner. In the center of the table is a bowl of white-flecked red camellias, three full blooms floating in water. These I picked days ago from the bushes behind the garage. They last a week in water, which is why I like them. Most cut flowers are dead by morning, just like all my friends. I move to the sideboard and pull a drawer. Laid inside are heaps of mismatched napkins, from damask to burlap. I take out three that are vaguely the same shade of green, and caper around the table setting them under the forks.

Through the window from the courtyard Gray and Mona call in unison: "It's ready!"

"Great!" I bellow back at them, tucking the last napkin, and then I look up—

And Brian is there.

For a second I think I've died. He's standing in the archway into the parlor, the dwindling firelight flickering over him. He can't be real, and for the moment neither am I. But he is more stunned than I am. He gapes at me, and his mouth quivers, speechless. He wears a dark suit and tie as if he's going to a funeral. Still it's more like a dream—I *want* it to be a dream. Somehow I've summoned him up by too much invoking his name.

Then he says, "Tommy, I should've called. But I didn't know how."

The beach house has no phone. Brian is apologizing. I'm very slow, like I'm still dreaming. Finally I say, "Mom died?"

"No, she's the same."

But then why has he come, and *how?* Nobody knows I'm here. Merrily through the kitchen the others come parading in, Gray with the steaks on a platter, Mona bearing the salad. They stop laughing as soon as they see the pair of us standing frozen. I turn helplessly to make the introductions, and suddenly I understand. Gray is completely bewildered, but Mona gives a brief shy nod in Brian's direction. It's Mona who's betrayed me! All that bullshit about the stranger at the theater, the *faux*-innocent speculations about my long-lost brother. Without being tortured even a little she gave out the full particulars of my whereabouts.

"Gray Baldwin, this is my brother, Brian," I say with chill formality. And as Gray steps forward to shake his hand I add with acid tongue, not looking at Mona, "I gather you know Ms. Aronson."

"I was out on business, Tommy," Brian says. His face is thicker and slightly doughy, the dazzle gone. "I just decided to wing it and come say hello. But then I couldn't find you, and then"—he makes a fruitless gesture, vaguely in Mona's direction—"I couldn't leave till I saw you."

I am so unbelievably calm, considering. "Well, you've seen me," I retort, giving no quarter.

Gray's super-WASP manners can't stand it. "We're just about to eat. Will you join us?"

"No no, I ate already, you go ahead."

There's a general fluster of embarrassment, everyone clucking apologetically. Gray and Mona hurry to take their seats. Gray beckons insistently to Brian, indicating that he should sit, even if he's not eating. I stand stonily, and Brian makes no move.

Gray and Mona are serving the dinner so fast it's like Keystone Kops, a blur of slapstick. Finally, because even I don't have it in me to just say get out, I relent and nod curtly to Brian, and he follows my lead and sits. Instantly a plate of sliced steak and salad is plunked in front of me. Gray and Mona are already eating, as fast as they can, smiling gelidly at my brother.

I stare across at Brian. "So. What've *you* been doing the last nine years?"

He doesn't know if the question is real, or just a caustic put-down. Neither do I. "Oh, same old grind," he replies, studying his hands. His hair is still like fire. "I got married," he adds almost sheepishly.

I say nothing. Mona, downing the dregs of her margarita, gives it another go. "And he has a son. Seven, right?" She beams encouragement.

"Right. Daniel," Brian responds, and then shifts the weight of his big shoulders forward, almost yearning across the table toward me. "What about you, huh? She showed me around the theater. That's great."

"I've got AIDS."

Brian looks down. "Yeah, she said."

I turn to Mona. "I don't know why we're bothering. I believe you've covered the major points."

"Tom, give it a break." It's Gray, who never makes the slightest ripple of protest, so it must be bad. "Eat," he says.

And so I do. Anything to stop this racing panic of rage. I cut my meat into little pieces, tasting the char on my tongue like the ashes of all I've lost. I listen with genuine curiosity to the surreal conversation they have without me. As it's Brian's first trip to L.A., they speak of the weather, the smog, how it all looks like a movie set. I am already looking anxiously at Gray's and Mona's plates, realizing they are nearly done, and they aren't about to stick around for ice cream.

Brian is telling about his own house, on a marshy shore in Connecticut, 1710 and picture perfect. Again I hear the old chatter from Gray, the aunts and the ranch and the musicales, twenty-two miles of beachfront free as Eden. But now it isn't charming anymore. I feel threatened and helpless, not wanting Brian to know so much. It's as if my desert island is being stolen, right in front of my nose.

But the story fascinates Brian, who explains that he works for a builder, same job he's had for fifteen years. "Tommy knows him," he says, glancing a small remark in my direction, but nobody really looks at me. We are all just getting through this. Nevertheless, the last thing I will do is acknowledge Jerry Curran, the pigfuck who rode shotgun through my brother's arrogant youth.

Mona lays her fork and knife side by side on her empty plate. I give her a pleading look as she announces she has to leave for the theater. When Gray takes the cue, siding the dishes, drawling that he'll be heading back to the ranch, Brian looks as desperate as I do. Either of them might have stayed, I realize, if I hadn't been acting so truculent. Clearly I have bought this meeting one on one with Brian with my own special hoard of bitter pennies.

I have no choice but to follow Mona and Gray through the kitchen and out to the yard, chattering as if nothing's wrong. What's so unusual, after all? A guy's brother drops by to surprise him. It's the most natural thing in the world that they'd want to be alone. I lean my elbows on the windowsill of Mona's Toyota as she starts the car. She turns and plants a kiss on my nose. "God, he must've been beautiful," she sighs. "Now take it easy, okay? Fratricide is very hard to clean up."

"Don't worry, this is going to be short and sweet."

"And remember, I need forty-five minutes tomorrow night."

I laugh heartily, pulling back as she swings the car around. I haven't performed in fifteen months, since the week the first lesion appeared on my arm. I move to the pickup as it pulls out of the garage. I shove my hands in my pockets and grin at Gray in the truck. We never touch good-bye or any other time. "Thanks for dinner."

"I'll be down Monday to fix that screen," he says. "Remind me to check the fuses." Endlessly polite, Gray wouldn't dream of saying too much about my brother. Family is something you talk about at a distance of three generations.

"I thought I had run away far enough that no one would ever find me."

Gray chuckles. "Foo always said we never should've let 'em build that coast road."

"I'm with Foo," I declare, waving as he drives away, crunching over the gravel. At the end of the drive he doesn't turn and follow Mona down the infamous Highway 1, but shoots across all three lanes and heads straight up the mountain road through the moonlit chaparral. I turn and head back to the torments of Chester, Connecticut.

Brian is standing in the parlor by the fire. He's taken off his jacket and loosened his tie, and he's paging through an old scrapbook, yellowing photos of picnics out on the bluff, aunts in costume, miles of open space. "This is quite a place," he says cheerfully. "You rent it by the month?"

"It's free," I reply flatly. "Was there something specific you wanted?"

He closes the album and sets it down, wearily shaking his head. Just in that second, sullen and heavy, he reminds me of my father. "Tommy, we shouldn't be strangers. We never should've let all this time go by."

"Really? I was for giving it a couple of millennia—you know, like they do for toxic waste." He turns to me full-face, his arms beginning to reach toward me, and I have this flash that he's going to drag me down. I scuttle back a pace and hurl my next volley. "I believe where we left it was that I caused Dad's stroke because I was queer. Jerry Curran and Father whatsis were holding you back, remember? So you wouldn't kill the little fag. Am I forgetting the nice part?"

I can see the zing of pain across his furrowed brow. It excites me that I've made my brother wince—a first. "So I was wrong," says Brian, weirdly meek and powerless. He also seems to have a set speech he needs to get through. "I treated you terrible. I hated my own brother, just because he was gay. I don't want it to be that way anymore."

If it's meant to disarm me, it succeeds. Suddenly I feel drained and almost weepy, but not for Brian's sake. I step past him and slump down heavily on the sofa, the afghan curling instinctively over my legs. The whole drama of coming out—the wrongheaded yammer, the hard acceptance—seems quaint and irrelevant now. Perhaps I prefer my brother to stay a pig, because it's simpler. And even though he's not the Greek god he used to be, fleshier now and slightly ruined, I feel *more* sick and frail in his presence. Not just because of AIDS, but like I'm the nerd from before, too.

"You can't understand," I say, almost a whisper. "All my friends have died."

There is a long, long silence before he speaks again. He sits on the arm of a battered easy chair, and I feel how uncomfortable he is in this room. The dowdiness unnerves him. Our sainted mother kept her house tidy enough for brain surgery. But it's more than that: he can't stand not being on his own turf. He's always been a neighborhood tough, the same as Jerry Curran, their territory staked, pissing the borders like a dog.

"I didn't have any idea," says Brian, "that all this was happening. I'd read about it and push it out of my mind. Nobody we know—" He stops, thinking he's said the wrong thing. But I don't care. His ignorance is oddly comforting, proving I don't have to like him. "It just hasn't touched our world. Is there anything I can do?"

"Sure," I say. "Find a cure. And then we'll sprinkle it all over Mike Manihan's grave, and Ronnie's and Bruce's and Tim's, and we'll all be as good as new."

Protracted silence again. This could go on all night, at this rate. I see him stealing little looks at me, fixed no doubt on the purple on my cheek. I wonder how sick I look otherwise, compared to a decade ago. In between I had some years where I felt pretty sexy. Pumped my tits regular, rode my bike with my shirt off, and connected up with a run of men as dazzling as any on Brian's team. Now I feel pained, almost cheated, that he can't know what I was like, that I had it all for a while. Not that I was so beautiful, or anybody's hero, but a man after my own kind.

Then I hate myself for caring what he thinks. The whole idea of talking about myself seems like a kind of special pleading. "So tell me, what're they like? Daniel and—I don't even know her name."

"Susan." Visibly he relaxes. Home turf. "Oh, they're terrific. Best thing could've happened to me."

And he's off on a staggering round of clichés, as if none of the rest of this lurching conversation had ever happened. Susan teaches special ed, and Daniel plays peewee hockey. A pair of golden retrievers and a summer place in the Berkshires. Somewhere in there the crusts are cut off the bread. Brian is hypnotized by the sound of his own voice, pouring it out like an aria, morning in America. He makes it all sound like the fifties, a decade I only caught the tail end of, but even at three years old I wanted to poop all over it.

"We go see her on Sundays," Brian says, and I realize he's talking about my mother. "She's pretty bad. Barely knows who I am. But she seems to like seeing Daniel."

Within a year of Dad's death she was in a fog, and two years later she'd shrill into the phone: "Who? I don't have a son. I don't have any children at all." Somehow she remembered only her miscarriages, before Brian and me. I never called again.

"At least she's still in her own house," declares Brian with passionate Irish pride. This is the kicker, that our zombie mother gets to wander through her lace-curtain rooms, frail as a Belleek cup, instead of being a veggie in a nursing home. Nothing in Brian's voice betrays that he's bitter about having to shoulder this burden himself, or pay for the daily nurse/companion.

Then he segues into a peroration about his business, and here I really tune out. I remember the great drama that erupted when Brian graduated Fordham, deciding not to go after the glittering prizes of Wall Street, opting instead to throw in his lot with Jerry Curran. It was the only time I ever recall my father faltering in his worship of Brian, who had to woo the old man shamelessly to convince him Curran Construction would make him rich. Which it did, but more than anything else it let him stay on his own turf, so he and Jerry could strut and raise hell, till life and high school were one and the same.

"I don't know, maybe we got too big too fast," observes my brother with a labored sigh.

So things aren't perfect at Curran Construction. Since I haven't been following what he's said, I haven't a clue what's wrong. Last I heard they were pouring an interstate and building twin towers in Hartford. Brian stares at the blue-red coals in the fireplace, lost in a troubled reverie. This alone is startling enough. In the twenty-five years I knew him before the breach, I never saw him stop to think. He was always in motion, always grinning, as wave after wave of cheering greeted his every turn.

"The stress must be pretty intense," I remark, lame as a radio shrink. "Sounds like you need a break."

"Yeah, I need somethin'." The brooding is still in his voice, but I can hear him shutting down. It's not that he won't discuss it any further with me. He doesn't want any more commerce with his feelings. This is a peculiar phenomenon of straight males—the shutdown valve—which I used to think was the exclusive province of the Irish. Now I know it crosses all cultures, instinctive as the need to carry weapons. Brian turns back to me with a smile, as if he's never felt anything at all, and reaches over and slaps my knee. This is his idea of a kiss.

"You still a good Catholic?"

He laughs easily. "Sure, I guess so. We go to Mass on Sunday. Don't ask me when I made my last confession."

There's a Bing Crosby twinkle in his eye. I feel the old urge to flash my dick in church. "According to them I'm evil, you know. That's the latest doctrine, from God's mouth to the Pope's ear. 'Intrinsic evil.' " I spit this last phrase out like it's poison.

Brian writhes slightly on the chair arm. He wedges his hands between his thighs, clamping his knees together. "That doesn't mean gay *people*," he retorts. "That's just about . . . acts."

A regular moral theologian, my brother. "Oh, fabulous. You can be gay, but you can't have a dick. Pardon me while I piss out my asshole."

"Tommy, you know what the church is about. They think sex is for making babies." He grimaces and rolls his eyes, as if to bond us against the folly and the hypocrisy. "Nobody takes that seriously. Including half the priests."

"Excuse me," I hiss back at him, scrambling out of the afghan. "Maybe you guys get to wink at the priest while you fuck your brains out." He doesn't like my language, not one bit. "But they're still beating up queers in Chester, because Her Holiness says it's cool."

"Hey, ease up. It's not *my* doctrine."

"And sixty percent of the priests are fags anyway!" I'm wild. I have no idea where that statistic came from. It's like I've been waiting for a little doctrinal debate for years. "They *hate* us for being out. They liked it the old way, where you get to be special friends with the altar boys, and maybe you cop a feel off little Jimmy Murphy after Mass—"

"For someone who doesn't believe, you sure do get yourself worked up."

"Don't give me that smug shit." I can feel his coldness, the backing off, though he doesn't move from the arm of the chair. "I bet you get all kinds of points for coming to visit a dead man. Corporal act of mercy—you should get a big fuckin' discount in purgatory."

I'm pacing in front of him, panting with fury, and he sits there and takes it. But there's no satisfaction. I feel impotent and ridiculous—feel as if Brian has *won*. All I can do is wound him and push him away. I stagger against the mantel, my forehead pressed to the great splintered slab of wood that's anchored in the stone.

"Dad went to Mass every Sunday too," I declare with a wither of irony. "And you know what? He was still a scumbag drunk who hit me for nothing at all. He used to hit me for *reading*. And when I

finally told him I was gay, he told me I made him want to puke."
Then a very small pause. "Isn't that where you learned it?"
Nothing, no answer. He's still as a rock. "So you'll forgive me if I
keep my distance from all you good Catholics."

Brian stands and reaches for his jacket, thrown over the back of
the sofa. "I thought we could heal it up between us. I was wrong.
I don't want to upset you like this. You've got enough to deal with."
He shrugs into the jacket and turns to me. There is oddly no shyness
between us, and nobody looks away. Perhaps this is the proof we are
brothers. "Look, if there's anything . . ."

He lets it hang, and I shake my head. "You can't help me."

He nods, and we move together. Through the dining room and
kitchen, then out to the yard, shoulder to shoulder across the grass.
The silence between us doesn't feel strained, and is even rather
soothing. We are ending it before it comes to blows. This is so
sensible, we are practically acting like WASPs. The faint spoor of a
skunk feathers the night air, and the moon is still bright, casting ice
shadows across the gravel drive. We reach the boatlike rental car,
nosed in between two Monterey cypresses. I wish my brother no
harm and hope he knows it, but I say nothing.

Brian opens the door and half turns again. His mouth works to
speak, another set speech perhaps, but all that comes out is "Take
care."

I stand with my hands in my pockets as he fishes for the keys. We
will never see each other again. No drunken promises to visit, no
embrace to pass on to my nephew, no jokes. This is a surgical
procedure, the final separation. And then the key turns in the
ignition, and there's a clunk. Brian tries it again, this time pumping
the gas. Nothing.

It is so ludicrously a symbol of the deadness between us, I want
to laugh out loud. But it's so clearly not funny, the useless click of
the key as he tries it over and over, because now my brother is stuck
here. I know this a second before he does. In fact I can see the
bloom of shock in his face as he remembers there's no phone. It's
nine o'clock on a Saturday night, and the nearest pay phone is two
miles south at the Chevron station. I have no car and no jumper
cables. Our mogul neighbors with Uzi guard dogs are not the sort
you bother for a cup of sugar.

Brian looks at me, dazed and slightly foolish, like a man who
can't get it up. He seems to understand instinctively that he's

trapped in a movie twist. "Fuckin' piece o' junk," he grumbles, so raw you can almost hear the brogue of Gramp Shaheen.

"You'll have to walk down to the Chevron in the morning. When's your flight?"

"Noon."

"Oh, you'll be fine. Don't worry, there's lots of room."

My own voice amazes me, so solicitous and chummy. I open the door like a bloody valet. You'd think the bile and snarling never happened. But this is different, a matter of hospitality, like laying down the guns on Christmas Eve. Brian grabs his briefcase from the backseat, and we head back to the house. The skunk is nearer, or at least sending out a stronger warning. The silence between us is comfortable. We both appear to agree that this part can be handled in purely practical terms, no frills and no demands.

In the house I douse the downstairs lights, and Brian follows me up the spiral stair. "This is where I sleep," I say, pointing into Foo's room. Then we cross behind the stairwell, and I throw open the door opposite. "Cora's room," I inform him as we enter, by way of historical orientation.

In fact, this is where Gray stays when he spends the night, though he's never stayed over during my two months here, so assiduous not to intrude. I snap the light on the bedside table, bathing the room in peach through the old silk shade. This room's not so tatty, though, its green wicker furniture crisp as Maine. Brian nods approval, soberly indifferent, even when I open the balcony door at the foot of the bed, to the beckoning shine of the moonlit sea.

"We share a bathroom," I explain, pushing through yet another door. Even as I flick the light I wish I'd had a minute to tidy up. It's pretty gritty. There're prescription bottles all over the sink and counter, like Neely O'Hara in *Valley of the Dolls*. Funky towels on the floor and underwear strewn haphazardly. The plumbing hasn't been scoured in ages, and green blooms around the fixtures.

"Beautiful tile," Brian says gamely, as I snatch up shorts and toss them into my room.

"Look, you don't have to go right to bed. Maybe you want a drink or something." I'm rattling on as I scoop the prescriptions and push them to the far end of the counter. I open the cupboard above the tub, and eureka, there's one clean towel. I present it to Brian. "I think there's vodka in the freezer. Whatever you like. It's just that I get real tired."

"Sure, sure, you go to bed. I'll be fine." There's a crease of worry between his eyes as he studies my face. "I'll just do a little work and then turn in myself."

"I bet you were supposed to call Susan."

"No, that's okay. They know I'll be home tomorrow. I'll be fine."

As he repeats this ringing assertion of life, he lifts his free hand in an awkward wave and backs out of the bathroom. Gently he closes the door. I who will not be fine turn and blink in the mirror above the sink, which I usually avoid like a nun. All I can see is the lesion on my cheek. My sickness is palpable, and indeed I'm completely exhausted. I splash my face with water, then use the hand towel to scrub at the smegma on the sink. It's hopeless.

I stand at the toilet and pull out my dick—O useless tool, unloaded gun—and dribble a bit of piss, not a proper stream. The virus does something in the bladder to tamp the flow, or else there're lesions there as well.

I leave the light on for Brian and close my own door. I don't even bother to turn on the lamp as I shrug out of the crew-neck and kick off my jeans. I duck into the bed and under the old down comforter that's shredding at the seams, spilling feathers like a wounded duck. Moonlight streams in, blue-gray on the furniture.

And I lie there, I who sleep like the dormouse now, nodding off into naps two or three times a day, ten hours solid at night. I stare at the ceiling, and the rage comes back. My father with the strap, my useless mother whimpering, "Don't hit his head." Brian on the field swamped by fans at the end of a game. Laughing with his girlfriend, horsing around with his buddies. My memory is split-screen, the Dickensian squalor of my woeful youth against the shine of Brian. No slight or misery is too small for me to dredge up. I am the princess and the pea of this condition.

I don't know how long it goes on. At one point I realize I'm clutching the other pillow as if I'm strangling someone, and my teeth are grinding like millstones. Then I hear Brian and freeze. The water goes on in the sink, right through the wall behind my head. I can hear him scrubbing his face—can *see* it.

Because it's as if the sixteen years have vanished since we shared a room in Chester. I in my scrawny body have finished brushing my teeth, and Brian the god, a towel at his waist from the shower, steps up to the sink to shave. At sixteen he's got hair on his chest. His stomach is taut, the muscles cut like a washboard. I am so in awe of him that I have to force myself not to look, for fear of the dark incestuous longing that licks at my crotch like the flames of hell.

The water goes off. There's a shuffle of feet on the tile, and then I hear him pissing. But with him it's a geyser, a long and steady stream that drums the bowl like a gust of tropical rain. I am spellbound by the sound of it. I can feel the exact shape of my brother's dick—heavy and thick with a flared head—more clearly than my own. The pissing is brutally sensual, beyond erotic, and I'm not especially into kink. The stream abates to spurts, gunshots in the water. Then Brian flushes. The bar of light under the door goes out, and there's silence.

Still I stare at the ceiling, but now the rage is replaced by an ache, just like the empty throb that followed my little heart attack. Not that I want my brother anymore—not his body anyway. At least my own carnal journey has brought me that far, slaking the old doomed hunger. I used to jerk off sniffing his underwear, the uniforms he'd peel off after practice. But even with the incest gone, a darker yearning wells up in me, undiminished by years. I still want to *be* him.

For he's what a man is, not Tommy. From seven to seventeen I walked around with a sob in my throat, the original crybaby, mourning for what I would never become. And now it's come back like a time warp. I'm still wearing the glove I can't catch with, a Wilson fielder. I'm flinching in the middle of a scrimmage, terrified someone will pass me the ball.

This goes on for maybe half an hour, a sort of anxious misery, leaving me wired and desolate. I'm sick, I need my sleep. Eventually the rage comes back around like a boomerang, because it's also Brian's fault. I get up and grope into the bathroom, flicking the light, my ashen squinting face looking dead and buried. Fishing among my prescriptions, I palm a Xanax and down it. Neely O'Hara again. I turn off the light and take a silent step to Brian's door, cocking my ear. I don't even know what I'm doing. *Go back to bed*, I order myself, but that is the voice I have always ignored, the one that used to tell me not to pull my pud or stare at boys.

By inches I open the door into the darkness beyond, barely breathing, craning to hear. And there it is: the deep rolling surf of my brother's breathing, a soft whistle at the end. He sleeps a hundred fathoms deep, he always has. Please—I slept in the twin bed next to him for seventeen years. I step inside and stand there a moment to orient myself. The moonshine is strong, though it throws deep shadows on the clutter of wicker, crazy expressionist angles.

Brian in the bed is lit up clear, the white of the sheets like a luminous ground. He's turned on his side and facing me, one arm under the pillow that cradles his head. Bare to the waist, the top sheet drawn up only to his hips, so I can see the waistband of his briefs. He doesn't even bother with a blanket, for the Irish side is very cold-blooded. Unlike me, who's always shivered in the California nights, shrouded in quilts and comforters.

Yet the cold doesn't bother me now, even in just my underpants, as I move to the wicker armchair by the bed. Though I sit carefully, perching on the edge, still it creaks and rasps under my weight. I scan Brian's face for any stir, but he sleeps right through. Now I am only three feet from him, so close I could reach out and touch him.

But I just watch. His red hair is silver in the moonlight. The arm that's crooked under his head has a biceps as round as a melon. The other arm rests on his side, and now that he's bare I see that his chest and stomach are still in shape, if not so finely chiseled as when he was young. All evening I've been trying to find him battered and soft, but it's not true. He's beautiful still, and even the puffiness in his face has soothed in sleep. If anything, the greater bulk and mass the years have wrought have only made him more of a warrior, king instead of a prince.

Am I still in a rage? Yes, livid. The last thing I need is this mocking reminder that life goes on for straights, mellowing and ripening into an ever-richer manhood. In the glint of the moon Brian's skin fairly radiates with health. The bristling hair on his belly is thick with hormones. He'll be fifty, sixty, seventy, and still be winning trophies. And I'll be dead, dead, dead. Of course I know I can't blame my illness on Brian, but I can still hate him for being so alive. And the deep, deep irrelevance of his shiny life, with the peewee games and the goldens, I can hate that too. The white-bread sitcom cutesiness and the lies of the Nazi church.

I'm leaning forward with gritted teeth, my face contorted with nastiness. I'm like a bad witch, rotten with curses, casting a spell even I can't see to the end of. And maybe Brian picks up the vibes, because at last he stirs. A soft murmur flutters his lips, and he rolls from his side onto his back. His hands are on the pillow on either side of his head, so he lies defenseless. You could plunge a dagger into his heart.

Except I have shifted position now too, the roller coaster of my feelings bringing me up from down. Perhaps it's the Xanax starting to work. But suddenly it's like I'm guarding him, watching over the last of my clan, the only one whose luck has held. Oh, I still want him out of there. Back to his sweet vanilla life, every trace of him expunged, all the torrent of stinging memories he has brought in his glittering train. I wish to be left to die in peace. I don't need a brother—it's far too late in the game. But I stand watch anyway, keeping him free of harm as he sleeps, from curses and daggers.

Tears are pouring down my face, silent and futile, without any reason. Crybaby. Finally I think I will sleep. I stand, creaking the chair again, and I'm superconscious of every broken thing in my body. My eight lesions, my old man's bladder, my nerve-warped knee. I wrap my arms about myself, huddling in my smallness. I take a last long look at Brian, and on impulse I lean above him, hover over his face, and brush my lips against his cheek, just where my own cheek bears the mark. I've never kissed my brother before. He doesn't flinch, he doesn't notice. Then I turn and stumble back to my room, pleading the gods to be rid of him.

TWO

OME MORNINGS YOU WAKE UP WHOLE. YOU OPEN YOUR eyes, and the ceiling is swirling with light reflected off the ocean. The bright air pours through the balcony doors like tonic. It's not that you forget even for a moment that you're sick. But if you're not in pain, the sheer ballast of being alive simply astonishes. I fling off the comforter, filling the air with feathers like confetti. I rise and caper across the threadbare carpet in my Jockey shorts. I slip through the french doors, the first sight of the limitless blue never failing to catch my heart. I straddle the stucco balustrade like a pony and drink it all in. The smell of sea pine and eucalyptus wafts around me. I don't want anything else but this.

Except I don't really know if that fits Gray's plans. When he offered the place to me—*Why don't you stay at the beach for a while*—I don't think he figured to have me all winter. We weren't such very close friends to begin with. He was a regular patron angel of AGORA, five hundred bucks a year, and a big fan of Miss Jesus. We'd known each other in passing for years, plastic cups of Almaden at everybody's opening, but Gray was so buttoned-up and -down, so WASP-geeky, we never seemed to get very far.

Then it was funerals we'd see each other at. Gradually he began to seem like an angel for real, taking care of mortuary etiquette, comforting mothers and lovers. He'd always provided for artists to sojourn at the beach house, three- or four-week stints, a sort of one-man colony. But here I am two months later, my welcome long overstayed, not budging an inch.

I catch sight of a pair of birds sailing the updraft at the lip of the bluff. They're white like herons but fat as wild geese, with bands of gray at the head and neck. One of them lights on the post at the top of the beach stairs, and the other cavorts in circles, dipping close to the swords of the cactus. I can't say what they are. I don't know the names in nature, except what Gray has pointed out, patient as a ranger. I never learned anything growing up, the leaves and feathers of life, because I was too busy running from micks. The beach house is my second chance at a little natural history. Whatever they're called, the white birds are gorgeous. Alighting here as they migrate north, a moment for me and no one else. Whatever time is left, I have had these birds.

And then they explode in flight, flapping away in tandem as if somebody fired a gun. I reach out to them as they disappear north, wishing them well, wishing to fly in their wake, so buoyant am I. Then Brian appears at the top of the steps, coming up from the beach. Now I know why the birds fled. He is wearing a Speedo of mine, green and black stripes, and toweling dry his hair. Of course he looks extraordinary, sleek as a sea god. It's *his* desert island right now, no question about it. He is a man to match the vibrancy, the aliveness of the morning and the place. He turns his warrior's head to look down the coast. He hasn't seen me yet.

It's not that I'd forgotten he was here. But none of that had started churning yet, and in my mind he was still asleep. I was staking the day for myself. I didn't think he would slip so easily out and find the secret places. I call from my perch: "The blue hump's Catalina."

Brian turns with a grin. "Good morning! Jesus, is that water *cold!*"

"It's winter."

He strides across the grass, squinting up at me. "I didn't swim far, I'll tell you that. My nuts shriveled up like raisins. I think we have time for breakfast."

"We've got to get you down to the Chevron station."

Brian laughs. "I've been there already. The car's all charged. You just put on some pants and get down here."

He stretches a shoulder muscle as he speaks, turning it in a circle, like he's warming up for a game. I see him for one more moment nearly naked in the morning sun, almost gleaming, before he ducks through the arch below me and into the house. I retreat to the bedroom, rattled, glancing at the clock—9:40. I'm exhausted by Brian's energy. A two-mile jog to Chevron, and still he wanted a swim in the ocean. Myself, I haven't been in the water once since I got here, not including my toes. Sullenly I grab my jeans, dogged again by the gap between what Brian can do and I can't.

When I get downstairs he's dressed, tie and the whole bit. The dining room table is set for breakfast, melon and bowls of Cheerios and the muffins Gray brought last night. Brian ducks his head in from the kitchen. "Coffee or tea?"

"Tea." I sit down quietly at my place. Something I haven't thought about in sixteen years: my brother used to put breakfast out for all of us every morning. Half a grapefruit and oatmeal, milk for us and coffee for them. He might torture me all the rest of the day, till I was black and blue and curled in a fetal crouch, but he served me breakfast fair and square. The old man would usually be hung and bleary, my mother making birdtalk to cover his silence.

Brian appears with a pair of mugs and sets one down in front of me. "I would've made you some french toast—that's what I make for Daniel—but you didn't have any eggs."

We eat. I am sorry now I didn't wear a shirt. Not because I'm cold but because I did it to show off my lesions. Pure spite, to get back at him for the little Olympian swim show he just put on. I can feel him looking at the nasty one on my shoulder. The casement window behind his head is open, the wet Speedo hanging from the latch and dripping into the courtyard.

"I wrote down our address and phone number on the pad in the kitchen," says Brian, buttering his muffin. "In case—"

"—I die. Don't worry, I'll have somebody get hold of you."

"That's not what I meant. We should stay in touch."

"Okay." It's not worth the ugliness to tell him that this is the end, right here. I eat my Cheerios stolidly, vowing neither to be unpleasant nor to lose my temper. It's just another half hour.

"So what kind of plays do you do? Your own? I always thought you'd end up being a writer instead of an actor."

"We don't exactly do plays," I reply with infinite precision. Brian is recalling my thespian days at UConn, where I ran with a crowd of earnest misfits, putting on Shaw and Albee. Then summer stock in Williamstown, doing walk-ons and touching the hems of minor stars, and sucking them off late at night. I don't remember Brian ever coming to see me in a play, those being the years when he first recoiled from the horror of my gayness. Yet he seems to know I was a lousy actor, all too true. So over-the-top I practically ate the scenery.

"Yeah, what I saw yesterday, it was more like stand-up." He says this tentatively, taking a slurp of tea. If it was stand-up, he seems to wonder, then how come it wasn't funny?

"Performance is kind of a hybrid," I reply, and then I can't bear the PBS professorial bullshit in my voice. I can't be nice a moment longer or I'll scream. "Actually, I was pretty notorious there for a while. I used to do a thing called 'Miss Jesus.' " He looks at me blankly. "You know, Christ as a raging queen. Getting it on with Peter and Judas. Kind of a pain junkie." I'm amazed how proud I sound, and how confrontational. Of course it was the nature of the piece to stick it in people's faces.

Brian stares abstractedly at the hollow rind of his cantaloupe. "I don't get it."

"Well, it started with a chubby little pederast priest, Father O'Hanion, who liked his bottle and dicking twelve-year-olds. But that was too easy. Then I did the Pope in this silk organza gown, 'cause he was going to the Vatican prom. That was very interesting, but after a while it seemed like one big Polack joke. See, I wasn't trying to be *funny*." I deliver this truncated résumé with maximum cool. Brian's discomfort is visible. He neither eats nor drinks, and his hands grip the edge of the table as if he will lift it off the floor. "Then I thought, go for the big boy. It took a while to evolve, and it's always changing. Plus I adjust for the season—a Christmas pageant, and an Easter piece that's all in leather."

Ravenous now, I spoon a great dollop of jam on my muffin, eating as if I've just come in from swimming the Catalina Channel. Brian is slowly shaking his head. "How do you live like that, so pissed off all the time? What does it get you?"

I shrug. "It's a job. Somebody's gotta do it."

"Can't you stop being flip for just one minute? So you had a shitty childhood. So the church isn't perfect. So let it go."

"You were right the first time, Brian—you don't get it." We're locked eye to glittering eye now. It's a little like arm wrestling. "I'm glad I came from a fucked dysfunctional family. And growing up Catholic was perfect, like an advanced degree in ruined lives. 'Cause it's helped me a lot with my work. Otherwise I might be just another middle-class troll, dead from the neck up and eating lies like peanuts."

"They had hard lives," he hisses back in my face. "They did the best they could."

"For *you*. And your life turned out perfect. So you keep the shrine, okay?"

He explodes. "My life is not perfect!" It's almost a scream, so violent it backs me against my chair. He raises a hand as if to cuff me, then slams it down on the table, rattling the dishes like a 4.5. "I'm sorry you're dying, kiddo, but everyone has it hard. Nobody has it easy." The bitterness in his voice takes my breath away. His face is beet-red with the violence he can't unleash on a sick boy. He hasn't called me "kiddo" in twenty years either. It used to be half a taunt, half a sneer, accompanied by a body check.

He breathes heavily in the silence that follows, cooling down. There's no more point to breakfast. "Yeah, well I'm sure life sucks all over the place," I declare with a certain numb reserve, "but I don't have room for anyone else's. I'm better off by myself."

We don't move for a moment. It's exactly the same deadlock as last night, when he left the first time. My brother can't help me. There's too much blood under the bridge. And yet I can feel an uneasy flutter in my gut that somehow I've missed the key, or blinked when the answer flashed onscreen. Something about that un-perfect life and the business that got too big too fast. I don't really mean, even now with all the walls up, that he can't unburden himself. Of course I'd listen. Yet I know that's not going to happen now. We've tried this reunion twice, and it's crashed and burned. Only a fool or a pain junkie would try it again.

Brian stands but doesn't clear the table. That's my chore, today as it was a lifetime ago. He strides through the kitchen and out the back door, not waiting this time for me to walk in tandem. I have to bolt to catch up with him in the yard, where he's striding in the sunlight to his car. It's only at the last moment, before he gets in, that he relents and turns to face me. The anger still darkens his Irish cheeks, or is it a kind of torment? Then a rueful smile plays at the corners of his mouth as he speaks.

"You're still my brother, even if you hate me."

It startles me, the sentiment is so twisted. The perfect Irish bottom line. I'm standing with my hands dug in my pockets, and Brian reaches up and swipes at the hair on my forehead, as if he's trying to tame a cowlick. I realize it is a gesture from his life with Daniel, and I understand in that moment that he's a good father, better than ours.

Then he is climbing once again into his car to leave. But this time I am torn, feeling I ought to give him something back. The engine bursts into life, stoked by the morning's charge. He rolls it into a slow reverse, pulling it back from the cypresses. The front wheels crunch on the gravel as he points them out to the coast road. He looks at me one last time.

And I say, "I'll be sticking around for a while." Taking back all I have said about death, its imminence and its stranglehold. I shrug, terribly aware of my spotted torso, but shrugging that part off. "I'm here."

Brian nods. The big Chevy boat goes lumbering down the drive between two rows of oleander. He stops at the road's edge, and I see him crane forward to check for cars. It's clear. A last vague wave in the rearview mirror, and I fling my own hand at the sky. Then he turns and is gone.

Is it relief? Immediately I feel so weirdly light-headed, gliding back over the grass to the house. I know that I've held my own, and for once have given as good as I've gotten. That's the first feeling: a kind of swagger, like I've just walked away from a TKO. I come into the kitchen, and the first thing I see is the pad on the counter, the scribbled address. Pequod Lane in Southport. I'm watching myself for any pangs of loss, but I just seem glad that it's over.

Then into the dining room, and my eyes go right to the Speedo hooked over the window latch, no longer dripping. Here there's a tug in my chest, as if the pouch of the suit still holds the shape of Brian's basket. Again it isn't the thing itself, but the memory of all those jocks and sweat pants tumbled on the floor of the closet in Chester. Still I manage to sail right through, letting it all roll off me. I mount the stairs, delirious with the need to nap, knowing only that I have survived intact. With every hour that goes by, I can feel it, more and more of me will come back. No matter how quick I die, I will live long enough to be an only child again. It's a matter of will, and I am willful if nothing else.

I reach the door to Foo's room, and I'm gazing across the stairwell. I think as I cross over that I'm being a good housekeeper, checking the guest room. The bed is aswirl with the slept-in sheet, the pillow dented and askew. My lips purse, as if I mean to punish that boy for not making his bed. Then I float—there's no other word—drawn and yet strangely dispassionate. I tumble onto the bed, rolling into the sheet, muzzy with sleep already. My face in the pillow can smell Brian, but it's the least sexual thing imaginable. I can't even say the smell transports me back. All I can say is someone else has slept here first, another man. And there is no pain and no regret, not the slightest sense of loss. I sleep a hundred fathoms deep.

For hours. Dreamless and utterly still. It's the downside of the afternoon before I even start flopping about, turning side to side to grope the last pockets of slumber. Most of this is AIDS, of course. You go three or four days at a pretty normal clip, and then the virus requires a minor coma. I wake up dazed as Goldilocks, disoriented by the new room, and vaguely aware that the bears are due back any minute. Guilty; I'm not sure why.

And *sad*. That is the oddest part. I get up and pad out to the balcony, the sun on the water like molten flame, and I want to cry out with loneliness. But I swear it's not Brian. He may have been the catalyst, him and his perfect isosceles of family niceness, yet this one is all my own. For I've never loved anyone all the way through—or maybe it's no one has ever loved me back. You'd think I'd get the direction right, considering this is what scalds the most. I can handle being alone, even dying alone. It's not that I'm desperate for somebody now, or maybe I'm too proud to want it anymore. But the fact that I never really had it, never touched life that deep, I carry around like chronic pain, what they call in the disability biz a preexisting condition.

Till now I have managed to put it out of mind entirely during my two months at the beach. Somehow I gave it a rest, with no one to whine at and no one to pine for. But now I feel like I'm reaching for an actual physical man I can't have, just like I reached for those birds. He is always a foot from my grasp, or standing below on the terrace where Brian stood this morning. I admit I have mixed them up, Brian and the man I have never had.

I don't really mean to see him in icon terms, all buffed like the airhead beauties you pass in Boys' Town, wincing at their blondness. It's not the body I'm aching for anyway. I want to be known. The quirks and the edges, the bumps and the hollows—I want somebody to see it all whole. And I want to have had years of that, even if it has to be over now. And I haven't. All I have had is two months here, six months there, wrestling with men who never quite fit. It's strange, I don't have such a bottomless well of self-pity about my illness, but about the man who never was, the hole in my heart goes all the way to China.

Anyway, I'm perched on Cora's balcony like a gargoyle, feeling sorry. The sun hurts. I don't know what else to do except take it an hour at a time, letting the loneliness leach out till I am simply alone again. I'm staring down at Brian's spot on the terrace, fixed on his absence, because somehow this is the symbol for what I've missed. And suddenly there is a shadow and then a figure, as if my longing has materialized a man. The light's in my eyes, I can't quite see.

"Hullo," says Gray, one arm up to block the sun. "I decided that screen shouldn't wait till Monday."

I laugh. The sheer ordinariness of the remark just about knocks me over. The netherworld of lost men that's seized me in its operatic grip vanishes on the spot. "Let me grab a shirt. I'll be right down."

I spiral down the stairs, yanking on an oversize sweat shirt. Gray is already crouched by one of the parlor windows, his trusty toolbox beside him. He's replacing a rusty latch, pulling the old screws out and filling them with wood glue. He works at all chores with fanatic neatness and marvelous patience. I lean in the archway just behind him, watching. Nothing ever got fixed in my father's house in Chester, unless he could throw a beer bottle at it.

"I have to weed the goldfish pond," says Gray, always making a list in his head. "Brother get off all right?"

"Finally," I reply. "His car wouldn't start. He had to spend the night."

"Nice-looking man." Gray doesn't overstep, any more than he'd ever admit he showed up here today for purposes of gauging the fallout. "I always wished I had an older brother."

"Yes, well they're very overrated. I know they're supposed to tell you all about girls and keep bullies from stealing your marbles. In my case he was too busy pounding my head in the dirt."

He's got the new latch in place, bright steel, biting a screw into the jamb. He grunts with satisfaction. "But doesn't it change, once you grow up?"

"Ah, but I didn't grow up, so there you are."

He's finished. He takes a midget whiskbroom from the toolbox and sweeps up the shavings. The job is perfect. Gray should be in charge of the MX missile. He stands with his box in hand, eyeballs his workmanship one more time, and steps outside. I follow in his wake.

As we head up the grassy slope to the sycamore grove, I'm

surprised at how much taller Gray is than I, three inches at least. His rounded shoulders and pulled-in neck make him look much shorter. He never wears sunglasses, so the squint lines around his eyes are deep troughs. Skin very weatherbeaten too, since he wouldn't dream of moisturizing. Still, his face has a craggy noble form, set off by the fine slope of his patrician nose. He reeks of old money.

The sycamores are mostly bare, though the dead leaves cling in clumps on several branches, holding on to the old year. They're budded but won't come into leaf for another month, the closest thing to Connecticut here. We slog through piles of unraked leaves to the evergreen hedge beyond. Nobody's clipped these bushes lately either, so the arched entrance is nearly overgrown. Gray passes through first, holding the branches so they won't switch back in my face. Then we are in the green room.

The hedge, maybe ten feet high, encloses a rectangle of ground on the high end of the bluff, perhaps twenty by forty. In the center is a rectangular pool edged with a coping of granite. The water is black, as if it goes down for miles, with two distinct clusters of water lilies at either end. From one of these springs a yellow flower wide as a man's hand.

Gray kneels on the granite lip and peers in the water under the lilies. Then he reaches in and digs around and pulls out a ghastly clump of root and tendril, covered with brown scum. Gently he pulls it away, detaching it from the lilies. I move closer to see and nearly gasp with delight. For his churning and weeding—he's plunged in again—have sent the fishes racing. Orange and spotted, some two feet long, they whip and circle about in the midnight depths of the pool.

Nobody knows how many there are, but I count eight. A couple have been replaced, but Gray says most have been here since the place was built. Which is why I call this the Chinese garden, because it's all mixed in my head with wizened old philosophers contemplating fish as old as the Ming dynasty. A white-flecked goldfish breaks the surface, showing a flash of tail.

"They won't grow by the ocean, that's what everybody said. And that's why Nonny planted 'em." Gray's voice is mordant as he deposits another load of slop on the pile beside him.

Honestly, it's like watching Mr. Wizard, or an eighth-grade science project: stuff you can find in mud. Gray is completely undaunted as he pokes and fiddles with things. Needless to say, it's a Sisyphean task, keeping up with the breakage and wearing-out of an old house, the overgrown flora of five acres. I don't quite understand why the Baldwin Foundation, the titular owner, doesn't pay for regular upkeep, just to protect the property value. But then I have never figured out the queer adversary relations between Gray and that pile of money. Gray doesn't seem to mind at all being handyman and underwoodsman. I can also see that he likes the company when I trail around after him.

The nasty job is done. There's a grisly pile of roots and muck on either side of him now, and he grumbles that he'll wait for it to dry out before he shovels it up. "Haul it over to the compost," he says, making a mental note for later. He stands, retrieves his toolbox, and we head out of the Chinese garden.

Because I have slept the day away, the sun is already winking at the horizon. As we tramp down the slope from the sycamore grove, I say, "Come down to the beach with me, will you? In case I have another heart attack."

"Well, I gotta wash," he replies, holding up his bare arm, slick with muck from the fish pool. Then he laughs. "Hell, I can wash in the ocean."

We make for the beach stairs. Gray leaves his toolbox under a cactus, and we head down, me first. Behind me Gray asks, "You think he came because you're sick?"

I feel a startled relief that the subject hasn't been dropped. "No, he didn't know that till Mona told him. I don't know why. The Irish get sloppy sentimental sometimes." We're clopping down the stairs at a fair clip. It's easier to talk about this in motion, my back turned. "I didn't really let him talk," I admit, sheepish for me. "I think he wanted to."

"Well, next time," Gray declares briskly.

"Oh no, there won't be any next time. That's all she wrote."

We've reached the bottom, coming off the steps onto the smooth and trackless sand. The tide is inching out, about ten feet away. Gray shucks his Top-siders and rolls his khaki pants to the knee. Without preamble he struts into the shallows, bending down and splashing water up his arms. You can practically see the gooseflesh.

"How cold is it?"

"Nippy," says Gray, cupping his hands and splashing his face. "Foo used to say there's an iceberg off the point."

He turns with a grin, happily wet, then his eyes go wide. For I am already half-undressed, my sweat shirt on the sand, shinnying out of my jeans. I drop my eyes as I drop my shorts, for Gray has never seen me naked. As I trot toward him I can see he wants to tell me not to, but holds his tongue. I'm hollering at the cold when it's still just at my ankles. I take a long stride past him and dive headfirst.

It's unbelievably arctic, a thousand knives. I roar up and out like a whale breaching, my arms flailing the surface. A numbness locks the joints of my bad knee. But I'm not planning to swim anyway, not a stroke. I totter to my feet, fighting the surge of the undertow. I turn and face Gray, about hip deep, and slap my hands over my head like a seal, whooping. Gray still frowns with concern, but he's glad, too. I head in, scrambling through sand that sinks and shifts. I'm chattering with the cold, I can't wait to get out, but I'm delirious from the shock. The sand gets firmer, and I feel like I'm dancing. Panting and roaring with pleasure, I drop to my knees on firm ground.

"I would've brought a towel," Gray says fretfully, but with no reproach.

I can't believe how upside down I feel, reeling still from the zero cold, every inch of my skin slapped. A pang of victory rises in me like a shout, though I am jerked by shivers. The sensation is very specific: it's the first time my body has not been crawling in months. I'm washed clean. I sit back on my haunches, hair stiff, eyes stinging, and Gray is already holding out my clothes.

"Now don't get chilled," he admonishes me.

I clamber to my feet, shaking off like a dog. I don't feel shy being naked now. My nuts have seized just like Brian's did, and yet I feel the most insistent cockiness. It's the first time I've done anything in so long—I'm practically a man again. I hunch and let Gray pull my sweat shirt on me, feel him rubbing my shoulders and arms, bringing the blood back up. In that moment he seems like my coach, and I stand in the sunset, simple as a jock. I grab my pants but don't put them on, tucking them with my Reeboks under my arm. I start up the stairs, butt-naked and laughing. Fastidious Gray stops to bat the sand from his feet and put on his shoes clean.

Of course the eighty steps do what they always do—put me in my place. Twenty steps up and I'm wheezing, favoring the banister. Yet I'm remarkably undaunted. I set my pace and count off as I go. Gray has caught up behind me, but makes no move to mother. It becomes a point of pride that I don't stop to catch my breath. I can feel myself pushing and winning, countering all that useless sleep. The last ten steps my chest is stabbing with every breath, but I'm in no danger of a coronary, not today. The terns are wheeling at the top of the bluff as we come up, their dance to the death of the sun. I am with them for once, my heart careening.

"You go get into the shower," says Gray, a light hand between my shoulders. Still my coach. "I'll make us something hot."

I trot bareass across the terrace, the feeling of being a naughty boy not dissipating at all. It only seems to get stronger as I stand under the pounding spray, lathering myself. I actually pump my dick for a bit, and it even lifts its head a little. But I have another secret building, much more exciting than a half-mast hard-on. I can hardly dare to put it into words, even to myself. But the feeling of having broken my leper status in the iceberg cold of a sunset swim—that holds. Toweling off, I can still see all my dalmatian spots, but they don't assault me. I'm enough of a realist to know it won't last, this existential vacation, yet I'm ready to work it for all it's worth.

When I come down Gray has put out bowls of stew, heated out of a can. With hunks of coarse bread and mugs of milk, it looks like a true peasant's supper. "That felt great!" I enthuse as I sit at my place, tearing into the bread. Gray lays aside the old picture album, something I've never seen him look at. Gray never needs the old snapshots, since he carries the whole movie around in his head. "I'm going to jump in the water every day," I announce brazenly.

He smiles approval, but he's pensive. After the next bite he says, "I need to ask you a favor."

So WASP formal. I feel a thrill of panic low in my gut, because I think he's about to ask me to leave. "Sure, anything."

"Well"—he laughs dryly—"this is completely out of the blue. But Foo's decided she wants to come spend a day at the beach."

For a second I think he's lost it, like my father after the first stroke, mixing the seventies and the forties. Gray is smiling at me, shrugging. "Your *aunt* Foo?" He nods. "She's still alive?"

"Oh sure. Ninety-one and sharp as a tack. But she hasn't left the ranch in at least five years, and there's hardly anything left of her. We're afraid she'll break her hip just getting into the car."

These Baldwins are something else. Even as I listen—round-the-clock nurses, still in her own room at the ranch where she once slept with a nanny—I'm utterly buoyed by the old girl's indomitability. I thought the whole lot of them had been dead twenty years. In my head there even appears to be a relationship between my dunk in the ocean and Foo's return, as if the shock of connection has opened a hole in time.

"So what's the favor? It's her house. Of course she can come."

"No, but it's *yours* right now," he insists, one finger touching my wrist on the table. "And she understands that. When an artist's in residence here . . ." He opens his palms and lets the phrase hang, as if the ellipsis could lead anywhere, a symphony or the Great American Novel.

"But I'm not doing *anything*. I'd be honored to have her here. We'll have lunch on the terrace. Unless—" Now I get flustered. "Maybe she'd like to have it all to herself. Look, I can split—"

"No, no, we'll all spend the afternoon together. Perhaps Mona would like to meet her."

It's still not quite believable, the ancient world returning like this. I consider the bitter irony that a woman who lived here in 1912 might still live longer than I. Which sets me frowning. "You think she'll be scared of my . . . you know, my cooties?"

"Foo doesn't know from AIDS," Gray reassures me, grinning. "She's not exactly up on current events. She's still arguing about whether Picasso's a fraud. 'That gigolo from Barcelona!' "

Sounds like we'll have an iconoclast's ball. I'm bursting now with the news of my own return, prodigal and improbable. The restlessness of old Foo seems like the perfect omen. "Look, you don't have any plans tonight, do you?"

"Me? No." He looks at me, puzzled but game.

"Will you drive me down to Venice?"

A startled pause. I can see his mind running ahead, but not daring to hope. By way of answer, one last throb of caution, he says, "You're not too tired?"

"Let's go."

We leave the dishes where they are and head out through the kitchen. I grab my ratty parka, which Mona says makes me look homeless. Night has already fallen fast, the March sky pulsing with stars, even despite the pouring moon. The Big Dipper stands on the tip of its handle, just above the Trancas hills. Gray apologizes that he's brought the pickup instead of his car, a Volvo pushing ninety thou. We climb inside, laconic as a couple of cowboys, and Gray pulls out, the gravel spitting beneath us as we head to the end of the drive.

The stream of Sunday traffic is pretty steady. They're shooting by at fifty, fifty-five. Gray has to choose his point of entry on pure adrenaline. Suddenly there's a space of five or six car lengths, so he guns and peels out. And now we're in the flow, the great California beach migration. I flip the radio on, right to country: Reba McEntire, who's lost her man to a lady bartender. I put my feet up on the beat-up dash and roll the window down. The night air's sweet and briny. To the left the hills are remarkably bare, with only the random lights of a few châteaux. The seething boom of construction hasn't reached this far, not quite. Even on the bluff side there's empty fields between some of the houses.

I look over at Gray, who hunkers at the steering wheel, squinting into the oncoming lights. "You know, you spoil me rotten." He smiles softly. "I don't think I tell you enough what a wonderful man you are."

He can't stand compliments. His shoulders lift in a slow shrug, like an animal shying. Who knows what deep Presbyterian springs prohibit him from being stroked? "I'm just glad you're around," he says, ignoring the encomium. "Gives the place some life."

"Wait, I think you've got it backwards. I'm a dying man." But I say so with perfect jauntiness, and we both laugh. I don't feel dying at all right now.

Still, Gray isn't sure what's happening here and hesitates to ask. He knows we're going to AGORA, but why is up in the air. We could just be dropping by for the Sunday potluck showcase, when the marginal types come in to try out work-in-progress, usually deadly. But since I am half the proprietor, it's not so odd that I'd want to sniff around. I haven't given the slightest hint that I might want to perform myself, except my level of nervous energy. I'm double-juiced, and Gray knows it.

Traffic slows to a crawl as we pass the Colony, Malibu proper. Straddling the hills on the left is Pepperdine University, right-wing nuts in caps and gowns, white rich straight kids being drilled in the politics of oppression. We pass through the town center, a Hughes Market and a lone movie house and fourteen realtors, but as for the Colony itself you can only see the gatehouse on the right, Checkpoint Charlie. Beyond is the land of the hit series, minitalent vulgarians who are pulling down eighty grand an episode, and thus own a parcel of Eden. Graffiti swoops and zigzags along the walls on either side of the gatehouse, proving the grave assertions of reams of Sunday supplement pieces, that the problems of the city have reached the beach.

"You can tell there's something gnawing at him," I say, as we pass a gaggle of surf bunnies milling in front of Domino's Pizza. I'm back to my brother, and there's no reason Gray should have followed the segue, except he nods. "Maybe his life was so happy growing up, it all tastes flat now, like dead ginger ale. Maybe that's a good argument for having a tortured youth."

It's only half a question. We're silent as we ride on, the traffic clearing again. From here south to the pier the coast road rides at sea level, snaking between a crumbling set of hills and the barest strip of beachfront. The houses are cheek by jowl along that strip all the way to Santa Monica, perched on tiptoe above the tide, waiting—almost yearning—for the Big One.

"I don't think I had a youth at all, tortured or otherwise," Gray remarks, more wistful than I've ever heard him. "I turned thirty-five before I was ten."

"Yeah, I've seen the pictures. All these picnics and everyone laughing, except this one little serious guy with a book in his lap. You should have glasses an inch thick by now."

"I read books instead of living." He says this matter-of-factly, without any whine or regret.

I'm about to protest that reading was the very thing that brought him to that outré world of beats and jazzmen, a far bohemian cry from the ranch or the Cheez-Whiz mainstream of the fifties, but I hold my tongue. This is the most he has ever said about how it used to feel, being a lonely kid. Somehow I don't want to gloss it over. "Did you know you were gay?"

He shakes his head. "I wasn't anything."

"So when *did* you come out?"

"Assuming I ever did," he replies dryly, "I guess when I was thirty."

Nineteen-seventy, same as me, for I was starting to rattle the knob on the closet door when I was thirteen or fourteen. I assume Gray is being very precise here, that he had nobody to speak of between the onset of the carnal itch and almost twenty years later. I feel an immense and loyal sadness for the youth he missed, and even think it may have been worse than mine, despite the fraternal abuse and my exile among the piss-blooded micks of Chester.

We're coming into Santa Monica, and traffic seizes again, the Sunday night thrombosis. Gray goes left and leaves the coast road, ducking up an alley behind the stores on Chatauqua. He's got shortcuts forty years old. We scoot down another steep alley and cross up Santa Monica Canyon, coming around to Ocean Avenue through a neighborhood of perfect thirties bungalows. You half expect to see those exiles, Thomas Mann and Brecht, walking their Weimaraners. Then the Palisades are on our right, and we're high above the beach, with the pier like a paving of diamonds on the water.

"But I feel gay now," Gray declares with an unmistakable puff of pride, turning up Colorado.

"Yeah? Well, now that you mention it, you're looking a little lavender around the edges. Do you feel an irresistible desire to listen to *Judy at Carnegie Hall?*"

We shriek with delight. It's already the most we've ever said to each other. I almost wish we weren't going anywhere, that we could just ride around like this all night. Through the winter Gray and I have grown tighter, like roommates except we live in different Baldwin houses. Yet there's always been a line we never cross, the no-man's-land where you walk on eggs. I usually chalk it up to my illness, or to Gray's unfailing reserve and discretion. Tonight there's no line. We're easy and antic, tooling around in a pickup.

This is what a brother is, I think, lolling my head out the window to let the wind blast my hair.

AGORA's not exactly in the middle of Venice, but more on the interface with Ocean Park. It's still in the senseless crime district, but being as the neighborhood is more industrial, it's not quite so *High Noon,* crack on every corner. We head up a street that's leased to Hughes Aircraft, great hulking warehouses on either side painted puke-green, World War III being assembled within. At the end is a cul-de-sac that forms a sort of low-rent industrial park, four modest factories not much bigger than bloated garages, sprawled around a parking square.

Dumpsters big enough for eighteen-wheelers dominate the open space; and yet, improbably, from the center of the square rise four royal palms, freakish as giraffes. The palms are never pruned or watered, and more than one truck has smashed against them backing up. But they stand six stories tall and aloof, a smidgen of oasis.

Gray pulls the pickup in by the loading dock. There are maybe fifteen or twenty cars parked higgledy-piggledy, not a bad crowd for Sunday potluck. Half of these, of course, are probably the performers' cars—the exhausted ones with shredding vinyl roofs. I move to get out. Gray touches my arm, and not just with one finger. "Break a leg," he says quietly. "Or at least one heart."

"I'm not promising anything," I retort, as if it's still up in the air, but we both know nothing will stop me now.

There's a proper front entrance, with a spiffy canvas awning and a sputtering neon sign, courtesy of a donor. But we head in by the loading dock itself, a concrete bay faced with railroad ties and big old tires. The aluminum sliding door is open a couple of feet, and we slip in. There's still a strong smell of ink about the place, as if nothing is truly forgotten. It's dark, and we make our way toward the white stage lights.

Music is playing off a tape—awful music, post-punk, tone-deaf. Gray and I approach on cat's feet to stage right, just beside the bleachers. The performer, a woman in three shades of black, is doing the obligatory mime, a cross between T'ai Chi and a sort of mute primal scream. The straggly audience is, as I expected, about twenty strong, most in black themselves. Performance is always a bit of a funeral.

Across the way, stage left, I spot Mona standing against a post, looking as if she wants to start a gulag for bad artists. Something catches her eye, and she turns and sees me. Total shock, then a grin of dawning light. She jerks her head toward the office. Gray and I slip around behind the bleachers, where there are still cartons of cheap ball-point pens stacked in dusty corners. We won't run out of pens for several hundred years.

I walk in with Gray, and Mona flashes a helpless look of gratitude at him, as if this is somehow his doing. I am already scooting around the desk, covered with reams of grant applications, past the chaotic filing cabinets, drawers yawning open and choked with rotting props. I open the accordion closet door and feel a surge of excitement. My costume hangs just where I left it.

"They're even worse than usual tonight, if you can believe it," Mona says, and as if we needed further proof, the woman onstage spews out a torrent of invective, none of it intelligible but clearly about as amusing as a root canal.

I lift out my caftan, a coarse dun-brown wool. "I may only do five minutes," I warn them, shinnying out of my sweat shirt.

We don't exactly have a dressing room. Slipping off my jeans I feel no shame or strangeness about my spots. Gray and Mona are watching me, not even pretending to small-talk. They of course have romanticized this moment to such a pitch, they probably think the exercise will cure me. I'm much more nuts-and-bolts. I clamber into the caftan all for its own sake, the smell and the scratchy feel. My shoulder-curl wig lies on the closet shelf like a dead squirrel. When I shake it, the dust of old hairspray clouds the air, but the Dynel is in fact a miracle, no tangling and supple as ever. I draw it over my scalp and check it out in the mirror.

"He is risen," Mona says.

Then I grab my sandals and sit in the swivel desk chair to strap them on, the kind with the long laces that crisscross up the calf. "He wants you to come meet his Aunt Foo," I tell Mona.

She blinks in confusion at Gray. "She's alive?"

"Of course, dear," I retort breezily, as if I didn't ask the same thing. "There's always somebody in a WASP family who never dies. How else will anyone know where all the skeletons are buried? Where's my crown of thorns?"

Mona stoops to the nearest filing cabinet, tugging open a sprung and rusty drawer. It looks like it's full of electrical cable, but she lifts out from the back something wrapped in tissue paper. Carefully she peels the tissue away, revealing the crown undamaged. This is a true slice of Grand Guignol, with darkly twisted branches and thorns like fangs. Mona found it at a garage sale in Reseda. As she props it lightly on my head, she says, "But you haven't told me a thing about your brother. What happened?"

I peer in the mirror, cocking my crown at a rakish angle, more like a forties Adrian hat. "Oh, the usual. I fucked him. He cried a little."

She swats my shoulder as I stand up. I'm incorrigible. Gray says, "You want to go next?"

"Sooner the better. I might collapse at any moment."

The three of us head out into the darkened theater, each of them squeezing an arm on either side. I feel like Diana Ross being led to the stage at Caesar's Palace. As we come up behind the bleachers, we can see through the seats that the sullen performer is reaching the end of her piece. The music has fallen from its cacophonous heights, sounding now like fingernails on a blackboard. Sorrowfully, inevitably, the woman in the spotlight begins to shuck her black clothes. So raw and authentic. I am meanwhile preoccupied ducking in under the bleachers and lifting out my cross without making noise. It's in two pieces, a couple of four by fours. Gray is right behind me, so I pass them back to him. Then I grab my carpenter's toolbox.

Gray is already fitting the crossbar onto the stakepole. Though he has never helped me put it together before, he's got that handyman's intuition for how things work. He slots the crossbar into place and secures the toggle bolts. It stands almost eight feet tall. Mona waits by the low end of the bleachers, ready to dart onstage as soon as Lady Macbeth goes off.

We watch for the flash of her dreary nakedness, but the black shift comes off, and it turns out she has saved us a final stunning metaphor. Not naked at all, but wearing a black lace G-string and matching pasties, the tawdriest peepshow gear. The woman herself weighs in at one-forty, so she looks like a fullback in drag. She stands in her final tableau, defeated and yet triumphant, for this is a postfeminist reading. The music cuts out. The twenty gulls in the audience applaud.

Clearly I don't have the right attitude anymore about my fellow supplicants in the temple of High Art. Mona applauds with the others, smiling enthusiastically as the woman retrieves her fallen garments. She doesn't bow but gives a dimpled smile as she totters off behind an armload of clothes. Then Mona strides on, before the clapping has sputtered out.

"We announced in our February flyer that we'd be premiering a piece tonight, but it's not ready." Mona shrugs, no excuses. There is no groan of disappointment from the audience, which sits there dully, expecting nothing. "Instead we have a special guest," says Mona. Her onstage patter has always been very straight-on—the dyke Ed McMahon. "The performance artist who put AGORA on the map. A man who's actually been called the Devil—by a *reviewer*. It's just like they always say: nothing sacred, nothing gained. Ladies and gentlemen, my bossman, Tom Shaheen. *Miss* Jesus to you."

Gray is holding the cross. I turn around, and he lays it over my shoulder so I'm gripping the crossbar, very *King of Kings.* The loxes applaud rather spiritedly as I trudge around the corner of the bleachers and into the light. Mona has scooted off the other way, so as not to block my entrance. I lug my burden center stage, and by now you can hear a pin drop. I turn my head and rake them with a desolate look, as if they are indeed a crowd of onlookers on the Via Dolorosa.

I breathe deep and speak. "Welcome to the Second Coming." Beat. "The first time I had a wet dream."

They don't exactly laugh, but there's a small expulsion of breath from several quarters. I turn and drag the cross upstage, where I slip it off my shoulder and prop it against a black-painted platform, toolbox beside it. My music begins, starting with monks chanting. As a sort of warmup I strike a set of poses, limp-wristed and mincing, flouncing my golden hair, shivering with sissiness. All right, it's self-indulgent, but it gets across the persona with swift economy: this boy is a queen.

"I thought as long as I was coming back to Hollywood, I might as well come back as Jeffrey Hunter." Once more they don't laugh, a little louder. This group is too young to have seen *K of K.*

I move to my toolbox and pull out a hammer and spikes. Then I climb onto the cross. I turn over and position myself so I'm lying on it, then hook my feet through the leather thong on the stakepole. The crossbar also has leather loops at either end for my wrists, and I slip the left one through, my right hand free with the hammer. I am more or less in the crucifixion mode, but with one significant modification. In the past I have stripped off my caftan and done the cross part in a loincloth, my shoulders and back greasepainted with whip marks. But I'm not ready to parade my lesions in front of this motley crowd. Even my sort of exhibitionism has its limits.

I reach over and stick one of the spikes between the fingers of my lashed hand. Then I start hammering. Of course they can see quite clearly that the spike isn't actually going into flesh, but the effect is near enough. Nobody comes to this moment in my act, Jew or Muslim, without an overload of images of the Passion. So basically they're riveted by the nuts and bolts. But as I hammer and the spike sinks into the wood, I start to moan with pleasure. Here I can get pretty tacky as I raise the stakes, and only the bravest laugh now, and no one tonight.

I loll my tongue and grunt obscenely—"Yeah, do it!"—as I strike each hammer blow. My music changes to the Kings College choir, trilling the "Hallelujah Chorus." I rub the hammer against my crotch, groaning and panting shamelessly as I flex my spiked hand. It's at this very moment, in fact, that I have been attacked—once, a God-fearing lady from the Coalition of Family Values who stormed onstage and wrested the hammer from my grasp. But this group sits in polite shock while I go over the top, thrashing in ecstasy. Then I go limp. I turn and gaze raptly at my nailed hand, wincing now as I mimic that postcoital ache where you realize you went a little too far. Then I look at them.

"I bet you never realized I liked it."

Silence. I'm acutely aware, from the corners of my eyes, of Gray and Mona standing on either side of the bleachers. My bodyguards. I release my hand from the crossbar loop, unhook my feet, and climb off. I pat my crown into place and brush at the wrinkles on the front of my caftan. Then, as if to show there's no blood, or maybe to bless them, I raise my palms to the crowd. It's about half and half, men and women, and nobody over thirty.

"The thing is, I can't figure how everyone got it so wrong. Think about it: I found twelve single men in Palestine who were still living with their mothers. I mean, give me a break."

It's amazing how it comes back after eighteen months. Not that there has ever been a script. But a certain flow of attitude, the cheap one-liners popping up, has shaped itself in the course of time. I'm not remembering but reinventing, and the material feels live, like a snake in my hands.

"I think James the brother of John was straight, and Peter was kind of bi, but I always thought that was mostly wishful thinking. Otherwise—honey, this was always meant to be a gay thing. And celibacy? Please."

I sniff with disdain and give them a haughty left profile. Gray is hugging himself with delight. I love how much he loves this stuff, and tonight I'm doing it more for him than anyone. After all, he's been my patron all winter, and I'm his colony of one. I look back at the audience and point behind me to the cross.

"Not that everyone was into *this* kind of thing. I admit it, I was much more on the edge than the rest of them. But hey, my father's house has many mansions. And besides, I was like the CEO, with all the pressures and all the *tsuris*. Now you know how those guys at the top need to be sex-pig slaves on Saturday nights. The straight ones like their hookers to do the dominatrix thing, with cattle prods. Really, when you come to think of it, isn't crucifixion just another turn of the screw?"

"I don't have to listen to this shit!"

Ah. About halfway up the bleachers a lanky man is standing. The woman beside him is pulling his arm, telling him to shush. But he's in his own spotlight now, and there's only one way to go.

"I'm a Christian," he seethes at me. "And you're a sick fuck."

"Thank you for sharing," I purr in reply, as he clumps down the steps, the woman huddling behind him in his wake. "Blessed are the Rock 'n' Rollers, for they shall see Elvis."

But he won't be drawn in any further. He storms across the skirt of the stage, past a flinching Mona, and heads out through the main entrance. His girl makes sure the door doesn't slam behind them. Everyone else has watched them go as if it was all part of the act, which of course it was.

"Just like my brother Aaron, flies right off the handle. Of course it's been very hard on Aaron, bunking all those years with the Son of God. See, Aaron was non-Immaculate. We were always a little out of sync, because he'd be playing baseball and I'd be doing miracles. But you know what's weirder than that? He had a lot more trouble with me being gay than being God. He was the butchest kid in Nazareth, but something about it really threatened him."

This is all new, and I don't know where it's going. I never did a brother riff before. What's curious is, I'm not really thinking of Brian, not consciously. I'm actually in character. I've crossed that invisible line, and the man I call Aaron is right there in my mind. He's swarthy with lush brown hair and a beard, dressed in a caftan just like mine, the gleam of a Palestinian terrorist in his eye. Gorgeous. A real warrior.

"And he's a much better carpenter too, so he's the one took over the shop. Which was fine with me because, honey, I can hardly hold a screwdriver straight." I sigh and examine my nails, pouty as a princess. "He still lives in Nazareth, building condos. Married, coupla kids. And when people ask if he has any brothers and sisters, he says he was an only child." I shrug. I can tell the natives are restless, as if they know I'm off the track, and besides, I'm not even shocking them anymore. "I don't blame him really. He didn't want his name linked with the founder of a homo church. Too bad *he* can't have a Second Coming, because it would blow him away to see how it's taken off. Success he can get behind."

My tape comes softly up again, the Mormon Choir singing "Amazing Grace." By this point I am supposed to be into the Last Supper, strutting around and rubbing my privates—flashing them on a good night—and taunting them with "This is my body—eat!" Somehow I have lost the momentum, or else I'm just too weak tonight to pull out all the stops. I turn and shuffle back to the platform, picking up my toolkit and hoisting the cross to my shoulder again.

I start moving across the stage, dragging the cross after me. I've let the energy drop, which bothers me in purely theatrical terms. I usually go off with a bang, telling them about my Jesus game show, my intro into cable. I stop and give them a melancholy smile. They've really been pretty attentive, and I can feel they'd like another little spin, doesn't have to be a bang. So I reach down in, not sure what I'm going to come up with.

"You know what's funny? When I first got it on with Judas, he reminded me of Aaron. I don't know, something about that furry Jewish chest—chunky shoulders—little bit of a gut. Plus that love Buick of his, with a nice big mushroom head. It's like I was getting fucked by my own brother. You know?"

Nope, they don't know about this part at all, not a clue. I can feel them hunkering down in their seats again. They're expecting another simulated orgasm, me sitting on Aaron's pole. But that's my last surprise, to turn it all upside down, just like the G-string and pasties. Tonight I want to leave on a grace note, mellow as Tony Bennett.

"You always fall for the ones who remind you of the one you never got. I fell for Judas hard. I would've done anything for him. His little sister got thrown by a camel, and I raised her from the dead, but we kept that very quiet. I stole his dirty underwear. I watched him sleep all night. I knew they paid him money, and still I couldn't keep my hands off him. I think that's why he betrayed me, frankly, because I was one of those girls who love too much. It was really messy."

I knock my head a few times against the cross, to show what a flake I am. "So now that I've got a *second* chance, my first commandment is: God shouldn't date. Only anonymous sex in dark alleys." I nod and give them a wink. "See you there. I'll be the one with the Shroud of Turin on my face. Peace and love."

And I trudge off stage right, dragging the sins of the world behind me. They clap, all right, and there's even a whistle, but not much more than they gave to Lady Geek before me. Still, Mona is beaming as I come off, practically jumping up and down with excitement. She throws her arms about my neck and kisses my cheek with the lesion. "Welcome home, darlin'," she murmurs in my ear, and now the little audience raises the volume, applauding more vigorously. If nothing else, they approve the schlock reunion of Mona and me. I'm swept up in it too, I admit it. Mona disengages, and I turn to the crowd and throw a fist in the air like Rocky. They're almost cheering, for all the wrong reasons, but what the hell.

Then I duck around the bleachers, and Mona goes back on to announce the next one. Immediately I set to work to dismantle the cross, undoing the toggle bolts. There's something deeply satisfying about storing your props just where they came from, ready for the next performance. As I work the crossbar loose, suddenly Gray is beside me, holding the stakepole. We don't speak yet because we're locked in the mechanics of the chore. He holds the two pieces as I crawl in under, then passes them to me one by one. Then the toolbox.

Huddled beneath the bleachers I feel a rush of mawkish tenderness for my chosen profession, the bits of wood and hardware that turn a bare stage into ancient Judea. I peer out through the gap between the rows, right between somebody's legs, and see the next thing start. A young man in a dark suit is actually standing there with a dog, a bastard mix with an amiable air who sits nonplussed while the guy barks at him. This is not somehow a promising gestalt.

I turn and crab my way out, knocking my crown askew on an unseen strut. Gray has a hand out to help me, and when I grip it and rise to full height beside him, he unexpectedly hugs me. Manfully of course, clapping his hands on my shoulder blades, not really squeezing at all. But it's still the first embrace that's ever passed between us, and I'm just as unexpectedly moved. It's over before I can properly hug him back, but he lets an arm rest on my shoulder as we head through the dark to the office. Behind us I can hear a veritable symphony of barking. Impossible to distinguish what's man, what's dog.

As we enter the office Mona's crouched behind the desk, rummaging in the tiny Pullman refrigerator. "We don't exactly have champagne," she grumbles half to herself, as she pulls out old containers of cottage cheese and yogurt bubbling with mold inside. Then out comes a bottle of Miller Lite, and she stands triumphant. Gray points me into the swivel chair, then turns to close the door. Mona has scrounged three plastic champagne flutes from yet another groaning file drawer. She blows the dust out of each, sets them side by side on the desk, and starts pouring the beer.

"Mona," I say, "sweetheart—a *dog* act?"

She shrugs, unfazed. "It's supposedly an AIDS piece," she replies dryly. "I don't prescreen 'em. Maybe the dog's got AIDS." She hands me a flute of beer, mostly foam, then one to Gray. She lifts hers and gives me a look brimming with camaraderie. "To the Second Coming."

We grin all around, reach and click our flutes together like musketeers, then take a swallow. "For a second there," I say, "I thought Mr. Onward Christian Soldier was gonna deck me."

Mona clucks. "I felt sorry for the girl. She was supposed to perform."

"They probably thought they were coming to 'Star Search.' "

"Please. That whole group"—she tosses her head at the theater—"is just what the cat dragged in. Next time we'll get you a clever audience, and maybe a little press even." Her eyes widen behind her glasses, dazzled with possibilities.

"Oh no," I protest for the second time today, "there won't be any next time."

And with that the exhaustion finally hits me. My muscles go weak and rubbery. In the middle distance I see white spots, like there's not enough oxygen going to the brain. The weariness is so profound that the gig I just did seems like a fantasy. I'm a dying man again, who's been losing ground by inches for eighteen months. That can't have been me out there.

Gray, who hasn't spoken but never stops watching, crouches beside the swivel chair and lightly taps my knee. "Time to get you home," he says, infinitely solicitous.

I'm so relieved to have someone take charge. I nod, handing over my glass of beer. Careful not to prick myself, I take the crown from my head and pass it to Mona, who swaths it with tissue again. When I stand, all I have to do is lift my arms, and Gray pulls the caftan over my head, first swiping off the wig. I feel like a little kid being undressed, and the feeling is unutterably delicious. My dad never took my clothes off except to whip my butt, and my sainted mother could barely stand to touch us once we were out of the crib, I think because we were boys and constituted for her an obscure occasion of sin. I prop a foot on the chair, and Gray swiftly undoes my sandal.

"You know you were fabulous," says Mona.

"Too slow, no focus," I retort automatically. "No energy at the end." I lift my other foot to be unshod and announce to Gray, "I think you're supposed to wash my feet with your hair."

"No, the brother stuff was great," Mona insists, lighting a Merit. "It's the first time I ever thought of Miss J as somebody with a past. Before it's always been like this outrageous Bible cartoon. The *greatest* cartoon," she hastens to add, skirting all left-handed compliments, "but you know what I mean? You could do a whole incest thing."

"Yeah, really," I say, stepping into my jeans as Gray holds them out, the perfect dresser. "Maybe Brian'll come do a guest spot sometime, and we can have it out once and for all. He could hammer the nails in." I shrug on my sweat shirt again, take a step to Mona's side, and bend and kiss her nose. "Sorry, girl, I've scratched this itch. Ask me again in a year and a half, or leave a rose on my grave, whichever is more appropriate. We're outa here."

No protest. She smooths my brow with the flat of her hand, and it feels so cool I think I must have a fever. Gray opens the door, and we slip out all three into the dark. We scuttle silently across to the main entrance, and I only look back once toward the stage, in truth with a kind of thrill at what I've brought off.

The man with the dog has put on a pair of black glasses, and he grips a sight-dog harness attached to the animal. He's declaiming something very profound, you can tell by the rich stentorian tone in his voice, like high school Shakespeare. I block out the words. Mona creaks open the door, and Gray and I duck out, Mona giving my ass a pat as we go.

Under the awning Gray and I are bathed in rosy neon, and though I'm half collapsing I want to dance. There's nothing like leaving a theater after doing a show you love. It doesn't even require a crowd of fans at the stage door. You feel like you own the night, the moon and stars into the bargain. Better even than walking home after a night of love. I trot ahead of Gray into the parking square, stopping under the stand of palms and turning in a kind of pirouette. I fling up my arms and strike a heroic pose, like Isadora in the Parthenon.

"Felt pretty good, huh?" Gray asks with a grin, slouching with folded arms against the back of his pickup.

"What can I say, I'm such a star." I stroll over to where he stands and shadowbox him. He watches me bemusedly. Then I let my arms go limp and loll my tongue out, dumb with fatigue.

"Get in," he orders me brusquely, knowing when I've played enough, then heads around to the driver's side. I shuffle over to the passenger's door, and I'm just about to get in when a figure steps out of the shadows by the loading dock. Instinctively I throw up an arm, as if I'm about to be attacked.

It's a woman. Stocky, mid-forties, jeans and a T-shirt. For a second I think she's homeless and wants a handout. Then she speaks: "Mr. Shaheen?" I nod. "I just wanted to tell you—I'm an ex-nun—"

Painfully shy. Oh God. Believe it or not I never want to hurt anybody's feelings. I know there're people out there like Mother Teresa, singing lullabyes to dying babies. They've got better things to do than be grossed out by me. I stand there as she hems and haws, bracing myself for a guilt trip.

"I mean, that was really something." She looks at me with a kind of awe, then suddenly bursts out laughing. "I bet the Pope woke up in a cold sweat when you were on that cross."

I feel giddy, as if I've gotten away with something very, very naughty. "Thanks."

And now she's pumping my hand, hearty as a salesman. The shyness is gone. "You take care of yourself now. And you ever need any reinforcements, you call me." I realize she's slipped a card in my hand, even as she stands away and motions me into the truck. I climb in, smiling and waving. Gray rolls us into reverse, and my nun waves us away, calling out exuberantly: "Angels are all gay too!"

I stare at the card as we pass beneath a streetlight. KATHLEEN TWOMEY. SALVA HOUSE WOMEN'S CENTER. With a street address in Venice. I smile across at Gray. "I believe I have just lit one candle."

He's somewhere else. "You take your medication?"

"Mm—I guess I'm a little late. Won't kill me."

He leans a little harder on the gas as we retrace our way through Santa Monica. I swear, he's more alert to my schedule of meds than I am. I tilt my head back against the rear window, which rises right behind the seat. The truck's too old to have headrests, or even seat belts, one of a hundred violations Gray would be slapped with if he ever got stopped by the CHP. But I like the rattletrap feel of the truck, the musty smell of its cracked seat, the dash where nothing works except the two-watt panel light that makes the interior glow like a film noir set.

"What would Brian say if he saw that?" Gray shakes his head in wondering delight, expecting no answer. "What would my *father* say, for that matter?" He gives out with a hooting two-note laugh, shivering with pleasure at the prospect of the old man turning over in his grave. There's a real streak of anarchy there. And I love being the goad.

"Too bad I couldn't get AIDS in," I say, my eyes beginning to droop. I mean it: for all its goose of the bourgeoisie, Miss Jesus seems a little quaint to me now, not quite in the heart of the fire. Maybe I should've flashed my lesions after all.

"You could," he retorts, but leaves it at that, not wanting like Mona to pressure me to do it again. We're back on the coast highway, heading out of Santa Monica. My head's wobbly. Gray taps the seat beside him. "Why don't you stretch out here."

An excellent idea. I scrunch down and curl onto the seat, tucking my feet up under me. As I lay down my head I find it pillows just right on Gray's thigh. I try to pull back, not wanting to get in the way of his driving, but he says "That's fine," so I leave it there. As it is I can fall asleep on a dime these days, but here I don't quite go out like a light. Instead I'm in this half slumber, feeling the muscle play beneath my head as his foot rides lightly on the accelerator.

I'm totally safe. At one point, just as I think I might get cold, he takes a hand from the wheel and lays his arm across my chest, and the chill is gone. We are bearing home with the beach on our left, the mountains on our right. Everything is in place. And I am still alive.

T H R E E

HAT WHOLE NEXT WEEK WE WERE HIT WITH A WAVE OF storms out of the Gulf of Alaska, bitter driving rain and boiling seas hammering the bluffs. A mudslide down by Big Rock narrowed the coast road to one lane for three days straight, sending commuters into apoplexy. Two stilted houses at the foot of Tuna Canyon collapsed into the swirling tide, one of them owned by a starlet who gave sobbing refugee interviews to all the local affiliates. It would pour for five or six hours steady, sheets of it slapping the house in a mad rage. Then stop like a faucet turned off, and the black clouds would flex their muscles for the next onslaught, till the sky was like a vast mushroom cloud pregnant with nuclear doom. And then the rain again.

It was fabulous. I was content to build great roaring fires every day, from the cords of cedar and eucalyptus stacked in the cloister outside the dining room. Then I'd bundle up in the afghan and read from the leatherbound sets of authors, dozing every ten pages or so. At this rate I wouldn't finish *Emma* till 1993, but hey, who was waiting for a book report from me? That first day, the Monday after Miss Jesus, Gray came tramping in in fireman's boots and a yellow slicker that swept to his ankles. He stood on the fieldstone hearth, dripping and rubbing the chill from his hands—no heater in the pickup either—and said with an imp's grin, "This is all your fault, you know." Then pointed up. "You pissed Her off."

We laughed and had a cup of tea, and afterward he spent a couple of hours tinkering over the property, checking for leaks in the red-tile roof, lashing a couple of flapping shutters. He said he'd be back next day with groceries, and we set the lunch with Foo for the following Monday. I'd long since stopped protesting that he didn't have to keep me provisioned, but in fact I guess I'd gotten pretty spoiled by his almost daily attentions. For Tuesday came and nearly went, and I was scrunched on the sofa wondering if Emma would *ever* stop cock-teasing Mr. Knightly, when my heart leaped at the sound of the back door opening.

I went to the kitchen and came face-to-face with a hulk of an Indian chief. Two-twenty-five and blue-black hair, weathered profile craggy as the buffalo nickel, wearing a Stetson and a buff suede jacket. I must have blanched, for he smiled apologetically and spoke with curious elegance for one who looked so adamantly untamed. "Mr. Baldwin sent me," he said, gesturing with the sack of groceries as he set them on the counter. "He's got the flu. He didn't want you catching anything."

I thanked him. He was called Merle, some kind of overseer at the ranch—which, despite its having evolved into a conference center and think-tank institute, still had horses, and fences to mend. Thrown off balance, I sent him away with a hasty get-well to Gray. Only when I'd curled up on the sofa again and picked up Jane did I realize how disappointed I was that my patron and friend wouldn't be coming by. First time I wished the beach house had a phone.

Still, I'm very good at being solo. I holed up cozily for the next three days, venturing out whenever the rain would take a breather, sloshing around my acreage. The ocean was too furious below for me to go down to the beach, and the beach stairs shuddered from the battering of the surf till it seemed they would tear away from the bluff. The goldfish pond was brimful, the overflow coursing away and digging channels in the lawn. But the water in the pond was icy clear, and the fish seemed to love it, flashing about in figure eights, bright as new-minted doubloons. Everything loved the rain, the sycamores and the beds of ivy, even a pelican flapping its wings in exultation out on the terrace.

I didn't think much about Miss Jesus, never being the sort who hungered for reviews, but I did think now and then about Brian. I tried to remember when his birthday was—August?—and how I might send him a card. The address in Southport still lay scrawled on the pad by the stove. I wondered what he and Daniel did on Saturdays, if it was ever anything else but sports.

And Thursday afternoon, when Merle showed up again, I couldn't wait for news of Gray. Feeling a good deal stronger, said the big man, who looked to be about forty-five. "He says to tell you lunch is on for Monday. He's just playin' it safe, with the germs and all." Again he had brought me food, which he unpacked out of the sack. Gray must've given him a list, for then he went outside and checked the drains and dragged the barrels out to the end of the drive for trash pickup.

In the kitchen I tore off the sheet with Brian's address from the pad and scribbled a note. "Who is this warrior chieftain you send to me? I miss your plain and earthy WASPness, and he is no substitute. Mona and I will take care of the Foo occasion. You just get better. I thought *I* was the sick boy. Love, Miss J."

I folded the paper and ran out just as Merle was climbing into the pickup. I handed it over, smiling, and he looked away as he took it, awkward and uncomfortable. I wondered if perhaps he couldn't read himself, or was I treating him too much like a servant? I could tell that Merle and I were destined to be out of phase, though he gave me a hearty wave as he drove away.

Next morning I walked in the rain all the way to the Chevron station, garbed in an ancient voluminous slicker that had been hanging in the pantry since the days of Captain Ahab. Also a brute black umbrella with a six-foot span—the aunts did not go in for dainty things. The rain wasn't heavy, but the wind was brisk and buffeting, and I felt like the Morton's salt girl. Panting with exertion, I folded myself in the phone booth and dialed Mona's number in Westwood, reversing the charges. Which she accepted— a bit reluctantly, I thought.

"Don't worry," I said in a wounded tone, "I'll pay you the fifty cents."

"It's not you, Tommy," she sighed. "Daphne just left."

Christ. Why is it one's friends never behave and never seem to learn? Daphne is Mona's ex—ex-*torturer*—a shrink by profession and beady-eyed, with a chip on her shoulder the size of a two-by-four. They've broken up ten different times, new girlfriends right and left, but something draws them back together to reenact their misery. I braced myself for the details, but Mona was too embarrassed or bored to go through it all again. She shook her self-absorption, inquired if I was surviving the typhoon, and I zeroed in on Monday's lunch.

"Get a bunch of ridiculous salads at Irvine Ranch," I instructed. "Curried pesto, that kind of thing. And fruit and cheese for dessert."

"Wait—what should I wear for this old lady? My Chanel suit?"

"Darling, it's the *beach*. Funky-cazh."

"And what if it rains?"

"The rain will stop," I intoned with a gravel of authority, tough as John Huston. "You just get rid of that two-bit Jungian sociopath, you hear? Or else *you'll* be the old lady, wondering where it all went."

She whimpered uncle. I've found that since my illness I can cut right to the chase with my friends, demanding that they jettison the bullshit from their lives. I am like the toller of the bell: my very presence seizes them with how little time is left. Exacting a promise that Mona would be at the house on Monday by eleven, I ventured back into the rain again. This time heading into the wind, the umbrella held before me as a shield. Every footstep felt like lead. My command that the storm would end seemed laughable and puny.

Then a red van pulled to the side of the road in front of me. A lift! I whumped ahead through a thirty-foot puddle and pulled the door and clambered in. The driver was one of those perfect surfers, Redford-blond and a Maui tan, even after a week of rain. His surfboard stuck through the seats between us, white with zaps of Day-Glo green. We chatted beachtalk as we rode the two miles up the road. He clearly loved the rain as much as I, and had seen a whole family of seals that morning, huddled under a lifeguard's platform.

It was a less-than-nothing encounter, yet he put me in mind of Brian, this nameless boy in his twenties reeking of health. When we reached my driveway and I got out, he grinned out his window and said the storm would be over in forty-eight hours. "And then the waves'll be *banzai!*" he enthused with a mock salute, peeling off into the rain. Leaving me desolate, shocked by the storm of his beauty, trapped in the spotted frailty of my body. I stumbled down the muddy drive, shot through with an unconsolable grief for the man I had ceased to be.

Oh, I got over it. Another night in front of the fire, dozing over *Emma*. A whole package of frozen waffles for breakfast. At two in the afternoon, bundled up in my afghan, Emma and Mr. Knightly finally took their fatal turn in the garden. "If I loved you less, I might be able to talk about it more," he says to her with exquisite feeling. And I found myself swallowing a lump along with the last of the Lido cookies. Then I heard a rattle at the back door, and leaped up to go greet Merle.

"She won't use a wheelchair," he said, unpacking still more food, "and she'll never get acrost that lawn with her cane, 'specially if it's this soggy. So I'll come down here with 'em and carry her into the house."

"Okay," I replied, juggling logistics. "So we'll be five for lunch."

He shook his head as he drew an envelope from his jacket. "I won't be eatin'."

"Well, of course you will. There'll be plenty."

"No thanks," he retorted, snapping slightly, as he handed over the envelope. His firmness in the matter brooked no further protest on my part. He obviously had his own fierce reasons, having to do with a certain pride of place. Not a class thing at all, somehow, unless *he* was the upper class, too aloof to break bread with the rest of us. He nodded curtly, issue closed, and headed out the back door with another list of yard chores.

I pulled out Gray's note. It was written on cream-colored paper thick as a biscuit, with a crest embossed in forest green. Very Baldwin. "He's half Chumash and half Malibu, a marriage of the two purest strains in the region. It's *his* land we're on, make no mistake. My temp is normal again, and my head's stopped throbbing. I'll be frisky by Monday, and then we can all try keeping up with Foo. I miss the beach house—I love it in the rain. You dress warm. And EAT."

Immediately I grabbed the pad and pen. Brian's address, now a loose sheet, fluttered off behind the coffee maker. As I bent to write I flashed on me and Gray as a couple of eighteenth-century gentlemen, with a footman to bear our letters back and forth. Who needed the telephone?

"Miss Mona and I expect you all about 12:30. Don't be late, as we will be nervous wrecks. I don't think the Native American likes me. I feel so unprepared for Foo—never got a chance to grill you for details. Indeed the rain is magical. It seems months since I've seen you. Have you changed? Don't you dare. T."

This time I put it in an envelope. Merle took it from me with studied indifference, squinted up at the mackerel sky, and then said, "Storm'll be out of here tomorrow." We're all weathermen in these parts.

And still that night it came down like the Flood, with a wind that shook the windows in their frames. I lay on the sofa and listened, arms around my knees as I fixed my eyes on the fire, and hated to see the tempest go. Its fury matched something inside me, cheap as a pulp romance, though I couldn't have put it into words. I fell asleep to a mad squall drumming against the ocean side of the house and woke up just before dawn. The fire was blue and orange coals, and the rain was a bare drizzle. I stumbled up to bed.

By midday Sunday the clouds were rolling away, fast-forward, eastward over the hills. I opened the parlor windows to rid the place of stale wood-smoke, and nearly swooned in the heady rush of freshness. I had to be out. I grabbed my parka and, almost an afterthought, the notepad and pen from the kitchen counter, stuffing them in my pocket. Outside the air was crystal, the clouds speeding overhead as white as cotton, all the gray rained out. I headed straight for the beach stairs.

Tramping down, I could see the white surf roiling below me. The last twenty steps had sprung free from the bluff, hanging by a thread and waterlogged like a beached wreck. Gingerly I descended, feeling the last steps sway and strain. Though the tide was officially low, the storm waves heaved and smashed, leaving a bare few feet of beach between the bluff and the water. I walked south for a while, my hood up and my face glazed with the salt spray. The water was magnificent, mad with power, spewing seaweed, foam that seemed a foot thick.

I'd gone a few hundred yards when I was stopped short by a huge pile of rocks extending out into the rushing tide. A crag of the bluff had apparently split off and tumbled down. One slab of sandstone teetering on the pile was covered with grass, which meant it had hurtled all the way from the top. Part of the aerospace mogul's lawn. He must be crazed, I thought with wicked satisfaction, to see his zillion-dollar shorefront crumble away. This slab alone, maybe ten by twelve, was probably worth a hundred grand.

I turned and wandered back, my southward footprints already nearly vanished along the wet sand. I thought of the Malibu tribe, which probably commanded these heights and beaches a thousand years before the Baldwins. There was an old story that made the rounds of the tanning summer flocks—that the Malibus invented the surfboard, not those big Kahunas in Hawaii. I couldn't help but feel a pang for the kingdom Merle had lost, though he certainly didn't act like a man dispossessed. In the wild of the storm's aftermath, it was hard not to think Los Angeles itself was the mirage. Impossible that all that urban shit and negative entropy lay only a half hour south of this new world.

I reached the base of the steps, rapturous as Crusoe. I could see that the hollow behind was clean as a bleached skull, the high waves having flushed it. I ducked under the steps and sat on the stone sill, protected from the wind. Sat there I don't know how long, watching the clouds break now and then to a piercing glimpse of blue. When I brought out the pad and pen from my pocket, I honestly thought I was going to jot some nature notes. I was startled as if by a blip of ESP when I brought the pen to the paper and wrote: "Dear Brian—"

Oh. It took a couple of moments for my head to catch up with my heart. Then I started writing in earnest. "I just wanted you to know I'm glad you came. I don't exactly forgive you for the past—not the abuse when I was a kid and certainly not the dumb-fuck attitude about being gay that severed us for good. But I sort of see you as somebody else now. We'd still fight, no matter how much we saw each other, because the old blood never forgets. All the same, I think you're probably an okay guy—"

I stopped at the wimpy idiocy of that remark and contemplated the surf again. Just then, a black-green crab two feet between the claws came scampering out of the foam and stared at me. It swayed on its pontoon legs and bugged its eyes, positively prehistoric. Then it skittered sideways down the beach. I bent over the pad once more, telling myself this was all a first draft.

"I'll probably never meet Susan and Daniel, so give them my love. I wish all of you long life. What I've learned from this thing is just to say what I feel—"

That didn't sound remotely true, not to mention self-important. It was probably best not to try to organize my feelings ten feet away from the roaring maw of the ocean god. Besides, I was getting a chill. Slipping the pad in my pocket I came around and started up the stairs, which groaned and shuddered under me. The first twenty steps I was ready to jump away if the stairway gave, hoping I'd land in the sand and break no bones.

The wind still whipped about me, flapping my parka like a flag. Halfway up I stopped to catch my breath, slumping against the banister. Runnels and rivulets trickled on all sides, and there was a great gash where a bank of the ice plant had broken away. I climbed more slowly, scoping the beach below, for the moment loving the isolation, and more convinced than ever that I was the first explorer here.

I reached the top, gasping as usual, but as charged as the day I jumped in the water, exactly a week ago. As I tottered across the terrace, the clouds above me gaped, and a shaft of sun shot through, splashing the side of the house. It was going to be perfect tomorrow. I went in by one of the parlor doors, thinking I'd set the table now, still grappling with whether to set it for four or five, so the Indian couldn't say no. Instantly I noticed something in the air, but I couldn't place it. Sweet, like a floral air freshener out of a spray can. I walked through the archway into the dining room.

In the center of the table was a great vase of flowers, pink lilies and callas and tuberoses, drunk with the promise of spring. The vase I knew—a green Craftsman pot, with an overglaze of white seeping down the green like icing—for it usually sat on the sideboard. I could already feel my heart racing as I circled the table, knowing something had gone awry. A folded note was propped against the vase where it faced the kitchen. I picked it up and opened it.

"You must be out for a walk—or a date with Judas. I was so restless I had to get out myself, so I must be all better. Thought you'd like a centerpiece. Now don't fuss too much—Foo's even plainer and earthier than I am! See you tomorrow."

No signature. He never signed. For some reason this made me furious, and I glared at the stupid flowers, though I knew it was all frustration because I'd missed him. I turned and bolted through the kitchen and out to the yard, but of course he was long gone. I trudged across the spongy lawn to the driveway. The tracks in the mud and gravel were very clear. You didn't have to be a Chumash scout. I stamped my foot in one of the ruts, flattening the imprint of the pickup's tread. It was only when I saw bits of white paper in the mud that I realized I was ripping up the note.

Fuck this epistolary life! Stung with disappointment, I headed back into the house. I was gearing up for a real pout, sick to death of being by myself. I couldn't have said what I wanted then. Gray seemed only a symptom. Certainly I longed to talk to him again—had felt it all week, ever since the night we drove to AGORA. But the missed connection sent me back to a larger solitude, the old glum certainty that nobody knew a fraction of me. And nobody ever would now because there was no time.

I hung up the parka and felt the weight of the pad in the pocket. There was no chance at all that I'd finish the letter to Brian, not now. What I'd learned from this thing, I thought with corrosive sarcasm, was how to feel sorry for myself. I stamped upstairs and burrowed under the covers, wincing at the optimistic sun flashing among the broken clouds. And slept for want of anything better, because I was damned if I would sort out all the tempest of emotion.

Which was basically how Mona found me Monday morning. Not in bed, but stubbornly unsorted. The day was as flagrant as all its promise, gaudy cerulean, every leaf and flower craning at the sun. I set the table for five. Mona sailed in at 11:30, foxy in a white silk dress, plumping down her bags from Irvine Ranch.

"You'll be proud of me," she said, nuzzling my cheek. "I made Daphne give me my keys back, and I'm having my number unlisted."

"Mm," I replied tepidly, sniffing at the pasta salad. She'd done as much three different times. I believe she once dug a moat and filled it with alligators, and still Daphne got through.

"Are we in a pissy mood?" she asked.

"Cabin fever," I grumbled, pulling serving dishes from the china cupboard, preparing the transfer from plastic. "Haven't talked to a soul all week."

She wandered into the dining room, and I heard her gasp at the flowers. "Who sent you these?"

"Gray left them."

"Oh, of course," she replied. I perked at the queer inflection in her voice, kind of smutty-sardonic, even as she continued. "I'm surprised he didn't leave you a diamond solitaire."

Icily I stepped to the doorway. "What's that supposed to mean?"

She smiled. "Sweetie, he's so in love with you."

I stared at her. Because my throat constricted and I couldn't speak, I blurted out "Ha!" Darting back into the kitchen, I muddled about among the takeout containers, but now I was in a genuine panic. I felt as if I'd come to after a spasm of dementia, and couldn't remember what happened in between. Total blackout. *Let her be wrong*, I pleaded with the powers of the air.

She stood in the doorway, puffing a Merit, studying me through the smoke. "That's news to you?"

"I think it would be news to *him*," I said, somehow failing to give the irony its proper topspin. "We're barely friends."

"Oh boy. And here I thought you guys were an item." She cringed slightly, then looked helplessly about for an ashtray. I handed her one of the empty takeout tins.

"Why don't you wash the fruit?" I suggested dourly.

I figured I'd finish unloading the takeout, then excuse myself to go up and take my pills. And maybe get ten minutes alone to stop the racing in my head. Mona pulled out the peaches and grapes, spraying them clean in a colander. She knew she'd made a misstep with her idle gossip, but already she was over it, back to chattering about showing the door to Daphne. Gray was no big friend of hers. So what if he had a crush on me? All she really cared about was my welfare, and if I was oblivious of Gray's tender feelings, then the matter was closed. Besides, her kind of passion was the battering kind, accusations and smashing dishes—*Wuthering Heights*, not *Emma*.

But even if I had been oblivious before, now I was racked with guilt. Had I given Gray the wrong signals? Because if I did, he was on his way to getting very hurt. I dumped the calamari salad in a cut-glass bowl and flashed on the drive home last Sunday night from AGORA. I should never have laid my head in his lap. That was the moment I must have led him on, though it certainly came to nothing. He'd let me off at the end of the drive and gone on his way up the mountain road.

But listen to me, trying to play innocent—a disgusting ploy of Catholics, lapsed or otherwise. Mona saw something in Gray, the two times she met him, something more than the puppy-dog loyalty, the fine-tuned self-effacement. She saw a man in the throes, and for being so blind and self-absorbed, it was all my bloody fault.

Mona gasped beside me. "I almost forgot, you're an item all by yourself today!" She wiped her hands on a dish towel and grabbed her alligator bag—endangered species are not on Mona's list of priorities. She rummaged through and produced a newspaper clipping, triumphantly handing it over. "This morning's *Times*."

It was a column from the Calendar section, called "Backstage." A weekly effusion by Nancy Marlowe, a lady of indeterminate age who you felt was the very last person on earth who still wore a hat and gloves to matinees. Mona tapped a fingernail on the final item, headed "Second Coming?"

There was an unannounced special guest last Sunday at AGORA, the performance space in Ocean Park that's always on the cutting edge. "Miss Jesus" made an appearance. First performed three years ago, Tom Shaheen's piece produced a mini firestorm of protest, with picketing church groups and statements of outrage. Shaheen is the only artist ever to be officially censored by the County Board of Supervisors, as a "public threat to decency." The controversy all but blurred the genuine cracked brilliance of the work. It's good to hear that Shaheen has surfaced again. Rumors of his demise are apparently greatly exaggerated.

"Don't you love that 'cracked brilliance'?" enthused Mona. "Just what *I* always say about you."

Well, well. Good old Nancy Marlowe. Silently I took back a decade of snarling venom I had vented over that lady's mawkish "theatah" notes. "Does this mean if I live long enough that I will achieve a mainstream following?"

"Hey, why not? Play your cards right, and before you know it you'll be opening for Madonna."

"Or wait—how about a benefit performance in Jerusalem, before all the world's religious leaders? Arab and Jew, Muslim and Christian, clasping hands at last! The NEA'll fund it in a minute."

We were very merry, practically dancing, me waving the clipping about. I lied about reviews; I'm as shameless as everyone else. We were riffing on it all, but dimly at the back of my mind I could see the special Tony, voted by the Board of Governors, presented by Miss Lansbury to the cracked and brilliant Tom Shaheen in his wheelchair. I grabbed a banana to use as a mike.

"I want to thank the Ayatollah and Mother Teresa for coming tonight, as well as the Senior Nazi from North Carolina. It's a special thrill to be honored by your peers. And to Father Mulcahy of Saint Augustine's, if you're out there, thank you for showing me the way every Friday after catechism class—that if Our Savior took it up the bum, then so must we."

Mona was laughing uproariously, and then her eyes flicked over my shoulder, and she blanched a little, as if we'd been caught *in flagrante*. I spun around—and there was Gray, poking his head around the kitchen door. "Sorry to break up the workshop," he said with a grin, "but the caravan's here."

I shot a glance at the clock above the stove—12:17. They were early! Leave it to WASPs. Gray had already ducked out again, and through the kitchen window I could see Merle striding by, carrying an improbable bundle of bones and linen in his arms, across the shamrock green of the lawn toward the front terrace. My ten minutes alone upstairs had been snatched right out of my hands. I followed Mona dumbly through the dining room and parlor, nothing thought through and no face prepared. We threw open the double french doors, and there between Merle and Gray, on her own two feet now and propped on her owl-headed cane, was the Ancient of Days herself.

"Foo," said Gray, not loud but close to her ear, "this is Mona and Tom."

And she turned with a loftiness and fluidity untouched by her bone-thin frailty. Her hair was in a thick braid wound on the crown of her head, white with glints of yellow still. Her eyes were giant blue behind magnifying glasses. The thousand lines and creases of her face sprang into laugh lines as she grinned and bobbed her head at Mona.

"How-de-do," she said, then peered delightedly at me. "So you're the young man I can't talk about with the vicar."

I squirmed but couldn't look away from her great blue gaze. "Well, I . . . I'm sorry if I . . ."

"That's all right, the vicar's a simpering fool. Why wasn't your picture in the paper too? Who does your publicity?"

"Uh, nobody."

"Just as well. Make 'em want to see you in the flesh." She turned to Merle. "Why don't we have our drink out here?" He nodded and headed back across the lawn, and I wondered if he was her personal servant. "I'm having a bullshot," Foo announced. "You're welcome to join me. I bring my own ingredients because people don't always keep beef broth. Me, I live on beef broth, with or without the vodka."

Leaning firmly on the cane, she pattered in baby steps across to one of the outdoor chairs. Gray hurried over to cradle her as she sat down, and once settled, she beamed with pleasure, gazing out over the bluff to the aching blue of the white-capped sea. I declared that I would go see to the drinks, and Mona and Gray piped up that white wine would be fine. As I rushed back to the kitchen, I realized I hadn't so much as locked eyes once with Gray.

Merle was already fixing Foo's cocktail, so all I had to do was fill two wineglasses and a Coke for me. I'm on too many pills to be drinking at all, but certainly not at noon. Beside me Merle measured the vodka very carefully, half a jigger, as if he knew the lady's capacity intimately.

"I set a place for you," I said, as offhand as I could.

He grunted softly by way of reply, setting all the glasses on the tray, which he handed to me. He didn't follow me out, but I had the impression he would join us for the food. This gave me a nice little liberal lift, as if I had done my part to heal the breach between red man and white. When I came outside the three of them had their chairs grouped in an arc, and they were laughing.

"I was the *baby*," Foo exclaimed, the joke on her, as if who could believe this wizened thing had ever been so young. "Just thirteen when we built this place." She took a stiff gulp of the bullshot as soon as I handed it over. "And Cora was twenty-seven, and Nonny was twenty-two." She seemed quite fiercely proud of getting the numbers exactly right. She waved her glass at Gray. "Your father was three the first summer we lived here."

"Foo, you should have a hat. You'll get too much sun."

She harrumphed. "I can't get enough of anything anymore, except beef broth," she said, then tilted her face to the sky. "It feels grand. I could die right here and be happy."

"Well, don't die before lunch, please," her great-nephew admonished dryly. "Mona and Tom have gone to a lot of trouble."

Mona and I burbled a protest, no trouble at all, and Foo threw an insouciant look in my direction. "Sunstroke wouldn't be such a bad way to go, now, would it?" I shook my head. "Quick and clean. You could toss me right off the bluff." And she gestured with the glass toward the brink, as if toasting the whole vast watery grave between here and Japan.

She wasn't drunk. It was just high spirits, that and a clearly practiced facility for saying whatever she liked. I glanced across at Gray, locking eyes at last, startled to see the worry in his. But I understood immediately: he was fearful the talk of death would pain me. His mouth crinkled as he gave a tiny shrug, as if to say she was incorrigible. I couldn't have cared less. But the other was so obvious now, the way his uncomplicated gaze lingered on my face. How had I managed to miss it before? Even to notice how happy he was. He smiled at me over his wineglass with an openness that choked me with dread.

Somehow Mona had got the old lady talking about the musicales, springing to life those sepia snapshots out of the albums in the parlor. Foo gestured across at the slope of lawn where the audience used to sit. She evoked the long summer twilights listening to Mozart trios, and art songs floated across the evening by women in rippling Fortuny dresses. Foo herself wore a long linen caftan, embroidered in a sort of Navajo motif. On both wrists she sported clusters of silver bracelets, which jingled like a tambourine as she swept her arms about.

"And how did you get the name Foo?" asked Mona, catching the careless frankness of the lady's tone.

Foo gave a hoot. "My full name is Faith Rue Baldwin," she said, ringing it out impressively. "Now really, doesn't she sound like a Puritan drudge? The only thing I ever had any faith in was Franklin Roosevelt. God has never been my dish of tea. The only god I ever met was Henri Matisse. Not Picasso—definitely not Picasso."

"Why don't we go in and eat?" suggested Gray, not exactly cutting her off or dismissing the drumroll of opinions, but clearly no reply was needed.

Foo struggled to rise, and Gray was there beside her, a hand at her elbow. I looked around for Merle, expecting he would carry her in, but apparently she meant to go on her own steam. Mona stepped forward boldly. "May I?" she asked Gray, and he stepped aside neatly, letting her take Foo's arm. "You boys go on ahead and put out the food," instructed Mona, pacing her step to Foo's.

Boys? Bizarre as well as impertinent, since Gray had fifteen years on Mona. But we let it go, for the two women had quite evidently clicked, and Foo was adoring the attention. Gray and I headed into the house, shoulder to shoulder, and I murmured behind my hand: "I only think it's fair to warn you, Mona's on the rebound."

We were laughing as we jaunted into the kitchen. There was very little to do, since Mona's four exotic salads were all in bowls in the fridge. I pulled the long baguette from its paper sack, turned to Gray, and tapped him with it on both shoulders. "You rise from this battle a knight, Sir Graham," I said, and he murmured back, "My lord." Then he snatched the bread and brandished it like a samurai, moving to the cutting board to slice it.

I hauled the salads out and plopped a sprig of basil in the center of each. Then I was in and out of the dining room, setting them on the table. I saw that Mona and Foo had reached the french doors. They stepped into the house and stopped for a little rest before proceeding farther. I dashed back to the kitchen for the final bowl and looked around for the salt and pepper. Gray stepped toward me, the basket of sliced bread in his hands like an offering, and I looked at him. His face was calm and still, a pond without a ripple.

"I really missed you," he said.

I could feel the heat rising from my neck, my first blush since high school. Even two or three hours ago, wouldn't I have taken that remark as perfectly innocent? Now I spoke with a falter. "Yeah, me too, but—we have to talk." I sounded ludicrously grave.

His brows furrowed a millimeter. "About what?"

Behind me through the doorway I could hear Foo and Mona trekking across the parlor, the old lady pointing out favorite bibelots. "About how you feel," I replied miserably. "I mean, how *we* feel."

He looked at me so strangely, for a second I thought I'd got it all wrong, another jog of dementia. Then he smiled, relaxed and easy, infinitely reassuring. "I'm not asking for anything, Tom."

Which left me feeling like a king-size dork, so I tried to toss it off. "Good, 'cause I'm lousy at relationships. Even when I'm not dying."

He chuckled—always leave 'em laughing—and reached over and squeezed my shoulder, but not anything like a lover. Man to man, neutral as Switzerland. I grabbed the pitcher of iced tea, and we headed into the dining room, just as Mona and Foo arrived at the table, *kvelling* about the spread. Gray moved to seat his aunt so she faced the yard. "Where's Merle?" I suddenly remembered, staring at the empty place.

"Oh, Merle won't be joining us," Gray replied smoothly, whisking away the fifth setup and stowing it on the sideboard. And my small liberal victory shriveled and died on the vine.

We sat boy-girl-boy-girl, Mona across from Foo, Gray across from me. As we passed the food, Mona continued to charm the bloomers off Foo, coaxing memories of her sisters and the old days. I'd heard a lot of this before from Gray, and truthfully didn't hang on every word. Cora appeared to have the gift for dance, and Nonny for writing skits, and one was a suffragette and the other neurasthenic. I'm afraid they tended to blur in my brain. I was content to have the surviving member of the trio, all her eccentricities intact. Foo was the past rolled into one.

My own radar was focused on Gray. He didn't seem to be jarred or brooding because of the line I had drawn between us. He threw in his own memories of the aunts, his summers here as a kid. After

Pearl Harbor, the house on the bluff was designated an official lookout by the War Department. "And I'd stand out there all day with a telescope, five years old, and look for enemy subs," he said, grinning across at me, no shadow of awkwardness.

The residue and aftertaste were all on my side. I hadn't even told him I was flattered or touched at all, which I was. Or let him speak his heart, his own way in his own time. Why did I have to jump in like the marines landing, before there was even a situation? And why was I the one hurting now, while he sat across the table laughing and full of life?

"So, Tom," said Foo beside me, breaking into my fruitless circle, "I'm afraid I can't get out at night anymore, or I'd come and see your show."

"Oh, that was just a one-shot deal. I'm not really performing."

"But how can that be, with such a nice provocative notice? And from Nancy Marlowe to boot—the original Philistine."

At this point we were extremely tête-à-tête, and I tried to smile at the others and bring them in, but Gray was turned half around in his chair, pointing Mona toward something outside. "Well, I'm sort of retired," I replied lamely.

"At *your* age?" Foo was stung with dismay. "It's not those Holy Rollers, is it? You mustn't succumb! We need artists like you sticking it up their whoopsis every day!"

She was really quite exercised. I looked down at my plate. "No, it's not that. Actually I'm . . . not well."

Curious, how reluctant I was to tell her. For the first time I wanted to protect someone from the nightmare. What did she need it for, ninety-one and barely ambulatory? I looked over at her. She was mortified—didn't know what to say. And I didn't realize the others had heard the last part. There was silence all around the table, till Gray said gently, "Auntie, do you know what AIDS is?"

She looked every one of her ninety-one years just then, but you couldn't mistake the Baldwin backbone as she sat straight up. Her blue gaze deepened, austere and heroic, the old pioneer stock. "Of course," she replied with a faint edge of disdain, as if someone had imputed that she'd gone senile. Then she reached out a bony hand and covered mine on the table.

I could feel the silver bracelets, cool at the tips of my fingers. Her grip was rock-firm as a lifeguard's, as if she would pull me bodily from the whirlpool. Her eyes shifted from me to her nephew. Her profile was like the prow of an ancient ship. And when she looked at him, a shudder of grief and sorrow transfigured her face. In a blaze of understanding, I knew that she knew he loved me, just as Mona had known. There was such a terrible silence then. It probably only lasted five seconds, but I couldn't bear it, that circle of faces so grim and melancholy.

"Really, I'm fine," I said, morbidly plucky. "I'm not going to be checking out anytime soon."

Mona and Gray looked startled. They were accustomed to hearing quite the opposite, my sardonic version of Foo's "Toss me off the bluff." But I'd said as much to Brian when he left the other day, and figured I owed the same to these, my loved ones. Not that I couldn't be wrong. For all I knew I'd wake up dead tomorrow morning. But that wasn't how it felt right now, not since the night of the Resurrection, nor all through the ravishing storm.

Foo sighed. "It's disgusting, how some people get to live as long as me." She looked bitterly round the room, then out to the parlor, as if the house was somehow to blame.

"Well, but I never expected life to be fair," I retorted, "did you?" Her hand still held mine as fiercely as ever, but now I could feel the force had shifted. It was I who had to pull her from the whirlpool. "Besides," I said softly, "nobody has it easy." None of them needed to know I was quoting the brute tormentor of my youth.

"Cora was sixty-two," declared Foo, and I knew she meant the death year. "That was thirty-three years ago." She shook her head in wonderment, and still with a certain tenacious pride in pinning the numbers down. She made a scoffing sound. "And then some people end up twenty years in bed and don't even know who they are anymore." She looked at me again, demanding nothing and holding nothing back, as if she'd been saving all these years the love left over from those she'd lost.

"All my friends died," I said, something of a non sequitur, but knowing too that no elaboration was required. Then I nodded across the table. "Except these two. They're not allowed to."

Hand in hand we looked at Gray and Mona. Only then did I see how deep their silence was, and what a great gulf had suddenly yawned between their side of the table and ours. For we were the ones, old Foo and I, who skirted the fields of death, who could feel the breath of the dark farmer on our necks. It was so odd to see the two faces, Gray's and Mona's, so aligned: respect, even awe. It made me feel about ninety years old myself.

"Well, now you've got three," declared Foo, her voice as firm as the clasp of her hand. "And I want you to know I'm very honored to have the Antichrist living in my beach house."

It broke the funereal air, and we laughed. The rest of the meal, we stuck to lighter fare. Mona and I told Foo about my death threats during the first Miss Jesus tour, one after another on my answering machine. Then the voodoo doll and disemboweled cat, left outside my apartment door.

"By then I couldn't tell if I had fans in a devil cult or what," I said. "But the death threats were all from born-agains. 'Hi, my name's Donny Lee, and Jesus is Lord, and I got a bullet here's got yer name on it.' I never got a burning cross, though. Those guys were too busy harassing gooks and niggers. And wouldn't they all just *love* to know I've got the big A."

Foo was having a ball. Her own forays in the arts had been of a much more elevated sort, and I doubted she'd ever had a First Amendment crisis. Nevertheless, she'd developed a taste for anarchy, just from having lived through so many decades of drivel and hypocrisy. *What the hell* was her attitude about almost everything, especially institutions and all political parties. It thrilled me to make her laugh, and nothing seemed to shock her. The only grandparent I ever had was my dad's dad, by then a shell in a wheelchair, spewing hate and ethnic slurs at everything that moved. Foo was like getting a second chance—finally, one's own kind.

"Hey, what time is your show?" Gray asked her as we drained the last of the pitcher of tea.

"Two-thirty," she said, gasping to hear it was only ten minutes off. She turned apologetically to me. "You'll forgive me, Tom, I can't miss 'A Woman Alone.'"

Mona clapped her hands. "My favorite soap!"

Already we were a family that didn't stand on ceremony. The women rose immediately to retire to the parlor, where a prehistoric Sylvania black-and-white perched on the hi-fi cabinet. I'd never once turned it on, but apparently it worked. Again Mona led Foo slowly, as I started to clear the table, once more calculating when I might slip away for a medicine break. And Gray said briskly, "Leave all that. Come on, show me where the steps are broken."

Why not? I didn't really want to get away from him. Didn't even mind if we talked some more about It. As we headed outside through the cloistered arch, striding across the lawn to the bluff's edge, there was something peculiarly raw and vital—manly, I almost said—about sharing the land today in its pristine state. I was happy to be with him, glad we had put behind us the worry of misalliance.

"She always knows more than I think she does," he said with a comic shake of his head. For a second I thought he'd seen what I saw—the spasm of sorrow as Foo realized her nephew had fallen in love with a dead man. But all he meant was AIDS. "You watch, she'll be on the phone tomorrow to the library, wanting everything they've got."

"I'm officially adopting her," I informed him. "I want papers drawn up and everything."

As we started down the beach steps, the sun on the water was blindingly bright. Which was why we didn't see Merle till we were practically on top of him. Gray was in front of me, heading down the second zigzag of stairs. Then he stopped so short I collided into his shoulder. Merle sat on the step below, his lunch spread out beside him. He looked cornered, almost cowering. "I thought you were off to a meeting," said Gray, breezy and neutral.

"I'm back," came the curt reply. His black eyes didn't leave Gray's face, never once flicking to mine. He moved to gather his lunch together—Big Mac, double fries, and a shake.

"No, don't move," interjected Gray, stepping over.

Hastily I followed suit, but hyperaware of the cold glare that he cast like a spell as I passed him. Gray picked up the pace, and we thundered down the next thirty steps to the midpoint landing. Soon as I caught up, I murmured out of the side of my mouth, "Why do you suppose he treats me like General Custer?"

Gray laughed. "Ignore it."

"My family were all bigots, but I don't think they had any active role in the Native American genocide. They were still picking potatoes back in Ireland."

"He's just very protective."

"Of you? But you can take care of yourself."

And he really guffawed this time, darting away and down the stairs, as if I would never catch him now. He had the wild innocence of a kid sometimes, which sprang in part from never having to grow up and get a job. He might be the family loser, but would always be the youngest too, unworldly in ways that amazed me. I trotted down in his wake, recalling out of nowhere how at fourteen I longed to be urban and sophisticated, trapped as I was in the provinces. And I got what I wanted, and now it meant nothing. Reaching the place where Gray stood, leaning out over the banister to study the damage below, I realized how I had come full circle. Exiled from the jaded city, and a simple man for a friend.

"How bad is it?" I asked, bracing myself beside him and craning out to see. "Doesn't it look like it's torn away from the pilings?"

"Yeah," he answered ruefully. "That whole bottom section's gonna have to be rebuilt. Cost an arm and a leg." He tilted back up to a standing position and ran a hand through his hair. "They'll probably just let it rot."

"Who? The Foundation?" He nodded. "But that's crazy. They can't let this place fall apart." I was indignant, not least because I thought he was being wimpy. *Make* them fix it.

"Sure they can," he retorted with some impatience. "Once Foo's gone, this will *all* come down." He swept an arm upward, to the top of the bluff. "There's four lots up there, minimum. Eight, ten million bucks, just for the *land.*"

"But wait—" My head for business got worse, the higher the numbers went. "What about you? It's yours for life, isn't it?"

He gave out with a sharp, one-note laugh, the sound of a man who'd learned to mock his fate. "Oh no—they cut me right out, those lawyers. I can live at the ranch for as long as I want, but that's it. No frills."

I was in shock. In an instant the house on the bluff had been stolen right out from under me. Till this moment, nothing seemed as provisional as I. Now my whole island—the six-story firs, the fish as old as the century—was suddenly finite, mortal as the frail and final Baldwin sister with the owl-headed cane. The last thing I figured I had to worry about was me outliving the beach house. Not anymore. I thought of the broken cliff in the swirling tide, that patch of the mogul's lawn. Nothing would hold. There was no safe place.

"I don't get rich people," I said at last. "How could your dad take everything away like that? What did you do to him? You're such a pussycat."

Gray looked at me bewildered, as if it couldn't have been more obvious. "I told him I was gay."

Of course. Did I think I had the monopoly on fathers who wanted to crawl in a hole and die of shame? The vast tract of Baldwin lands didn't make a smudge of difference. When it came to hetero paranoia, throwing up at the thought of your blood kin sucking dick, a kingdom was as good as a tenement.

"Well, I hope she lives to be a hundred and thirty," I said. "And I hope the old man died screaming in pain."

His mouth crinkled, just as it had when Foo came out with something audacious. "You're so Sicilian," he declared, which I chose to take as a compliment.

We tramped back up the stairs, me still feeling burned and cheated, as if I'd lost an inheritance of my own. It was going to be neck and neck as to who went first, me or Foo and the beach house. Right now I wouldn't bet a sawbuck on any of us seeing next Christmas.

Gray was a step behind me. I could feel him poised to take my elbow if I needed it, just like he did for his aunt, and I didn't like the feeling. Then he hesitated and turned to look down the beach, this being the best vantage before the stairs rose through a cleft in the bluff, cutting off the view. As I watched him drink it in, a muzzy smile on his face, I thought: *He's going to lose more than I am.*

After all, I would be long gone. This place was his last perk as a Baldwin. Foo would go, and then the beach house, and then he'd just get old, no place to come and putter anymore. Curiously, there was never any question in my mind that Gray was safe from AIDS, though he'd never admitted his antibody status to me. I was sure he'd have a full and natural life, and with his genes that could be forty more years. The nice thing was, it didn't make me bitter. I only felt protective as I stepped up behind him and laid a hand on his shoulder.

"You have to understand, he's been through hell," Gray said thoughtfully, as we watched the break of the waves below. "I've known him since I was a kid. He used to be a surfer—down there." He nodded south to the pipeline of the Trancas Wash. I couldn't figure out *who* he meant, then realized it was Merle.

"Which hell would that be?" I asked, trying not to sound sarcastic, as if AIDS were the only inferno worthy of the name.

"Drugs." And he shrugged his shoulders beneath my hand, a gesture that felt hopeless.

"Oh. So that's the kind of meeting you meant."

He nodded. "For years he was a dealer, up and down the beach. I didn't have any idea." And I realized the shrug had been mostly about his own stupidity. "He got busted. Six and a half years in Lompoc. Now he's clean."

I don't know what astonished me more, Gray Baldwin talking about dealing and getting busted, or the image of Merle as a surfer. Yet it was possible even now to see behind the Indian's massive barrel shape—fat like a badly aging football jock—the young warrior with the blue-black hair and muscles for days.

"He really does have Malibu blood," continued Gray. "His grandfather used to trace it all back for him, just like the 'begats' in the Bible. Back before the missions came and herded them off their land." More Catholic crimes, I thought, making a mental note for my next Pope show. So I almost missed the throwaway line that followed. "We used to be . . ." Another shrug, barely a ripple. ". . . for a while."

No noun there. Its absence felt like a small electric jolt in the pit of my stomach. "You were lovers?" My hand slipped off his shoulder.

"For a *minute*," he retorted, hearty with self-deprecation. "It was years ago—feels like a hundred." At last he turned with an easy smile. "But I think he's still very possessive. Anyway, that's why he treats you like General Custer. It's probably not even conscious."

I stared at him blankly. "You and *Merle?*"

"He thought you and I had something going. I told him no, but . . ." He let it trail off and shrugged yet again, but this time careless, like *What're you gonna do?*

Then he resumed climbing the stairs, his lanky arms swinging on either side. I scrambled after, stung into silence. It wasn't even Merle that was so flabbergasting. Frankly, I'd never thought of Gray with anybody. I assumed, from all that self-deprecation, that he'd only had the most fleeting encounters. Blow job here and there, falling for guys who wouldn't put out, the usual dog-and-pony show of longing and self-loathing. By contrast, Merle was so fucking *real*.

I hadn't even reached the top of the steps, my lungs puffing like a leaky bellows, before I scored myself for this one too. It was all my own arrogance that had put Gray down as a man of limited carnal knowledge. My ridiculous worldliness. At least he had an ex still woven in the fabric of his life. My guys, I couldn't track down a single one if you paid me a bounty, for they had all disappeared like thieves in the night.

And here was the oddest thing of all. By the time we reached the landing at the top, I'd completely revised my opinion of Graham Cole Baldwin. Suddenly I found him fascinating and utterly unpredictable. His whole vanilla persona had vanished on the spot.

He waited for me on the landing. I usually panted and whined right about now, especially when I had an audience. But suddenly it was important to me to show how energized and invigorated I felt. Hardly pausing for breath, I darted across the lawn and threw myself into a cartwheel. The tilt in my belly spilled out in a squeal of laughter. I landed on my feet, but the centrifugal force wasn't finished. I pitched over into a second wheel, giddier now, catching a glimpse of Gray topsy-turvy. This time I landed on one foot, wobbly, and should have called it a day. But I went for a third and could feel my arms buckle beneath me. Halfway through the wheel I crumpled to the ground in a heap.

I tasted the green of the rain-soaked grass and rolled over onto my back, gasping with laughter now. The dome of blue sky was deliriously bright, the shapes of the trees wavering at the edges of my vision, an afterglow of dizziness. Gray came sauntering up and stood over me, hands on his hips, the sun behind him. I stretched my arms luxuriously over my head, feeling the shirt pull out of my pants, leaving my belly naked. I felt—no other word—sexual. Like I wanted to show off, I who'd decided long since that I had nothing left to show.

"If this boy doesn't calm down, Mrs. Shaheen," drawled Gray, "we're going to have to put him on Ritalin." He held out a hand. "Now come on, before you get all wet."

I could feel the chill of the damp in my shoulders and butt. "Please, sir, I haven't got muddy since I was six. I need regression therapy."

He grunted and grabbed my arm, pulling me to my feet in a single motion, without any yank. Suddenly we were face-to-face, an inch away, and he was grinning. This was more disorienting than all the upheaval of my late acrobatics. "What can I tell you?" I said, working to keep the banter up. "Sometimes I get these urges."

I broke free then, or else I would have kissed him. It seemed perverse even to me, a moment of instant replay from my reckless youth. Now we were ambling comfortably across the terrace, my arms swinging at my sides, mimicking his country gait. Gray appeared to have noticed nothing unseemly about my sprawl in the grass or the bristling proximity of our lips, but then I couldn't be sure anymore what he saw. Or what he wanted.

But I had the sinking feeling, as we reached the french doors, that all the others had got it wrong. Mona, Foo, and Merle—every one of them so convinced he had lost his heart. It was just their own romantic claptrap. Each of us pulled a door wide, and we walked in blinking our eyes from the dazzle of the afternoon. They'd got it all backward. They were protecting the wrong man.

I was the one in trouble here.

The TV screen was the first thing that came into focus—rolling credits, superimposed on a freeze frame of a guy and a girl embracing. He was stripped to the waist, and she was buttoned up in a high-neck Victorian collar—standard procedure on the soaps, where the men did all the tease-and-flash. Then I made out the two figures on the sofa, Mona and Foo. The old lady seemed to be resting her head on Mona's shoulder, but when I came around closer I saw that Foo was slumped against the back cushion, softly snoring. Mona slouched beside her, legs tucked up under the white silk dress, still as a cat.

She winked at me and Gray, pointed a finger at Foo, and mouthed her words at a bare whisper: "She fell asleep in the love scene. Just like Daphne—only Daphne does it in real life."

Gray leaned forward and peered at his sleeping aunt. He reached a hand to her shoulder and seemed about to wake her, but Mona stopped him. "Give her another fifteen minutes. Then I'll make her a cup of tea."

Gray nodded, content to have a woman's opinion in the matter. Then he said to no one in particular, "I think I'll go find Merle."

As he headed out through the dining room I felt like spitting after him, as if taking my cues from the soap: "I don't care *what* you do with him!"

When I looked at Mona she tilted her head in a puzzled frown. "What're you scowling about?" she asked, innocently enough.

"Nothing!" I snapped, and she drew a stern finger to her lips, so I wouldn't wake Foo. Mouth slack, folds and wattles expressionless, the old lady looked as if she'd sleep through a nuclear attack. But I moved to Mona's other side, which happened to be the spot where

I'd scrunched through the week of rain. I curled up beside her. She seemed untroubled by my own brief squall, perhaps because she'd ridden more than anyone the hills and curves of my personal roller coaster. She clasped my hand and squeezed it.

"I'm still not sure," she whispered, "but if I had to bet the farm I'd say no." I looked at her, bewildered. Did we all talk to one another like this, finishing sentences hours later, picking up strings of conversation no one could possibly follow? "Foo," said Mona impatiently. "She doesn't appear to be a daughter of the mother goddess. If you catch my drift." Got it: not a dyke. "I gave her lots of openings—talked about all the bad girls I've been through. Now I didn't come straight out and ask, but it looks as if she might be just a spinster after all. A fabulous one, however."

The tube had done its schizophrenic shudder through nine commercials and settled on the news. An overcoiffed anchor was reading his TelePrompter like holy writ. Someone had invaded a bleary country, and a senator was ranting. Due to the convex black-and-white screen, it seemed like news from the fifties.

"You want today's scoop?" I asked Mona out of the side of my mouth. "Gray and Merle used to be a thing."

"The Indian?" A brief pause, while she processed this. "Well, I'll be damned."

"It's worse than you think. I've decided I like him."

"The Indian?"

"No—Gray. And he's not nearly as smitten with me as you suppose. Which I hardly blame him, because that would be practically necrophilia."

There was a miniscreen above and to the right of the anchor's head, on which now flashed a man's face, pudgy and surly. I knew this man but couldn't quite place him. Mona began to speak, always ready to play Miss Lonelyhearts, and I dug a finger into her arm to silence her.

"In Hartford, Connecticut, today," the anchor intoned, "a grand jury investigation of racketeering in the construction business had a major setback. The inquiry into the billion-dollar ripoff of federal housing funds by builder Gerald Curran"—My Jerry Curran! The demon meanie of Chester was going to get his at last!—"had scheduled a star witness for today's session. But this morning a bomb went off in the Southport home of Curran's partner, Brian Shaheen, killing Shaheen, his wife, and son. Without Shaheen's testimony, the trail of Curran's money—through savings and loans in eleven states—will be very hard to trace."

And he went right on to the next item, the tragic death of a Thoroughbred who'd won the Triple Crown. For a moment I thought Mona hadn't picked up on the name, she was so quiet beside me. I had an instant's fleeting hope that I could slip away upstairs without anybody knowing. Then I felt her fingers close about my arm, wanting to be there for me. I didn't exactly take it wrong, but couldn't bear the thought that I would be required to have a reaction.

Horror is not the same as grief. That's what I learned in the long surreal minutes that followed. Grief I'm a pro at—been through it three different times in the last two years. Rivers of tears at the drop of a hat. This was terribly dry instead, as if my eyes, my very blood, were shriveling in a heat like radiation. No feeling seemed to work. But I don't mean numb either. The pain was like revulsion, rejecting the world the way a body rejects a transplant, preferring death to invasion. Mona held on, her grip as firm and unequivocal as Foo's had been when my own death was announced. She made it clear it was my move.

I wonder how long we would have sat there motionless, watching the weather and sports like zombies. But then I heard the bang of the kitchen door, and my heart started racing again—had it stopped entirely? A moment later Gray came walking in, and the breeziness of his stride hurt like a physical pain, as if he had only come in to mock my sudden paralysis. And something in me recalled, like a desperate reach across a chasm, the luxury of my roll on the grass—was it ten minutes ago? All gone. Nothing but death surrounded me.

"I put the kettle on," said Gray, and at last a feeling surfaced, gulping for air. White rage. *So how's your buddy Merle?* I wanted to sneer, as he leaned toward his slumbering aunt. "Hey, Foo," he said softly, "how 'bout a nice cup of bouillon?"

"His brother got killed," said Mona, the words sounding brittle and foolish, like a joke that died.

I turned to look at his face, the puzzled frown of unbelief, his eyes darting from Mona to me and back, the wrench of pain. As Mona haltingly filled in the details, a grim parody of broadcast news, I felt a sharp and guilty pang of relief that the two of them were here. As if I had somehow outwitted the deepest pain by having this family instead, and not those far-off blood strangers who'd just been obliterated. This spasm of coldness only lasted a moment as well. But I remember thinking, as Mona and Gray tossed the horror back and forth, that they would come up with something for me to feel, if I just stayed dumb and motionless.

Then Foo woke up. She made a couple of beeping sounds and flailed the air in front of her face, wiping the cobwebs away. Her great blue eyes swept the room like radar, then lighted on Gray. I don't know how he looked to her, but she said, "What's wrong? Am I sick?"

Gray crouched down beside her. "No, Auntie. Tom just found out his brother died."

The old lady's hands fluttered in her lap. Then her blue eyes, vast as the winter sea, came to rest on my face. "But"—she hated to get her facts wrong—"I thought he was an only child."

And there the unreality broke. I came to my shaky feet and staggered forward, snapping the TV off. I turned and faced my made-up family, every one of them helpless. How would I ever protect them? I held out my arms, and Gray rose up to meet me, cradling me close. I could feel my weight let go as I slumped against him, neither brother nor lover. And then I cried.

F O U R

FINALLY I CALLED MY MOTHER, BECAUSE I COULDN'T THINK of anyone else. All the cousins and uncles and neighbors of my childhood had disappeared—not so much as a Christmas card in the nine years since my father died. The past had taken Brian's side against me, ever since our brawl at the old man's funeral. Well, to be fair, I guess I cut the whole lot of them as much as they cut me. But here I was now, with no ally close to the tragedy, no one to throw an Irish arm around my shoulders and tell me life was a bitch. I must have cried nonstop for a couple of hours, but some of that I think was just the old feeling of being left out.

I don't even remember saying good-bye to Foo. It was decided in the kitchen that Merle would take her home, and Gray and Mona would stay with me. By then I was wrapped in the afghan, curled in a ball on the sofa. Mona put a mug of tea and a box of Kleenex on the coffee table, and when the afternoon shadows began to lengthen, Gray laid a fire. I had fallen away from sobbing—barely ten minutes of that—into a sort of exhausted blubber, like something on the stove at a low boil.

I couldn't exactly see in my mind the blasted house in Southport. It was more like a loop of war footage, bodies blown limb from limb by land mines, naked children running on fire with napalm. Then all my own deaths came back, Bruce and Tim and Mike Manihan, thin as Auschwitz and racked in their final comas. Somehow I couldn't make myself focus on Brian. As for Susan and Daniel, I'd never seen so much as a picture of them. So I more or less blubbered instead for the whole frail world, with a liberal dose of self-pity into the bargain.

It was dark by the time the crying stopped. I realized I was staring blankly into the fire, and that Mona was sitting beside me, stroking my leg. Gray was hunched in the easy chair, elbows on his knees. "I guess it was Jerry Curran who did it," I said in a toneless voice. I tried to imagine this and failed, unable to see around the adolescent image of my brother and his sidekick, joined at the hip as they rollicked through high school. I slapped the arm of the sofa beside me, turning my two friends' heads. "But we don't really know *anything.*"

Mona pushed her glasses up, tight on the bridge of her nose. "Remember Leslie?" Yes—the twisted affair before Daphne, a grad student at UCLA. Miss Bulimia. "Well, she teaches at Yale now. I called her and had her read me everything in the New Haven papers."

She's so hands-on, that Mona. Briskly she picked up a spiral notepad beside her, consulting a scribble of notes as she filled me in. Apparently the Curran investigation had been a big story for a couple of months, with allegations of a huge skimming operation involving federal highway funds. Obscurely I remembered Brian talking about repaving I-91, new bridges and cloverleaf inter-changes. I leaned forward expectantly, suddenly ravenous for details, as if the filling-in would soften the explosion.

Jerry was already under indictment for the highway fraud, out on bail and crowing he was innocent. Meanwhile the grand jury had turned up another whole can of worms. While probing Mob control of the unions in Connecticut, they uncovered another ocean of diverted funds, this time in low-cost subsidized housing. Curran Construction was the builder of record in almost every case, a network that spread over eleven states. Thousands of units at a hundred grand a throw, paid for and never built. And when they followed the gush of that hemorrhage of cash, it all disappeared in the laundry, surfacing in squeaky-clean vaults in Zurich, untraceable.

"Your brother's been giving depositions all along," said Mona. "He and Curran have stuck to the same line since the beginning— that the Mob set *them* up. But then about two weeks ago, something changed. Brian made a secret deal with the prosecutors. He'd settle for a perjury rap, in exchange for which he'd connect all the dots around Jerry Curran. Today he was supposed to testify behind closed doors. Except somebody let out the secret."

The dollar amounts went right by me, as well as the intricate three-card monte by which the money was siphoned off. For the first time I actually took it in that my brother was a crook. No depth of slime surprised me when it came to Jerry Curran, but Brian— Eagle Scout of Eagle Scouts, darling of whole orders of Brothers. Say it ain't so.

Gray snorted and reached to poke the fire. "Sounds like Brian found out he was gonna be left holding the bag. So he decided to sing. And ol' Jerry killed the canary." The gumshoe cadence was filtered through a layer of black irony. Nonetheless, his grasp of the gangster modalities amazed me. I was still groping to catch up, trying to figure where my brother's trip to L.A. fit in.

"Oh yes, and Curran's made a statement," Mona declared. "Leslie saw it on the local channel. He's choking back the tears, and he blames the killings on secret forces out to destroy them both. I guess that would be like the Black Hand."

I shook my head. "Poor Brian. He should've kept playing baseball."

"Leslie's going to fax all the coverage in the morning. Daphne's got a machine in her office." The dyke underground strikes again.

"Tom," said Gray, discreet as a vicar himself, "is there someone in the family you can call?"

Why, I nearly asked, for it was all over now but the useless tears and bad dreams. Then I realized somebody might want to know my feelings about the death arrangements. I recalled how good Gray was at funerals. And sat there trying to think of the cousins and uncles by name, but they were all gone, or at least I was. Let Susan's family take care of all that, I thought. I knew right then I wasn't going. I didn't care if everyone thought it was terribly bad form.

"No," I said, shaking my head slowly, "but someone should probably call my mother."

I knew of course that the someone was I. So did Gray and Mona. We stood up all three, no further ado, as if we had no time to waste. It was going on eight o'clock, almost too late to call back East. We straggled out through the kitchen, Gray foisting a banana on me, which I ate as we strolled to Mona's car. Then I remembered I didn't have the number, and had to duck back in.

My chewed and battered Filofax was stowed in the drawer of the zinc table. I lifted it out, crammed with prescriptions and lab results, and turned to the phone index. These days it was mostly a log of dead friends and specialists. I flipped to S, and there she was: *Nora Shaheen, 130 West Hill Road* in Chester. Though I hadn't dialed the number in seven or eight years, it printed itself anew on my brain like a serial number from an old prison term.

I tossed the organizer back in the drawer and the banana peel in the sink. I spun around to go and caught a glimpse of white on the counter. Then stared: the slip of paper with Brian's address, curled up next to the coffee maker. Haltingly I reached for it. The butt end of the banana was sticking out of my mouth, like a retard monkey. I read the scrap of his handwriting and thought of the unfinished letter I wrote on the beach.

The missed connection stung my eyes. A sob was in my throat, till I nearly choked on the fruit. *Brian, I'm sorry,* I pleaded in my head. Feeling him really dead for the first time. The apology was for him and me, for what I had kept from happening between us a week ago, because of my stubborn resentment.

I was weepy when I reached the car, and Gray and Mona said nothing as we drove to the Chevron station. Mona parked up snug beside the phone booth, but they waited in the car while I made the call. Gray had written out his credit card number for me, which I accepted without complaint, since it would have been pretty tacky to call collect. My stomach knotted as I punched the number in. *I don't have a son,* I could hear her saying.

The nurse/companion was hostile, right from the start. She'd been fielding calls from the cops and the distant cousins all day long. She was querulous when I gave my name, resistant to my assertions of family ties. "He was my *brother*," I stated emphatically, at last eliciting a disoriented "Oh." She obviously hadn't a clue that there was another one out there.

"I'm sorry for your loss," she said, straightening the collar of her dignity. Catholic, without a doubt. "We thought it was better not to tell her."

"*Who* thought?" I demanded crisply, but secretly relieved. At least I wouldn't have to hear my mother cry again.

"Me and the doctor," she replied, at once apologetic and defensive. "Mr. Shaheen, she don't know any of 'em when they come. She likes the boy, but it don't register who he is."

I pulled back from her use of the present tense, wincing as if I'd burned myself. I could hear Brian at the beach house, talking about the kid and his grandma. "Yes, well that's fine," I said, suddenly feeling stuffy in the booth's close quarters. "And what are *your* plans? I mean—"

"Money-wise?" Miss Mary Alice Lynch had clearly given this some thought. "The lawyer called. He says I'll be paid by your brother's estate, but it might take a couple weeks before it starts coming. Well, I can't wait like that. I'm a woman alone." Even through the tension I wanted to bleat with laughter at the phrase. "Besides, without family around, it's too much responsibility. I'm elderly myself. She's probably better off in a home."

Sweat had sprung out on my forehead, and I could feel the shirt clammy against my torso. The terror of suddenly having the Problem dropped in *my* lap made me want to scream. But I did the right and gutless thing, purring and kissing her ass with compliments, begging her not to act hastily, wheedling from her the lawyer's number.

"Please—Mary Alice, you can't leave now," I beseeched her, cozy and desperate. "I'll make sure you're paid. But I hope you understand, this is a very hard time right now." I practically gagged on these sentiments, and hoped she'd put it down to the choke of grief.

"Well, all right," she replied in a martyred tone. "You'll be coming in for the funeral?"

"Actually, no." I could feel her stiffen three thousand miles away. "See, I'm in the hospital myself. My doctor won't let me."

"Mm," she replied primly. I imagined she could hear the traffic whizzing by on the coast road.

"But I'll be checking in," I assured her, oozing spunk. "I'll get right on this, I promise. Thanks for everything. Brian always said you were a saint. Bye now."

But she wasn't finished with me, was Mary Alice Lynch. "Don't you want to know how she is?"

The curdle of contempt reminded me of every nun in grammar school. But she had all the marbles, and she knew it. "Oh sure," I replied, suitably chastened. "She doing all right?"

"No, she's slipping," sighed Mary Alice, taking a noisy sip of something vile like Postum. "Hardly gets out of bed anymore. And she doesn't always get to the bathroom, if you know what I mean."

I stared glassily out of the booth to where Gray and Mona waited. Mona was smoking, sending a billowing stream out the side window as she and Gray talked gravely, bending close. I ached to be with them.

"But you know what?" asked the nurse/companion, her voice

suddenly pregnant with feeling. "I think she knows. She's been agitated all day. I had to double her medication and give her a good massage. It's like she knows her boy is dead."

I could hear the tears begin to gather in her voice, sloppy as an Irish wake. "Look, I'll have to call you later," I said quickly. "My doctor just walked in—I'm having a spinal tap. Don't worry, I'll see that you're taken care of. Bye."

I set the receiver back in the cradle and leaned my forehead against the glass wall beside me, squirming at the awfulness of what had just transpired. Then I pulled open the accordion door and walked out, stunned to think I might actually have to get involved. Almost in answer my knee began to throb, sending tendrils of pain along the nerves to my ankle. As I hobbled toward the car I berated myself with a sneer: Whatever made me think I *wouldn't* be stuck with the problem now? As if through a crack in a wall I started to see what Brian had shielded me from. I opened the rear door and slumped in Mona's backseat, on total overload.

The two of them were terrific, of course. As soon as I'd related the details of my chat with Mary Alice, Gray piped up that he would call the lawyer. Then, as Mona swung around onto the coast road again, she called back over her shoulder: "I hope you're not thinking of going, Tom, because we don't think it's a good idea." I perked up instantly, pathetic with relief. The pain in my knee reduced by half. But because I was silent, Mona seemed to think I needed more convincing. "I mean, if your mom doesn't even *know* about it. Who are you going for? You can cry all you want to here. Besides, we don't think you should breathe all that airplane shit."

"Yeah, you're probably right," I replied, subdued and laconic, and the two of them in front smiled at their small victory.

We drove the rest of the way in silence, and I thought about the weird team of my mother and her nurse. Put-upon and self-vindicating, Mary Alice was clearly a carbon-copy version of the type. That thin whine of martyrdom had skirled at the edges of every sitdown meal of my childhood. Now my mother herself, it sounded, lay in an ever deeper fog, the pictures on her dressing table mocking her like total strangers. Mary Alice did all the living in the house. It was utterly grotesque, the perfect end to our luckless nuclear family. And the final twist would be the shell of my mother surviving me.

Mona turned in at the drive and let us out, promising to be back in the morning with all the faxes. She leaned out the window to hug me, pulling me down to plant a smeary kiss of cherry Revlon on my cheek. Then she gave a husky whisper in my ear. "You've got to *live* now," Mona said staunchly. "That's all you've got to do. First things first."

I gave her back a watery smile, not quite sure if I was being given advice about grief or AIDS or what. We waved her away as she lurched off, spitting gravel, then turned and made for the house. It had never been stated specifically that Gray would stay the night, but now it was a foregone conclusion, for we were carless. No more did we have plans for dinner, or any agenda at all. Yet it seemed both right and proper, almost a ritual, as he moved about the kitchen, pulling ice cream from the freezer, bowls, bananas, Hershey's sauce. I sat on the stool by the zinc table, lazily watching.

He hadn't asked if I wanted the dizzying sundae he now constructed, one for each of us, but I was happy to go with the drift. The wordlessness between us was as comforting as the piling on of ingredients. And when the confections were done, sprinkled pecans and bananas sliced on top—he's got this thing about me and bananas, goosing my potassium—Gray drew up a second rickety stool, and we dug in. Numb and atavistic, like beasts at a trough. It was very, very soothing.

I was down to scraping the bowl before I spoke. "It's like there's two Brians," I said, not sure at all I could draw this picture. "And the one that got killed is the one who was here last week. That guy could die like anyone else. But the other one—Brian the god, with his perfect body, who couldn't make a wrong move if he tried—that one's still back in Chester. Like nothing's changed."

Gray nodded pensively, licking his spoon.

"And I'm sad for the one that died, him and his poor decent family. He was sweet to me, you know? Made me breakfast." A flush of tears caught me unawares, making me gulp and bat at my eyes. "But the other one—I can still smell his sweat. It's like we're still sharing the same room. And I hate him because he won't look at me. To him I don't even exist."

A long silence, since Gray had nothing pithy to say in reply, for which I was grateful. After a while he reached across with his napkin and rubbed at my cheek, wiping the lipstick off. Then he sided the dishes into the sink. Again without consultation, we headed upstairs to call it a day, dousing lights as we went. When we reached the upstairs landing he headed across to Cora's room, not stopping to hug me, but I didn't mind. Instead he turned at the door and smiled: "Now don't forget, I'm right here."

I nodded as he stepped inside, and found myself touched beyond measure by his delicacy and restraint. Whatever upheaval he'd caused me earlier, down by the beach, had dissipated. I wanted nothing from him now but his clear head and his instinct for empathy. The jealousy I'd felt over Merle, and the consequent seizure of need, seemed for the moment completely mad. But then I'd always been very good at curing myself of love.

I closed the door to Foo's room and started to get undressed. Out of my pants pocket I pulled the square of paper with Brian's address. I stared at the scribble of writing, running a finger across it like Braille. I was struck by a certain morbid fascination, to think the address on Pequod Lane no longer existed, blown to bits like the people who lived there. So much for suburban calm. Then I had a sudden pang, wondering what happened to the pair of retrievers. Were they playing outside when it happened, chasing rabbits? And when the big explosion came, did they run away in terror? Would they ever come back, or would they go wild, trusting nothing of man again?

I was so weary I was punchy. I tucked the paper in the corner of the mirror above the dresser, then shrugged my clothes to the floor. I took a step toward the bathroom—and heard the water go on in the sink. It wasn't that I'd forgotten Gray was there, but what slapped my face was the memory of Brian. I sat down heavily on the bed, dazed by the proximity of the water's hum, the sudden shadow of the night we shared. The noise seemed like an awful mockery of how close we almost came. Then, just as abruptly, the faucet turned off. I actually clutched the blanket with both hands, dreading what would come next.

There was a dribble of hesitation, probably because he's so modest. Then the full stream, drumming the bowl. I couldn't bear the intimacy of it. A wave of shame burned my face, for all the carnal thoughts I'd ever had about my brother. This was the proof of how dead he was, another man pissing, what seemed so raw and disturbingly alive about Brian himself, only a week ago. I felt more than a little nuts just then, because at the same time I shrank from the rawness of Gray. Almost as if I didn't want to know he had a dick.

The toilet flushed, and I heard him padding back to Cora's room. But the drama wasn't over. I had to go myself, but couldn't stand that Gray would hear me. It wasn't just irrational, it was right back to being twelve years old. Hating to show myself naked in front of Brian, especially my clumsy member, terrified he'd see my morning hard-on. I stared at the bathroom door, my bladder throbbing.

Then, acutely aware of how surreal this all was, even in some way soothed by it, I got up and slipped out onto my balcony. Instantly the crisp of a winter's night raised gooseflesh on my arms and legs. The wind was up from the ocean, shivering all the trees. I thought about everyone fussing around me, always trying to get me to bundle up, as if a chill might carry me away.

I stepped to the railing, my skin like wax in the moonlight, looking across the slope of lawn to the sycamore grove and the secret garden. I held my dick and thrust my hips forward like a naughty *puto*, feeling the muscles unclench. I let it out with a shudder of release, and a moment later could hear it falling on the oleander, just outside the dining room.

Truly it sounded like rain, a most specific and concentrated squall, like a small memory of last week's downpour. By now I had quite forgotten the excess of shyness that drove me out here. It seemed nothing more nor less, as I let it go in the wind, than a proper tribute to Brian, man to man. I hated to come to the end of it. There's so little that really connects you to the dead, you cling to whatever works, no matter how bizarre. Death wins anyway, but sometimes you give it a squirt.

When I came inside again, a glimmer of Brian stayed with me, something to do with the naked freedom of my body on the balcony and how it echoed him. Because when Brian walked naked—in the locker room after a shutout—he moved like something unearthly free, untouchable by years. And I climbed into bed holding that image close, without any envy for once. I didn't hate him, want him, or even miss him. Because I had him right then in the exact center of my mind, still as the eye of a storm.

Dreams are another matter, of course, and the night had its own psychodrama waiting in the wings. I'm never very good at dreams, coming in late and leaving early, usually speechless and all alone. But not tonight. The scene was crystal clear as Chekhov, without any woozy edges at all. Brian and I in our room in the house on West Hill Road, him in his baseball whites and me buck naked. He was trying to coax me out to play, pulling me toward the door and laughing, no roughhouse at all. That was the most vivid feeling, my certainty that he wouldn't hurt me. And we definitely wouldn't be playing a sport, so there was nothing to win or lose. He wasn't out to best me.

"Come *on*," he kept saying, tugging me irresistibly.

I swear I could smell the funk of his sweat. But I wasn't laughing, because I had this terribly urgent thing to tell him. "Let *me* go first," I insisted, groping to get past him to the door. I couldn't have said what was out there; maybe it was nothing. But if it turned out to be the monstrous force I feared, an annihilation ravenous for blood and bone and soul, then I was the one it wanted.

And Brian wouldn't listen. He pulled me into the crook of his arm and reached for the doorknob, ready to tumble out onto the lawn. "Please—you stay here," I begged him, tears of impotence choking my throat. Only one of us needed to go, and I was the one prepared for it. Then he opened the door to a crack of blinding light, and suddenly seemed to understand. He shoved me back and fell out into the light like a skydiver. I woke as the door shut in my face.

I was shivering and very confused, and my head on the pillow was bathed in sweat. Almost by reflex I stumbled out of bed, pulling off the clammy T-shirt. I staggered into the bathroom and grabbed a towel behind the door, hooding it over my head, rubbing the damp from my hair. The dream was sharp inside me; I was still shaken that Brian had gone out that door, but couldn't connect it to anything actual.

A night sweat brings its own aura of unreality, turning you into a strange hybrid, half-somnambulist, half-nurse. Part of my brain was trying to recall if there were any dry pillowcases, but I didn't want to turn on the light and jar myself too far awake. I groped in the linen cupboard, hounded by Brian's fall and a piercing sense of having missed my chance to play with him. And then I remembered—he was in the next room!

It's something about the loss of electrolytes when you sweat hard. Your brain goes fuzzy, and you take what refuge you can in mirages. I can only say, as I lurched for the connecting door and into Cora's room, that I was back to a week ago, and Brian was here for the night. But I can't begin to convey the singular moment of relief, seeing him in the bed, putting the grim finality of the dream behind me. I moved toward him, delirious with feeling. What did I mean to do, climb into bed with my brother? All the taboos against incest seemed to vanish in that moment of recovery. *Here I am, Brian,* I wanted to cry out. *We can play now.*

And the figure turned over and showed his sleeping face, and it was Gray.

Strange, how fast reality works. In an instant I knew the truth again, that I'd sleepwalked through a second reverie, that Brian was gone forever. My knee was already on the bed as the wave of desolation hit me. Then Gray's arm moved, lifting the covers back to make room for me. He was more asleep than awake. It was all instinct, a man who kept his promise to be here if I needed him. And frankly, my last bed having crash-landed, I had nowhere else to go right now. Hurting with grief I ducked in under the covers, letting him fold his arm around me.

I lay on my side, absolutely pliant as he tucked me up against him, till I was enveloped in a kind of bear hug. I needed every inch of it just then. Brian's death throbbed like an open wound—or no, like a missing limb. Nothing of the dream remained except the picture of him in his uniform, young and a hero, at the peak of his force. Downstairs I'd said to Gray that this Brian had somehow escaped the explosion, at least in my head. But here in the dark the two Brians came together at last, like the hairs on a gunsight. The young one was just as murdered, as gone as the man who fumbled back into my life and almost touched me. And if *he* was dead, my cruel and dazzling tormentor, then I'd lost the only thing in the world I'd ever compared myself against. It was like the moon losing the sun.

So I sank as deep as I could into Gray's embrace, solid as a cave. The rhythm of his deep breathing lulled me. I only had the briefest moment's thought that he might not be so nakedly accommodating if he'd been wide awake. Surely his WASP modesty would set its invisible boundary wider than this. Not that we were in any danger, I in my briefs and he in pajamas. Pajamas! Must be the last man on earth, I thought as I burrowed against him. Not unaware, despite the aching emptiness that used to be my brother, of the deeper irony here.

Namely: what an odd way to end up in bed with a man. And deeper still, the knowledge that I hadn't been to bed with anyone in two years, which sometimes felt like twenty. And perhaps most amazing of all, I thought as I spiraled under, that it should come back as easy as this, cradling into a man's embrace. Like riding a bicycle.

The depression hit like a hangover headache, a migrainous second before I opened my eyes. The foreign country of Cora's room, its clutter of cool green wicker, only deepened my first sight of a world irreversibly out of sync. I was all alone in the bed. I sat up guiltily, shying away from Gray's side, as if I ought to be ashamed. For what, sleeping untroubled the rest of the night? I stood up irritably, startled to find myself hard in my shorts.

Make up your mind, I scolded it.

Then saw Gray's powder-blue p.j.'s, slung over the open drawer of the dresser. I smiled in spite of the hammering despair, thinking how neatly he kept a special set of clothes at the beach for when he stayed over. I shuffled into the bathroom and pissed this time in the toilet, slapping my dick first to bring the swelling down. As I groped through my dresser, determined to wear all black, I thought of myself the day before as manic and out of touch. Only now did I really appreciate how dead was dead—as if I'd forgotten the lesson of my friends, the nightmare depressions that crashed down on me as soon as the funeral cars dispersed.

I put on a black turtleneck and black jeans, refusing to comb my hair besides. I felt suitably austere as I thudded listlessly down the stairs, already making out Mona's voice in the kitchen. Jesus, she sure hadn't wasted any time getting here. Fixing my face with a scowl that announced in no uncertain terms, Not Before Breakfast, I headed in. They both stopped talking midsentence and looked over expectantly. I gave them a vague wave, as if to say *Go right on, don't mind me,* and poured myself a mug of coffee.

Plainly they wanted to hear from me, but saw it would be an intrusion right now. They could see how I was—black. Gray stepped aside neatly from the fridge so I could reach in for the half and half, then forced himself to address Mona, hunched on one of the stools. "So—you both finally agreed it's over."

"Yeah," said Mona. Like Gray she sounded painfully stagey, watching me as I took a powdered doughnut from a box on the counter. It was as if they were the food police, counting my calories for me. Mona continued, half-distracted, "But she still knows me better than anyone, and just how to push my buttons. This morning she tells me she's found me the perfect girl. Like she wants to set up a blind date. So I smashed the clock on her desk and threw a bunch of files out her window."

I stepped to the zinc table and sat on the second stool. Only now did I see there were several sheets of paper spread out on the tabletop, faxes from the New Haven papers. A headline jumped out: 3 DIE IN BOMB BLAST. Then my eye went to the picture below, tantalizingly fuzzy. Brian and Susan and Daniel, waving at the camera from the back of a speedboat. Susan and Daniel wore life preservers puffed around their chests. All you could really tell was that she was blond and had lots of teeth, and the boy was darker. Brian was turning from the wheel, for of course he would be captain. No shirt and no life preserver, because of course he couldn't drown. On the stern of the sleek craft was lettered IRISH EYES, and under that SOUTHPORT. My brother's toys.

"That's yesterday's," Mona declared, the pretense having vanished that they could talk about Daphne or anything else. "Here's this morning's."

She pointed her fingernail to the article closest to her: SHAHEEN WAS READY TO BLOW WHISTLE. Underneath was a photo of Brian and Jerry Curran, arms around each other's shoulders, toasting the camera with cans of beer. In their visored hats they looked as if they'd just finished a round of golf. I never would've recognized Jerry without the caption. He was big as a house, his linebacker's frame having swelled and bloated with the years to the size of a pizza don. His leering grin was cruel and repugnant as ever. And beside him Brian seemed all the more untouched by time. The triumph was palpable in his face. He'd lucked out into a life where he'd never have to stop playing.

My eyes shifted across the gray of paragraphs, not ready to read the details yet. Another double picture: on the left a saltbox house with a trellis of roses along the side, set on a rolling lawn with a split-rail fence around; on the right a chaos of rubble, chimneys sticking up at either end. Before and after. What they call in the real estate business a start-over.

"It says there's a wake today and tomorrow," Mona announced. You could tell she wanted to brief me as simply as possible, so I wouldn't have to read through everything. "I sent some flowers and signed your name. White roses." I nodded and chomped my doughnut, a dust of powdered sugar falling onto the pictures of the house. "There's police guarding the funeral home. Little late for *that*."

"I think I'd like to be alone now," I said.

A beat of silence, in which Mona tried not to take the flatness of my affect personally. "Sure, I'll go outside and read," she retorted, reaching to the floor to scoop up her bag.

"No, he means *all* alone," said Gray. "And I need a ride to the ranch, if you don't mind."

Mona minded. She'd grown up in the chicken-soup belt of the Valley, arriving today with no plans but to sit shiva, nondenominational of course. She shot a look at Gray in which was a barely concealed pang of betrayal, as if he'd just given in on a nonnegotiable point. Mona herself couldn't bear to be alone in crisis, especially when pointed objects were hurling between her and Daphne. But she swallowed it on the spot for my sake, though it went against every pop-psych book she eagerly devoured. She slung the bag over her shoulder and went right to the door.

Gray followed after, not catching my eye with a freighted glance. In yesterday's clothes he looked endearingly rumpled. As I stood in the doorway, watching them cross the yard side by side, I did one of my total flip-flops, wanting to call out and take it all back. What the fuck did I want to be alone for? I couldn't even pout right without a proper audience, let alone heave with sorrow and remorse. But here they were, my two best buddies, taking me at my word. They both waved curtly as they piled in Mona's car, clearly not wanting to come across overemotional.

Because that was the vibe I'd been giving off from the moment I came downstairs: that I was feelinged out.

Yet even as the car drove off, I realized I'd got it wrong again. I didn't want *them* to stay, just Gray; and I hadn't wanted the two of them out of there either, only Mona. That's how grief makes you lonely. All day long, from breakfast to Johnny Carson, you don't know what you'd like or what might help till you've slammed the door on it. In addition, you usually catch your thumb in it when it slams—which was more or less how I was feeling now, as I brooded back into the kitchen. I wanted to thank him for letting me sleep with him, even if it made him blush and hunker his shoulders. Wanted to speak it aloud to prove it had really happened.

I picked my coffee up from the table of clippings and drank the sour dregs. I cast a glance at random down the columns of print, wanting to know more but also to avoid the forensic details. I settled on a paragraph which said they'd just come home from a weekend at their country place in the Berkshires. A *little spring skiing*, one of the neighbors informed a reporter, as if that had any bearing on the tragedy.

Farther down, it said my brother's Mercedes was stolen, presumably surviving the blast because it was parked in the street. This meant the killer must've been out there waiting in the dark and watching—the explosion came at 4:00 A.M. The midnight-blue Mercedes had been recovered in a parking lot at LaGuardia, keys in the ignition.

I skipped to the next article, which proved to be a glowing list of Brian and Susan's civic leadership—Little League, Junior Kiwanis, Young Republicans. Brian was on the national council of the Eagle Scouts of America, swear to God. But the main gush here came out of the mouths of the princes of the church. The archbishop of Hartford himself was planning to do the funeral Mass. He'd made an official proclamation mourning the loss of such a fierce soldier of God, making no mention of Brian's pending indictment.

They must have donated plenty, I thought—nice team uniforms for every parochial school in the archdiocese. The bug-eyed parish priest in Southport weighed in with his own plea for prayers. "We have lost a whole family of Christ," he remarked, among other lugubrious things.

"If you mean Miss Jesus, Father," I said out loud, "you're right. She's feeling more than usual like a fucking orphan."

I'd had enough of the press accounts. I grabbed another doughnut and headed outside to the beach stairs. The day was as crystalline as yesterday, which didn't quite fit my Hamlet mood and costume. On the far horizon, however, billowing scallops of cumulus rode the water's rim. There was hope for another Alaska storm, just what I needed.

I clumped about twenty steps down the stairs, then sat and looked through the bars of the railing. A couple of gray terns were wheeling near the cliff face, nothing to do but scud the currents. Lazily I broke off bits of my doughnut and lobbed them. The birds came plummeting down and didn't miss a crumb, swooping around in relays. For a minute I could pretend they were my birds, coaxed from the wild and trained to my command, but as soon as the doughnut was finished they were gone, cavorting away along the bluffs. And I was alone, just what I'd asked for.

It came like a crazy idea, right out of the blue, another flip-flop. What if I went? I felt it like a delicious jolt of belligerence, defying I knew not what, since I was the one who'd begged off. But what if I just showed up?

The scenario fell into place full-blown, with a nice border of black comic anarchy. I could hitch a ride to Santa Monica and be there before Wells Fargo closed. That's where AGORA keeps its gasping bank account. I could quick withdraw a thousand bucks and be on a plane by one. It seemed the perfect touch, that I should embezzle the cash to attend the obsequies of my brother the crook. Of course I'd pay it all back somehow, but then that's what they all say, isn't it? Don't ask me why, but it seemed especially crucial to pull this off without telling Gray and Mona.

So I'd just make it to the funeral home in Southport before the viewing was done for the night. Except viewing wasn't quite the right word, since all three caskets would be discreetly closed. I would be the messy part, leaving those nameless cousins and neighbors speechless. And Father Dildo too, who would probably just be finishing a sonorous rosary for his little family of Christ. Before you could say "intrinsic evil," I'd turn that decorous Irish wake into the Masque of the Red Death.

As each one came and shook my hand they'd see the kiss of purple on my cheek. And then the horror would dawn that they had touched me. I didn't have to worry that the mick bigots of my clan had developed any reasonableness around the subject of the fag virus. They'd probably plunge their hands in fire as soon as they got home.

And tomorrow at the funeral, maybe I'd be all alone, just Father Dildo and I. Standing in the graveyard behind Saint Augustine's, burying them all beside my sotted redneck father. Unless Jerry Curran had the balls to show up. Ah, then I would make a scene to pale the blood feud that erupted over our father's funeral meats. The priest would have to tear me away from Jerry's throat. And if I was lucky I'd get a bite in, sinking my viral fangs in the flesh of his cheek.

Was it all just self-important, shaming the dead to gratify my own stunted ego? Well, so be it, and frankly, there was even worse where that came from. Because I wouldn't even have to see my mother. I could take a last ride over to Chester and spit a final time on all the rabid playgrounds of my youth. Churn up every last dollop of lingering bile, and make it a witches' sabbath.

I gripped the rails of the banister like prison bars, astonished by my own dark passion. There was only one issue here—did I mean it? Would I really go, breathing all that airline shit like Mona said, coming back with who knew what new twist of infection? The answer seemed to frame itself in the bluntest terms: Was I man enough? Ridiculous, I know. Politically incorrect, the worst kind of macho posturing, but there it was. If I didn't go now I would die the same androgynous loser I'd been from five to twenty. Though nobody's heart would lift at the sight of me, I had a right to be there. Maybe even a duty, as much to my exiled kind as to my brother.

Oh yes, I was going.

It's how I make all the big decisions, adamant and out of nowhere. I stood up and leaned over the banister, taking a last deep breath of ocean. I'd be back in three or four days, but I needed to bring this with me in all its sublime clarity, a vision of my true homeland. As I made my way up the stairs I realized I had no suit—could barely throw together a clean shirt and pants. I'd need my ratty parka for the icy damp of Connecticut. Tough shit, if the swells of Chester thought I looked like a bum.

The spring in my step was wonderfully resolute as I came to the top of the stairs. All the shrinks will tell you, even crazy Daphne, you have to have closure. Now the decision was made, of course I'd call Gray and Mona, maybe from the airport—once I was on my way.

I stepped from the landing onto the lawn, and froze. Twenty feet away on the terrace, sitting at the foot of one of the chaises, bent over a book in his lap was—Tom Shaheen. The dream had rooted deeper than I thought, or I'd lost much more than electrolytes. It was me as a little kid, black crewcut and shoulders slumped, reading in secret so my father wouldn't beat me. I felt an overwhelming sense of protectiveness, even as flashes of stars bloomed across my vision. No question but that I was going to faint.

And then the boy looked up, guardedly checking me out, and I knew he was real. My seething memory hadn't called him up. I scrambled to think—did Merle have kids?

"I'm Daniel," he said evenly. Statement of fact, no more.

I nodded dumbly, pointing to myself, but couldn't seem to say my name. I grappled to understand. Somehow he had survived—escaped—got himself out here. Because I was all he had left. I could see the exhaustion in his pallor, the joyless blank of his eyes, and didn't know where to begin. I walked toward him, my brain still wanting to run to the airport and the lavish melodrama of my prodigal return. I put out my hand to shake, my tongue still tied, and stumbled out, "I guess I'm your Uncle Tom."

"I guess," he replied with a rueful smile, but taking my hand manfully, a reflex clearly learned from his father.

I stood there floundering. How do you comfort a kid who's lost everything? If he got here by himself, then he had more wherewithal than I. I still could hardly believe how much he looked like me—only not so fragile, even after what he'd been through. "What're you reading?" I asked, loathing myself, as if the banality of all grown-ups leered at him out of my fatuous smile.

He raised the book from his lap and showed me the cover: *Treasure Island*. My ego burst to the surface again, for I could have told him exactly the crook of the tree where I'd read it myself, skipping confirmation class. As if it would matter to him. I bit my tongue on the book report, as he waited politely for me to speak. I didn't want to feel it, but it was there. The same helpless panic as when I'd talked to my mother's nurse, the impossible thought that this had all become my responsibility. And I couldn't do it—*wouldn't*. I had my own dying to get through, and that was that. No more room at the inn. It was horrible. I'd known this boy for thirty seconds, and already I was trying to palm him off like a Dickens foundling.

"Are you all right?" I asked, trying to focus, reeling with inadequacy. "Have you eaten?"

But before he could answer, the french doors opened from the parlor, and my brother stepped out. It was oddly anticlimactic, not like Lazarus clapped from the dead. *Oh, right*, I thought, awakening at last. The midnight-blue Mercedes at the airport—they'd missed their deaths entirely. Brian walked gravely toward me across the terrace, in jeans and a Fordham sweat shirt. "Tom," he said, and the guilt in his voice amazed me, "it's just for now. We had nowhere else to go."

I felt terribly embarrassed for the boy, that he should have to hear his father squirm. I avoided Brian's eyes and smiled at Daniel again. "I'm glad you came. It's a big house for just one person."

Then I felt the force of Brian's hand on my biceps, tugging me off to talk in private. It was such an eerie echo of the dream, pulling me toward the fatal door, that I shuddered as I followed him into the cactus patch. He felt the tremor and drew his hand away, misreading it as revulsion, I think. For his eyes flinched in shame as he looked over my shoulder to sea.

"I'm sorry, I should've told you when I was here. My life is totally fucked." Then he clenched his teeth in self-contempt. "And I've got no right to dump it on you."

I felt light-headed, like someone about to laugh at a funeral. I reached my hands and gripped his shoulders. "Hey—I'm glad you're alive, Ace. Nothing else matters."

For a second I thought he was going to cry, just from the break in the tension. I liked holding on to his solid mass, but my touch was easy, nothing to weigh him down. He shook his head bitterly, as if to deny himself any release. "We were supposed to be *back*," he said, meaning Sunday night. "We only stayed over in the mountains because she was getting her period. She didn't want to be sick in the car. Otherwise—" He stared in stupefaction at the water. He was going on the assumption that I knew everything.

"But I thought—" I didn't know quite how to say this. Certain details might be too unbearable still. "Didn't they find—I mean, there's a picture in the paper of these body bags." Three of them lined in a row on the lawn, a picture I couldn't look straight in the face.

"Ita and Kim," said Brian, wincing again in shame. Then he must have seen how puzzled I looked. "Sorry—the Vietnamese couple. They've been with us for years. They had a little girl." He gave a helpless shrug of despair at the insanity of it all. "They didn't do *anything*. Except trust me."

"So nobody knows you got out of there," I declared, cutting impatiently through his guilt.

"Now they do. Susan called her sister this morning. The coroner just had a news conference, to say they made a mistake." As he turned his body to face directly out to sea, my hands fell away from his shoulders, reluctantly. "Tommy, I just need a few days to figure my options. I'm not gonna get you in trouble."

"Hey, not to worry. Trouble's my middle name." I think what startled me most was that I had no sense of judging him. The blood went deeper than what he'd done. This from me, who'd never felt a blood tie in my life, unless you included hate.

"There's a lawyer out here," he said. "That's who I came to see before, soon as I realized Jerry was setting me up. He's trying to work out an immunity thing. So maybe I'll check in with him." He shrugged again, no more sure of this than any other plan.

"But nobody knows you're *here?*" I asked precisely, relieved when he shook his head.

"We spent the night in a motel down by the airport, full o' hookers." He laughed at the layers of absurdity. "All we got is what we've got on, and one duffel bag from the weekend. We caught a cab up here, took my last thirty bucks. I'm scared to use a credit card."

His voice betrayed a sort of permanent astonishment, as if he couldn't believe the abruptness of the change, from having so much to nothing. Safe by the skin of their teeth, overnight they'd turned into a little band of refugees—like Ita and Kim on the South China Sea. I turned to look at Daniel, reading his book again. Strangely, he seemed not astonished at all, even rather used to it by now. Just like me. My first conscious memory, four or five years old, was a sinking feeling of having no expectations. Life would just do what it did.

"The papers didn't mention the dogs," I said.

"Dead."

I nodded, studying Daniel, trying to figure how high he'd already built the wall. Then Susan appeared in the parlor doorway, blonder than her picture, stunning even forty feet away in a lilac jogging suit. I lifted a hand and waved, smiling brightly at this woman I'd never met. She didn't wave back, seemed uncertain whether to step outside, as if she had trespassed far enough. "Come on out!" I called cheerfully.

Brian's head swiveled around as I made a move toward her, and he grabbed my arm, harder than he meant to. For a second it felt like a punch from twenty-five years ago. "Tom," he murmured, squirming again, "she doesn't know about . . ." It died in his throat, but I saw his eyes lock on my cheek.

Okay. Gently I pulled away from him and continued toward my sister-in-law. For some reason it didn't enrage me that he hadn't told her. Usually I want it screamed in people's faces. Right now there was too much else, especially when I saw the pained embarrassment in her face, and beneath it, stark as a skull, the fear. "Finally," I said, brimming with warmth, sticking a hand out.

She barely touched it, her small cold fingers limp. She mumbled hello and stared at her son. By now Brian had strode up beside us. "I told him it's just for a couple of days," he said to his wife—defensive, almost stilted.

But I'm not sure how much I really picked up. I was too busy overcompensating. "Let's get you settled," I announced—the perfect hostess, who knows just how weary her guests must be from the trip. Imperiously I led the way into the house, and the two of them followed without a peep. Up the stairs, me chattering over my shoulder a shorthand version of the aunts' tale.

"We'll put the two of you in here," I said, sweeping us into Cora's room. I blinked at the swirl of dishevel, having forgotten we'd slept there. With two men's underwear strewn about, it looked like more than sleeping had been going on. "We'll get this made right up," I declared, as if I had a chambermaid at the end of a bell pull.

They stood there grimly serious, which I chalked up to the terrible disruptions of the last two days. I ducked into the bathroom and pulled from the cupboard a fluffy stack of towels, for I'd finally done a proper laundry in preparation for Foo's visit, as well as a vigorous scour of the bathroom hardware. I set the towels down on the green wicker chair and beckoned them out to the hall again. At the far corner of the stairwell a low arched doorway opened onto four narrow steps. They followed me up to a small round room with windows in every direction, a sort of squat tower.

"Nonny's room," I announced with pride. It was sparsely furnished with a single bed and a rag rug, and otherwise cluttered with boxes, having evolved by default into a semi-attic. "He'll love it up here, it's like a lighthouse."

This didn't seem to perk them up at all. Susan looked mortified, as if she was being reduced to charity. I let her be. Four different AIDS support groups had drummed it into me: you have to let people have their process. So I stepped to one of the casements and threw it open, looking down on the terrace below. "Daniel," I called, and he tore his eyes from Long John Silver, squinting up at me. "This is where *you'll* stay."

"Thanks," he replied, rigorously well mannered, but made no

move to run up and look. They all seemed so defeated, but could you blame them? When I turned back, Susan was sitting on the foot of the bed staring at the floor, Brian standing above her, a pang of grief in his face as deep but not as clean as death. It was so obvious they needed to be alone. I murmured about checking the linen and beat it out of there.

As I stripped the bed in Cora's room I could hear Susan raising her voice, hammering at him, shrill with rage. I couldn't make out the words and didn't want to—or only the one word *not*, repeated like a curse. I will *not* do something-or-other, she swore at him. This was *not* what she wanted. I put these beautiful creamy sheets on the bed, the border embroidered in garlands, probably bought when the house was built. I shoved Gray's scattered clothes in the bureau and fussed about with a dust rag, all the while hearing the blur of accusations through the wall. I think what jarred me the most was that my brother appeared to be taking it all in silence.

I stood there a moment, surveying my chamberwork, winded and softly coughing. I thought: *Can't they just be glad to be alive?* Awfully Pollyanna coming from me, who bit people's heads off when they told me I looked terrific. Or as one or two former friends had said, *Be glad you're alive today.* So no, I didn't expect my brother and his family to be giddy with relief. They were up to their nuclear neck in problems. All I could do—and I liked this part—was make them a place that was safe and calm.

I came out into the stairhall and was starting down the steps when Brian emerged through the arch from Nonny's room. I gave him a bland smile, not wanting him to know I'd heard his wife's tantrum. He leaned over the banister. "Things aren't so good with Susan and me."

I nodded dumbly. He turned away and lumbered into Cora's room, closing the door. I hurried downstairs, suddenly fearful that Susan would appear. *Don't take sides,* I warned myself, knowing the mire was deeper than I was used to, even including Daphne and Mona smashing clocks.

I saw through the parlor windows that Daniel hadn't moved an inch. Even I, who'd been such a desperate reader at his age, wondered how spellbound he really was. Stevenson was no slouch, but still. I'd done my own share of staring at books till the print ran, when the pain of my father and Brian was too much. How old was he—seven, eight? I'd forgotten exactly, and with no kids anywhere near my orbit, had no skill at guessing. All the same, I had an irresistible longing to go out and sit beside him, stumbling around till I found the words to tell him I understood.

Understood what—that life sucked? Who said the chaos of his life was anything like mine, eons ago in the Donna Reed graveyard of the fifties? I told myself *Not yet*, painful as it was to see him out there all alone, finding his island in a book, not trusting the one he had landed on. Let him get settled first. The last thing I wanted to do was come to him from a place of ego, wanting him too much to be like me. Let me want him to be like him, I thought.

And turned away from his melancholy figure and headed through the kitchen out to the yard. Keeping it simple. I stopped at the potting shed behind the garage and pulled on canvas gloves, grabbing the hand clippers and a basket. I was back to the care and feeding of my guests, and figured they could use fresh flowers, especially if they'd be holed up bickering and cutting losses.

The roses grow on the south side of the driveway hedge, the hottest spot in the whole five acres and the most protected from the sea. Several bushes were bright with blooms big as a man's fist, bursting into the sun after all that rain. Like I said, I never bring roses in myself, because I can't stand the swiftness of their passage, here and gone. Happily Brian and Susan wouldn't have all that superstitious baggage. I clipped the stems long, laying them one by one in the basket, yellow for Cora's room, red for Nonny's. There wouldn't be quite a dozen for each, but nearly.

The sweat was pouring off me, and as I wiped the back of the glove across my forehead, I heard the sound of tires in the drive. An instant goose of adrenaline—what if it was the FBI? I didn't know precisely who was after Brian. I tossed my head back coolly and walked to the end of the oleander, prepared to stand my ground and demand to see a warrant. I came around the hedge. It was the pickup. The door opened, and Gray stepped out, flustered already and red in the face, not expecting to run into me so fast.

"I won't get in your way," he blurted. "I just didn't want you to be here all by yourself."

"Gray—you won't believe it—"

"I'd never intrude, I hope you know that." He didn't know what to do with his hands. Jammed them in his pants pockets.

I laughed to see him so awkward, the laughter startling him. "Gray, listen—my brother's alive." A waver of doubt clouded his eyes, like maybe I just got religion. "He's *here*. They're all here." He stared over my shoulder at the beach house, still wary, an old frontier stubbornness that demanded proof. "It was this family that worked for them who died. They weren't even there."

Slowly the disbelief ebbed from his eyes, and he turned them again on me. He smiled his crinkled smile, followed up after a beat by a tiny snort of laughter. Then he glanced at the basket on my arm. "May I quote you?" he said, mocking me ever so gently. " 'I hate roses.' "

"No, I don't. I just don't like them dying on me."

"Oh."

He was grinning at me now, but then I may have started it. There was really no one else who could fully appreciate the craziness of the last day, all the way to death and back. Well, Mona could of course, but she wasn't here. I don't know what other people do with the aura of good luck that follows a false alarm. But for me, standing there like the rose queen, it was like waking up from a nightmare to a world of second chances—Scrooge after the ghosts. I thought nothing and weighed nothing, because there was nothing to lose. I picked up a yellow rose and held it out like a specimen.

"Lord Graham, I hope you won't think me out of line, me just a poor tenant and all. But before that funeral started yesterday, I could swear I was falling in love with you."

He took it between two fingers, careful of the thorns. Sniffed it, but not floridly. "Oh really? I thought that's what *I* was doing. According to Merle and Foo and Mona."

"Yes, well, they got it backwards." I think I was waiting to see him blanch, or shuffle from one foot to the next. Those Jimmy Stewart moves of his, so earnest you wanted to put him in your pocket. I was amazed how cool he took it, frankly, and so I breezed right on. "Don't worry, you don't have to do anything about it. I mean, *we* don't have to. I just decided to tell you." I shrugged. "I'm terrible with secrets."

He gave me the most remarkable look, blazingly frank, beyond anything he'd ever allowed himself with me. I did the blanching. "They didn't get it backwards," he said, savoring the repetition. "I've been in it for months now. I just happen to be great at keeping a secret."

There was a dangerous merriment there. "I warn you, my lord, some people say I'm a dead man."

"Yeah, so I hear. Same ones who say I'm a hundred years old."
His turn to shrug. "You get what you get. Besides, death's very
overreported around here, don't you think?"

He opened his arms wide, taking in all the island. Seeing my
chance I moved to embrace him, still holding the shears and the
basket. It was a hug of relief more than anything, not especially
sexual, more like survivors meeting in the aftermath of a wreck. I
was looking over his shoulder toward the house and saw Daniel in
the kitchen window, watching. Oh shit, *now* he puts down his
book. Who would he tell, I wondered, his mother or his father? And
I knew the answer because he was me. He wouldn't tell anyone.

"I won't come in," said Gray, easing away.

"Of course you will," I protested. "You'll meet them. You're
my—" Mouth went dry. No word yet.

"Tomorrow's soon enough."

He waved the rose like a little flag. I saw that he needed his
shyness to curl up in for a while and catch his breath. He was right,
of course—I still had to get my refugees squared away. So I let him
go without a second thought. Waved him down the driveway after
our sixty seconds' swap of declarations. We seemed to have found
our own way to smash a clock. He tooted once before he gunned
across the coast road and into the Trancas hills. And for once,
turning back to the beach house and my blood, tomorrow seemed
like a good idea. Because now there would be enough time.

F I V E

CURIOUSLY IT FELT ALMOST ORDINARY, THE FOUR OF us together in the house. Not the same thing as *normal*, mind you, but they had their rooms, and I had mine. At least we weren't on top of each other, the way it had been on West Hill Road the last time I did the family bit. Susan stayed upstairs for the first day and a half, so I didn't see her at all. This I chalked up to female mysteries, recalling Brian's remark about her period. In any case, the connecting bathroom between our rooms required an extra alertness in the locking of doors. Once I went in to brush my teeth and caught a faint whiff of bitter musk—a woman's blood. Instantly I thought of my mother, the only woman whose smell I'd ever known. Yet it didn't faze me at all, this coming full circle. It only served to reinforce the sense of natural history that clung about the beach house. The arrival of my brother's clan seemed inevitable as the cycle of seasons.

Almost ordinary, especially when Brian and Daniel and I gathered for meals in the dining room. For supper that first night, Campbell's soup and peanut butter sandwiches, the three of us hunched at the table without a word. But I mean, it didn't seem awkward in the least. It was as if we'd been having supper like this for years, no need to speak. And the next morning at breakfast, coming down to find my brother in the kitchen making french toast. It moved me in a very uncomplicated way, to find myself part of the ritual of Brian and his son.

Only I knew where the maple syrup was, a tin at the back of a cupboard with black molasses rust around the cap. Sitting there scarfing it down—four slices, six slices, trying to keep up with the kid—I almost forgot the upheaval of my brother's plight. Till Daniel drained his milk, set his glass on the table, and addressed his father gravely: "Where will I go to school?"

"Don't worry, we'll work all that out," said Brian, with a slight burr of annoyance. "You're still on your Easter break."

The boy nodded sadly. My cheeks were bulging with toast, ridiculously piggish, but I wanted to reach out with my napkin and gently wipe the milk mustache from his upper lip. I didn't. "May I be excused?" asked Daniel, and his father nodded, and he slipped away from the table. I watched him pick up his book off the sideboard and head outside. The book was like ballast, the last thing holding him down from flying away.

"I'm seeing that lawyer tomorrow," said my brother, no lingering look after the figure of his fleeing son. "Not here," he hastened to add. "At his office. I'm not giving anyone this address."

I smiled at him. "I guess the idea must be to find you one of those witness protection things. Change your name. Whole new life." Even as I said it I couldn't prevent the creep of envy in my voice. It sounded marvelous.

Brian laughed harshly, his upper lip pulling back in a sneer. "Yeah, those programs are total bullshit. You know what the rate of survival is? 'Bout fifty percent make it two years before somebody catches up with 'em. Great odds, huh? Just like they swore I'd be testifying in secret." He scoffed in disgust, leaning back in his chair, hands behind his head. The swell of his biceps was taut against the sleeves of his T-shirt.

By midafternoon a cover of clouds was starting to seep across the sky. Soon the sun was pale, dilute as lemonade. It wasn't clear that a storm was coming, the ambiguity of March leaving it up in the air. But they'd started to argue again in Cora's room, or Susan at least was harping, harping. Once again I couldn't hear the words distinctly. As it happened I was lying on my bed, jeans to my knees and playing with myself. Idly enough, only half-hard, but truly it had been months since I'd fiddled with it at all. I suppose I was testing the waters, for Gray's sake as much as my own. But as soon as I heard that nattering drone I buttoned right up and went downstairs, determined to avoid all domestic incidents.

Daniel was in the parlor, perched on the sofa and huddled over the coffee table. He looked as if he was studying a map with an X for buried treasure. Tentatively I moved to the doorway, reluctant to intrude. He didn't look up. Now I could see that he had the million pieces of a jigsaw spread out on the surface of the table. He'd already pieced together three or four ragged islands and a foot of border.

"Hi," he said, then scooted over on the sofa, making room for me. This gesture of accommodation made me flush with unexpected pleasure. I sat beside him, careful not to touch his knee with mine. I bent over the puzzle, which seemed like nothing but a fractured mass of gray. "Are you seven or eight?"

"Seven and three-quarters," he said, laying in a corner piece.

"Birthday's in June?" He nodded. "Maybe we'll have a party." He shrugged, not impolitely, but as if to say who knew where they'd be three months from now. He tapped in another piece, bridging two of his islands, all of it gray to me. "What's this supposed to be?" I asked, feeling stupid and aphasic.

"A statue," Daniel replied, and reached beneath the table for the box. He handed it to me.

I gaped at the picture on the cover: Michelangelo's *David*, in three-quarter profile, standing in the rotunda at the Accademia. But all I could see at the moment was his dick. I glanced again at the coffee table, the shrapnel pieces coming together. Now in dismay I could see that one of the islands was David's thigh, another his shoulder and left pec. My eye darted frantically among the jumble of unassembled pieces, trying to find the crotch shot. I excruciated, in a daze of embarrassment, wanting to cover the boy's eyes or drag him bodily away. This stupid bohemian house! Why didn't it have a *normal* puzzle, a nice barn in Vermont? Inexorably Daniel filled the picture in, piece by methodical piece.

I realized I was terrified that Brian and Susan might walk in and think this was my idea. And that shocked me back to sanity, because what, after all, was wrong with Michelangelo? Instantly I knew, sitting like a giant beside this little boy, what I was really afraid of. That Daniel would turn out gay, and they would blame me and curse my infected ghost. That's why I shrank from touching him, even my knee.

Once I saw my own fear of being implicated—of tainting him—I realized how the old self-hatred still had its hooks in me. Because what I really meant was that I didn't *want* him to be gay, to run that gauntlet of misery and solitude. Where the hell was all my pride that had marched in a hundred parades?

"Uncle Tom, are you on television?"

I winced at the family name, feeling at the moment all too worthy of the scathing contempt with which the phrase was freighted. For I had just sold my people down the river, all for the sake of what the Aryan masters call "family values."

"No," I retorted guiltily. "Who told you that?"

"Mom said you were an actor."

"Oh. Well, I'm not really that kind of actor." As if he knew there was any other kind. I was startled to find myself ashamed not to be on a hit series. Me and the Cos, so the kid would have something to brag about in school. Some dim, unsettled place in me wanted to race to my apartment in West Hollywood and grab my box of clippings—show him all my raves in *Drama-Logue.*

Yet he didn't seem remotely disappointed, or curious to know what other sort of actor I might be. He accepted me all on my own, a given, because I was his uncle Tom. As I watched him, aching with tenderness now, he fitted two pieces of the puzzle together. Now we could see David's hooded brow and his piercing eyes. I understood that I couldn't keep Daniel from learning the world, of men with men or anything else. Suddenly he looked up at me, the giant towering over him, and smiled wanly. "I like my room," he said, clearly wanting to please me.

"I'm sorry about your dogs."

He frowned, and his shoulders moved in a barely perceptible shrug. "Yeah, they were great," he said, shifting his gaze to the puzzle again. So stoic. Such a fatalist.

Me.

I stayed a while longer, even attempting to lay in a couple of pieces myself. But I've always been lousy at close work, and found myself trying to jam together shapes that were not cut out to be. I scanned the field of shards a final time, still hoping I could palm the piece with David's dick, so the assembled whole would sport a fig-leaf of negative space. But the fucker eluded me.

I stood up to leave and didn't touch Daniel, who for his part seemed philosophical as to whether I stayed or went. No words required about seeing each other later, since we just would. And I walked away with such an overwhelming sense of him, his concentration and his cool, I couldn't any longer distance him by calling him a mere shadow-image of me. For once in my life I'd met a kid as real as the one I left behind in Chester. If anything, I was the shadow of him now, not the other way around. Was this how parents put away their childhood, the vaporous image evaporating in such bright light?

I napped that day like a stone at the bottom of a well. When I woke, the breeze had blown the balcony door open. Still the air and the milky sky had the tease of rain. The prestorm in California sometimes goes on for days, leaden skies with mackerel swirls, swelling till you think they'll burst, and then they clear off without so much as a drop. A sort of stratospheric coitus interruptus. Now I longed for another five-day Alaska blow, like the one that turned things upside down last week, leaving me half in love with Gray. I wanted it for Brian and his family, to cabin us together safe and sound, the eye of the storm. I wanted to show Daniel pelicans on the lawn.

I brushed my hair in the mirror, a scowl of irritation at the KS spot on my cheek. I didn't have room for AIDS right now. I had just shut the door behind me, moving toward the stairs, when Susan stepped out of Cora's room. She shied like a deer the instant she saw me, her instinct to run back in and hide. But the Catholic girl won out, too proper to be so rude, and she nodded a pained hello.

I was shocked by the change a day had wrought. It wasn't just that she'd been crying, welts of red that narrowed her eyes, or the rumpled lilac sweat suit, no other clothes to wear. She looked lost—almost amnesiac. As if a cry was roaring in her head—*Where am I, where am I?*—insistent as the surf against the bluff. Her sunlit hair, pulled back in a bun, was dull as straw. It seemed she hadn't washed.

"You want me to put on a pot of tea?" I asked, sweet-tempered as Emma.

At first she acted like she hadn't heard. Her face was taut with racing thoughts. Then she stepped to the railing, the well of the stairs between us. "I'm sorry, but—" She swallowed. One hand rubbed the hip of her sweat pants. "We don't approve of your life-style."

I think I just blinked a few times, as if I could change the channel. Her words were even more sententious here, echoing in the stair hall. "Yeah?" I said, but not pugnaciously. It was almost as if I wanted her to elaborate, play out all the twisted reasoning.

"We wouldn't be here if we had any choice," said my sister-in-law.

I don't know why I didn't feel rage, maybe because she looked so fallen. It all seemed like such a pathetic joke, her clinging with white knuckles to her bigotry. If anything made me want to sneer in her face, it was that "we." Didn't sound to me, given the shrill of bitter words coming out of their room, as if "we" were going to pull through. And I might have added, where was she getting off with her high-and-mighty, now that her husband was wanted in eleven states?

But what I said was, "I don't really care. I'm doing this for my brother." I even hoped it didn't sound unkind. "I think you've got enough to worry about, don't you? I'm nothing." I started down the stairs.

She leaned out over the banister. "For years," she declared, "I didn't even know you existed." And this time *she* wasn't being unkind, just amazed. No response seemed necessary. For years I didn't know if I existed either, lady. But it was as if she couldn't let me go, even though I was of the devil's party. "He keeps things in, and then it's too late. I didn't find out about this whole . . ." She groped in frustration. No noun was awful enough. ". . . till the FBI came to my house."

She'd blurted much more than she wanted, especially to the likes of me. It must have killed her to have no phone. She needed to talk to her sister, her suburban mommy friends, so she could shake the air with how cheated she felt. "Well, that's between you and him," I said evenly, looking up into her hunted eyes. "You should really try to get outside. Take a walk down to the beach."

I know it was patronizing, but that's all I had. She'd let me in by the wrong door. I continued down the stairs, light on my feet. Though I felt no rage for my sake, Daniel was another matter. I bristled to think of him being guided by this defeated woman. I thought of Foo and her ramrod strength, fierce with no illusions. Then my mother, futile and helpless, ironing and vacuuming, desperate to make some order before the old man came careening home. The wrong people had all the babies.

So what do you want? I asked myself as I swung around the newel post at the bottom. *Custody?*

I laughed out loud at the absurdity of that, trundling through the dining room. When I came in the kitchen, Brian and Gray were perched on the stools, leaning toward each other across the zinc table. Their faces were so close they might have been about to kiss. I stopped dead, forgetting they'd ever met. As Gray looked up to greet me with a smile, I saw they were bent over a scribbled page of calculations. Jesus, but things moved fast around here.

"Brian says we can fix the stairs ourselves," Gray announced proudly.

"You better get a couple extra drill bits," said my brother, all absorbed in the list he was making. "And we want a good waterproof sealer."

The connection didn't surprise me: two men so good with their hands, and both so restless. It only surprised me they'd made it so quick. Very deliberately I crossed to Gray's left side, making as if to peer at their calculations. But when I leaned down I nuzzled Gray's temple with my cheek, planting a soft kiss on his forehead. Then I draped an arm around his shoulder as I crouched in earnest and studied the specs. This whole maneuver was out of bounds, of course. Gray didn't exactly startle, but I could feel him grow very still under the weight of my arm. Public display, male to male, was miles down the line for him. As for Brian, for whose sake I was making the point, he affected a fine indifference, but that didn't mean I hadn't scored.

"We'll get it all done tomorrow," said Brian, "before the storm. Piece o' cake."

On the page in front of him was a crude rendering of the stairway joint, a new design to reinforce the pinning where the steps had broken loose. Beside it, a list of materials and tools. My brother the builder, who'd flung up subdivisions overnight and poured whole interstates, was manic with excitement. He started to talk about how they would pulley the wood down the face of the bluff, when I butted in: "You're busy tomorrow."

"I'll be back before noon," he retorted cavalierly, brushing me off, and I wanted to tell him coldly, to damp the fire of his eagerness, *Go take care of your wife.*

Then Gray piped in. "I'll bring Merle. He's an ox."

And before I could catch my breath the meeting was over. The two men stood, Gray easing out of my arm, and they exchanged a sort of grunt-and-nod, like some mystical butch code between two workmen. They seemed to like each other, but more, seemed to be sharing a bond from which I was excluded. Not meanly, not out to hurt me. Yet suddenly I was back in Chester, the last one picked for every game. Please—if you don't think being a sensitive plant isn't a full-time job.

So I found myself half trotting beside Gray across the back lawn, as he strode toward the pickup. And I said, "You can't keep leaving like this."

He laughed. "I'll be back tomorrow. I've got to get all this stuff." And he waved the list.

He was already gripping the door handle. I pushed his shoulder and turned him toward me. "I want some time alone," I said, more stubborn than I meant to be, almost an ultimatum. I leaned up and kissed him openmouthed. He didn't back off, but it jarred him, I could tell. This was fine with me, who was feeling the need of a shake-up. I let my lips linger a moment, grazing his more softly, and when at last I pulled away, he turned his head like a reflex toward the house.

"You think somebody's going to punish us for kissing?"

"No," he said slowly, his gaze moving off the house and into the trees, the long branches of the eucalyptus swaying in the breeze. "But maybe we shouldn't rub their noses in it."

Consider my buttons pushed. "Are you comparing my love to a pile of shit?" I inquired with nuclear irony.

"No. I just don't think—"

"I heard you the first time." A wave of cold fury had me in its grip. "I've spent enough of my life hiding and being ashamed, thank you. They should be *grateful* to see a little romance. They're kind of running on empty themselves."

"Hey, I'm on your side, pardner." A tight smile froze his lower face. "I'm just a little more discreet than you are."

"I don't *want* to be discreet." What was I defying so, in this runaway train of my heart?

"Then maybe you don't want me."

The worst was, he didn't say it with any sort of nastiness or threat. Rueful more than anything, with an undertow of unbearable self-denial. He lifted a finger and touched my lips, as if he'd already reached the stage of mournful recollection. Then he turned and climbed into the truck. And I was stung into silence, not trusting myself to say anything right. I smiled bravely and fluttered my hand in a hopeless wave, like somebody drowning, but somehow trying at last to be discreet. He gave me back a look of wounded tenderness, reversing with a lurch, then rumbling away up the drive.

I stood there till he was out of sight, not wanting him to miss me if he looked in the rearview mirror. The pewter sky above the

Trancas hills was dull as a dead fish. I realized I had loaded Gray with all the baggage I'd felt around Daniel, my own wrong-headed leeriness. Devastated, remorseful, hands balled into fists, I understood I might have lost this thing with Gray before it even got started.

But I think I must've lost some time in there as well. I don't remember going in, or anything till I came to myself, sitting at the kitchen table staring at the sketch of the beach stairs. It was dusk outside. The house was deathly quiet. My knee was throbbing, like an old man's barometer. I studied the sketch in the failing light, as if it could tell me where I'd fucked up and how I could mend the break.

I'm not sure how long I sat there hurting. Nothing broke the stillness all around me, till my head perked up at the sound of feet outside the kitchen door. Too much to hope it was Gray, even as I recalled his passionate impulse yesterday, roaring down from the hills because he didn't want me to be alone. Then I heard the mumble of voices as the door opened. Mona stepped in, a taller figure behind her. It was really rather dark by now.

Mona flailed at the wall, and the overhead light went on. "Hello," I said.

She jumped. The other person was Daphne. "What are you doing sitting in the dark?" asked Mona, rattled and faintly accusatory. But just as quick she seemed to regret it, hurrying over and taking the stool beside me. She clasped my hand on the table and looked searchingly into my eyes. I was acutely aware of Dr. Daphne watching from the sidelines, making her little Freudian mental notes. I pointedly didn't say hello to her, thus giving her volumes for her next report on the war of attrition between lesbians and the world of men.

"Tom," said Mona, "we have something to tell you." The look in her spectacled eyes was witheringly intense. What were they doing, getting married? Perhaps they wanted a sperm donation, but surely not from me. "Tom," she repeated, lowering her voice to a smoldering hush worthy of Dietrich herself. "Your brother's not dead."

"Oy," I murmured low in my throat, shutting my eyes.

But she must have heard "Oh," for she started to chafe my hand and purred, "I know, I know."

Of course I trusted Mona's loyalty implicitly, despite her having finked on my whereabouts to Brian—was it just ten days ago? But Daphne was something else entirely, truculent and arch, in addition to which she hated me. Who knew if she'd keep my brother's hideout a secret? I brought my free hand to my face, covering my eyes as if I was reeling, but really just stalling for time.

"Don't be afraid to feel," said Daphne, in a distinctly oracular tone. Now I understood that she'd been brought along as a sort of shock consultant. I peeked through my fingers at her, willowy and tall, with a tumble of auburn hair to her shoulders. She carried herself on the balls of her feet, lithe as a dancer. I never said she wasn't beautiful, just an arrogant bitch.

"They all survived," Mona went on gently, filling in the details beamed by Leslie from Yale.

All I had to do was let her finish the update, then declare I needed to be alone. "To process," I'd say to Daphne, soulfully earnest, then get them out of there. "He may try to contact you," said Mona, and I thought, *Five minutes and they'll be gone.*

But once you've got a houseful, nothing goes quite the way you planned. Too many variables. The variable in question came pattering in from the dining room, and Mona and Daphne stared. Utterly single-minded, Daniel went straight to the fridge. He opened it, ducked his head inside, and emerged a moment later with an apple. I had about a millisecond to think, as the two women's eyes came back to me.

"Teddy," I said spiritedly, "you'll spoil your supper."

Daniel's teeth were already sinking into the apple. He gave me a glazed look of confusion, then understood in a flash and recovered beautifully. He took the apple out of his mouth, mumbled a curt "Okay," and returned it to the fridge, teeth marks and all.

"Say hello to Mona and Daphne."

Dutifully he stepped forward and gravely shook both their hands, Daphne first. As he stood by Mona I reached out and ruffled his hair, the first time I'd touched him. I couldn't believe how small his head felt under my hand.

"Teddy is Foo's great-nephew," I said, making it up as I went along. Then to Daphne, "This is Foo's house." She nodded, accepting it all at face value, too self-absorbed to be suspicious. Daniel gave me a pleading look that said *Can I go now?* I smiled at him indulgently. "Don't you have a puzzle to finish?"

And he was out of there like a shot. Even so, by the astonished look in Mona's eyes I knew she knew exactly who he was. So I turned her earnestness back on her. I clutched her hand and said breathlessly, "I can't believe it, it's like a B-movie miracle. Maybe Brian and I will get a second chance after all." I blinked across at Daphne. "All the stupid fighting seems so unimportant now." Daphne beamed, loving every cliché, and feeling no doubt that she'd cured me on the spot.

"He's still got to go to jail, you know," said Mona pointedly. "And these are very violent people he's involved with."

I stood up. "Where there's life there's hope. Right, Daphne?" The killer shrink nodded, eating out of my hand. "Now if you girls will excuse me, I think I need to be alone right now. To sort all this out."

"Wait—" said Mona.

"Maybe I'll call you," I suggested with a winsome smile to Daphne, moving her toward the kitchen door.

"Of course, any time," she replied, rifling her bag and producing a business card. Mona scrambled after us, protesting that she wasn't finished, but Daphne gave her a laser look that would have turned a lesser woman to stone. Mona shut up. Daphne gripped my shoulder and gave me a sage smile. "Keep a dream journal," she declared, and I gasped at the rightness of that.

Mona was a study in silent desperation. Daphne led the way out, already putting together a paper in her head on her latest triumph. Mona leaned up to hug me and whispered in my ear, "What if *you* get in trouble?"

I squeezed her. "Trouble's my middle name, baby."

She had no choice but to keep the secret and go. I flipped on the light above the back stoop as she moved to join Daphne, walking across the lawn. I felt an unexpected twinge of jealousy, despite the whacked-out nature of the bond between them. Tall and short, oil and water, they obviously gave each other something besides broken clocks and ulcers. I'd always cheered their myriad breakups, never having liked how meek Mona was around Daphne, deferring to her self-proclaimed genius. But seeing them together now, as they stepped around a squish of mud, dainty as little girls, they were doing a whole lot better than Gray and I. And they had more time besides, to work out the kinks. Oceans of time.

I was blue when I came back in, and bluer still when I opened the fridge, to find that Gray had thoughtfully laid in dinner for us. A roast and potatoes and artichokes. I started to peel the potatoes, deciding I would apologize for everything. I didn't want to be right anymore, I wanted to be in love. And oh, how I wanted this ache of a kiss gone wrong to go away.

Then Daniel stuck his head in, to see if the coast was clear. "Good job, Ace," I said, Ace being Brian's moniker on the ballfield.

"Was that your girlfriend?"

I didn't even know which one he meant. Maybe he didn't either. "No, not exactly," I said, wondering why the qualifier. Did I want to seem a *little* butch? "Mona's my business partner," I said, which must have satisfied him, for he rooted into the fridge again and retrieved his apple, no more questions.

I liked him being there, perched on the stool, neither of us speaking as he watched me trim the spuds. And when I was done and had them boiling, I rubbed the roast with garlic and mustard. As I put it in to sear, I turned to him and said in the most conspiratorial voice, "You think you can convince your mom to come down and have supper with us?"

He made a circle of his forefinger and thumb, giving me the high sign. "Piece o' cake," he drawled.

I didn't go in with any expectations. When Daniel came down later and told me yes, she'd join us, I took it in stride. Neither an excess of sentimentality nor any hope of resolution. I was going for the ordinary, plain as the mismatched forks and napkins. My only point of comparison, after all, were the dinners from hell on West Hill Road, the old man stinking of Seagram's, my mother fishing pathetically for compliments on the prison swill she fed us, Spam hash and tuna surprise.

At around seven I called Daniel from his puzzle and sent him up to fetch the grown-ups. I was just bearing in the platter of meat and potatoes when they came straggling down the stairs, still slightly dazed, like a family of deer after a forest fire. Susan had managed to pull together a skirt and sweater, heather to match her eyes, and her hair was bright and sleek again. Apparently she'd decided to make the best of it, commenting cheerfully on my table, offering to light the candles. I wasn't under any delusion that she'd shifted her ground about me, but for the family's sake she must have felt they needed to show a united front.

She sat across from Brian, Daniel across from me. Immediately my brother mumbled that we would say grace, and we joined hands around the table. "Father, we thank you," Brian intoned, blah-blah the gifts of the earth. I stared stonily forward at their three bowed heads. Holding hands was a nice refinement on the bleak dinner prayers of West Hill Road, my mother clutched like a rosary. "And, Father, bless us for being together again with Tom." He squeezed my hand as the three of them said "Amen."

Quickly I sent the platter around, jabbering across at Daniel, who'd never eaten an artichoke. I enjoyed rattling off my little lecture on the dismantling of the spiny succulent—feeling pretty avuncular, actually. Daniel listened soberly, dunking a leaf in the drawn butter, chewing off the edible part, his face intent as a fawn in clover. He loved the part about throwing the spent leaves into a common bowl in the center of the table. Brian and Susan were eating quietly, an occasional murmur of praise for the chef. I had the easy feeling that we would keep the flow of talk to simple matters of feeding.

Then Daniel looked over at me and said, "Who's Teddy?"

I stammered. "Oh, just a guy I used to know. We were roommates for a while. He—" *Died*, I was going to say, then amended that. "He was sort of an actor too."

I felt cornered and embarrassed. How could they not see in my blushing face the raw and crazy passion I'd had for Teddy Burr, the first man I loved in Hollywood who wouldn't love me back? Then an eruption of impotent fury at myself, acting as if there was something to be ashamed of. I clamped my teeth on an artichoke leaf, trying to think how to reverse this reflex of self-censorship. Swearing to parade myself instead, at the very next opportunity.

But Daniel was way ahead of me in the openness department. Following my lead he cleared away the cactus hair, baring the artichoke's heart. Then he turned to his father and spoke with studied nonchalance. "So, Dad," he said, "what have you guys decided? Where we going?"

Brian and Susan exchanged a look across the table, in which they zapped each other with guilt right between the eyes. "We haven't decided yet, pal," replied my brother. "Don't worry, you'll be the first to know."

" 'Cause I have this book report I gotta give," persisted Daniel. "The day we get back from vacation. And I'm supposed to go first."

"What book is that, honey?" asked his mother, stalling now herself.

"*Treasure Island*," I piped in, and she gave me a look of unutterable disdain—as if it were any business of mine.

"Sorry, pal," said my brother, trying to be soft, the repetition sounding hollow and cheap. "You're not going back to that school. It'll be someplace else, here or . . . someplace." His voice seemed to deflate as it came to the blank wall of his future.

"But, Dad," insisted the boy, struggling not to whine, "there's only two months left. What if I get held back?"

My brother's hand slammed the table, and my stomach went tilt with an old fear, that he was about to hit *me*. "That'll be enough, soldier," barked Brian. "You're not the only one in this family who's got some adjustments to make. So you just wait for your marching orders, okay?"

Daniel seemed to shrink to half his size, as if he'd been struck by a witch's curse. His mouth set in an inverted U, he took a bite of potato to keep from crying, then swallowed it like a lump of pain. Aside from my useless empathy, I was riveted by the field of force here, riddled as it was with bloody crossfire. I swiveled my head instinctively to Susan, whose turn it seemed to be. *Ah, family values*, I thought in my bitterest core, the mile-deep gold mine of West Hill Road.

"Think about *my* students, Daniel," she said, with a teacherly twinge of singsong. "One can't hear, and two have Down's. No one in my class can read like you. Think how much they'll miss me."

Even as she was unconscious of the smarm and condescension in her tone, she seemed to be making no other point than to toot her own horn. And to stick it to my brother for spiriting her away from her good works. Until this moment, I'd forgotten she was in special ed. I tried to like her better for taking care of those whom fate had fucked. I failed.

When I smiled across at Daniel I tried not to seem too much his ally, not wanting for his sake to turn this into us against them, because he had to live with it, better or worse. But I swear I could see in his eyes, in the vastness of what he left unsaid or had no words for yet, I saw the cool resolve of a kid who'd already started to pack the bags of his feelings. It didn't mean he'd run away in five or even ten years. He'd be smart enough to stick it out and let them pay for his education. But emotionally he was out of there. Long gone, just like me.

We fed in silence after that. We couldn't really talk about the future, because for them there wasn't any yet, and as for me, forget it. They all seemed to be feeling hopelessly misunderstood by each other, bruised into silence. In the days of our old family, even before I could talk, I gave up the idea of being understood. Perhaps these three just had nothing else to say, with their house and former lives in smithereens. I wondered if an outsider, wandering in right now, would even know they were a family. Because if it was Mona and Gray and Foo and me, anyone would know.

When Daniel asked to be excused, Susan made him stand in front of her while she wiped his mouth with a napkin. This seemed to me a pointless gesture of humiliation, but Daniel appeared indifferent. Told he could watch a half hour of TV, he scurried into the parlor. I said I'd take care of the dishes, but here my sister-in-law's suburban pride asserted itself. So we all three bore the wreckage of the feast into the kitchen, and as my brother filled the sink and rolled his sleeves, Susan took care of the leftovers. Her scullery instincts were excellent, for she went right to the drawer that held the food wraps. She slicked a sheet of Saran over the rest of the beef roast, then opened the fridge to stow it. And balked slightly.

"Oh, sorry," I said, laughing as I hurried to her side. The whole top shelf was cheek by jowl with medicine, leaving no room for the platter. "My lady pharmacist always gives me six months' supply of everything," I declared, shifting and stacking containers of pills. "She's a delirious optimist. Plus Mona brings me these Chinese herbs marinated in rice vinegar. Which tastes like sheep's piss."

There, I'd cleared nearly half the shelf. But when I stepped aside so Susan could shove the platter in, she was standing immovable, a blanched look on her face. Her bewildered eyes raked me up and down, then settled at last on the purple spot on my cheek. My God, he still hadn't told her. Out of the corner of my eye I saw my brother stop washing at the sink, staring in our direction. Then Susan tore her gaze from my lesion and gaped at the platter in her hands. All she could think of, I knew, was that I had cooked it. For a second I thought she was going to fling the platter across the room, or into my face.

But she leaned over and set it down carefully on the counter before she turned on her husband. Suddenly she was quivering, and the ice in her voice was as deep as the polar shelf. "How could you bring us here?"

"Susan, we can't catch it—"

She almost yelled. "How do you know that he hasn't touched our son?"

Brian winced and wouldn't look at me. "Honey, don't be crazy," he practically pleaded. "We're all on overload right now. But we have to—"

"You can't do this to me!"

It was a scream out of *Medea*. And now she was on him, pummeling his chest with her fists. Brian, his arms still wet from the dishwater, was trying to wrap them around her, as if he could turn it into a mad embrace. Susan hadn't stopped yelling, but the words didn't make any sense anymore. "Sickness," she shrilled a few times, flailing to slap his face. It was more like a fit than a fight. I glided along the counter and swung the kitchen door shut, my only concern to somehow protect Daniel, hoping the TV was turned up loud.

Brian attempted to grab her wrists, but she smashed through and clawed his cheek, drawing blood. He roared, a final trumpet of warning, and then I heard her shriek: "You're the same as him!"

I knew the look on Brian's face from a long time back—cruel, remorseless, dancing on the edge of the void. With one hand he yanked her hair, snapping her head like whiplash. Then he clouted her hard, cheekbone and temple, sprawling her to the floor at his feet. Still he held her by the hair, both of them panting grotesquely.

Drips of blood began to spatter the floor, I guessed from Susan's mouth. The two of them seemed to catch sight of it at the same time, and the shock of the red broke the spell. He let go of her hair. She came up off her knees, hand to her mouth. Quickly Brian tore off a length of paper towels, ran it under the faucet and held out the sopping wad. Susan took it and turned away, holding it to her mouth as she made for the door I'd closed. Her eyes grazed mine as she left, the madness gone but the hate pure.

Brian leaned heavily on the sink, propping himself on his hands, head sunk in his shoulders. From Susan's first moment of horror, all through the battle, it was as if I wasn't there at all. She'd accused me of molesting Daniel, probably thought I had spit in her food—her revulsion completely unfettered. Yet I felt no wounds of any sort. I just kept thinking: How could she be so *stupid* not to figure out I was sick? Really, what was the point of all that rabid homophobia, if not to feed the paranoia around AIDS?

And in the same breath I felt extraordinarily detached, near invisible. None of this was about me. Not a single blow.

"I better go put Daniel to bed," Brian declared stiffly, moving to go.

I said nothing. I wasn't there.

And once I was sure they had all gone upstairs, I went into the parlor and built a fire. Curled in my corner of the sofa, toasty under the afghan, I thought about Gray and how I would apologize tomorrow. The relationship we were struggling to begin didn't seem half so crazy now, compared to the competition. And I saw clearer than ever how the abuse had come down like a wayward gene from my father to Brian. It wasn't just an adolescent's meanness, mauling his baby brother. He had this well of violence in him, and so did his wife, and they danced a constant tango of taunt and explosion. Coldly I wondered which of them hit the kid.

In the middle of all that, Brian came downstairs. He didn't speak at first, moving right to the fireplace and leaning against the mantel, staring in. After a minute he sighed. "She's cracking from the strain, Tommy. She doesn't know what she's saying."

"Uh-huh," I replied, mostly to be polite.

"She doesn't want to be rational. She wants her life back."

"Yeah, me too." But without sarcasm. I was amazed, in fact, how sympathetic I felt just then. I didn't like her at all, but I understood.

"I know this is going to insult you," said my brother, turning now to look at me. "While we're here, she wants to prepare the food for her and Daniel. Separate." A dry sound like a dead laugh escaped him. His hands at his sides lifted in a helpless shrug, as if to say they were tied. His disgust was palpable.

I pulled the afghan closer around the hunch of my knees. "It doesn't matter," I said quietly.

When he turned back to the fire, I had the feeling he would've preferred it if I'd flown into a rage and pummeled him, just like she did. For I saw now that he wasn't the same as our father, after all—who attacked without warning, like a preemptive strike, raining down blows when you least expected. Brian the bully, my father's legitimate heir, had somehow been put to rest. Now it required Susan to beat him up till he lashed out, a goad to draw the bully from his cave. He shook his head wearily.

"I'm not sure they can keep me out of jail."

"Oh, these lawyers are pretty smart," I retorted, realizing only then how I sounded like all my useless friends, ducking the unpleasantness. *These doctors are pretty smart,* they said.

"Would you believe I didn't know about any of it for years? It was all Jerry's thing. And when I realized what was going on, I tried to look the other way. Except I kept getting these bonuses." Another dry and dusty laugh. "So I figured what the hell."

The confession ceased abruptly, if that's what it was. Still I felt not the slightest urge to judge him. "Sure, I believe you," I said, staring down at the puzzle on the coffee table, about two-thirds complete. You could definitely see it was *David* now, but still he had no dick.

"They're going to take all my money. This RICO law." Strange, how he didn't sound bitter. He'd gambled and he'd lost. End of story.

"Didn't you put some away?"

"You mean like Switzerland?" His voice quickened with irony. "Naaah—I didn't think that far ahead. I'm a putz of a gangster, Tommy." He stretched his pitching shoulder, kneading it and rolling it around, as if he ached to throw a few balls. "Fuck, I had about two mill in stamps and coins at the house. In a safe." Again that parched laugh, almost a cackle, like someone on whom the truth has dawned, say at the final frame of "The Twilight Zone." "Safe from what, huh? Either the fire got it or the cops did."

Funny, what you remember when. As kids we collected two-bit stamps and coins. Pennies we scrounged and pressed into slotted albums; worthless stamps ordered in bulk from the back pages of comic books. For all our fighting, I couldn't recall that we argued over any of that. I could see us just sitting together in the kitchen, filling our albums, when it was too rainy to play outside. What ever happened to those, I wondered. The hours more than the albums.

"You can live without money," I said. "I've done it for years."

I meant it facetiously, but he didn't laugh. He continued to gaze intently at the fire, unblinking, till I thought he would scorch his eyeballs. Then he said very distinctly, "I can't imagine what I'm going to do."

Slowly he swung away from the mantel. Though he faced me now, I wasn't sure if he could just see dark after the dazzle of the flames. One hand seemed to grope before him, and then he was leaning down. Toward me. Instinctively I huddled deeper, turning my face to the cushion, always protect your face. Then I felt the flat of his hand between my shoulders and his lips against my hair, just above the ear.

"G'night Tommy," he said. "And thanks for putting up with us."

He lumbered away, leaving me in a stunned silence. My jaw was so slack I couldn't even return his "good night." He'd never embraced me before, nor I him. We wouldn't have dreamed of such a thing. Though I knew it was a gesture left over from kissing his son—the very same spot above the ear, I was sure of it—I was no less overwhelmed.

And what a pushover I turned out to be, racing now to forgive him every slur, every torment. What did it say about my self-respect, that I would happily give the world away for certain kisses? Such a needy little devil. Even then, it wasn't all roses. In some dim and cankerous recess of my heart, I felt a spurt of triumph over Susan. I thought: *So, did you get a kiss tonight, honey?*

My wickedness shocked even me sometimes.

I was in bed in twenty minutes, bareass under the molting comforter. But I must have fallen asleep with the light on—not reading, just staring around my room and thinking of Gray. I forgot about my brother and all the craziness, the beach house bursting with people. I just wanted to sleep with Gray—period. This was called taking it one step at a time. "Low and slow," as my brother used to say on the field. I don't remember which sport.

So the light was on, which must have drawn him. It was two or three o'clock—I don't know if I ever looked. I felt a tug on the comforter, and I swirled up out of sleep trying to remember who was sick, who needed to go to the hospital. My eyes blinked open, expecting a figure looming over the bed. Nobody there. Then I dropped my eyes a couple of feet, and Daniel was leaning on the edge of the mattress, propped on his elbows. He wore pajamas with cowboys all over.

"What's wrong?" I whispered, half sitting up.

"Can't sleep," he said, lips pursed in a coy pout. "Can I sleep with you?"

"No," I said sharply, wide awake now, and suddenly frightened by my own nakedness under the comforter. "I don't think that's a good idea," I said, softer because he seemed a little hurt.

"But I get scared." His voice trembled. "I keep having dreams about my dogs."

Oh, I could see the manipulation, plain as the quiver of his chin, but that didn't mean it didn't work. "Well, why don't you just sit up here for a minute?" I said, scooting over to make room for him, tucking the comforter tight around me so he wouldn't get any ideas about crawling in under. He hopped right up, sitting cross-legged against the pillow. His knee touched my chest. "Don't be afraid of dreams," I said, a trifle singsong myself. "That's how we get rid of a lot of bad shit—I mean stuff."

He studied his toes thoughtfully. "All they do is fight."

"Yeah." We weren't talking about the dogs anymore.

"If they don't stop fighting, how are we gonna figure out where to go?"

The weight of the world on his shoulders. It must have seemed to him an impossible obstacle course, between here and being safe in school again. "They'll be okay," I said, a comment that struck me as being about as empty as my paean to the smarts of lawyers. "Just give 'em a little more time."

Happily these banalities didn't fill him with contempt. He scrunched down and tucked in closer to where I was curled on my side. I sucked my belly in, trying to keep some distance, but it was useless. He was completely unselfconscious, burrowing like a bear cub. I had an awful feeling he was going to ask me to tell him a story, and all my stories were X-rated, picketed by the likes of Susan. In vain I cast my mind to try to think of a fairy tale that was clean, animals singing and dancing in a circle, cuddly and neuter.

Daniel said drowsily, "I used to have a picture of you in my room. I found it at Gramma's. I kept it in my toy box."

How could I not be flattered, being let in on his secret? *Being* his secret. "What kind of picture?"

"You and Dad. When you were little."

I had a sudden fierce desire to see it, then remembered the fire. Black-and-white, but taken by whom? My parents weren't the type, in the long unraveling of their lives, to memorialize their kids. A hundred pictures of Brian, yes, in all his myriad uniforms, but not of the two of us. "How old—" I started to say, then realized the kid had fallen asleep, practically in my arms.

His breathing so light I had to hold my own to hear it. And for a moment there was nothing else but this, me cradling my nephew in the curl of my body. Thinking, *What if I'd never met him?* And *What would he remember*, years from now when I was gone? It would only be the briefest meeting, that I knew already. Soon they would go, wherever they had to, leaving me to the hourglass of my disappearing island. But at the moment, I couldn't get it up to feel melancholy or cheated. No matter what else, I'd had this taste of being an uncle. And I enjoyed it most shamelessly.

I was gently stroking his head, patting him like a dog really, not having a lot of practice with human puppies. It couldn't go on—I was too aware of the dangers of his parents freaking out. Inching away, I slipped noiselessly off the bed, one hand shielding my genitals. It seemed very important somehow that he not see me naked. *David* was quite enough for one day, thank you. I glided across to the closet and slipped my seersucker robe from the hook behind the door. I drew it on, tugging the belt tight. Then I walked around to where he lay, one hand batting idly at an itch on his nose.

I'd never done this before, but figured he wouldn't be any heavier than my cross. I crouched and scooped him into my arms, lifting him up, ready to hush his protest. The deadweight of him shocked me, and I staggered. But instantly he helped me, groping his arms about my neck and holding on, still fast asleep. I reeled around and clumped to the door, gently heaving him onto my shoulder so I could reach the knob.

As we came out into the hallway I started to get the hang of it. We moved in perfect balance, like a peasant hauling water. We skirted around the stairwell, and only now, as I passed his parents' door, did I feel a thrill of fear. If Susan should come out right now, if I tripped and made too much noise, words would be said whose scars would never go away. For a second then, it was a high-wire act, teetering forward on the balls of my feet, the boy secure in my arms.

Through the arched doorway and up the four steps. As we came into his room I'd forgotten the windows all around. I was used to it only by day, drenched in sun and wide open to the rimless cerulean of sky and water. Now in the dark there was only velvet black all around, scattershot with the diamond glints of stars. The nightshine was sufficient for me to find the bed, no jarring lamp required. I bent over and laid him softly down, cradling his head onto the pillow. He slept as deep as his father. I covered him with a light cotton blanket, tucking it under his chin. Then I glanced out to the ocean, the last watch of the night.

The moon was down. I could see the clouds rolling across the sky, milky pearl and amorphous, still unsure what they were bringing. *Let it rain*, I beseeched the heavens. Then looked down at Daniel one last time, reaching out and stroking his cheek with the back of my hand. I didn't kiss him because—I just didn't. But I was so glad he was in my house, sleeping in my tower.

I sailed down the steps and whirled around the stair hall like Isadora, as if I was capering round a Greek vase. And in the middle of one of those leaps, I bashed my head on the wall fixture—a bronze tulip sporting a single bulb. The light flickered as I grabbed the side of my head, swallowing the groan, though I'd made enough noise already to wake the dead. I reeled into Foo's room and shut the door, lurching forward and tumbling onto the bed. *Laughing*. I don't know why the pain was funny, except it was. Hilarious.

I wanted to take care of them all. How's that for the son of a drunk? Always wanting to fix things. I could see Mona's groaning shelf of books on codependency, the pinnacle of her self-help Ph.D. Please—I've been through the program. But I knew right then, as the worst of the throbbing began to abate, I wouldn't let them out of here without a little headwork. Wouldn't let them fall into total dysfunction, the legacy of West Hill Road, without a fight. I probably had a slight concussion, but I was too ornery to black out.

Still faintly whinneying with laughter, I stood up shakily and moved to the bureau. Right away I saw in the mirror the swelling bruise on my left temple, a small seep of blood along the hairline—just about the spot where Brian had grazed his lips. Maybe that's why the pain struck me so funny. Brian's address on Pequod Lane was tucked in the corner of the mirror. One of my most Italian qualities: I never throw anything out. Complete pack rat. I opened the top drawer of the bureau. My Jockey shorts were folded neatly on one side, good little Catholic boy, and on the other side a battered leather box tooled in gold, of the sort in which Fred Astaire would have stowed his studs and cuff links, but used by me for a catchall.

As it happened, the box had been given to me by Teddy Burr, may he rest easy. I opened it, just the stray bubble of laughter now and my head starting to spin in earnest. My UConn class ring, my upper retainer, my cock ring. I lifted out a card and squinted at it: *Daphne*. Oh sure. How about a nice hundred-dollar hour with Dr. Dyke, a little family therapy as we all stared at the smashed clock on her desk. No thanks. Then I picked up the card that lay beneath it.

Kathleen Twomey. Salva House Women's Center. My lesbian nun fan. *Angels are all gay too.* I tucked it just above Brian's address in the mirror.

I could've turned away then, I was ready to crash. But I burrowed once more in the box, brushing aside the ephemera—buttons, shillings, subway tokens—and lifted out a crumpled snapshot, furred around the edges. Brian was probably ten, in his baseball whites, a bat across his shoulders. A few feet behind him, more or less blending into the shrubbery, a small child is turning away, blurred because he's in motion. Only I would know it was myself. And not by the slightest stretch of the imagination would you say it was a picture of the two of us. I just happened to be walking by when my father recorded his Little League hero.

Was Daniel's picture from the same roll? Was there one with the two of us arm in arm? I was really going to faint if I didn't lie down. I remember closing the box and the drawer, I remember wanting to prop the picture in the mirror's opposite corner. But you get to a point where you've pushed your limits so far you're dancing on thin air, and the best thing to do then is free-fall, knowing your bed is right there—the way it would be in a normal house.

S I X

WOKE TO THE SOUND OF MEN AT WORK—CALLING RUGGEDLY, heaving brawn—and the first thing I thought was *What did I miss?* I rolled off the bed and stared point-blank at the digital Westclox. 11:23! Damn, how I hated to lose half the day to this thick cocoon of viral sleep. Not including the entr'acte with Daniel, I'd been under for almost twelve hours. I wouldn't admit I needed it, that the pace and tension of the last days were a marathon next to the dreamy weeks I'd passed here solo, me and Emma. I stood up to a thunderbolt of pain on the side of my head, recalling my dying-swan *jeté*. I tottered over and peered out the balcony door.

All I could see was Merle, standing among the swords of the century cactus, bellowing down the bluff. Stripped to the waist, his ruddy torso massive but without any waste of fat, he was playing a rope through his gloved hands. He leaned against the weight of the load he was easing down the cliff face. With a sweatband around the crown of his head, he looked as tribal as I'd ever seen him, a shaman at the edge of the world, wrestling the bonds of an awful ceremony. Above him the cloud cover had banked in again, moiling and dark with rain.

I felt a mad surge of adrenaline, because I couldn't stand it that they were all getting ahead of me.

I was dressed and downstairs on fast-forward, eager to join the men, only stopping to duck in the kitchen for my morning pills. I didn't plan on Susan, who stood at the stove in her lavender sweats. We both balked. A slurred "good morning" passed between us, flat as a hangover, as I made a bead for the fridge and she went on stirring her pot. I shook out my fourteen pills; went to the sink for water.

When I pitched back my head to drink, she said blandly, "I'm making them soup and sandwiches. Would you like some?"

I felt my first spurt of contrariness, as I lowered the empty glass. Dr. Jekyll having just taken his morning draft, Mr. Hyde turned to his sister-in-law. "I thought I'm supposed to eat separate," I said, drawing the last word out with fine contempt.

Susan shook her head wearily, sighing. "That's not what I said," she declared with brittle firmness. "I'd just rather you not prepare food for me and my son. Look, I'm sorry you're sick."

At last she looked directly at me, struggling to change the tone of this whole encounter. Now I could see the puff of swelling, purple on her upper lip. It seemed to freeze her lower face in a permanent sneer. "It must be terrible," she said.

Don't even try, I wanted to tell her. I saw she was studying the lump by my temple, probably wondering who had battered me. "Mostly it's all the friends I've lost," I replied, "and nobody cares. But I haven't been sick sick. Yet."

She looked down at her pot of soup—vegetable-beef, bubbling with a skim of fat. "You must despise people like me." Spoken very evenly, with a certain ring of self-knowledge, but no intention of changing either.

"I only despise the people in charge. All politicians, left and right, who bathe in each other's slime. And every creep above the rank of monsignor, all the way up to His Hitlerness."

She shook her head again, with bitter rue. "That's your business. But I wouldn't blame God for the sins of the church. You never know. He could turn out to be your last chance."

Superior as a Jesuit. She stirred the pot, serene as if the souls of the damned were being rendered into soap. "Oh, don't worry," I said, "I've got a fabulous thing going with Jesus. We're like sisters."

She frowned in some confusion. Quickly I turned and headed out before either of us softened and called for a truce. After all, she still believed the very touch of my fingers was ripe with death. But I had to admit, striding along under the pergola and out to the cliffside terrace, Susan was a much more stimulating opponent than Mrs. Beaudry of the Coalition of Family Values. Or my drunken moron father. By comparison, the skirmish just concluded was High Theology.

The lip of the bluff was deserted, Merle having gone below to join the others. I could hear them barking orders at one another as I headed down the stairs, raw as any construction crew. Running beside the stairs was a groove in the cliff where the rope had worn away. Far out, the ocean had almost a yellowish cast, dull gold over the gray, oddly apocalyptic. *Why not a typhoon?* I thought merrily, my heart leaping as I came around the midpoint landing and saw them gathered below.

My brother and Merle were grappling with a vertical four by four, swaying it into place against the rock, while Gray squatted and wedged it tight, agile as a sherpa. Close by his father on the landing, Daniel straddled the toolbox, drill in one hand, hammer in the other. I trotted down the last flight to join them, but only Daniel looked up to greet me, beaming at the sight of me.

A blurred half-cheer went up from the three men as they anchored the four by four. Then Brian and Merle set to work bracing it with two by fours. I haven't a clue how anything is constructed—the only thing I've ever built is my cross. But they seemed to be shifting the weight of the structure deeper into the fold of the cliff. This would allow the final flight of steps to the beach to lie securely in a bed of rock. I didn't see how they would make it work, and anyway, the anarchic bone in my body wondered why they were bothering, given the force of the coming storm. Doubtless I was reacting to my brother's vivid enthusiasm, the sweaty physicality with which he threw himself into the job.

Then Gray hoisted himself onto the landing, springing to his feet near Daniel and me. When he saw me there, he broke into the same uncomplicated grin as the boy, who crouched between us over the toolbox, watching his dad intently. I felt a burn of shyness, for once not wanting to speak first. Gray cocked his head to one side, drinking me in. "Don't ever let me go away like that again."

"Please—you should have pushed my head in the mud and *then* left."

We laughed. There was nothing further to apologize, since we'd both taken all the blame. Yesterday's tiff had been about discretion, hadn't it, and Gray had clearly won the point. For here we were, not kissing in front of the kid. And then the focus shifted, my brother grunting like a foreman, wordlessly beckoning Gray to help. Gray turned and in one stride was back with the program, wedging himself between Merle and Brian, gripping the two by fours while the other men hammered them fast. The three of them together looked like seamen playing sails, bonded by the drill of heavy labor.

Brian, in jeans and a frayed football jersey—FORDHAM 38—was powerful as ever, wonderful to watch in motion. The muscles in his forearm swelled and rippled as the hammer drove home. A different sort of strength from Merle's, who heaved to like a stevedore, sheer brute force. Yet it was Gray between them, lean and fierce and holding the thing together, who drew my eyes. For I found him more striking today than ever, a man full-blown and radiantly untortured, perfect mate for a winter harbor. This was remarkable all by itself, since with me it's always gone the other way, the heat of a man evaporating sometimes by the hour.

"Tommy, bring over those braces," Brian called out, startling me. He'd given no indication that I was even there. Rattled, I looked about me in confusion, not a clue what I was looking for. The landing was littered with lumber and tools, all of it foreign to me. But Daniel, quick to save my ass, scrambled from the toolbox and reached for a paper sack. He rooted in and drew out a bunch of L-shaped doodads with holes for screws. He handed them off to me, and I hurried over to where the others waited.

"Here—right here," Brian ordered me, slapping the place where the beams joined. I ducked in next to Gray and reached to press one of the L braces exactly where he said. "You got it upside down," Brian snapped impatiently, poised beside me with screws and driver. I flipped the brace over and held it in place. He started the screws, working with burning intensity. The perfume of the white pine was enough to make you woozy. "For Chrissakes, Tommy," he barked, "hold it steady!"

Already my fingers were numb from pressing. But I poured all the force I had, lasering in on the brace, making it right for my brother. Simultaneously I winced from his surly tone, furious that I'd got myself caught up in this macho game. I could hear as if through a hole in time my brother sneering as he popped me flies, and me running around like a chicken, terrified the ball would hurt if I caught it, which I never did. Oh, how I didn't wish to be transported back to 1965.

"Other side," commanded Brian, and I dutifully moved to lay a second brace—right side up—on the opposite face of the join. In doing so I pressed up next to Gray's hip beside me. Meanwhile it felt as if Merle was hammering nails in my ear. When Brian leaned around to secure the brace, his shirt swept over my face, and I smelled the head of sweat in his armpit.

Instantly I was reeling from the sudden raw explosion of carnality, as if the dogs of my old hunger had been set on a hunt to the death.

I was twelve again and totally neuter. As Brian worked the screws, his pitcher's arm was six inches from my face, the coarse thatch of red hair thick from wrist to elbow. I felt helpless, held against my will, and worst of all, utterly disconnected from Gray.

Finally we took a break, all of us disentangling from the corner we had carpentered together. The others murmured with satisfaction, again that wordless Neanderthal tongue—a shared male shorthand, clearly neither gay nor straight, since only Brian among us was unbent. Even I produced a small rumble, like a pup's first growl. Except I was also exhausted and slightly light-headed, not having strained so hard in years.

Merle was already dragging down some boards with which to underpin the stairs. Gray crouched by the railing, reading the label on the waterproof sealer. Then out of nowhere I felt Brian's hand clap my shoulder. "Thanks," he said, pleasant as could be.

I blinked at him as he squatted to huddle with Daniel. Did he not remember the sneering words? Was it all just part of the team push, jostling and sniping, no hard feelings? Was that how it felt to him in Chester, torturing one minute, teasing the next? I could hardly trust my own perception, not here, not on any field where Brian ruled. I moved toward him. "How'd it go this morning?" I asked.

He looked up at me impassively. "Pretty good, I guess," he said with a certain reserve. "They'll do a deal."

Then he turned again to his son, who was furiously unwrapping a paintbrush. Brian had given him leave to slather the new wood with sealer, and the boy was wild to get started. Gray took the screwdriver to pry off the lid of the can, while he lobbed Daniel a couple of handyman tips on how to work with the stuff. Nobody needed me.

I happened to turn around as Merle was lighting a cigarette, staring at me as he blew out the match, his eyes glittering with mistrust. I knew he was reacting to the proximity of Gray and me. *Eat your heart out,* I thought, sick of his jealous silence. And yet I gave him a winning smile, because deep down I knew he was only trying to protect this gentle man who'd touched us both. And I wanted Gray protected.

But I'd had enough of mixing it up with the guys. When Gray stood up, moving to lead Daniel and his brush over to the job site, I said, "Can I have the pickup? I need to go down to the Chevron."

He nodded, fishing a hand in the pocket of his baggy jeans. His hair was all mussed. I suppressed an impulse to reach up and smooth it down over his bald spot. Daniel waited impatiently beside him, burning to go to work. Gray held out his ring of keys, twenty or thirty bristling in all directions, like a tenement landlord. "Start it in second and pump it easy," he said.

"Really? Just like me," I retorted dryly, but he didn't quite get the double entendre, or chose to ignore it. So I let them be and scampered away up the stairs, hovering for a moment at the next landing to give a backward glance. All four were busy again, strutting and flooring the new structure. I felt an unexpected rush of pride, as if I had brought this whole thing off myself, pulling together my two families. They moved below me in harmony, like pioneer neighbors gathered to throw up a barn in a day.

Still, the uphill climb was a killer after that little stint of construction. Three times I had to stop, panting, hanging over the railing as I kneaded the stitch in my side. By the time I reached the top of the bluff I practically had the dry heaves.

Happily Susan was nowhere in sight as I staggered upstairs for my wallet. I very distinctly didn't want anyone seeing me weak and frail. This was a notable change for someone who used to shove my symptoms in people's faces, mostly Mona's, like some kind of existential badge. Just who was I trying to spare, I wondered, me or them? But I knew the answer. I'd come to that slippery place, rife with the shoals of denial, where I wanted to be as alive as all of them.

I splashed water on my face and resisted the urge to curl up for a nap. Coming downstairs, the mass of keys jingling in my hand like a leper's bell, I braced for a second encounter with Susan. But the kitchen was empty. A plate of sandwiches sat on the counter, slicked with plastic wrap. I slipped a hand in under and drew out a half of tuna fish on white. Downing this in two bites—I'd had no breakfast—I moved to the stove and lifted the lid on the pot. Soup smelled fabulous. I grabbed a big spoon and ladled up a mouthful, potato and a hunk of beef. I gobbled it, smacking my lips—then had to decide, with a devilish snoot of irony, whether I'd stick the tainted spoon back in for a second bite. If only Susan had walked in then. But I demurred, replacing the lid and plopping the spoon in the sink, saving countless thousands from certain death.

I hustled across the yard to the pickup, wondering if I had enough cash on me to gas it up, thus giving Gray a little back. I opened the door and slung myself inside. Nearly crying out in shock to discover Daniel sitting on the passenger's side, quietly waiting. "Can I go with you?" he asked plaintively, accustomed to *no* as an answer.

"I thought you were putting the sealer on."

He shook his head gloomily. "I screwed it up," he said. "And then I spilled some. Dad took the brush away."

Yanked it away, I imagined. I was flooded with double feelings, wanting to make it all better for Daniel but also to punish my brother. He'd always been a stupid perfectionist, his rigid marine defense of neatness in the house of a slob drunk. By way of reply I cranked the key in the ignition and popped us forward in second, making a neat U-turn. I pumped the gas easy, just as instructed, and rolled not quite to a stop at the end of the drive. No traffic. We sailed out onto the coast road, heading south.

I was trying to think of something to say to cheer him up, when he suddenly asked, "Is that where Ricky Gun lives?"

I glanced over. He was gawking out the window at the turret and gated arch of the Norman castle. "No, he lives on the other side," I said, disheartened by his awe of the rock star. I still wanted Daniel to see the beach house the way I did, as a desert island unencumbered by the world's dreck. But here he was, a child of MTV, possessed by ear-splitting superheroes. Who had even told him the sequined Mr. Gun was our next-door neighbor? He certainly didn't miss a trick.

Then he said, "Gray's your friend, right?"

"Yes," I replied carefully, my stomach beginning to clench. "Why?"

"He's really nice."

And that seemed to be that, just a moment of piercing sincerity, where the kid had managed to say exactly what he felt. I was the one who was thrown, suddenly riddled with questions. Had his parents said something about Gray and me? And if Daniel knew about Gray, did he also know about AIDS? I could feel my hands gripping the wheel for dear life. I understood in that instant that I had to be as open as this boy, and that nothing real would hurt him.

"I'm very lucky," I said, "because he lets me live in his house. And he brings me food so I never go hungry. It's a really good deal."

I turned to flash a grin at him, and suddenly a roar was on my left. I swiveled to look. A Jeep was passing with screaming teens, inches away. Directly ahead, in our lane, a dump truck heaped with gravel lumbered along. There was hardly twenty feet between us and the dumper, but the Jeep wanted in. It gunned and nosed for the gap. As it fishtailed by our front bumper I braked and swerved right, thudding us along the shoulder. Daniel was sprawled on the seat beside me.

It was over in seconds. We regained the pavement, the Jeep lurching out to pass again and disappearing round the truck, teens howling, bound for a head-on crash before they were out of high school. "You all right?" I whispered at my nephew in a strangled voice.

"Uh-huh." He picked himself up and sat by the door again, completely unfazed.

I was a wreck. Creeping with horror, I realized we'd set off without any seat belts. The frigging pickup *had* no seatbelts, one of its legion of violations. And what if Daniel had been thrown against the dashboard? Then what would I say to his parents—the split lip, the broken teeth? I was shaking. Daniel, bless him, was oblivious, craning around to check out a couple of rubber-suited surfers zipping up. But I had this bone-zero realization that I'd almost failed him, and along with that, an overwhelming sense of what it meant that his life was in my hands.

I slowed the pickup till we were barely doing thirty-five, which only made more people pass us. The responsibility was almost unendurable. I think I came the closest to comprehending Susan's fear—of me, the virus, everything after the bomb. For how would she ever keep her baby safe now? For a minute I couldn't even bear to look at Daniel, all that trusting innocence.

At last the Chevron came into view on the left, and I edged into the turn lane, wincing with dread at the oncoming cars, letting fifteen chances go by. I waited and waited, till a car was honking behind and the stretch of road to the south was empty. I coasted in next to the phone booth and stopped, my hands still so tight on the wheel I thought they'd have to be pried loose.

"You stay here," I declared, which was fine with Daniel. He was happy to peer out the window at the exotic beach types going in and out of the scruffy convenience store beyond the gas pumps. I walked across the gravel and accordioned myself in the booth, but making sure I was facing the pickup. I drew the card from my pocket, dialed the number in Venice.

"Salva House," a woman's voice answered. I asked for Kathleen

Twomey. "She's with a group right now," came the reply. "Why don't I give you her machine?"

And after two clicks and a beep, my ex-nun's recorded voice spoke. "Hi, it's Kathleen. I'm out of the office. Please leave a name and number where I can get ahold of you. If you have no phone, or you feel you're in danger, then come right down to Salva House. We're always open. Remember, nobody has to live in a battered place." Then a long beep.

"Hello," I said, suddenly shy, "this is Miss Jesus calling. Remember me? The queen of Judea. Listen, I've got this . . . uh . . . problem. I mean I don't want to dump it on you, but maybe you'll have some ideas. See, my brother and his family kind of dropped out of the sky on me. This is the Irish branch—very low communication skills. And if they don't start talking, there's going to be this terrible explosion."

Really? What did I mean by that, exactly? Perhaps it was just a free-associated image of the bomb that had ripped my brother's house. "Don't worry, it's nothing urgent," I reassured the machine, except I didn't sound very convincing. "I don't have a number, but I'll call you back, okay?"

As I rang off, startled by the urgency even as I denied it, I saw Daniel lean out the window of the pickup. A fat old dog, three colors of shepherd and retriever, came trotting over from the convenience store, wagging its tail shamelessly. Daniel's whole upper body was out the window as he reached to scratch the dog's ears. I whacked the door open and called in a too-loud voice, "You stay in that truck! And leave that dog alone!"

In a flash the canine took off, tail between legs. Just as quickly Daniel pulled in and sat down. Because of the glare on the windshield I couldn't tell if he was upset, but I felt like a jerk. What did I think, that the dog had rabies or Daniel would fall on his head? Total overreaction. Guiltily I huddled back into the booth, determined to make it up to him. Then I dialed Mona's number in Westwood, relieved when she answered in person.

"It's like Ibsen around here," I said by way of hello. "And my Norwegian is very rusty."

But she was in no mood for drollery. "Are you sure you can't get in trouble?" she demanded rather shrilly. "You're harboring a fugitive, aren't you?"

"That's not how it works," I retorted with some superiority. "He's making a deal with the prosecutors. After he testifies, they'll get him resettled."

"You shouldn't be around kids. They're full of germs, and they've always got colds."

I laughed. "I believe the drift of paranoia goes the other way, doesn't it? *I'm* the Typhoid Mary around here."

"I'm serious, honey. You don't need all this stress. Who's taking care of *you?*"

"I am," I purred in reply, but of course she had a point. For all I wanted to do right then was get off the phone and go take care of Daniel. "Listen, take this number down." I read off Sister Kathleen's information from the card, asking Mona to keep trying till she connected. "Find out when I can call her. I think we need some facilitating."

As good as done. Mona lets nothing slip between the cracks. Then she said, "So how's Gray?"

"Oh, we'll be okay, if we ever get any time alone. We sort of banged heads yesterday—"

"Yeah, he told me."

And right there I saw how tricky it all was, the nexus of power lines that strung us all together. Even if I didn't have a phone, Mona and Gray did. I suddenly had this vivid picture of the two of them chatting late into the night, Mona in the role she was born for: lovers' confidante. It was only a couple of weeks ago that they barely gave each other the time of day. And now she was Juliet's nurse.

"So," I said, drawing out my sharpest needle, "I gather Daphne's been given back her key to your ball and chain."

"Meaning what, precisely?"

"Looked to me like you two are wife and wife again."

"Lies and gossip," Mona drawled. "I only brought her for *your* sake, in case you had a breakdown. Daphne and I are officially free, white, and over thirty. All that craziness is behind us."

"Mm. I'd still hide all my clocks if I were you."

But my heart wasn't in it, impatient as I was to get back to Daniel. Admonishing Mona once more to call my nun, I got off the phone and padded back to the truck. Daniel looked up brightly from reading an old torn newspaper on the floor, seemingly unbruised by my having barked at him. I leaned my arms on the driver's door and poked my head in.

"You want to go in there and get an ice cream?"

"Great," he said briskly, scrambling out on the other side.

Coming around to join him, I noticed how he set his pace to mine as we walked across to the store. I would have done anything for him just then, for he made me feel like I was a fellow to be emulated, as he studied his way to becoming a man. I held the door open, and he walked in wide-eyed, casing the place with instant attention. Myself, I can't find anything in a 7-Eleven; the system eludes me. But Daniel turned immediately down the first aisle and headed for the freezer case in back, as if by radar.

I followed in his wake. Already he had the glass door open, reaching inside, practically disappearing among the frozen goods. He pulled out a very upscale concoction on a stick, wrapped in designer paper. "I like these," he said soberly. "What do you like?"

The same. Graciously he handed me the one in his hand, then reached in for another. As he closed the freezer door and marched toward the front, carefully ripping the wrapper away, I felt the most curious envy of his single-minded concentration. Just then he didn't seem unhappy at all. I wondered if he had some special fortitude I lacked, that let him slough off the rages and confusions of his household. He looked so carefree, scanning the racks of magazines by the counter as I pulled my wallet out to pay. I certainly couldn't recall any single equivalent moment from my own cracked boyhood, or any free ice cream either. So maybe he could survive intact, given a little breathing room and a few side trips to the Chevron.

"Why don't you get one of those?" I declared, watching him pore over the comic books at the end of the rack.

He turned, ice cream stick in his mouth, as if amazed I'd even noticed. He shook his head. "No, they don't let me."

"C'mon—pick one. You can't just live on book reports."

Listen to me, the resident barbarian, coaxing a seven-year-old away from Robert Louis Stevenson to schlock. His eyes alight with guilty pleasure, Daniel turned to the comics again and instantly plucked one up. Knew exactly what he wanted. Brimming with largesse I smiled at the dullard cashier, waving my wallet to indicate the two sweets and the reading matter. As he gathered my change from a ten-dollar bill, slow as a cow, I glanced at the cover of Daniel's comic.

All-New Tales from the Crypt, with the twisted bug-eyed face of a man clawing his way out of the grave. Well, I wouldn't have chosen quite that one, but if that was what he wanted. I pocketed my change, and the two of us headed out. Besides, I rationalized, wasn't it psychologically sound for a kid to see his nightmares played out in story form? Bruno Bettelheim and all that.

We'd almost reached the pickup, Daniel once more gauging his pace to mine, when a voice called out, "Hey, dude." I looked to my right, and there was my Redford surfer, pumping gas into his red van. He pointed up at the smoky sky. "Looks like another doozy, huh?" His teeth flashed white against the cocoa tan of his face.

"Yeah, let 'er rip," I retorted, and would've turned away, except Daniel had stopped in his tracks beside me. He stared riveted through the open side door of the van, where the surfboard was stowed between the seats, sleek and tense with power as a loaded gun. I rested a hand on Daniel's shoulder and smiled at the hunk. "Can he see your board?"

"Hey, my pleasure." That vast California enthusiasm. He flipped the gas hose to automatic as Daniel and I walked over. Then he beckoned the boy into the van and started rattling off the specs. As usual I was deaf to all the technical jargon, but I delighted in the mesmerized look on my nephew's face. He reached out to touch the slick white fiberglass, its zaps of Day-Glo green like mystic script.

As for Redford himself, flawless in his orange jams and a county lifeguard's windbreaker, this was the dude I had ached at the sight of, back in the thick of the last typhoon. Before I fell in love with Gray; before my brother's family came. Strange, but now I didn't desire him at all, or feel any less a man than he. Silently I gave him back the riotous promise of his youth, the effortless beauty that looked as if it couldn't ever die. And I seized with greater savor at my own life, mirrored now in this terrific kid who rode with me today. I felt absurdly proud, chest puffed out, as the surfer led Daniel out of the van.

"Your first board's the most important," Redford intoned, sincere as an adman, " 'cause that's where you learn your moves. So go for the top o' the line."

Daniel nodded in awe, as the other winked at me and moved once more to straddle the gas hose. I don't know who was more deliriously happy just then, Daniel or I, as we walked back over to the pickup, slurping the last of our ice cream. I swear, you'd think I'd fathered the kid myself. And I was on red alert when I pulled us out to the edge of the road, waiting for an opening in the line of passing cars. I willed away all reckless teens and scooted in behind a Winnebago, stately as an ocean liner, proceeding up the coast at cruising speed.

I thought Daniel was reading his comic book. In any case my eyes were glued to the road, no distractions. Then, with a casual air that seemed entirely unrehearsed, he said, "My last year's teacher got sick. She had to leave right before Christmas and didn't come back till March. We had a substitute." I could feel his eyes turn to look at me. "Is that what you're doing?"

I swallowed hard. "Kind of," I said. "I guess you could call it a leave of absence." I licked my lips, suddenly dry as ashes. "But I don't have a substitute. There's only one of what I do."

He nodded, mulling this over. "So how do you feel?"

When was the last time anyone asked? Not that Gray and Mona didn't care, but they tended to figure it out rather than putting it point-blank. "Well, pretty good," I offered. "I get tired easy. Dizzy sometimes. My knee hurts." Was that the whole ball game? I shrugged. "Manageable."

I knew his eyes hadn't left my face. It flashed on me that he was the one taking care of me and not the other way around. "Are you gonna die?"

The sky itself seemed to darken perceptibly. This was getting too Bette Davis, even for me. "Did your parents say that?"

"Uh-huh."

"Well, eventually. Not for a while. See, I have this disease that nobody understands yet."

"AIDS," said Daniel quietly, but not flinching in the least. "They told us about it in school."

Didn't miss a trick. "Yeah, so it's hard to predict. Could be a year, two years—" I made a vague motion with one hand, like somebody groping in the dark.

But it struck me that he knew more about the subject than his mother, and wasn't afraid of it either. Indeed, he seemed to relish the notion of being grown-up about it all. Perhaps he'd heard Susan at a particularly off-the-wall moment, proposing fumigation and quarantine. He reminded me of myself again, who always preferred the company of adults, my parents excepted, because the kids of my acquaintance were all frivolous and mean.

Then I felt his hand touch my arm reassuringly. "Uncle Tom," he announced with spirit, "I hope you don't die for a long, long time."

"Thanks, Daniel."

It really wasn't lugubrious at all, or even misty-eyed sentimental. We were just being very real, like a couple of guys in a foxhole. I put on my blinker and slowed, waiting for five hundred yards' clearance before I made the left into the driveway. Somehow it didn't surprise me that a boy who'd only learned about death four days ago, when his dogs were snuffed, was better equipped to face it than his elders. He hadn't had enough time to build up a lot of bullshit about the issue. The oleanders on either side were waving rhythmically, wind off the ocean, as we came to the foot of the drive. I stopped beside the garage, wilted with relief to have got him back safe and sound.

Yet no shadow of our mortal talk pursued us as we tumbled out and made across the lawn. It was in my mind that we'd go right out to the bluff and check on the progress of construction. Enough time had gone by since Brian relieved the boy of his paintbrush. Maybe we'd jump in again and be useful. We should have gone there direct, and I don't really know why I detoured into the kitchen first. Maybe I thought he should have some soup—ice cream was hardly a proper lunch. I banged the screen door wide, and the two of us tramped in.

Instantly I saw I'd taken a wrong turn.

Susan stood at the sink, stacking the dishwasher beside it. When she turned to face us, there was almost a look of demonic glee across her features, a smile of horrible triumph. She ignored me. It was all for her son. "Where have *you* been, young man?" she hissed.

Daniel seemed to shrink beside me. "We just—"

"Who gave you permission?" Almost a shout. Swiftly she crossed toward us, her wet hands spraying. She hunkered down and grabbed Daniel's elbow. I heard him gasp. "Don't you *ever* leave this house without telling me."

"It's my fault," I protested.

"Stay out of this," she growled, not even deigning to glance at me. She snatched the comic book out of his hand, glared at the cover. "Junk," she sneered, dashing it to the floor as if it was witchcraft. "Now go to your room."

"I'm sorry, Mom—"

"Sorry's not good enough. Now go."

Why was I silent? She was practically quivering with loathing. Clearly the boy didn't have any options. Head sunk between his shoulders, he shuffled out through the dining room. Was it all just territorial that I hadn't stuck up for him, tacit acknowledgment that hers was the only real power here?

Then she turned her hunted eyes on me, murderous with hate, and I realized I'd held my tongue to protect Daniel. What was between his mother and me was ugly enough; it shouldn't be laid on him. For if looks could kill, Susan and I stood armed with fire enough to scorch the earth. "And you," she spat at me. "You leave my son alone."

Like water off a duck's back. "Don't you see," I asked, maddeningly reasonable, "he's just trying to stay out of your way while you guys figure out your life."

"Oh really? And now you're an authority on children, is that it?"

"Hey, pick on me, that's fine. Don't pick on him."

God, how she hated the medium cool of my demeanor. She gripped the air between us with her fists and seethed in my face: "I'm. His. Mother." Rung down like Old Testament law, immutable and pitiless. There was no answer, and no escape for Daniel. She wheeled around and crossed again to the sink. With a supreme act of will she began once more to rinse dishes and prop them in the dishwasher. I could still hear her breathing heavily, as if her heart were hammering.

"He's a great kid," I said to her back. "So you must have done something right." I didn't mean it as any further volley in the war. A left-handed compliment, to be sure, but I figured to leave it at that and made for the dining room.

"This place isn't right." Her voice had altered, the fury gone. The revulsion was still there, only now it wasn't just her brother-in-law but the very walls of the house. "We don't belong here. Your . . . people are a different breed."

I stopped in the doorway. "Susan, if I disappeared, your life would still suck right now. Even if you were staying with white folks."

No answer, but then I expected none. I'd said as much before. Honestly, if it gave her any comfort to think of me as the enemy, it was really no sweat off my ass. All I wanted from her was that she not fuck over her kid. I tramped upstairs, empty inside, wanting to go across to Daniel's room and divert him from his exile. But for now at least, it wasn't worth the potential for further explosion. So I took my usual refuge in Foo's room, staring at the ceiling, not quite able to shake the feeling that I too had been sent up here as punishment.

The noise of the men working filtered in through the balcony doors, their voices hearty and curt amid the hammering. From this far off I couldn't really separate one from another, though a sudden bray of laughter wild as an eagle was clearly Merle. Because of the blowup with Susan, I felt separate from their workers' cheer, as if they'd all been chosen to play but me.

Underneath was a mix of guilt and powerlessness, for having got my nephew into trouble. Of course it was my fault, not to have thought it through that he would need a pass to leave the base. I wondered if he blamed me. Wondered if the outing had been worth it, despite the verbal lashing from the commandant. No to the first, yes to the second, I told myself firmly. After all, the kid was probably used to the scathings of his mom, the banishing and confinement. Now at least he had the taste of ice cream on his tongue.

You can't exactly sleep with all that hammering, but I must have gone into an alpha state, my brain pulsing with the throbbing noise. All I know is, I heard the silence when they were done, sharp as the crack of a rifle. Eyes wide, I tingled with alertness. A minute or two passed, and I heard their voices closer as they climbed to the top of the bluff. Again they were indistinguishable, relaxed now and joking, a bunch of guys sauntering home from work.

Silently I slid off the bed and glided to the balcony doors, but careful not to show myself. Merle appeared first, then Brian, then Gray, each carrying tools and odds and ends of boards. They straggled through the cactus and onto the lawn. "You guys want a beer?" asked Brian, brimming with comradeship, as if he'd just come off the field.

"Some coffee," said Merle.

They laid their burdens down at the edge of the terrace, then moved toward the house. Swiftly I slipped out onto the balcony. As I leaned over the rail, Merle had already disappeared under the pergola, Brian right behind him. "Sst," I whispered sharply. Gray looked up, grinned when he saw me, started to speak. I laid a finger on my lips.

Then I slung a leg over the rail and peered down the side of the house. With hardly a pause for breath I reached out a foot and groped, touching one of the sculpted beams that roofed the pergola. Recklessly I shifted my weight, feeling the pure tilt of midair before I landed in a crouch on the beam. I teetered a bit, then reached down and gripped the beam. Kicking out with my legs I swooped down and swung by my hands, dropping neat to the ground directly in front of Gray.

"Count Zorro," I declared with a small bow.

"You're crazy."

"Not quite. But I have most definitely had enough of everybody else." I grabbed his hand. "Now show me what the big boys did."

I tugged him after me toward the bluff, though he groaned that he was beat. Only now did I feel the first sprinkle of rain in my face. It thrilled me, pushing me forward with even greater urgency. Gray was laughing behind me, useless to protest. As we pitched headlong down the stairs, I tossed off a breathless account of my outing with Daniel and run-in with Susan. I couldn't tell how much he caught, but it didn't matter. Just to feel the pressure lift, as if in the sheer rush of words was my real life, whatever I could share with Gray.

Reaching at last the sturdy final landing, its bright new wood and glinting nails, was almost an anticlimax. I staggered for the railing. Gray caught at my shoulder and spun me around. "It's tacky," he said, letting me half collapse in his arms instead.

Who cared how tacky I was anymore, I thought belligerently, then realized he meant the wood, still fresh with its slick of sealer. This struck me so funny I howled with laughter, falling ever more limply into his embrace. I might as well have been crying, for all the sense I made. But Gray demanded no logic, holding me fast while I caught my breath, rocking me softly, till I felt the rain again on my face and there was no sound but the wind.

"Alone at last," he whispered in my ear.

We didn't say a word about the new construction. Arm in arm we headed down the bottom flight of steps, which lay securely now in the fold of the rock. Perhaps it was enough just to christen it. As we stepped down onto the sand I realized I'd stopped taking my daily walk, because of the clambering required around the broken steps. The air was colder here at the base of the bluff, whipping in off the water. Still the rain was mostly drops in the wind, tapping at our faces, barely leaving them wet. The full storm would come with the night, the dark perhaps an hour off, the light on the water already dim and leaden.

Gray pulled me close and nuzzled my hair. "We can't stay. You'll catch a chill."

Oh, but I wasn't going back in that house again yet, with its minefield of family drama. I turned and dragged him after me under the stairs, where the shallow cave faced south, cutting the seaborne wind. It was dry in there, feathered with a light down of sand. I crawled in first and sat cross-legged, grinning out at Gray. With a game shrug he ducked in and lowered himself beside me. "Are we going to play pirates?"

"No—desert island. You think we could finally have a little make-out session?"

About time. He smiled and put his arms around me, gently drawing us down till we lay face-to-face on the floor of the hollow. Now that the moment had come, the jangled urgency had passed. In the dusky light we looked in each other's eyes, very, very quiet, the way you would watch a star-shot sky. With one hand he smoothed the hair back from my forehead. For the first time I felt the luxury of how solid he was, his rangy frame and his big hands. I liked feeling small, burrowed against him. I couldn't even begin to say how long it had been since I'd held a man for real.

He brushed my lips with his, lightly, attenuating the moment till we were breathing together. Hunger wasn't part of it, not then. Perhaps we were both too grateful to waste it being frantic. When we opened our mouths at last to drink each other in, it was astonishment rather than passion shivering in me. I never expected another chance. I'd shut this part of me down for good, like a summer house, the day they told me my antibody status. And given how bad I was at love, there had almost been a perverse relief in letting the whole thing go—the way a spinster feels at fifty, when everything's finally frozen over.

But you'd never have known any of that now. I kissed as if I'd been kissing all my life. I tugged his flannel shirt, pulling it out of his work pants. Then slipped my hands along the taut of his belly, reaching the patch of fur at his breastbone. All *terra incognita*. I'd never even seen this man with his shirt off, let alone his pants. I liked discovering him by feel instead of by sight. And for the moment anyway, I didn't even think about my dick, or Gray's either. This from an old-school pig who used to root for the prize like truffles, usually without preliminary.

Kisses beyond counting, and then Gray pulled back a couple of inches, smiling wryly. "I suppose you think you discovered this place yourself."

"Well, it's true that I'm something of an explorer in these parts." I could feel his heart beating under my hands.

"Just so you know, I used to sleep down here before you were born. My sleeping bag and a kerosene lamp—right over here." He pointed at a cavity in the wall, just above my head. "And Nonny would pack a survival kit so I wouldn't starve."

"Oh ancient one, teach me the secrets of your cave." I leaned close and bit his chin, then along the line of his jawbone, tasting the salt of his day's work. Darted my tongue in his ear, making it rush like the sea. "And tell me, were you ever raped by a shipwrecked sailor?"

"No. Dammit."

"Me neither. More's the pity. Happily for you, however, the U.S. Navy has just landed." With that I wriggled down and grabbed at his belt. He made as if to protest, hands moving to shield his crotch. The last modest man! "Excuse me," I said, batting his hands away, "if this is going to get serious, I need to check out the equipment."

He laughed by way of surrender, pillowing his arms behind his head. I went to work in earnest, undoing the belt and then the button fly, one by one. I was playing more than anything. This didn't even seem like sex, in the past such a grim inexorable procedure of getting down to business. For underwear he sported dun-green boxers, army surplus, which struck me at the moment as more endearing than erotic.

I slipped a hand through the opening, groped about and got a gentle grip around him. He gave a soft hiss. The member in hand was half-swollen and pretty hefty as I lifted it out. Uncut. "Well, well," I murmured. "Good for that old pioneer stock. Leaving the wild in its natural state." I squeezed and stroked it, pulling the lip of the foreskin back. With my other hand I tugged out his balls. Then I bent and licked the head. He groaned and stretched, his dick pulsing harder. It was getting to feel like sex after all. My mouth moved down and took him full in.

"Wait," he whispered, his hand reaching into my hair, not quite pulling it. "I need a shower."

I came up off him. "Tastes great to me," I mumbled, prepared to dive right back.

But he lifted my head with his hands, forcing me to look at him. His forehead was creased with trouble, so that I had a sudden pang that I was giving a lousy blow job. "Please," he said fretfully, "I don't want you getting any germs."

I mean really, what a world. "Hey, it's good honest blue-collar sweat," I protested, resisting with every fiber the notion of living my life in a bubble. I hadn't had so much as a taste in two years, in part to avoid these grisly negotiations. "I won't let you come in my mouth, I promise. Do I have to suck it through a zip-lock bag?"

"Am I more afraid than you are?"

"That I'll get sick? I think it's probably fifty-fifty."

And I bent once more and touched the head with my tongue, but no thought now of the full maneuver. I didn't feel annoyed that he'd interrupted the flow. On the contrary, the whole occasion seemed to go just the way it was meant to, and felt no less that we were making love. My lips lingered a moment longer, nothing urgent here, nothing to prove. We'd do a better job of it in a bed, I thought. But I wasn't sorry the scene in the cave had veered from carnal to intimate. We needed to go by degrees—next time, let him undress me. Let it go back and forth, so no one got lost in the shuffle.

Was it a flash of color that made me turn my head? I certainly wasn't startled—just lazily swiveled my head to look out, my lips still grazing the tip, even as the muscle relaxed. I saw Susan an instant before she saw us. She was moving past the mouth of the hollow toward the stairs, bundled up in a motheaten cardigan she'd borrowed from Cora's closet. Her blond hair blew about her head, lavishly sensual for once. She turned her face from the wind and looked directly in my eyes.

And froze, her cheeks blazing up with a mix of horror and embarrassment. She was hardly five feet away. Truly I must be shameless, for my first impulse was to laugh at her rotten luck—but I swear, it wouldn't have been a cruel laugh. The next instant she was out of there, before I had even raised my head, moving around to the foot of the steps and hurrying up.

I realized Gray hadn't seen her, stretched out as he was toward the back of the hollow, and the roar of the surf drowning out her footsteps. The laughter spilled out of me, helpless, to think I had just set back the evolution of Susan's tolerance by at least a decade. That look in her face, as if she had stared into the bowels of hell.

And we weren't even having sex! It was all too twisted, requiring the convening of Vatican III. Gasping at the absurdity, I squirmed up next to Gray in the sand.

I think he thought I was crying even then, for he threw his arms about me and held me close. I don't know what tipped it, frankly, maybe just the swift unqualified protection of his embrace, but now I was crying for real. No noise, and not even much in the way of tears, like the rain out there that would not stick. I suppose I was crying for Daniel's sake, so many years to go before he could escape the bad deal of his blasted family. Crying for Gray and me, starting out already scared, no handle on time. Crying mostly with relief, because I didn't have to come up with a reason. Gray was going to hold me, no matter what.

In a minute the squall had passed, and I snuffled and ducked my face against his shoulder to dry my eyes. Only then did I realize I wasn't going to tell him about Susan's late appearance, because I wished to protect his modesty. Once more he smoothed my hair back from my forehead. "You think I can put on my pants again?" he asked playfully, as if the mood had never shifted down.

"Please—before you freeze your nuts." And while he put himself back together, tucking his shirt in all the way around, I added: "What if I fall in love with you very hard?"

He did up the buttons of his fly, tongue between his lips. Then the belt. Then he looked over, and the cave had grown so dark I could hardly see his eyes. "Don't worry," he said, "I can keep up with you."

I've never been much for declarations. It's been my experience that telling a man you love him is like a trapdoor in the middle of your living room floor. They disappear that fast. This casual openness of Gray's—to follow my heart wherever it led—was thus no less than a revelation. And I certainly wasn't going to jinx it now with further demands and codicils. Agreeing to love in principle, fair and equal as the laws of a just republic, was something I'd been waiting for all my life. Say no more.

I scrambled out of the shadows and knelt at the lip of the hollow, letting the wind buffet me. At the western rim, the day was guttering out in a swirl of mercury, the rest of the sky iron gray. It was drizzling now, though the shelter of the rocks above still kept us dry. I was mad with exhilaration as Gray moved up behind me and squeezed me in a bear hug, head on my shoulder. We watched the break of the waves in silence, the last white glow of force before the stormy night took all the power to itself. I think I could have stripped down and gone in even then, rolling in the shallows like a seal, because I was in the mood to dare the planet.

But I contented myself with shouting "Now!"

And the two of us, single-minded, leaped from the cave and chased around to the stairs. We ran up laughing, past the new construction, and I flashed on Susan, even now probably trudging into the house, chilled to the bone. Would she tell my brother what she saw? Oh, not that it mattered at all. I was so far past shame and discretion, tilting against my lover as we dashed around the midpoint landing, trying not to laugh so I'd save my breath.

But Susan—my bursting heart wanted to tell her how beautiful she looked, with the wind wild in her hair. And that she had so much to love, a man and a boy of her own, it couldn't help but turn out fine. They had all the time in the world. And right now I didn't begrudge them.

"Stop!" I gasped, panting with surrender as I slumped against the railing. Four steps ahead Gray spun about with a grin, his own breath heaving. For once there wasn't that ominous crease of worry between his eyes. My reeling from the sprint upstairs had nothing to do with AIDS, or at least we played it so.

"You look like Heathcliff," Gray observed, gliding down the railing toward me, face glistening.

I threw back my head in abandon, a very queenly Olivier, and bellowed at the lowering sky, "Cathy! Cathy!"

Gray reached a hand, and I clasped it, letting him draw me to him. We were really getting soaked now. He shook his head, as if hardly believing his eyes. "Every minute I'm with you," he said, "I'm making up for lost time. But it all goes awfully fast." He shrugged. Nothing to be done about it. "My life used to be so slow you couldn't even see it move."

I nodded, accepting the compliment, but suddenly needing to unburden me as well. "Gray, sometimes I have these—they're like blank spots. And I realize I've lost the last five minutes." Why was I telling this now, at the very moment we were free? Not surprising, the crease came furrowing down between his eyebrows. "It's like my brain's taking a station break."

"Now?"

"No. But yesterday, after you left. A few times. I suppose it's the virus." I had to look away from the aching intensity of his eyes, down the vertiginous slope of the bluff. "That's what I mean, about falling too hard. It's all very *Dark Victory.*"

Again he pulled me close, so that my mouth fell against his neck. It wouldn't take much, I realized, to become the boy who cried "Wolf!" around here, if you could always count on a hug like this. "Let's just keep living now," he declared, as if he'd thought it all through long since. "And we'll fall as far as we fall."

Is that a prince? Another prolonged embrace, as I arched him backward against the railing and smothered his mouth with mine. The seascape staggered beneath us, yielding up in that one moment of winter dusk—the gaudy expressionist angles of cliff and water, desolate, unrelenting—all the process shots of the wilder shores of passion. Sometimes nothing is wanting, no matter how long you've wanted it. Who noticed the cold and the wet, for the sheer quick of being dead center in love? Like Susan declaring the law of her Motherhood, written in stone, I seared it into my brain: *You will not forget this kiss.*

Yet we pulled away from it as casual as ever, for we also knew how to keep it light, being men on whom no irony was lost. Darting across the landing and up the last flight, I announced with fierce insistence, "You're staying over. I don't care what the Catholics think."

"Stop choreographing," Gray protested.

"I have to. And now we have to get out of these clothes and drink hot chocolate. And a roaring fire."

We reached the top together, walking shoulder to shoulder. Now the night had fallen complete, but the way was clear through the cactus, shiny in the rain. As we reached the lawn, Gray dropped in a runner's crouch to tie his shoe. I stood and waited, watching the house—lights in the parlor and up in Cora's room. Then I saw Brian at the edge of the pergola, light streaming out from the parlor doors behind him. He was shaking something. His hand was waving. He was—

I started to run before I really saw it. I think I screamed "No," but maybe it wasn't out loud, for my brother didn't turn till I was almost on him. He held Daniel captive by one wrist, hoisting him up so the boy dangled a few inches above the ground. His pants were down to his knees, and Brian slapped at his bare butt. As I dashed toward them in the rain, a fury as old as the ocean roaring in my head, I heard the sharp crack of my brother's sick power, scoring the flesh of his child. Then I barreled in like a fullback, and Brian looked up in shock.

I smashed into his chest, reeling him back against a column. He dropped Daniel. His livid face, with its stupid Irish anger, couldn't quite seem to place me. I was flailing blows, pummeling at his shoulder, and for a moment he took it like a dazed bear. He was all armor. No way was I hurting him. But now I found my voice again, and it shrilled the air like a war cry.

"You want to break his arm? Is that what you're trying to do, bigshot? Just like your dad?"

I *saw* how the words knifed home, and I wanted to dance. Even as he snatched my wrist midair, and I only had one fist left to drum it in. "Easy, Tommy, easy," he grimaced, but he wasn't in charge and he knew it.

"You got a problem, babe," I sneered at him, shoving the heel of my hand against his shoulder and then again, taunting him like a bully. "You like to hurt people, don't you? Well, we don't allow that dirty little secret anymore. They take kids away from guys like you—"

Then Gray was grabbing me from behind, dragging me off him. A red heat flushed the cords of Brian's bull neck as his fury rose to meet my own, that I should dare to rob him of his son. But now I was twisting and yelling at Gray. "You hear what my old man did? He pulled my arm right out of the socket—just yanking me around one night. Remember that, Brian? Remember me screaming?" A ghoul's laugh erupted from me, as if I'd just gotten some cosmic joke. "No wonder I can't throw a fucking ball."

Gray held me tight around, but with no pressure to censor me. Brian slumped against the column, looking aghast and vaguely disgusted. Then my eyes lighted on Daniel, huddling back in the shadows, pants still around his knees. For his sake I swallowed my raving on the spot. But nobody spoke. The floor was still mine. My impulse was to reach out and hug him, help him get dressed, but that would only force him into taking sides, and I was not the solution here.

I still didn't know where the memory of my father came from, so buried was it until the trigger of the scene under the pergola. I only knew I hadn't dreamed it. A twinge in my shoulder had never quite forgotten. But if this much pain was blocked inside me—

unremembered, shut like a final closet—there must be more. For the violent nights of my father were grim as clockwork.

"Daniel," I said gently, "put your pants on, and go on upstairs. Your father and I won't hurt each other, I promise."

The boy looked back at me gratefully, but shifted his eyes to his father, no move possible without a go from the top. My gaze held on my nephew, so I didn't know if Brian nodded yes or looked away in shame. Daniel hitched up his pint-sized Jockeys, then his jeans. He didn't appear embarrassed or even very interested in the charged air that crackled among the grown-ups. But then, I knew better than anyone how quick these things got buried. Kids like me and Daniel carried our own shovels.

Once he'd walked into the house, Gray released his grip. I looked at my brother, hands hanging heavy at his sides. There was definite shame here, the Catholic kind, wild for absolution. "Yes, I remember," he said with an odd dignity. "Mom and I took you to the emergency room."

"Oh."

Now he was way ahead of me. For all my own recollection stopped on the dime of the agony—my arm dangling like a broken wing, my long scream for relief in a house where no one knew me. I didn't remember the E.R., or my mother and Brian, or mending in a cast. I would have stood there blankly, groping the past and coming up empty, if Gray hadn't moved to take charge.

"Tom, you're shivering. Let's go in." And so we did, Brian following awkwardly, Gray moving right to the fire to stoke it. "Take those clothes off," he ordered over his shoulder.

I began to unbutton my soggy flannel shirt, aware of my brother standing off to the side. I stripped the shirt and dropped it on the hearth in a wet heap, as the fire blazed up. "See, it all gets passed down," I said, hearing at last the chattering of my teeth. "He hurt me, and then thirty years later you hurt Daniel." If it made him squirm to hear it, nevertheless he stood his ground. I kicked off my shoes, then started undoing my pants.

"But it's not going any further," I declared—tough being a new taste, like metal on my tongue. "Because you're going to work it out before you leave this house, all of you. All of us. It stops here."

I kicked off my pants, drenched and clinging, sloughing them like a snakeskin. Now I stood bareass before my brother and my lover. I stepped up close to the fire and bent and shook my hair. "I'll get you a robe," said Gray, slipping the afghan around my shoulders. He headed for the stairs, to do his own undressing in private. I turned to Brian. I don't suppose I'd ever faced him naked before, no hiding the man I was.

"I'd never hurt Daniel," he said.

"Uh-huh. And you probably think you never hurt me. Well, you're wrong." Then silence for a moment. The fire was white-hot up and down my back, practically singeing the hair on my legs.

"I know I should have stopped him, Tommy." Meaning our father. "Sometimes I tried. But he just seemed to hate you." He shook his head and hung it at the same time, overwhelmed by the craziness.

"You're tearing each other apart, you and Susan. There's someone I want you to talk to." He nodded. I almost would've said he was relieved to hear me taking charge. "I've been through a couple of programs myself. Children of lunatics, that kind of thing. It helps."

He looked at me, and I swear his eyes glanced down at my crotch. "You still hate me?"

"No. I love you—in spite of myself, believe me. And that's why I won't let you turn into him. If your life's going to start all over, you might as well be a *really* new man. Without weapons."

He nodded again. Gray was coming down the stairs in a robe, carrying another over his arm. Brian took this as his natural cue, and they passed each other with a shy smile, painfully aware of not wanting to intrude. They looked like brothers themselves—the nice sort. And I turned and stared into the flames with the queerest thrill of dread, heart pounding, realizing for the first time that I was the head of the family.

S E V E N

USAN REFUSED, CATEGORICALLY.

I heard them arguing deep into the night. Even through the double bathroom door, and with the rain growing steadier by the hour, I could pick out certain phrases as she railed at him. The very idea of *counseling*! How dare it even be suggested—as if she disdained the whole field of the talking cure as gibberish, another sort of witchcraft. And that *I* should have been the one to propose it, invert and blasphemer that I was. I couldn't actually make out the specific words of my damnation, but got the picture.

I can't stay here, she told him again and again. Or else what? She'd go mad. No, worse: her very soul was threatened now.

I don't know if she told him about seeing Gray and me on the beach. I dozed in and out, curled as I was in the arms of my fellow blasphemer. I didn't care anymore, so far was she from being able to hurt us. And all her shrewing and lashing out didn't compromise for a moment the lulling safety of the rain, or keep me from the deepest fathom of that first night with Gray. Nor the morning after, surfacing into passion, loving before we were fully conscious. The drone of Susan and Brian through the walls, raw and numb with misery—had it gone on all night?—was no more than distant gunfire, a civil war in another country.

We came belly to belly, Gray on top of me, his sweet heaviness like an anchor in the harbor. This was the oldest act of love, our two dicks rubbing as we kissed, innocent as boys at camp. Reaching the top, I groaned with a near roar of delight, which surely carried into Cora's room. Gray was as silent as I was noisy, gulping in air as he let go, then strangling out a soft delicious whimper. We lay still for several minutes, catching our breath, no words, all lost time accounted for at last.

Then I watched as he got up and fetched a towel to clean us off, darting in and out of the bathroom, not wanting to encounter the heteros. But the squalling had stopped in Cora's room. Doubtless my little crow of ecstasy had hustled them down to breakfast. Gray smiled as he tenderly wiped my belly, then moved to the chaise to pull on his yesterday's clothes. I couldn't stop studying his tough and lanky body, still so new to me. No extra fat, and the sleek form of an ocean swimmer. His being fifty had no downside; he was simply a full-grown man. And lying there lazily under the comforter, I took the most wanton joy in being the younger one.

"Doesn't sound like she's crazy about the idea," Gray declared as he shrugged on his workshirt. It was the first I realized he'd heard the din from the other room. I always thought WASPs had an extra sleep gene that helped them ignore such things entirely.

"I'll talk to her," I said, but as if I didn't stand a chance. "Some people don't really believe there's a way out. You get to be an abuse junkie."

"I still haven't even met her." He sat on the bed beside me to put on his shoes. "She laid out the lunch for us yesterday and then ran upstairs. I don't think she'd know me if I met her out there in the hall."

She'd know your dick, I thought, suppressing a smutty grin. "Are you running off again?"

He narrowed a look at me to see if I was pouting. Satisfied I wasn't, he gave a rueful shrug. "I better go check on Foo and Merle. They didn't know I'd be out all night."

"They know where you were," I remarked dryly.

But I was just teasing. I could feel the pull of the ranch, and all his responsibilities there, even as he lightly stroked my cheek with the tips of his fingers. I could only guess how ingrained were their habits up there, who put out the Wheaties, who fetched the mail. Yet I felt no jealousy whatsoever, and only wished that he not be stuck taking care of too many of us. I turned my face into the palm of his hand and kissed it softly, to let him know it was all fine. Completely fine.

Then I scrambled out of the bed, and he said, "You don't have to get up."

"Oh, is that so? You mean I can lie here all day and eat bonbons and play with my winkie?" I faced him naked with a hand on my out-slung hip, cocky as a Donatello bronze. His eyes swept me up and down, brimming with delight, rendering all my spots invisible. "Please—I have to see if they've killed each other."

I pulled on a pair of sweat pants, nothing underneath, deliciously aware of him watching every move. It was like a striptease in reverse, slipping on a tight white T-shirt, then a lumberjack's wool shirt over it, giddy with eros. As we moved to leave we glanced against each other, and grabbed another kiss, his hand running down my spine and cupping my butt. Then we were out the door in the stair hall, and instantly I felt the slightest drawing away, as Gray struggled manfully with the specter of Discretion.

But now I only wanted to make it easy. I darted down the stairs, laughing, so we wouldn't make our entrance like a couple of love-drunk satyrs.

Brian and Daniel sat at the kitchen table, plowing through stacks of french toast. It was a tribute to our intimacy that they barely nodded good morning, so intertwined had we become in the dailiness of things. Even so, as I groped for the coffee, I felt an eerie shiver that they should be sitting so peaceably, as if nothing were out of control. Just an echo, probably. I'd sat through too many mornings after, the stink of stale Seagram's like an aura around my bleary old man, my body throbbing from the previous night's assault.

Then Gray walked in, and this time Daniel looked up with a bright smile of welcome. "Hi," he said cheerfully, managing to convey his pleasure that Gray had stayed the night. I handed Gray a mug of coffee.

"Susan went out," said my brother, flustered, not even sure himself why he sounded so apologetic. "To call her sister."

"Hey, I could've given her a ride," retorted Gray, and Brian murmured that was okay, she felt like taking a walk. I pictured Susan trotting down the coast road to the Chevron, whose phone booth had become a sort of annex and index of the jumble of our lives. I imagined her desperation, stumbling along in the wrong shoes, wondering over and over how she'd ended up so lost and far from home.

"Look," said Brian, "this isn't right, us eating your food like this. I just want you to know I'm keeping track."

He was talking to Gray, who protested briskly, and I looked at Daniel. He stared at his plate guiltily, then laid down his fork, as if resolved to starve from here on in. The wave of rage I felt just then for Brian—*Not in front of the kid, for Chrissakes*—only showed how powerless I was. Like my mother wringing her hands and whining *Not his head*.

Then Gray drained his mug, never one to linger, and was heading for the door. I bolted after, sloshing coffee over my wrist as I slipped outside, flinging the rest of it onto the camellias by the steps so I could keep up. "Call Miss Mona," I instructed, half running beside him. It was drizzling and blustery, but a lull in the larger storm. "Make sure she tells Kathleen the wife won't budge. *Now* what am I gonna do? I thought they could have a nice little session of family therapy, just the three of them—"

My mind was racing faster than my voice, already breathless. And as if that wasn't enough, I felt this crazy desolation because Gray was about to leave. Honestly, when was it ever going to be enough, so I didn't think it was all about to vanish, every time he got into that truck?

Then he was pulling me under the eaves of the garage, holding me by the shoulders, steadying me with his eyes. I come from people who always looked away. In the whole of central Connecticut, no one ever looked you in the eye—or me they didn't anyway. "Just be with your brother," he said. "Mona and I will brainstorm. And Miss Balanchine? Remember what they taught us at the Kirov. Less choreography is more." He drew me close and buried his face in my hair, breathing me in, not seeming to care who might be watching.

"When are you coming back?"

"Tonight," he said, as if he couldn't have been more certain, and even better, as if the answer would be the same tomorrow.

So I let him go—slouching seductively under the eaves, Donatello again, instead of that needy creep of abandonment. As I turned back to the house, I let the idea play in my head that I had it for real this time, a man who would know me to the bone. For the space of a held breath I seemed to float over the wet grass, the mist in my face like the worst cliché, dew on the fucking roses. Happy—was this what happy was? Because if it was, I had most definitely never felt it before.

And it only took me the fifty feet between the garage and the kitchen door to learn the most obvious thing in the world, the canker in the rose: I could not bear to lose it now. My chest seized with a pain that wasn't physical but worse, such that my heart attack two weeks ago seemed like a sissy bout of hypochondria. Even AIDS. Dying was nothing to losing. I felt like the last person on earth to learn it, as if I'd been absent the day they taught it in nursery school.

I tramped into the kitchen, shaking the wet like a dog, wondering if I could stand how sad at the bottom happy was. My brother sat at the table where we'd left him. Daniel was gone. I had a selfish urge to rush right through and up to my room, so I could hoard and savor the lifetime of cheap emotions suddenly restored to me. Brian stared at his empty plate, lost like me in one of my blanks. He'd rather be alone anyway, I thought, clamping my mind against Gray's advice, *Just be with him.* I took a tentative step toward the dining room, and the movement seemed to jar him from his trance.

"She wants to leave me," he said, more to the plate than to me. "She'll take Daniel to her sister's. Minneapolis." He smiled wanly at the final word, as if geography were the only thing he could put his finger on in all of this.

"Just till you get resettled," I said, so firm it almost sounded like an order.

"No, she's had it. She wants me out of her life."

"But—" I wanted to whimper with exasperation. "That's why you have to *talk* to somebody. You can't make decisions like this."

Finally he looked at me. He seemed fascinated by my insistence, but also untouchable, alone out there on the pitcher's mound. "You don't understand," he replied, not unkindly. "I don't blame her. It disgusts her, what I did. Thou shalt not steal." The last bit spoken completely straight, Charlton Heston on the Mount.

"Uh-huh. How about thou shalt not lose thy house in Connecticut. Or thy Volvo station wagon. Or thy slot in the Junior League. Isn't *that* what she's really pissed about?"

His face went rigid as I tossed off my commandments. "She's very religious," he retorted tightly. "Whatever you think of her."

"Sorry." Last thing he needed was my shit. On the other hand, exactly how *did* one be with one's brother? "I think what I really want is for *our* parents to go get help. Little late, huh?" He didn't answer, but didn't look affronted anymore, so I slipped in another jab. "You just going to let her go?"

He chortled a one-note laugh, devoid of humor. "She'll prob'ly be better off," he declared bitterly. "She's even ashamed to call a priest. I don't know what we got left." His voice was harsh, but all at once he seemed to have trouble swallowing. "Except Daniel."

This time when he turned to me, his exhausted eyes were dazed with panic, an animal frozen in the lights of a speeding truck. He raised his arms toward me, fingers clutching the air, as if he wanted me to lift him bodily out of the chair. Then, with a groan that sounded just like mine an hour ago, he cracked and the tears came. Halting sobs, his face a sudden twist of agony.

I found myself holding him, no conscious memory of getting there. I stood beside his chair, cradling his head against my stomach, his massive arms clinging about my waist. Jesus Mary and Joseph. The world could not have been more upside down than it was right then. I was scared and thrilled at the same time, without a clue what was needed, therefore mute. But after half a minute, the more he buried his face against my shirt, I felt like a kind of rock, if only by default. Stillness was everything. I would stand there all day if necessary, till all his pain had spilled.

"He's—my—" But he couldn't form the words through the sputtering gasps that racked him. He tried to pull away, disgusted to be so out of control, but I held him fast. My hands were full of his thick red hair, bearing him like fire, but fire that no longer scorched and charred. So close for once in our lives that I couldn't tell where he left off and I began. As long as I was here, though, he wouldn't go out that door in the dream, pitching into the void. And with one finger of perfect detachment, I hoped that Daniel could hear all this.

"I don't—want to hurt him like—"

Like the old man hurt me, I silently finished the thought. He was pleading the court for mercy, just at the very moment when I finally stopped being a judge.

Then the squall was over, sudden as it came. His arms relaxed their grip around me, and I felt a throb of regret that now he would draw back, like a man pulling out. When it didn't happen, when he let his head stay resting against my belly, breathing deep as he pulled himself together, I thought I would burst with loving him. I would have done anything—taken a bullet, gone to jail in his place—to keep him from losing another thing.

I hadn't forgotten his own Jekyll-and-Hyde. All of that still waited to be wrestled and cursed and exorcised. But here was my brother turning to me. In the quick of our fumbling clasp, something wrong that went to the core of the planet—a fissure that leaked molten rock and brimstone—knitted at last and healed. I was taking care of Brian.

"I can't even think anymore," he said, his voice husky and drained.

I looked down at his warrior's mane, crowned since birth with laurels. "Don't think, just feel."

He nodded against my belly, then stood up—graceful even in that, unfolding like a diver. His eyes weren't very red or puffy, considering. He looked relieved. "Tommy," he said, "we need to talk about something." Yes, yes. Anything. "The lawyer wants to bring the agents here." Agents? Was he selling his story already? "They'll take a deposition, for the hundredth fuckin' time. And then we'll try to work out this witness protection thing."

"The FBI," I said, catching up at last, then looking around the kitchen with vague alarm, as if I'd left some nuclear secrets lying about.

"They think it's safer here than the federal building. Or the lawyer's."

I nodded. Sure, whatever worked. But wait, could we go back a little first? I wasn't ready to change the subject yet. Indeed, I'd barely begun to see what the subject *was*.

"So I'll set that up for tomorrow or Saturday," he said, swiftly clearing the dishes, more businesslike with every passing moment. The flood of raw feeling already began to seem a mirage. "With any luck, we should be outa your hair by the middle of next week."

"Look, I'm not in any rush—"

"And don't worry about Mom. Before they froze me I set up a trust that'll pay for the nurse. Won't be long anyway."

"You could stay here."

He was looking past me out the window at the rain, and I thought he was thinking it over. Then he said softly, "Here she is now," and I realized he hadn't heard me at all. Where had the other Brian gone, the wounded one who needed me? When the door opened behind me and Susan came in, I saw in my brother's face a spasm of tenderness and relief, as if he'd been worried the whole time she was gone. "So how's Michelle?"

"It's fine with her," said my sister-in-law. "She's got plenty of room." So matter-of-fact, they might have been discussing baby-sitting arrangements, and not the disintegration of their marriage. As I turned, Susan was furling the aunts' umbrella and hooking it on the coatrack. Then she slipped off the voluminous black slicker, hanging it on the next free hook. Husband and wife exchanged a shy glance of the central Connecticut sort, not quite eye to eye. Yet in that very misconnection was the longing to take it all back. The love between them was so obvious, to me at least, who'd become something of an overnight authority.

"Did you tell him?" she asked, meaning Daniel.

"No, I . . . not yet." He shrugged, no excuses. But she didn't seem perturbed to hear it, only nodding once, as if she understood completely. I wasn't sure why they were speaking so freely in front of me. Maybe they felt they'd reached a point where they didn't deserve their privacy anymore. Maybe they were just too tired.

Me, I wanted to scream. How could they let this get so out of hand? All they had left was each other. Who the hell else would want them?

"I'll go find him," said my brother gently.

"I'll go with you," she replied.

Now they were sweet and polite, when it was time to go break the kid's heart. They moved together into the dining room, and I heard them shuffling up the stairs, talking low. Why was I so furious? It wasn't just desire to protect my nephew from the fallout. More than anything it was the cavalier unconcern with which they were throwing their lives away. And Gray and I would have to fight for every precious month together, digging out foxholes in winter ground. I couldn't help the sour taste of injustice rising in my gorge. Narcissistic and petulant, that's what they were. They'd had it too good too long.

I stepped into the dining room, fists clenched with outrage, only now aware that the rain had redoubled again. It was dark as dusk already. Somehow I couldn't think—didn't know how to—that Brian and Susan might really find each other unbearable. Fueled as I was with the triumph of love, I couldn't imagine the dead-end wall they'd come to, or why they couldn't find the will to vault it.

Let them go, I commanded myself, determined to stay in my own joy. I called up a picture of Gray as I moved through the arch to the parlor. His flinty weathered strength, a profile stark as a sea captain's, and yet possessed of so much lightness, years of pent-up laughter spilling out of him, drunk with contentment. Drunk on me.

I was breathing easier now. I looked down idly, and there on the table was the finished puzzle of David, every piece in place, dick included. It seemed ludicrous that I ever wasted a second fretting about its propriety. The hero stood colossal, his white gaze unblemished by my bourgeois fit of respectability. For what came into play now, quickening my sight, was the filter of the night just past, the flesh of the marble before me burnished with the heat of our embracing.

Here was our icon, Gray's and mine, the warrior stripped for passion, nothing withheld. To the rest of the house it was only a statue, hardly likely to haunt the dreams of a seven-year-old. You needed to be where I was, in the throes of flesh and hungry again already, to see where the carnal met the exalted, perfect as David's massive hand cradling the stone.

I raised my eyes to the window, blinking from so much seeing. The ocean wind blew the rain against the glass, rippling the world outside like the wall of an aquarium. The terrace chairs were upside down, hunkered against the umbrella table. And just at the edge of the lawn was—what? A rock that moved. I took a step closer. The black shape swayed and stuck up its snout. A seal! I uttered a small cry of delight, then instantly felt dashed that I couldn't show it to Daniel. I thought of running to get him, but remembered they were upstairs briefing him, finishing off his childhood.

No, the seal was just for me today. The wild improbability of the moment—how had it ever climbed this high?—was one with the fine upheaval of my heart. The animal plonked through the grass, tossing its head as if it were bobbing a beach ball on its nose. I think I even heard it bark. As it sashayed in among the century cactus, making for the beach stairs, I let it go gladly, not needing to show it to anyone. I caught a last glimpse of its black shine, liquid as patent leather. Eighty steps down to the beach on flippers—a daunting feat, like me and my eighty steps up on a bad day. I trusted the beast had found the journey worth it.

I backtracked to the sofa and burrowed in under the afghan, thinking to watch the rain for further apparitions, then falling asleep as fast as Foo in front of the soaps. I vaguely heard some clumping down the stairs and the back door slam, my brother's voice calling, but none of it had a thing to do with me. When they were done disintegrating their family, then maybe we'd all sit down to lunch, and they'd come to their senses. I still harbored a stubborn conviction that love would win out in the end, against all odds. Against all evidence.

When I felt the tug at my shoulder waking me up, I flashed back to West Hill Road, my brother giving a sharp nudge to get me up for school. I opened my eyes with a scowl, assuming it was Brian, his touch as rough as ever. But no, it was Susan, her ashen face only inches away. "We can't find Daniel," she declared, equal parts hysteria and despair. I sat up and swept the afghan off me, trying to shake the sleep. "Do you know where he is?"

This time I heard the accusation, cutting through the panic with a razor edge. But worse than all that was the pleading, as if I had the boy bound and gagged in the attic and she was begging for mercy. I stood up abruptly, backing her off. I could smell the dank of her hair from her running outside in the rain. "I haven't seen him since breakfast," I said, as gently as I could.

She huddled into her folded arms, her face tight with pain. "We'll find him—" I started to say, reaching a hand to touch her elbow, and she shrilled at me with scathing venom, "Why don't you have a phone?"

Displacement. I'd been there a thousand times with AIDS, screaming in line at the bank. I took her arm firmly. "Where's Brian?"

A sob caught in her throat, as she flung out the other hand toward the bluff. She strangled something out, which sounded like "He's dead."

I didn't wait around to ask which one she meant. As I ran out through the kitchen and grabbed the slicker, hauling it on as I bolted outside, I prided myself for staying cool. Because I believed without question that nothing was terribly wrong. The boy was safe and poking about somewhere, enjoying the rain. This was all just a mother's overreaction.

Yet the rain was driving down in sheets as I tramped across the side lawn, wishing I'd brought the umbrella for a shield. He couldn't actually be *out* in a storm like this—the first small voice of worry hissing in my ear. Already my pants were clinging wet to my legs below the tent of the slicker. I crossed the terrace, buffeted so intensely I thought the wind would blow me over. Please—let him be somewhere inside. Even the stiff swords of the century cactus were bending like reeds. My hair and face were drenched, my shoes squishing, but at last I reached the top of the beach stairs.

I clung to the railing. The ocean below foamed in the tempest, white-green and pitiless, seething to litter the shore with broken ships. No one could be down there, I thought. And as if to mock the puniness of my thoughts, a solitary figure appeared on the beach— Brian, in just his shirtsleeves, soaked to the bone. His hands were cupped to his mouth like a megaphone, and doubtless he was bellowing the name of his son, roaring like Abraham, though I couldn't hear. But my brother's vast powerlessness, here at the end of the world, chilled me deeper than the northwest wind. On the ribbon of sand below stood a man whom the gods could not cease from stripping away, till nothing was left but a howl.

Why wouldn't they take his son as well?

I backed away from the brink, numb with horror, trying to tell myself the beach was covered and I should search up here. I swung about, my back to the wind, and gaped at the ramshackle house as if I'd never seen it before. No safe harbor there. On the ridge the sycamores and eucalyptus were shaking wildly, dancing almost. I lunged that way, swept along by the wind, falling once to my knees and gripping the grass, the soil beneath as soft as pudding.

I clambered through the sycamore grove, fallen branches cracking under my feet. As I staggered into the Chinese garden the wet firs slicked across my face, sharp with the perfume of polar North. Within, the rain still came in buckets, but the wind was quiet. Of course there was no one there. I could hear myself panting and suddenly felt queasy. I bit the inside of my cheek hard, tasting blood, trying to focus. Where would I go if I was seven? The surface of the fishpond was hammered with rain, hiding all the gold. Would I run away to hurt them, or hide and make them crazy? Which would bring the crisis to a head?

I swiveled around and crashed through the evergreen hedge, back to the keening of the wind. The panic had rooted in me now. As I skidded down the slope of the ridge, tearing the spongy fabric of the lawn, I kept telling myself he was doing this deliberately—hide-and-seek. In a minute he'd swagger out and wonder what all the fuss was about. But if I was so sure, then why was I so scared?

I staggered against the corner of the pergola, gripping the stucco column like an anchorage. I stared dully through the parlor windows, alien and orphaned by the storm. The scruffy plush of the parlor furniture, the crackling fire and the nice relations—all of it seemed like another life, a daydream I had wakened from at last. The world was chaos after all. And then there was no wall anymore between me and the unthinkable: *He's dead.*

I pitched along the side of the house, moaning now, reason flung to the winds. I looked down and saw my right foot was bare, streaked with mud. Somewhere I'd stepped out of one of my shoes, without even knowing. A wave of black laughter convulsed me, because I couldn't feel the slightest difference between one foot and the other. Please—let him be all right. If he was dead, then what was I praying for? And to whom? I was all contradictions, tilting against the newel post by the kitchen door, the runoff from the roof above like a waterfall on my head. Some rescue mission.

By then I must have been on adrenaline overload, or shellshocked from the rain and cold. I should have gone in. I was flirting with hypothermia when I lurched across the back lawn, making toward the garage. My head was fogged with grief already. I had the clearest picture that I would find my nephew in there, hanging from a roofbeam. When I reached the gravel drive I finally felt which foot was bare, from the stinging of the crushed stones. It was better that I should find him. Maybe I could even cut him down before his parents had to see him.

The big sliding door was stuck and rusty, because nobody kept a car in there. I tugged at the handle, bracing my foot on the frame, creaking it open a bare few inches. Then I wedged my shoulder into the breach and shoved, widening the gap bit by bit till I could slip inside. The light was silvery gray through the dusty windows. Panting with dread I looked up into the gloomy eaves, tracing the crisscross of the beams. Nothing there of course, no seven-year-old at the end of a rope.

So why was I shuddering? Why this high-pitched moan?

Because this was what I always swore to do in my bitterest hours: hang myself from a rafter of the barn on West Hill Road. Then let my father try to answer what he had done to his son. It was my trump card for years and years, ready for when I couldn't take it anymore. I kept the rope coiled in the loft like a sleeping snake. And couldn't say even now how close I came, though the bleating cry of loss erupting from me here made it seem as if I'd done it. In fact, I'd found a way to be a dead child without going all the way.

Then I was crying with something like relief. The garage was cold as a meat locker, but the panic had receded some, so the chattering of my teeth was purely physical. No one had died here. The memory of West Hill Road flipped over, and I saw very clearly my child self, swinging my feet at the edge of the loft as I read through a stack of library books. Secretly, so my father wouldn't hit me. It was a wonder I didn't go blind from so many hours in such dim light. And the rope always coiled beside me, like a spy with a cyanide pellet. I don't know why I never thought to run away. In my day Catholics didn't.

So I couldn't have said which seven-year-old was missing anymore, me or Daniel. But I did begin to see how deep things went between parent and child. How the terror of something being wrong—an injury, a kidnapping—dredged up all the most ancient fears. You became a lost kid yourself.

Wiping the rain and tears from my eyes, I turned my head, and dimly through the dusty window saw the prodigal's return. I couldn't be sure at first, because the other figure beside him carried a wide red umbrella, huddled over them both. I darted to the window and smeared a wet hand across the grimy pane. They'd just reached the kitchen door. Daniel, without a doubt. I didn't recognize the blond young man who collapsed the umbrella and followed him in.

When I burst outside the rain in my face had turned from winter to spring. The stones in the drive didn't even graze my foot. I skidded across the lawn as if I were riding a skateboard. For once the nightmare had turned out to be nothing but hide-and-seek, and I was a boy homing in to touch base. It never occurred to me to be angry at Daniel. All the horror had lifted, and I was back to being happy, the memory of Gray in my bed returning with a rush.

I flung the kitchen door wide and strode in with drunken glee. I must've looked a sight, shoeless and muddy and drenched. Daniel and the blond young man—platinum as Mona—sat on either side of the zinc table, dry and chatting amiably. The young man blanched at my Ahab demeanor, but Daniel as usual took it all in stride. "Uncle Tom," he said excitedly, "look what Ricky gave me."

The table was strewn with compact disks, but still I was a beat behind. The young man, rail-thin and looking slightly cornered, stood up and offered his hand. "I'm Ricky Gun," he declared, the voice right off the East London docks. My own hand must have been cold as a bog, but he shook it firmly. Straight, I remember thinking. "Your Daniel found a hole in the hedge and came to visit me," he said, not unamused.

I wouldn't have recognized him from Adam, not being a devotee of MTV. He didn't *look* as if he pulled in thirty million a year. Utterly ordinary and without sequins. Yet even as Daniel chattered breathlessly, unrolling a poster of Gun and his band and holding it up to show me, I experienced a moment of coldblooded perspective. To wit: this scrawny man was the apex of the glass pyramid of entertainment, while I was and ever had been at the very bottom, despite being the drag Messiah. And I wanted to kill for envy, not because of his zillions or even his shining good health, but because he was my nephew's hero.

"Daniel," I declared, waving my arms to make him stop the presentation of his loot, "your parents are looking all over for you. They thought you got lost." Neatly excusing myself from the general panic.

Daniel didn't appear to take it in, shuffling and clicking his CD's together. Ricky Gun was already edging by me, stooping to pick up his red umbrella. How could the boy not understand he needed to prepare a chastened face? "I'm at the Forum in May," said the rock star, and I realized he was talking to me. I turned to his smiling face, all his East London teeth neatly capped and bonded. "I'll drop off some tickets," he announced cheerfully.

None of us will be here, I thought, but I let them make their nice good-byes. Daniel stood at the kitchen door and waved his new friend away. And just then I heard the yelling, blowing in through the parlor doors like a bad wind.

We hardly had a second to get ready. I hissed at my nephew to warn him, but he was still mooning after Ricky. The shouting filled the house, too shrill for me to make out the words. I took a step toward the kitchen table, thinking to hide the evidence of a merry outing, when the two of them burst through the swing door from the dining room.

My brother in front, blown by the storm, stared wildly, his face chalk-white and stark as a lone survivor. His wife behind him seemed to ride him like a harpy, her own features twisted beyond recognition. They stopped in their tracks at the sight of me, beasts at bay. I shrank back guiltily. They looked as if they were chewing it over whether to grind me up in little pieces before they resumed their rampage.

Then my brother's eyes flicked to the left, catching sight of his son. I couldn't see Daniel react, but expect he just stood there very still. A piercing groan tore from Brian's heart as he scrambled by me and fell to his knees, seizing the boy to his soaking shirt.

My eyes were fixed on my sister-in-law, who looked beyond demented now, or anyway beyond help. Her mouth was a rictus of fury as she screamed: "Where have you been?" The same as what she screeched the day we went to the Chevron, Daniel and I, but this time there was no reply that would ever be the right answer.

I responded evenly: "He went to visit the neighbor." Playing down both the glamour and the adventure.

She didn't hear. She gripped the top of her head as if it would explode. A sound like gnashing teeth, and then she threw herself into one of the kitchen chairs, sending the CD's flying as she sprawled her elbows and buried her face in her hands. She wasn't exactly crying. The muffled noise she made was a kind of surrender, as if to say she couldn't take it anymore.

I turned to the others, Brian still gripping his son in a frantic wet embrace. Daniel looked at me over his father's shoulder, his own face composed and patient, what the Irish call long-suffering. Something close to irony passed between us then, though we were both far too well behaved to give it full expression. Yet it proved to me again what outsiders we were, the two of us, how far removed from the ruckus and upheaval that his parents lived on, just as mine had. He was a keeper of secrets like me, innocuous and seemingly impassive, biding his time till he could be free.

Suddenly Brian released him, giving him a push toward Susan. The boy shied slightly, and Brian coaxed him, murmuring some variant of the Sixth Commandment. Dutifully Daniel moved past me to his mother's side. He reached a hand and touched her shoulder. "Mom, it's okay," he said softly. "Nothing happened." And for once she didn't snarl and tear into him, but let the tears come instead.

My brother rose to his feet and pulled off his sodden sweat shirt, wrestling it over his head. The sudden nakedness of his torso, witnessed only by me, was oddly thrilling—the warrior stripping his armor. A great pool of water spread around his feet, which a

Catholic boy would never track through the house. He turned with
the heap of cotton in one hand, unsure where to set it down till I
reached out, and he passed it to me like a football. I moved behind
the kitchen door, still open to the storm, and pulled the lid of the
washing machine and dumped it in.

By which time Brian had kicked off his seeping mocassins and was
shucking his wet jeans. He danced on one foot, then the other, to
tug them free. Again he handed them off to me, his body all
glistening wet. Where his Jockey shorts clung against him, his dick
was vividly outlined, better hung than *David*. I couldn't quite put it
together, the massive presence of my brother's flagrant nakedness
and the queer tableau of mother and son beyond.

Then Brian hooked his thumbs in the waistband of his briefs and
yanked them down. No excess of modesty there. I was the only one
who blushed, as he kicked off the shorts and caught them up in his
hand, his thing swinging between his legs, the burning bush of red
hair—all of it charged as ever for me. Madonna and child weren't
even watching. Totally unselfconscious, casual as a locker room,
Brian lobbed the Jockeys to me, since I had designated myself to the
wash detail. I stared at him more or less dumbstruck.

He was already turning away when he happened to glance
through the open door, where the rain drummed steady on the
kitchen stoop. And I saw the most amazing change. Suddenly it was
Brian doing the blanching. His mouth went into a funny grimace,
and he actually brought up a hand to cup his genitals. His face was
as red as his hair. I was behind the kitchen door, so I saw nothing
but him, spinning around and ducking out of sight through the
swing door, a stripper who'd just spotted a cop.

Daniel still stood with his back turned, half hugging the bent
form of his mother. Then a knock on the door an inch from my ear.
"May we come in?" asked a musical voice.

Daniel turned and Susan looked up, and the last thing I saw
before the others walked in was a gleam of relief in Susan's eyes,
wanton with hope. Then I was seeing a three-quarter view of
Kathleen Twomey—in the modified habit of a teaching nun, royal
blue with a shoulder veil, very Vatican II. Mona behind her, in a
black trench coat out of *Shanghai Express*, saw me first and gave me
a shit-eating grin.

Then Kathleen smiled beatifically and laid a hand on my arm.

"Tom, it's good to see you," she said. "Please introduce us to your family."

Her eyes were brimful of the jest of her Halloween getup, but only they betrayed her. Otherwise she was a fount of serenity, playing it absolutely straight. I couldn't pretend to keep up with it all anymore. I went on automatic, treating it like a play, relieved for the moment not to be the star. "Susan," I said, smiling across at my sister-in-law, who stood up from the table and hastily straightened her lilac jumpsuit, like a shanty Irish housewife. "I'd like you to meet Sister Kathleen."

"Sister," whispered my brother's wife, almost curtseying as they shook hands. "This is our boy. Daniel." A protective arm around the kid's shoulder, not a clue that a minute ago the walls shook with shrieking and ranting.

"Welcome to California, Daniel," Kathleen declared with hearty good cheer. "I'm sorry it's not sunny, so you can play outside. You'll have to believe us, it's *always* sunny here. Right, Tom?" Her voice boomed with laughter at the folly of the storm.

"Oh, he gets out," I murmured dryly, raising a brow at my nephew, but more than anything wanting to rattle Susan's First Confirmation rosiness. It reminded me of my mother simpering at Father Donegan. Mona leaned forward and introduced herself, like the donor in a medieval triptych, but Susan hardly noticed. Her face was swooningly open only to Sister. She wanted all A's in parochial school.

"I understand you've had a lot of trouble," offered Kathleen, and the compassion wasn't the least trumped up. The room was charged with an extraordinary air of release, that the trials of my brother's family were already revealed, no shame anymore. "Maybe we could pray together," Kathleen suggested, and there was something almost seductive there.

Susan nodded gratefully. Clearly this would be one on one, not a circle of us on our knees. Mona and I drew back, impeccably discreet. Kathleen leaned down to Daniel, lifting his chin with a finger. "We'll be back in a bit, and then I'd like to hear how you're doing in school. Tom says you're quite a reader."

Daniel shrugged, modest to a fault, but you could tell she'd struck the right note. At last, someone to give him some hardball counsel on where he should show up for school at the end of Easter break.

As Susan and Kathleen exited through the swing door, I was amazed how ethereal the latter looked in her habit, especially compared to the civvies I'd seen her in before, butch as a telephone lineman. I could hear them going upstairs to be private, and assumed my brother had covered his nakedness. Daniel was meanwhile regrouping in a heap his Ricky Gun paraphernalia. I turned to Mona as she unwrapped the trench coat, letting it slink on the back of a chair.

"I thought she said ex."

"Oh yes. Very ex." Mona hauled open the refrigerator door and pulled out the milk.

"Well, then?" I persisted. "Isn't there some kind of law about impersonating an officer? A hundred million years in purgatory?"

"So who are you, Miss J? The Inquisition?" She poured out half the quart in a saucepan on the stove. "Get out of those pants, will you? They're soaked. Daniel, I'm making hot chocolate."

I realized I was still wearing the black slicker, the last one of us suited up and ready to fight fire and flood. I shrugged it off and hung it back on the coatrack. Indeed, my green fatigues were horribly clammy. As I undid the buttons I half turned away, no locker room exhibitionist like Brian. Even though no one was watching: Mona crouched at the table with Daniel, letting him spill the excited tale of his encounter with the music god.

I shinnied the pants to my ankles and stepped out of them, bareass, feeling at last a throb of frostbite in my foot. I ducked behind the kitchen door, crammed the wet pants in the washer, then opened the dryer to grab a clean pair of sweats. As I drew them on, then knee socks over, I yielded to the coziness of the moment —however manufactured, however perverse in light of the *sturm und drang* just passed. Miss Mona served up the hot chocolate in big chipped mugs, producing yet another tin of shortbread from her bag.

Oh well, I thought as we supped like a trio in *Pooh*, you took the R & R where you could get it.

Afterward, Daniel excused himself to go to his room. As he gathered the CD's in his arms, Mona happened to ask if he had a machine to play them. He shook his head no, but didn't appear especially troubled by the contradiction. The raw consumer goods were comfort enough just now.

When he scooted upstairs, Mona and I drifted in to sit by the fire, as the rain threw itself in curtains at the west windows. *Sotto voce,*

Mona told me all the machinations of her three-way contact with Gray and Kathleen. It was Gray apparently who pushed the nun disguise, having heard the intractable squalling in the night from Cora's room. Kathleen, it turned out, had jumped at the chance, a bit of a drag queen herself.

I lay with my head in Mona's lap, letting her stroke my hair, delighted to think what a crackerjack team we all made. The waiting drew out to an hour, Kathleen upstairs with Susan and Brian, but we didn't mind. Even as I dozed I waxed sentimental, Mona patting me like a big sister. There were never enough times like this. Mostly we ran in and out of the storm, a hasty kiss in passing. But this was all I ever wanted, a lover in my pocket and a best buddy like Mona, so attuned she could finish my sentences for me. A man could get to be very greedy, shooting the dice for time to savor it all.

When Kathleen came down I sat up, the two of us blinking at her expectantly, but not breathing a word. We let her stroll to the hearth and warm her hands, looking contemplatively into the flames. I was so used to her as a nun now, I could hardly recall the dyke in flannel. As she turned to us her eyes swept admiringly over the fireplace stones, the tiger's-eye paneling, the wrought-iron sconces. Then she looked at us with a deep shrug. "It's up to the two of them now."

"Did you get them talking?" Mona asked.

Sister tilted her veiled head and held up her finger and thumb a half inch apart. "A little," she said wryly. "I left them praying. They're good Catholics."

But here I couldn't tell if she was being ironic or not. I blurted out: "Are you?"

She laughed lightly, a teacher the student thinks he has stumped. "No, dear. I thought I made myself abundantly clear. I believe in Miss Jesus."

"What about God?" And why did I sound so earnest?

"Oh." She rolled her eyes and frowned, as if this was more than she signed on for. "I let God take care of the universe," she said, waving a vague hand at the rain outside, but more dismissive than anything. She couldn't be bothered with the universe. "Me, I stick to taking care of battered women. God has not dropped by lately, unless I was out for coffee." In that moment, the depth of her own estrangement from the church seemed bottomless.

Yet her ebullient good humor remained somehow intact. "However," she declared vigorously, holding up a triumphant forefinger, "I think I can get her into a group in Minneapolis. Run by some Catholic Workers. Pretty radical types if you're coming from horsey Connecticut, but I think she can handle the stretch."

"Wait," I protested, scrambling to keep up, "isn't there some way to keep them all together?"

She shrugged again: up to them. But I saw where her sympathies leaned, to let them split, if only because her own skills lay in the healing of women alone. Still, she pushed no agenda, separatist or otherwise. She was simply here among us, nursing the feelings along, without any judgment call. That was perhaps the least Catholic thing about her—no moral high ground.

"He talked about you and your father," she said, her voice quickening now in my defense. Correction: she had no problem judging the violence in men. "Sounds pretty awful."

I neither spoke nor nodded, nothing being required. As Mona laid a quiet hand between my shoulders, I looked into the fire, feeling a small triumph of vindication, just having somebody else know. It also gave me secret pleasure that my brother had been teller of the tale. I had a moment's fix on my father's face, puffed and surly, that endless snarl of racist poison, his all-consuming hatred of everything not Irish working-class. Did I hate him anymore? It didn't compute. I'd sowed his grave so long with salt, a sort of perpetual curse that went on without me, like the Masses of Remembrance my mother used to pay up for thousands of years, mail order from the Trappists.

"I'd better go see Daniel," said Kathleen, "before he thinks I forgot him. I swear, I feel like a waitress in this outfit." She pulled at the hips of the shapeless blue dress. "When they went polyester, that was the last straw."

"He keeps it all buried," I said.

"They all do," she replied automatically. "But I'll tell you one good thing. I used to teach second and third grade. So I know exactly where he is in long division." Actually rubbing her hands together, as if she was getting the chalk off. She tossed her head with spirit, balking at the veil, and moved to the stairs again.

"Kathleen—thank you—"

"Oh, don't even try," she retorted, striking a languid pose across the banister, gazing heavenward. "It is my mission, after all. And besides—" She grinned down at me slyly. "I've already got it figured how you return the favor. A small command performance for my girls."

"It'll be easy," said Mona, the pat on my shoulder suddenly getting awfully chummy.

"My drop-in group," explained Kathleen, "except I call it the dropped-*on*. I'm always trying to teach them how to be angry. You're the perfect thing."

With that she floated off to her next consultation, knowing she had me trapped, tit for tat. Mona sat there like a mouse, figuring I might blow a piston. But I couldn't have been more equanimous, trusting Sister's instincts. I already had the gig figured as a sort of USO show, like Mona's beloved Miss Dietrich performing for the combat troops. "We'll do it some Monday night," I said, because AGORA was dark Mondays.

Mona nodded, in a slight daze to find me so amenable. "You really *are* in love," she remarked, as if I'd had a conversion.

But I was somewhere else. "Just when you guys arrived, Brian was standing there naked."

"Please—don't think we didn't get a good look."

"I realized something today. I spent fifteen years trying to find that exact body and drag it into my bed." I happened to be looking at the jigsaw *David*, spread out before us on the coffee table, but the full-blown Brian flooded my mind, more real than the men I groped to recall. "Teddy Burr, for one. Those same big shoulders and flame-red hair. It didn't even matter that we lived on different planets. He did every drug he could get his hands on, and screamed at me and had tantrums. But for a little while there, it was like fucking Brian."

I shook my head in wonder, touched by a finger of self-disgust like ice along my spine. "Welcome to my dysfunction."

Mona laughed ruefully. "But he is beautiful," she insisted. "Who could blame you for mixing *that* up with love? Hey listen, Daphne's my cousin Amy, right down to the nipples."

I sighed. "It takes so long."

Mona sighed even bigger. It sounded like a contest. "At least you found someone."

"Perilously close to the finish line."

She didn't try to answer. We stayed curled up for another long time, waiting to see who would come down next. When the footfalls came, I recognized Brian's step. Without a signal Mona was up and hurrying toward the kitchen, as if she had something burning in the oven. As I turned to smile at my brother I was surprised to see the windows already dusky, throwing back the firelight. The days just flew and vanished, I thought, with an ache that wanted to hold them still, all my double family, letting nobody leave. Brian came to stand behind the sofa, wearing a sweater from Cora's closet, something old of Gray's. I could smell the camphor. I couldn't read his face.

After a moment of fire watching, he said, "Thanks for calling Sister Kathleen. We're so far from . . ." He left it unfinished, but I could see the sturdy Gothic spire, the monsignor in his picture hat, the long slope of graves behind Saint Augustine's, the Fordham brothers cheering. God, in a word.

"She sees a lot of families," I observed, not wanting to blow Kathleen's cover, unsure how much she'd revealed.

"They'll leave Monday for Minneapolis," Brian announced calmly, and I felt a stab of failure sharper than anything I could remember. Not Kathleen's fault, though I'd hoped she'd turn it around; and surely not mine. But there was a flaw we shared as a family, all the way back to my dad's old man in the wheelchair, drooling like a bulldog—a lack of faith that anything would ever come out right. The only hope, the only unqualified triumph, was Brian on the ballfield. And that was packed in mothballs long ago, jittery and flickering as the old eight-millimeter strips of film, recording shutouts and touchdowns. Otherwise we were a clan of losers.

"Will she let you see him?"

"Sure, but I won't." His voice was tough as a staff sergeant's. "Not for a couple years anyway. I want them to get settled up there like I never existed. Or else they're always gonna be running from my name." All thought through, completely unemotional. I could even tell his strength was coming from *acting* strong. "Fuck, if I survive two years out there," he said, gesturing with a vague hand at the storm outside, where he'd howled like Lear. "Hey, who knows? Maybe we'll live happily ever after."

For the first time I picked up the frisson of excitement as he contemplated being on his own, *out there*. Nothing could convince him he wasn't a marked man. Yet there was a perverse relish about the cat-and-mouse, dodging the hit squad he'd unleashed, dispatched by the bad characters he'd been in bed with. Who knew, maybe he was right. In my mind he was already running, hand to mouth and off on the next train. But what struck me just now was how much he wanted to earn his family back. Somehow, being a wandering nobody was a sort of quest to come home.

"Whatever I can do," I offered, feeling less than useless. "I'm in love with your kid. He's the best."

"I'm sure you know the feeling's mutual."

Well, yes. "Will you leave right after they do?"

"Couple days."

He was standing directly behind me now, one hand resting lightly on the back of the sofa. As I lolled my head to the side his hand was magnified, grizzled with red hair and coursed by rippling veins, massive as the warrior on the table before me. I leaned toward him and touched his wrist with my forehead, rubbing against him gently. For a moment he didn't move, accepting the contact shyly. Then, returning the intimacy, he shifted his hand and rested it lightly on my head, sheltering me.

I was overcome with feeling, to think we had tamed together the brother who used to hurt me so indifferently. I had no illusion about what lay ahead. We both still had miles to go, out there in remorseless weather—but no longer reeling under one another's baggage. Brian and I were home free.

"We should talk about us some time," he said, "before I go."

"You mean before I go," I retorted, teasing him with my demise, almost playful.

"You know what I used to think? That I made you gay. Like it was all my fault." He spilled out a soft self-mocking laugh, and his fingers rustled my hair. "Like I tempted you."

I would have spoken. I would have laughed with him. But something in me had suddenly drifted, and I was blank. And yet not quite the same as before, since I'd never noticed these episodes till they were over—two minutes lost, five at the most. This time the blank was in my body and not my head. I was still completely present, hanging on my brother's words, nestled in his hand, but my nerves were shut off and my limbs like driftwood. I lay in a slump against the back cushions, frozen.

At first I didn't even panic. More than anything I was embarrassed that I had no words to answer Brian. Yet he didn't seem in the least troubled by my silence. After all, as he'd just finished saying, we could talk about us anytime. I could feel him twirl a lock of my hair between finger and thumb, no inhibitions. Then he turned away, leaving me to doze by the fire.

Only now was I swamped with a wave of terror, unable to cry out, locked in the cell of my body. I started to shiver, despite the heat from the fireplace. Sweat sprang out on my forehead as I tried to scream and nothing came.

A stroke, just like my father. I could see his specter in the flames, the horrible sag of his right cheek, as if his face were melting. The slurred speech and the groping hand, a man drowning from inside out. I strained to move, frantic now, feeling the blood pound in my head from exertion. Some muscle must have twitched in response, for my shoulder shifted on the cushion, pitching me down prone on the sofa.

And when I felt my brain begin to flicker too, I thought, *Let it be over now.* Death being better than the vegetable state of the last long year of my father, or Teddy Burr in a shriveled coma, only able to blink his eyes to tell us he wanted to go.

For a while there I was already gone. Though I heard Kathleen come down the stairs, laughing with Daniel, it was happening on another plane entirely. My eyes were fixed on the fire, the substance of me all mercurial, transparent as the flames. From very far away Mona's voice joined them. A small pinprick of my brain still attended their human interchange. Time for them to depart, said Kathleen. Time! The very idea was so frail and poignant, nothing to do with me anymore.

Then Mona came close, and I knew she was standing above me. "Should we tell him we're leaving?" she whispered.

"No, let him sleep," hissed Kathleen in reply.

Yes, by all means. Let me get out of it easy as this, like falling off a log. I had already left the husk of my body, or seemed to be sitting on the edge of it, like the kid who used to read himself bleary in the loft. Gently Mona unfurled the afghan and lay it across my motionless form, curling it under my chin. *Go now,* I thought, *before I start missing you.*

Good old Miss Mona, always does what she's told. She grabbed up her bag and hurried away, a last whiff of *Blue Angel* floating in her wake. Then total silence, once the two women had left the room. *Now,* I told myself, *go.* As if I needed that one more push to slip off the edge and be under the ocean, all the storms behind me.

Can you really make yourself die, by sheer force of will? If so, then why had all my friends gone out with such ghastly protraction, flailing and eaten up, every exit walled up but the last groveling hole? All I can say is, for a few moments I thought I'd got through it painlessly, a Houdini escape from my body's broken vessel. I'd already passed through the flames. I was waiting on the other side, patient for the bus to heaven.

Then my line of sight to the fire was severed. Someone was blocking the way. I didn't want to focus, didn't want to come back, but I could see it was Daniel. He slouched against the sofa, careful not to wake me, but I could tell he wanted to be in my orbit, as if I was some kind of safety zone. And as soon as I realized that, I wasn't dead anymore. I was locked again in a body that didn't work, struggling again to scream.

Daniel turned. Even I could hear the low toneless wail coming out of me. "Are you okay?" he asked, then leaned down to peer in my face. "Uncle Tom, why are you crying?"

I kept screaming in my head, and the thin wail continued. Feeling began to thud into my arms and legs, like the blood unfreezing, horribly painful, the bends of reentry. I must have reached out a hand like something climbing out of a grave, because the boy stepped back fearfully, not knowing what to do. I could hear myself blubbering now, and a great writhe ran through my body.

"He's sick," said Daniel urgently to someone I couldn't see.

I clutched my hands in front of my face like a prayer, stunned and still disoriented, my nerves going every which way. Then Gray was by my side, wrapping his arms around me. "It's okay, it's okay," he said. "I'm here."

At last the cry broke from me, a wail of release that sounded like coming. My unbound arms seized him around his neck, and I could feel my body lift as he drew me deep into his embrace. I was sobbing with relief, gulping in life like air, though the dark still beat against the windows, wanting in.

"I couldn't—" I gasped, but there was no verb big enough to encompass all that had been robbed from me. Gray rocked my torso, making a hushing sound, as if he understood it all without my saying. My face was against his neck, kissing and crying and holding on. "Don't—leave me," I choked out, desperate, a child too scared to go back to sleep.

"I'm not going anywhere," he whispered, soothing me down, one hand stroking my head.

And when I finally took a real breath, I was looking over his shoulder. Daniel stood against the table, still too frightened to move, the desolation in his eyes enough to break your heart. I reached out a hand, and that was all he needed. He threw himself against us, gripping us both and burying his face, burrowing like a dog in a thunderstorm. Now we could let all the tears be his. His boy's grief was something else, of course, but right now all that mattered was his letting it out. For here was the crux of the difference between my nephew and me: that I had been the crybaby of Chester, and Daniel Shaheen the hero's son had never shed a tear.

We made a most peculiar threesome, I daresay, Gray and I holding each other's eyes across the sobbing figure of the boy. Did his mother and father hear it all and lean over the stairwell to see what was going on? Did it make Susan flinch that he hadn't come to her? And was this what the Coalition of Family Values meant, when they talked about queers recruiting children? Surely I was a special case, Lazarus raised from a sudden grave. In any event I only wanted one thing for Daniel—that he learn to cry when he lost something, or how would he ever be sure he truly had it, or know what to look for again.

The oldest wish of the race, that the child should have it easier. So: let him not grow up among people who learned too late how to feel. I knew about this, down to the marrow. I looked across into my lover's eyes, flashes of amber in the firelight, knowing it could be stolen at any second, the next time pitching me all the way down, broken on the sand.

Not that I had any regrets for the life that brought me here, not a minute of it. The slightest turn might have diverted me from the perfect balance of our three hearts. At last, to feel everything down to the marrow. If it only lasted a moment more, it had come to me in time.

E I G H T

FIRST THING IN THE MORNING I CALLED THE DOCTOR. Overnight the storm had mostly cleared, the early sky pillowed with white clouds rolling off to the east. As I stood in the booth at the Chevron, the brittle morning air was so cold I could see my breath. Sometimes the bite is as sharp as the Oregon coast—or even Maine, where my father used to drag us for a week in June, doubling up with our mick cousins while the uncles wallowed in beer. I left the accordion door open, so as not to feel cut off from Gray, who waited a few feet off in the pickup. His eyes never left my face, his untroubled smile a magic circle of reassurance.

Which I badly needed, for I felt like a fugitive turning his ass in. I had to talk my way through an answering service and two nurses, explaining again and again that I had to speak with Dr. Robison now, since I had no number to leave. They all acted deeply offended, as if I was worse than a welfare case. I hated to use the word but finally bit the bullet: *emergency.* On hold for half a minute, I put out my tongue and flicked it obscenely at Gray, who laughed, a billow of smoke in the morning chill.

When Robison came on, I felt an instant flush of shame. Haltingly I chronicled my symptoms, the random blanks and then the bad event of the night before. Hearing myself now, I experienced the most peculiar memory trace—recalling the sweaty confessional in Chester, mumbling my boy's impurities through the grille to Father Donegan. I felt the same claustrophobia, even with the door open to the ocean air. And when Robison cut me off, directing me to report for tests to the neurology unit at Brentwood Presbyterian, I felt the same Catholic emptiness, punished without being heard. A lost soul, unforgivable, knowing it in my gut when I was twelve,

181

because what the good Father was calling mortal sin would be my life.

I walked to the truck in a stupor. I told Gray where we were going, then slumped against the door in a daze of dread. None of it was any kind of surprise. We'd both known when we left the beach house, cutting out before anyone else was up, that a gauntlet of tests was in the offing. But now it was real. Gray let me be as we headed down the coast road, beating the rush hour. I had my own horrors to face, just steeling myself to walk in the doors at Brentwood Pres. The place where Mike Manihan died, eighty-five pounds and purple with lesions all over, like a rotting eggplant.

But then, there wasn't a hospital in the county where I hadn't sat one vigil or another. They dotted the city like the torture centers of some deranged tyrant. Nothing about them spoke to me of healing or sanctuary. Once you passed those portals it was all downhill, a delirious descent into the magma of pure suffering. Everything you ever loved was checked at the door, exchanged for a suit of prison grays. Later they sent somebody around to pry the gold from your teeth. Sorry, but they were out of local anesthetic.

We parked underground, in B-13. Carefully Gray jotted it down on the back of the parking ticket, as if there was any way out. In the elevator to the third floor he slipped his arm around my shoulder, and the orderly riding up with us instinctively stepped aside, fearing contamination. At Neurology Reception, I filled out about thirty-five forms, attesting to my abject poverty and formally begging the state to underwrite my care.

Twenty minutes later I was in a peach-flocked johnny gown, sitting in a wheelchair waiting for a CAT scan. The chair was mandated by hospital regulations, in case I had a foaming seizure. Gray waited on a bench beside me, grazing a finger along the back of my hand. I looked to the side and caught sight of us in the mirror steel of the double doors that led to X-ray. Already we seemed transformed, rocketed into the last stage, invalid/inmate and care-taker. My mood alternated black and blue.

By the time they'd run me through the Frankenstein maneuvers, zapping me with rads enough to light up Santa Monica, I felt as if I'd been disappeared. When they wheeled me out of X-ray, Dr. Robison was standing there in his white coat talking to Gray. They were almost exactly the same age, except Robison tipped in at two-seventy-five, a coronary waiting to happen. I'd always been oddly touched by Robison's girth, since it was so clearly a stress response to losing a patient a week. It was no picnic being a gay doctor. He'd pulled three plugs on friends of mine, so we'd known each other in combat.

"I can still count backwards," I announced grandly, wheeling into their midst, "and I can name you every Best Actress back to 1935, which should've gone to Garbo for *Camille*. My role model, I might add."

Robison grinned. "Sounds like end-stage dementia to me."

"Just start the morphine drip and let me sail, Doc."

Gray seemed more disoriented than I, hearing this manic banter. He didn't understand that I'd roped the good Robison—a Westside doc in a silver pearl Mercedes, not known for his care of indigents—by the fact of my small fame as a fringe comedian. Jocularity was *de rigueur* in all of our encounters. I fully expected to be gagging out one-liners around the ventilator tube when we got to the short strokes. Perhaps I was just overcompensating, guilty at being treated free, but I felt like Robison's last laugh.

"I think we better do a spinal," he said gently. At which my jaw locked involuntarily, and the free-floating anxiety seemed to hiss out of my ears. "You'll just be in overnight."

I licked my dry lips and nodded yes, unable to think of a quip. But even as Robison squeezed my shoulder and toddled off, all I could really see was my nephew. Two days left, and I would be spending one of them here. The beach house seemed impossibly distant from this place of torments. To get back there I would have to run away, change my name, go underground as deep as Brian. And something in me berated myself for losing it, as if this had all happened because I'd taken my desert island too much for granted.

"He says it could be nothing," Gray observed mildly.

"I want to die at the beach house. Not here."

"You're not going to die."

He said it without really thinking. In the silence that followed, as I raked him with a baleful look, I had no wish to punish him. It was only that we needed to share an awful moment of reality, eye to eye, the same unwavering gaze we had exchanged last night by firelight. Yes, I would die. Not today, unless the spinal technician was wired on uppers and let the needle slip. But this morning was the beginning, here in this castle whose only law was pain. Gray's eyes were suddenly sharp with an inexpressible mix of rage and grief. He must have wondered, now if not before, what he had signed on for.

Yet the moment served to help us catch our breath, honing our priorities. I stood up from the wheelchair like a cripple at a Baptist revival, and embraced him fiercely. "Just get me through this one," I whispered in his ear, as if I wouldn't be asking the same the next time and the next. What I meant was he should walk me through it a step at a time, because I couldn't put another foot in front of me alone. His arms gripping tight around me were all the response I needed to shake off the ghosts who roamed these halls.

As we turned toward the elevator a nurse called out, "You have to stay in that chair!" Gray and I swiveled our heads together, looking down our combined noses. She stood imperiously by her cart of meds, tipping two hundred herself. And we laughed more or less in her face, as if her bark had pricked a private joke in us—indeed, as if we had diplomatic immunity. She didn't repeat her command as we proceeded chairless into the lift.

The small victories get you through.

Fifth West was the AIDS wing. Here the smell of disinfectant was twice as pungent, as if the green-suited janitors went for overkill when they swabbed these floors. A black kid at the nurses' station, twenty-five and rail-thin, clearly on the bus, grandly assigned me to 509, purring like a concierge. Room 509 seemed far enough away from 531, where Mike Manihan had ridden out his last convulsions. As Gray and I headed down the hall, I pointed out the coffee closet and, farther on, the day room. Rigorously I averted my gaze from the open doors to patients' rooms.

But we paused at the door to the day room, with its shelves of videotapes and New Age bromides postering the walls. A frail and ancient boy in a gown just like my own looked up from the card table, where he was doing a jigsaw. I tried to stare at the puzzle, not *David* this time but a stupid Norman Rockwell barn on an autumn hillside. Tried to turn away without connecting.

And the boy took a labored breath and said: "Tom?"

His hollow face was bright with recognition, which only made it worse that I hadn't a clue who he was. Gray seemed to draw closer to me, blindly protective. "Ed Bernardo," said the wraith, pointing a bony finger at himself, and the worst of all was that I recognized the name and nothing more. The dwindling body before me was still a stranger—or no, he looked just like everyone else before the end.

"We got arrested," he said, persisting, more and more animated. "Saint Vibiana's."

I gasped, I hope not in horror. "Of course," I blurted, a ghastly grin on my face, my temples pounding with the memory of the *real* Ed Bernardo. "Gray, this is Ed. We laid down in front of the archbishop's limo together."

Ed Bernardo laughed, sending himself into a fit of coughing. He looked as if he would die in front of us. Now I saw the tubes trailing out of his gown to the IV pole beside him. Not a friend at all, really, just a buddy from ACT/UP. Off and on over the last two years we'd picketed and railed together, our little band of urban guerrillas not going quietly, thank you. This was before the last wave of fatigue had beaten me down and my knee began to throb, rendering me too bitter and solipsistic for activism. Now I just wanted to turn and bolt, pressing myself against Gray.

But Ed had somehow segued from coughing to laughing, practically holding his sides with mirth, or trying to keep his tubes in. "Tom," he gasped, "I heard you were *dead!*"

Oh it was priceless, how black the humor could get. I gave out with a chortle in response, and then the three of us were whinnying merrily at the absurdity of keeping track of who was still alive. When in doubt—no Christmas card two years running—assume the worst. And as for the gray areas, the half-dead, look at Ed Bernardo, for Chrissakes. Was I really so sick I could laugh at *that*? The fifty pounds he'd shed, the straggle of thirteen hairs on his head, where he used to sport a ponytail. His mottled face, at once gray as a dead fish and weirdly ruddy, as if he'd stood downwind of a hydrogen bomb. Yet we laughed like kids in a graveyard.

Swearing we would compare notes later on, I shunted Gray and me out of there, and we careened down the hall to 509. If I had just seen the shadow of where I was going, it was no more than what I already knew from a hundred other nightmares. What was there for Gray and me to say about it? Everything and therefore nothing. I ordered lunch instead, every dish on the gimpy hospital menu, as if we were staying at the Beverly Wilshire. Myself, I was not allowed to eat before the procedure, but I had this crushing desire to take care of my lover.

As it happened, the food arrived at the same time as a tiny

Filipino nurse who wanted blood. So Gray had to negotiate his minestrone and greasy Monte Cristo while tube after tube of blood was milked from my arm. Gallons of it, it seemed to me, who wilted against the pillows, Garbo-like. By the time Miss Manila left, I felt as if I'd been ravaged by a vampire.

I closed my eyes and pretended to doze, not wanting to vent my gathering despair on Gray. Unbelievable how fast the world was lost in here, how trapped I was already in the system. I used to swear I'd end it all before they'd ever check me in, my small final protest against the stealing of the real Tom. No Ed Bernardo dwindling for me.

But I hadn't done it, had I? I'd walked in here on my own power, freely giving up my name and self. And all because I'd been ambushed by love, and would do anything now to squeak through. It wasn't Gray's fault, yet I couldn't help but feel a certain helpless sorrow, to think I'd surrendered my chance to check out early.

Next came the blinking intern—Dr. Polluted, I thought he said. Looked about nineteen. He bristled with excitement, ready to reel off his minilecture on spinal taps. Airily I waived this last chance to hear my rights. I knew every raunchy detail of the procedure, because in my circle people had spinals more regularly than civilians had their oil changed. My jaded attitude severely cramped his budding bedside manner, but hey, we might as well cut to the chase.

"Just get me my Demerol, will you, Dr. Polluted?"

"Dr. *Belushi*," Gray corrected, as the intern scurried out. Which struck me even funnier, as if I were about to be spinal-tapped on "Saturday Night Live." Then Gray moved to the bed and engulfed me in a hug, admonishing me to take it easy, swearing he'd be right outside. Over his shoulder I watched a nurse wheel in the instruments on a cart. She sported a plastic oversuit worthy of a nuclear plant at core meltdown.

"I love you," I whispered to Gray, but couldn't shake the feeling that we were fated to different orbits from here on, barely able to touch as we passed, tracing our doomed parabolas. But I snookered a hand between the buttons of his shirt and pinched his nipple, for his sake swallowing the whole third act of *Camille*. "Now don't you dare try to fuck me while I'm under," I warned him in my smuttiest tone.

The nurse/astronaut moved in as he stood away. She untied the gown and bared my butt, jabbing the left cheek, my best side. The swooning began almost instantly. Belushi's entry in his own spacesuit was already a kind of dream. A stickler for protocol, he stood over me and gave me the lecture I'd just refused. I didn't care, my own muzzy brain having taken refuge at the beach house, flying there swift as a bird. I remember being arranged into a fetal crouch and told I must hold very still, an irony to someone who was wheeling over the Trancas bluffs.

Then I heard the doctor say, close to my ear, "You'll feel a prick." And that made me want to make another smutty quip: *Prick has to be pretty big these days for Miss Jesus to feel it, Doc.* Then I felt the sting, which wasn't funny at all.

It was hours later that I surfaced, one eye blearing open, feeling more than a little amphibious, not yet ready to leave the sea and walk upright. Hazily I saw Gray across the room, hunched over the telephone and murmuring low. It seemed to me that if he was all right, then I was. And back I went under. When next I groped awake, hours later still, the TV in the ceiling corner was on at whispering volume, Gray standing before it watching. Local news: I recognized the bimbo making happy talk. So it was evening.

But another cloud of nap intervened before I grogged up on one elbow and spoke: "Water." From Garbo to Helen Keller in a single day—what a range.

Gray cradled me in his arm and gave me sips. "Mona insists I leave a message on her machine, every hour on the hour," he said. "I feel like CNN."

I flashed him a doofus smile. "You're still here," I woozily observed, by which I meant not that he might have fled, but what a relief it was to find I hadn't dreamed him.

He stroked my hair. "Spinal fluid's clear. I talked to Robison. He ticked off about fifteen things you don't have."

"Good. Let's get out of here." I started to swim out of the covers, forcing him to pin me. No, not yet. Blood tests wouldn't be in till morning, still a chance I had some alien protozoa space-stationing in my brain. Besides, I had to stay prone for so many hours after the spinal, or else I'd get a migraine. I incidentally discovered I liked the feeling of being pinned, and made a blurry note that we ought to try some naked wrestling. I pouted my lips, and Gray obliged me with a kiss.

"Kathleen's been up at the house all afternoon. Brian called from the Chevron. He said to tell you he loves you."

Exactly. We all loved each other now, and nobody would get hurt anymore. And because my head was cradled so securely in the crook of his arm, I swooned under again. When I woke from that, there was only a nightlight on. I felt as if I'd been sleeping for months. My head was finally clear of drug, and I knew exactly where I was. Alone. *Get used to it,* I told myself, because when the black carriage finally came, there would be room for only one. And I felt for a long moment as if there had been no Gray at all. That whole delicious interlude of passion, the best week of my life, seemed like a movie I'd left in the middle of.

Grunting softly, I rolled up onto my elbow and reached the water glass from the bedside table. There was in fact a knot of dull pain behind my eyes, twin to the stinging pinprick at the bottom of my spine. I knew they were connected, brought on by the tiny leakage of fluid when the needle was withdrawn. The rest of my body felt wrung out, strung on the throbbing clothesline of my nervous system. I sipped from the glass and swallowed wrong, choking and spraying the pillow with water. I leaned my forehead against the siderail of the bed—

And there was Gray, curled on his side and sleeping on a low cot, about two feet below the level of my sickbed. I felt an instant flood of protectiveness, the tables turned, as if I were the one on guard here. Then castigated myself for not having told him to head on home for the night. There was no reason at all for him to be keeping such close watch, and giving up his comfort in the bargain. No reason except the preciousness of time. It was nothing but false bluster, my wishing him home in his comfortable bed. I was punchy with relief that he was here.

I reached a hand through the bars of the siderail, stretching toward the cot below. I couldn't quite see his face, turned toward the pillow, the softest whistle of breath regular as a distant horn at sea. I could just touch his hair with my fingertips, ever so light, not wanting to wake him. But I really believed, now for the first time, that I'd make it out of there. I didn't need the test results to tell me I was still alive. This had all been a test, like a lifeboat drill.

I don't know how long I watched, hovering there above him like a guardian angel. After a long stillness, maybe an hour, I saw the first gray outline of the window as the dark began to evaporate. I grew drowsy again and fought it, not wanting to leave behind the safety of the night. But even as I glided under, I knew what the secret was. We didn't require the beach. We were an act you could take on the road, a string of colored lights and a trunkful of costumes in the back of the pickup. Not the time or the place but the two of us were the whole show.

We bolted awake at the same time, when a nurse came brawling in, barking reveille. I squinted up as she stood beside the bed, holding what looked like an enema bag for horses, the nozzle on the hose about the size of a forty-watt bulb. "Turn over," she said with menacing glee, as I gaped in protest. Then she twisted her head and gave a puzzled look at a dangling tag on the bag.

"Wait—you're not Barton," she declared, a withering accusation, then stormed out as abruptly as she came.

"And so Alice stepped through the looking-glass," I said, by way of good morning.

We'd hardly washed up, sharing the skimpy towel in the bathroom, rough as a cheap motel. Robison walked in as I stood there naked, having just shed my johnny gown. I cocked my head defiantly. "Nothing, right?"

He shrugged his arms wide, big as Pavarotti. "Can't find anything."

"Which isn't the same as nothing," I remarked, with a rueful smirk at Gray.

"Oh, it's *something*," said the doctor. The conversation was getting more like *Alice* every second. "Not a tumor. Not an infection. Maybe stress. Sounds to me"—and he nodded at Gray as his witness—"like you've been racing around like crazy. Ease up, will you?"

"I'm just smelling the roses, Doc." I wiggled my hips like a saucy barmaid, swaying my dick brazenly.

"Don't worry," said Gray, "I plan to keep him on a very tight leash."

"Promises, promises," I drawled, pulling on my briefs and snapping the waistband.

Gray's voice changed. "And if it's not stress?"

This time Robison's shrug was more resigned. "Could just be . . . part of the process."

I brayed a one-note laugh. How was that for circular reasoning: AIDS was caused by AIDS. For a decade now we'd been hearing about "the process," my friends and I, except all of them had been processed into the grave. Yet I didn't intend thereby to cast any aspersions on Robison himself, who was as up on all the latest as any doc could be. My bitter hoot was for all of us, hostage to the inexorable creep of the viral breakdown. Treatment was still just a fistful of Band-Aids. Underneath, the process went on and on.

Yes, I told him, I'd check with him right away if the blanks got worse. And I let him finish with his own brand of touching wood: "You look terrific, Tom." This with the slightest extra weight on the verb, as if looks could be very deceptive.

And bang, we were out of there, scooting down the hall to the elevator. As we vamped impatiently, Gray pressing the DOWN button over and over, I happened to glance along the hall. A few doors down, Ed Bernardo was struggling out of his room, tangled up in his IV line. He wrestled with the pole like somebody dancing with a broom. Quickly I looked away, hunching my shoulders to hide.

"Nurse," I heard him call, exasperated, and then the elevator doors opened. I practically lunged inside, so determined was I not to say good-bye to Ed. Of course I was racked with cowardly guilt as we descended. For there went my chance to say the *real* good-bye, however couched it would have been in the code of denial. *Keep fighting, Ed.*

You look terrific.

Fourteen dollars in parking fees, and we were on our way. Driving back down Sunset in the lemon morning light, a day in jail behind me, I let the whole experience go with dazzling single-mindedness. Nothing more to be said about it. Yes, it had been our introduction to dying: Hell 101. All the more reason to hurry home, my fingers drumming impatiently on the dashboard as we sailed down the last long curve to the Coast Highway.

"So," I said deliberately, "any update on how it went yesterday with Kathleen?"

My brother's family came flooding back into my head at the first piercing glimpse of ocean, Catalina riding crystal clear across the bay. I only realized now, as we nosed through traffic at the intersection, heading north on 1, how profoundly I had put them all on hold. Part of the AIDS triage, where we got through the minefield of Brentwood Pres by shrinking the world to Gray and me alone. The rest of life had to fend for itself. Perhaps there was also an instinct that protected a man from too much missing. But now the image of my nephew rose again like a lump in my throat, and I was mad with impatience to be there again.

"According to Mona," chuckled Gray, "she had the three of them playing role games for hours. I gather Daniel let them have it between the eyes." Good boy. "He asked if he could stay with you."

The stab of feeling was so intense, I thought I would pass out. Eyes brimming, I stared past Gray at the ultramarine of the water. Not a chance in a million, of course, which Daniel knew as well as anybody. He'd faced the parameters of my condition better than his parents had, unafraid even to use the "D" word. He knew where this was all going.

And when I walked him up to bed two nights ago, after he'd cried his heart out, I tucked him into the covers and crouched by the bed. He said: "Can I be your brother?"

"Isn't nephew enough?"

He shrugged. "It's okay. But I always wanted a big brother."

"Well, you got one now." I leaned over and kissed his forehead, I who'd been so afraid to sit too close and touch his knee in front of *David*.

Now all I wanted was a little time, one last walk with him on the beach at sunset, so as to sink the memory of me deeper. Fifty years from now, when Gray was gone and Brian—all of us—Daniel would be the only thing left of me. Believing nothing else, I found myself longing for that small immortality.

"We could go and visit them," said Gray, without preamble. I looked across at him, one hand on the steering wheel, squinting like Gary Cooper. I knew he meant Daniel and Susan, once they'd settled in Minnesota. Were we so close now we could hear each other think? Better and better.

"No, I don't think so," I replied, with something akin to my brother's feeling that Daniel would have to grapple himself a new life, unencumbered by the past. Or was it that I couldn't face the image of myself, six months down the line? By then I might look like Ed Bernardo, and Daniel would have to freeze a smile, swallowing his shock. No, he should leave tomorrow without looking back, his memory of me whole.

I reached a hand across and rested it on Gray's thigh, recalling with delicious pleasure the night I'd stretched out on the seat not knowing I was being courted. Gray covered my hand with his, lightly. As we straggled through Malibu proper, stop and go, the

Mediterranean weather seemed to have brought out every surfer and bunny, shaggy and streaked with platinum. Achingly young, the Aryan beach bohos ducked in and out of waterfront shops, looking like none of them ever worked. Relentlessly straight, not an obvious queer among them, these starlets and Pepperdine frat boys.

In certain moods, of course, I'd have gladly lined them all up against a wall for the firing squad. Crime: AIDS indifference. Today, somehow, my release from the castle of pain had left me giddy with generosity. I loved us being the secret fags of Malibu, hand in hand as we inched our way through the stoplight at the pier, wishing them well in their deathless town on the water. Excepting time, they couldn't have more than we did.

Even with Sunday traffic and a pit stop for groceries, it was hardly midmorning when we reached Trancas. Still a whole day, I told myself as we rose up the hill to the beach house turnoff. As Gray waited for a break in the flow, blinker on, I gazed down the oleander alley of the drive, almost hallucinating the sweetness of the day ahead—a kind of wall-to-wall picnic, summer in March. Then we were rocketing down the drive, gravel spraying like shrapnel. Gray lurched the pickup to a stop beside the garage. I looked at the window I'd rubbed the grime from, the other day in the rain.

"Hey—who are *you?*"

I turned to see a man striding across the lawn toward us. Gray froze, halfway out of the truck. I saw the ridiculous clothes before I saw his face: Gucci head to toe. Green-and-red-striped sweater, black linen pants, white loafers. Looked like a music executive. Worse: looked like an agent. "Nobody works here today," he said, one hand shooing the truck. "Come back tomorrow." He seemed to think we were gardeners and didn't know English.

In tones as old as the Magna Charta, Gray announced, "This is my house."

Gucci blinked. He was maybe a couple of years younger than Gray, but it was hard to tell, because he'd had an eye tuck and some nose work. A regular queen, except he was straight. "You— you're—"

"Gray Baldwin," replied the Magna Charta. "And I'm talking to . . ."

"Nigrelli. Billy Nigrelli." He put out a hand to pump, and Gray noblesse-obliged. "I'm Brian's attorney." The deal maker. He flicked his eyes to me in the truck, and I knew right away he'd been told the whole story. "I'm awful sorry. We got the feds coming, we're kinda jumpy. How you feelin'?" This last directly to me.

"Fine, thanks," I replied with a thin smile. "Where's my brother?"

Billy Nigrelli shrugged toward the house. "He's gettin' them ready for the airport."

My mouth went dry as sand, but Gray said, "Getting *who* ready?"

"The wife and kid. We gotta leave in half an hour." He pointed at his wrist, bulging with a Rolex.

"No," I croaked, recovering my voice. "Tomorrow." But it sounded more like pleading than statement of fact.

"Hey, I don't make the schedule," retorted Nigrelli, defensive now. "The FBI moved everything up. They run the show." He shrugged again, a wheedling look on his face, no doubt just the sort he gave his clients when the verdict came back guilty. Don't look at me, Jack.

I whipped my door open and tumbled out. As I trotted across the grass I heard Gray's plaintive call behind me: "Tom, your head!" I ignored him, leaping the back stoop and banging the screen door wide. The duffel bag and a paper sack were propped by the stove, ready to go. I bolted into the dining room and started up the stairs, stumbling against the banister as a blinding flash exploded behind my eyes, pulling me short.

Easy, easy. I hunched over and gripped my skull, trying to give the pain room. Half a minute I stood there gasping till the thudding began to abate. Gingerly I mounted, one step at a time and gripping the rail. When I reached the upstairs landing I was fine, no traces of the aftershock except a film of icy sweat on my upper lip. I swiped it with my sleeve, threw back my shoulders, and made for the arched doorway. I was the grown-up here—no time to be sullen. Make him leave happy.

I came up the four steps into the peak of morning, smiling and casual. Because I'd heard no voices, I was startled to see my brother slouching against the window frame, staring out to sea. Daniel sat cross-legged on the bed, a little blue backpack beside him. Idly he plucked at the tufted bedspread, then looked up, his face bursting with sudden joy to see me.

"Told you he'd make it," he cheered, scrambling off the bed and running to hug me.

Brian turned. The sorrow in his sleepless eyes didn't change, even though he smiled. "Tommy," he said, then lowered his eyes to the boy, who clung about my waist. Brian's wistful smile seemed to underscore his pleasure that Daniel loved me so unreservedly, but also a bottomless melancholy. Almost as if he feared an embrace so raw with passion, stirring up all the agony of good-bye. The wish was plain in his face—*no more feelings*—a longing for Susan and Daniel to disappear while his back was turned. "What did the doctor say?" he asked, practically a whisper.

"I'm fine," I replied firmly, disengaging myself from the circle of Daniel's arms, but letting one hand rest on his shoulder. "Brain's clear. I'm just as demented as ever."

Brian's eyes narrowed. I could almost hear him making his own diagnosis. He forced his baseball grin. "Great," he said heartily. "Look, why don't you guys visit. I'll go check if she's almost ready."

He strode out past us, down the tower steps. Now he would try to avoid saying good-bye to his wife, face-to-face, just as he had with his son. I moved past Daniel and sat on the end of the bed, putting us on the same level. "How you doing, pal?"

He cast his eyes down. "I don't want to go."

"Yeah, it sucks."

For a second I thought he was going to cry, but he crinkled his lips and looked out at the water, gazing with his father's eyes. The milky skin of his face was near translucent, the best of the Irish. "Minneapolis," he said sardonically. "Yuck."

"You'll be okay. Just squawk if you need something. Don't hold stuff in." I was dazed by a sense of acceleration, no time to lob these pearls of wisdom or let them sink in. Then it struck me, jagged as the smithereens of sun on the morning sea, that all time was stolen. It never got easier to say it now. "Remember, everyone up there's going to be doing backflips, trying to help you and your mom. Let 'em spoil you a little, okay?" He nodded, but maybe just being polite. "If you want someone to bounce things off, someone outside like Sister Kathleen—"

He turned and gave me a hawk's eye. "She's a psychiatrist, right?"

"Sort of," I conceded. "But it doesn't mean you're crazy if you go talk to somebody smart. It'll *keep* you from going crazy."

He nodded again, judiciously. "What was the hospital like?"

"The pits. Look, I'll miss you a lot, but I'm really glad we met. It's the best thing that's happened since . . ." I couldn't think how far back. Before AIDS or a million years ago, whichever came first.

His eyebrows, faint as down, scrunched together skeptically. "What about Gray?"

"Okay. The *two* best things."

He squirmed onto the bed behind me, grabbing at his backpack. "I got you a present." He struggled to undo the rawhide knot, then plunged in his hand and pulled out a puff of tissue paper done up with red twine. "Mom wrapped it," he said, handing it over, about the size of a wallet. "She gave me the money. It's all they had at the gas station."

I tugged the bow and pulled off the twine, trying to think what I was giving him. Carefully I picked at the tape, not tearing the tissue paper. "It's not fragile," observed my companion, a trifle impatient. So I ripped my way in. A tongue of fiberglass fell out in my hand, about five inches long and Day-Glo green. "It's a surfboard."

"Very hot."

"And a keychain, see?" He jiggled the metal ring that looped through one end of the miniboard. "I know you don't have a car, but . . ." His voice faltered with uncertainty. "I would've got you something else . . ."

"But why? This is perfect. We'll put the keys to the truck on it." He flushed with pleasure to see me laugh, though what I was thinking was how eccentric Gray would look, sporting his keys on this clumsy neon banana. "Besides," I added with mock gravity, "this is my first board. And that's the most important one. Why?"

He grinned, delirious that I remembered. " 'Cause that's where you learn your moves."

"Right!" And I grabbed him close in a sort of wrestling embrace, as he laughed with abandon. For a second I seemed to hold hope in my arms, like a physical thing of pure energy. Then I sprang up, tumbling him onto the bed. "Come on, I've got something for you!"

It was a race, against time if nothing else. I barreled down the tower steps into the stair hall, Daniel right behind. A tiny cautionary voice inside me tried to pipe in with "Tom, your head," but I was on overdrive now. Daniel roared past me, rounding the turn of the stairwell. As I dived after him into Foo's room, he was already bouncing up and down on my bed like a trampoline. Yes, yes—shake this house with life.

I went right to the top drawer of the dresser. I pulled it open and reached in among my underwear for the gold-tooled box from Teddy Burr. "That picture you lost in the fire," I said, rooting through buttons and coins and rhinestones. "Me and your dad. Was it like this?" And I plucked out the rumpled snapshot, smoothing the creases and thrusting it toward him. He settled himself cross-legged and peered at it closely. I held my breath, not sure why it mattered so.

"Yeah," he said carefully, "almost." Studying even closer, cool as a scholar. "In mine you could see you better." So I was right, there had been a picture of me and Brian side by side, before I turned away in a half blur. Daniel looked up. "You mean I can have it?" he asked, nearly in awe.

"Sure."

His face blazed with delight as he bent to examine his treasure again. I felt triumphant, as if I'd restored some corner of the world that disappeared in the conflagration, a piece of the jigsaw. "I was eight," I said softly, looking down at the box of shards in my hands. Nothing worth anything—rusty tie clip, Monopoly token, a pin that said I DON'T DO MORNINGS. A sort of time capsule by default, the accidental savings of a man with no goods to leave. On a sudden impulse I plucked out the brass cockring, slipping it in my pocket, and held out the box. "Why don't you keep it in here?"

He took it from me and looked inside. Fascinated, he poked a finger into my UConn class ring and twirled it thoughtfully around his knuckle, so the garnet caught the light. "This is like all your stuff," he said, seeming to understand intuitively that indeed he had all of it there, whatever I'd managed to save. He looked up at me with a troubled frown, struggling to get this right. "Don't you want to give it to Gray?"

I shook my head. "Gray's got me."

He looked down again, letting the ring slip off his finger. Then he nodded half to himself, like a man deciding to accept a mission, and carefully replaced the photo of me and Brian in the box. I handed him the lid, which he gently laid in place. I thought perhaps I was the one going to cry. "Thanks," he said, tracing the gold tooling with a fingertip. "Is my dad gonna come back to us?"

"I don't know. He's got a long way to go."

"He'll be sad by himself."

"Yup."

"And then if you die—" He gazed up at me, unflinching. "Then we'll all be sad. How will we ever get happy again?"

How do you translate across the gap of twenty-seven years? "You

can still have happy *days*," I said carefully. "Like birthday parties."
But I wouldn't pretend: the world once broken would never be all of
a piece again. This kid was too smart to string along, too good with
subtext. "Then someday if you're lucky, you find the right person.
They let you be sad when you need to, but they don't let you stay
there a minute too long."

"Like you and Gray."

A light rap on the door, and Susan's voice said, "Daniel? You
ready?"

Curiously she sounded rather calm, and for once without the
overriding suspicion that Uncle Tom was molesting her son. I
stepped to the door and opened it. She smiled, startlingly beautiful
in a green print dress, the first real clothes I'd seen her in—courtesy
of Nigrelli, I later found out. She didn't appear remotely bent out of
shape that Daniel and I were alone in my room. "He just has to grab
his backpack," I said, as Daniel bolted between us, running up to
the tower.

We shared a chuckle at the irrepressible force of him. Then she
held out a square of paper. "Here's my sister's number. We want to
hear from you." She closed the paper into my palm, more intimate
than a handshake. "Brian said everything came out negative."

I shrugged. "For now."

"Thank you for being so good to our son."

And I swear, she reached her arms around my shoulders and
embraced me. If Kathleen was this good with my sister-in-law, her
battered women would soon be running corporations. Even so, I
could see how composed it all was, like the dress and the black
pumps, gracious as a lady in Connecticut. *This is what she was like
before*, I thought. She released me but kept her hand on my arm, no
fear of contagion at all.

I wanted to say: *Please take my brother back.*

Then Daniel came rushing out of the tower, his backpack slung
on his back, and there was no more room for Susan and me. She
bent and fixed Daniel's collar where the strap of his pack had ridden
it up. Then we descended the stairs in procession, Susan's blond
head regal, a girl who saved her best for entrances and exits.

Nigrelli was at the dining room table, arranging his yellow pads
and burrowing into a ponyskin briefcase. Across from him stood a
thick-waisted man in a cheap Hawaiian shirt, fiddling with a tape
recorder. Nothing about this potato-faced dullard suggested he was

FBI—no black suit and shades, not even a gun—but it seemed to be the case. Both men looked up as we came down, nodding vaguely, nothing verbal. Susan, more than ever like a queen going unbowed into exile, hovered a protective hand at the back of Daniel's head, averting her eyes from the lowlifes. I led the way like an equerry, sweeping the swing door wide and hustling us into the kitchen.

Brian and Gray stood by the back door, both with their arms folded, staring out onto the back lawn. Gray was the perfect one, I thought, to be there for my brother—wordlessly. He looked just like he did at funerals, staunch and without any airs, standing next to the person most in pain. Yet as soon as Brian saw us, he flashed his baseball grin. His eyes were dead, but he made sure they didn't connect with anyone else.

"Got your parachute on, eh, buddy?" he said, clapping a hand on Daniel's shoulder. I flashed on the other day, my brother kneeling drenched and clutching the boy he thought was lost, almost as if he could fuse them together. Now he worked to keep it all light, playing against the real thing about to happen. Smiling the way he'd smiled in my dream, as he pitched out the door into endless night.

Gray leaned down for the duffel bag, while I crouched and hefted the paper sack. We followed my brother's family out. A black man in a proper G-man suit stepped forward from his unmarked Dodge and greeted Susan. "Agent Evans," he declared proudly. "I'll be taking you to the airport."

Susan declined her head, maintaining a rigorous distance. Out of the corner of my eye I saw Brian lead Daniel past the camellias for a last brief huddle. Gray and I hauled the luggage and stowed it in the car's trunk. As we came around, Susan was already waiting in the backseat, the door open. I took up a casual slouch on the rear fender, startled to notice that Gray was making straightway for the house. Did he hate good-byes? No, I expect it was just the fineness of his feelings—above all not to intrude, the first WASP commandment.

I watched my brother and his son. The boy's head was bent, looking at the ground as he listened to Brian's pep talk. I couldn't hear a thing, but the moment was near hallucinatory. For they were the mirror image of West Hill Road, my father giving Brian a last bit of shorthand coaching before a thousand games.

And the queer thing about it was, this jealousy I'd carried like a clamp on the heart for thirty years released me at last. I saw for myself that the secret to being a man, withheld from me season after season, was never there at all in the pregame one-on-one. Brian and Daniel were clearly doing the best they could, but there was no special dispensation. The tentative shuffle of the boy's feet, the crouching stance of the father, the firm hand on Daniel's shoulder proof against nothing out there. It was only a waltz on the lip of the void.

I felt what I'd never imagined before: sorry for all the fathers, even mine, for the secret that couldn't be taught.

Then the huddle broke, and they strolled together toward the car. I wished Brian could see it from my vantage, because no one would have doubted who they were to each other. The sense I'd had when Daniel walked beside me, unconsciously matching his step to mine, was beyond mimicry here. Man and boy were the same. As they loomed closer it seemed like a grand achievement, something my brother had won, rather than just the mute work of genes. I would have given anything at that moment to gather them in my arms and hold them here, till they made the father-and-son thing work.

But I didn't, because I knew my place—not to show more feeling than my brother did. Now we were all bunched in the lee of the open door, and Susan was leaning out to embrace her husband. Again it was rather *pro forma*, good-bye Connecticut-style. Would passion have served them better, my brother roaring in pain and clutching the side of the car, dragging along as it lurched away? Daniel and I locked eyes across their last banalities, Brian swearing to write as soon as he got settled.

My nephew smiled and reached a hand behind to pat his backpack. "Don't forget," he said, "I got all your stuff."

I spread my arms wide, as if to take in the whole bluff. "Treasure Island, right?"

Brian pulled away from Susan, who scooted over to give Daniel room. The little guy clambered in, and there was an instant altercation, because she wanted him to take off the backpack. No way. "You can't wear this on the plane, young man," she declared, but only halfheartedly. Evans swung into the driver's seat, exploding the engine to life. I was standing shoulder to shoulder with my brother, trying to stay as motionless as he. Daniel struggled to poke his head out the window, but as the agent swung the Dodge in a half circle, the boy was thrown back on the seat.

Seat belt, I screamed in my head, but said nothing.

The Dodge roared down the drive, the oleanders on either side tossing in its whirlwind. Daniel had managed to prop himself up so he could look out the back window, but he didn't wave. His face was perfectly still, just like my brother beside me. I didn't blame either of them for holding back, all my death watches having taught me that the thing itself when it finally came was beyond feeling.

At the end of the drive the Dodge hovered momentarily. With the glare of the sun on the window, the boy was hardly an outline. And I suddenly realized, just as the car bucked out into traffic, that the last sight he had of us was the same as the picture lost in the fire.

Dust swirled in the driveway, the oleanders nodding. For a long moment we stood there silent, nearly at attention. I'd taken a blood oath not to be the first to move or speak. Anything else would have seemed an insult to my brother. I could hear a mockingbird in the sycamore by the garage, veering impatiently from song to song. More acutely than ever I felt as if I were straddling two worlds, West Hill Road and here.

"Well," he said finally, "kiss *my* life good-bye."

Tough—he wanted to play it tough. We broke ranks and swung toward the house, nothing required of me but to match his steps and keep it laconic. I thought of Gray in his funeral mode, mute and stoic. As we came in the kitchen Brian darted a look about, as if he wanted to grab a shield before doing battle in the dining room. "Some coffee?" I asked hopefully, and he gave me a grateful nod, heading on in.

I boiled the water in a trance of selflessness, not spilling so much as a sigh over Daniel's sudden departure. That would come later. Right now I had a mission of my own—to be what bridge I could for Brian, only a day before he took off himself. Every detail now, starting with this cup of coffee, would be our last transition. I suppose the enormity of small things was the residue of my twenty-four hours at Brentwood Pres, the phenomenal world surrendered. Here I was the nurse in charge.

I set the mug on a tray, along with a wedge of coffee cake—service for one only. When I batted the swing door open, Nigrelli and the agent gave me a pair of poisonous looks, that I should interrupt their man's work. Already Brian's face was dark with the blood up, fuming Irish, as he tumbled out a monotone of kickbacks. He smiled wanly as I laid the tray before him. Then, moving toward the stairs, I passed behind Nigrelli's chair and coughed with my mouth open, rippling his hair. I could see his head pull in like a turtle's, certain he'd been exposed.

They waited till I'd reached the top of the stairs before they began the questions again. "May of 'eighty-six," said Potato-face, "the interstate contract. What was the union involvement? Who was your bagman?"

"You've *got* all this," snarled Brian, and Nigrelli purred how they needed it all on tape in a certain order.

I pushed open the door to Foo's room—and Gray shot awake, half sitting up, as guilty as if he'd fallen asleep at the wheel. He looked bone-weary, rumpled as the clothes he'd slept in at the hospital. I crossed to the bed and motioned him to lie down again, but he wanted to know right away. "How'd it go?"

I shrugged wearily, kicking off my shoes. "Nobody cried."

"How are *you?*"

I ducked and burrowed against him. "I'm glad I'm not seven," I mumbled into his shirt.

We left it at that for a while, holding tight. Across the room I could see the dresser, its top drawer still yanked open. I felt a low thrill of victory, to think I'd dispersed my tangible wealth in a single stroke, like a millionaire trying to get into heaven. Daniel I couldn't bear to think about too closely—getting on that plane with heavy heart, his losses too numerous to count. I'd had the best of it surely, his presence here a burst of unexpected light. And the memory would be enough, because I still had Gray.

"That guy downstairs," he said sleepily. "I know him."

"Who? With the tape recorder?" Potato-face.

He nodded, his chin brushing my hair. "Yeah, been around for years. He's the one keeps the files on all the artists. I'm sure he's checked out Miss Jesus."

I bristled at this information, not having previously considered any interface between my brother's mess of problems and my own small conspiracy to bring the nation down. Loathing Christian Amerika so, hawking lungers at Family Values, I assumed I was on any number of lists, those who'd been naming names with foaming regularity all the way back to McCarthy. I couldn't place Potato-face myself, that sift of dandruff like epaulets on the shoulders of his aloha shirt, but I knew the type. What put me in a huff was that they couldn't come up with anyone better for Brian, the gaudiness of whose crimes deserved a triple-A agent, not some fourth-rate local cheese. And besides, how would Brian get the right protection from this jerk?

Maybe they didn't want to protect him very much.

Prickly now with paranoia, I lay there brooding as Gray dozed off in my arms. Poor guy, he'd probably logged no more than a few hours on that cot. Let him make up for it now, I thought, slipping out of his arms and pulling the quilt over him. Nurse Tom was more than glad to take care of the pair of them, my lover and my brother. Restlessly I moved to make my rounds, padding out into the hall again, soundless in my stocking feet.

"What did the senator say to you?" asked the agent, as I leaned my elbows on the banister.

"He didn't *say* anything. He was too busy pawing the cash."

"This isn't enough," sneered Potato-face. "If you want to bring a senator down, you gotta wear a wire."

"I don't give a shit if he comes down," retorted Brian, matching him sneer for sneer. "He can shoot his scum all the way to the White House, for all I care. I just want to bring down Curran."

"Yeah, well he says this whole interstate thing is you, not him. And I still haven't heard a fuckin' thing to contradict him."

Brian slammed the table. "He set me up, asshole."

"Confer with my client," Nigrelli piped in, smoothly declaring a recess.

I heard the screech of chairs shoving away from the table, and turned on a dime and retreated to Foo's room, in case somebody came up to take a leak. I burrowed beneath the quilt, ready now to hibernate in the curve of my sleeping friend, and feeling a good deal better about my brother, just hearing him seethe. Revenge—now there was a good place to go with the scalding emptiness over losing your kid. And there was something especially satisfying to me, hearing him ring down curses on the serial bully of Chester. It proved their long blood brotherhood was a hollow sham, convenient as the girls they'd fucked, or the priests who absolved their every sin because they were All-State quarterback and center.

Oh yes—piss on Jerry Curran please, and may he rot in Danbury Prison till the Irish give up whiskey.

We slept. Not very deep, no nightmares, though a certain amount of twitching and grappling, like dogs dreaming of chasing rabbits. I woke first, but what followed was all Gray's fault, for he was the one with the raging hard-on, throbbing against his zipper.

I had it out before he knew, my mouth already engulfing it as he came awake laughing.

"Wait—wait—" he protested, cradling my head and calling for time out.

But I had the ball as it were, and would not yield. Three deep swallows and I had him. He groaned, lifting his hips to meet me, his hands gripping my head like a basketball. I wanted it fast, picking up right where we left off in the cave. I needed the bond to be physical, to gorge on him, if that pinprick above my coccyx was ever going to stop feeling like the first kiss of dying. I growled and sucked, holding his ballsack tight in my fist. He loved it. But I also knew he was afraid to pump me back, to really fuck my head, because maybe my brain was tender.

"Wait—wait—" he pleaded, dragging me off him. We held each other's eyes. "I don't want to come in your mouth."

"I'll spit it out. I want it."

Not taking no for an answer. And no time please for one of those weird negotiations as to how safe safe was. I was already back on the case, consuming in the flesh what the heart so feared to lose, this pitch of being one. If Gray still had his reservations he kept them to himself. Besides, his dick had its own agenda now. I rode him hard, my throat wide open, pushing my face in the thick of his hair. He gripped my shoulders as he arched again, gasping a last wordless protest.

One thing I knew with every swallow: nobody sucked like this in the grave.

When he reached the top, I felt it a moment before, as his gasping broke to a low wail. The shot burst in my mouth with a soundless roar, tide from an inland sea. The first taste I'd had in years, so sweet I would've sobbed if my throat hadn't been so full. It kept on spilling, gout after gout, thick as a man's half his age. Then a moment of absolute stillness, my mouth consuming him whole, his back still arched like a pole vaulter. As if we'd agreed to freeze the moment and memorize it, even if there was no film in the camera.

Then he let go, his hips falling back on the mattress. I drew my mouth away, smiling up at him wickedly, my cheeks swollen with seawater. He shook his head on the pillow, irony warring with disbelief. Then sternly, jerking a thumb at the bathroom: "Now."

So WASP—they love to get things cleaned up. I rose from the

bed and turned tail, sashaying across the room, Miss Jesus at her tawdriest. In the bathroom I leaned above the sink and let it go, not spitting so much as drooling, savoring like a smutty connoisseur. Then grinned at myself in the mirror: *Nasty boy.*

Dutifully I ran the tap and took a belt of Scope, gargling and washing out. As I lifted the towel from the hook behind the door, I noticed the plastic bracelet on my wrist: *Shaheen, 509.* Swiftly I rooted in my toilet bag for the tiny scissors I used to clip my nose hairs. In a trice I was free of the last shackle of Brentwood Pres, dropping it in the wastebasket with a sneer of distaste, like a used rubber.

I poked my head around the door and grinned at my man. He was all zipped up, arms behind his head and looking very lazy. I affected a Lana Turner smolder. "Can we play doctor every day? 'Cause I really like the medicine part."

His chin jutted out, prepared to reply in kind. Then Nigrelli's voice drifted up from below: "Excuse me—can I help you?" It sounded as if he was just under the balcony, right outside the dining room.

"I don't believe so," replied a reedy voice, even older than the Magna Charta. "After all, this is my house."

Foo. Gray leaped off the bed and dived for the balcony. I pattered after, vastly amused already. "Auntie, what're you doing out of bed?" her nephew called accusingly.

"It's Palm Sunday," came the answer, as haughty as it was non sequitur. And when I appeared at Gray's side, she turned on the chaise where she was lounging and clucked at Merle. "Now I ask you, does this boy look like he's in the hospital?"

Merle stood mute as a tree. Gray said, "Don't come in, we'll be right down."

"Good. We can all have a bullshot."

We pivoted and headed in. Gray hitched the front of his pants, readjusting his dick so it didn't bulge quite so postcoitally. "Like children, the two of them," he grumbled sourly. "Can't stand it that they might miss something." Not amused at all.

As we came out into the stair hall, we could hear Brian's litany droning on. "Thirty grand a month to the *state* highway commissioner, seventy grand to the fed."

"You're talking 'eighty-five through 'eighty-eight?" We were already coming down the stairs, but Potato-face was on too much of a roll to rein himself in. "Mr. Shaheen," he pounced triumphantly, "that office had three different commissioners in the time you're talkin'—two Republicans and a Democrat. You saying you had 'em *all* on the take?"

"Uh-huh," replied Brian, heavy with boredom. "I got a better idea. Why don't you find me one who isn't." He shot me and Gray an antic look, full of bloody Irish. This was more like the Brian I remembered from the ballfield—untouchable, utterly cocksure, *Get outa my way.*

They stopped to let us pass, the agent's eyes following us, Nigrelli mauling through his briefcase. Gray trotted ahead of me, darting across the parlor and out to the terrace, so I heard Potato-face pick up the ball. "Brian, we got sixty million bucks unaccounted for, and you say it's kickbacks. You got allegations all over the friggin' map. What I want to know is, where's *your* stash?"

"Fuck you, turkey," retorted Brian, and then I was out the door and missed Nigrelli's next juridical move.

Gray was sitting at the foot of his aunt's chaise, the lady dressed in a Sunday purple suit, and a black hat with a veil that was getting a bit Miss Havisham around the edges. "No," Gray was saying, "you don't have time for a bullshot first. Tom's got to rest."

She threw out an arm to gather me in, and I crouched and gave her a careful hug, touching the rippled satin of her cheek with mine. "How's your head?" she asked, peering behind my ears as if I might have a chunk missing.

"It's fine, Foo. I'm fine."

"He just needs quiet," Gray persisted. "And no visitors. Next week you can come and have lunch."

She peered at him now, her goggle eyes brimming with self-possession. "And who was *that?*" she asked, one hand pointing vaguely toward the house. "Another artist in residence? A painter of the Picasso school, perhaps."

"No, he's just a lawyer. I'm sorry he was rude to you, Auntie. He's from Beverly Hills."

The old lady took this in with imperial indifference. On the table beside her were two cans of beef broth. Merle was nowhere to be seen, which was more nervewracking than usual. I had a vision of him skulking about like a Malibu shaman and getting blown away by one of the agents. Foo looked back and forth between us, very parental all of a sudden. "His *brother's* lawyer, you mean," she replied, with the deepest satisfaction.

So she knew. Gray passed a weary hand across his eyes, indicating it wasn't he who'd spilled my brother's hideout. Foo's goggle eyes were fixed on me, triumphant. I shrugged.

"Mona told me," she explained, "because I told *her* I'm an old dustrag nobody ever listens to, so who would I tell? I knew something was going on down here, because this one got very queer." She pointed at her nephew, then winked at me. "Something besides the two of you, I mean. *That's* been as plain as the Baldwin nose on his face since the day you moved in here."

"Okay, Miss Marple," drawled her nephew, "so you got it all figured. But this isn't the cocktail hour. The FBI's in there, and they don't like surprises."

"Exactly why I came," she declared, even if the logic was lost on us. "What if they tried to arrest you boys? I thought you might need me." When Gray looked at her blankly, almost stupefied, she added, "After all, Graham, I am the head of the family. And I believe the Baldwin name still has a certain influence, even in Washington."

"Yeah, with President Harding," came the retort. He patted her hand, which she must have found insufferably patronizing. "Foo honey, don't call us, we'll call you. Now where the hell did Merle go?" Abruptly he jumped to his feet and headed around the side of the house.

Foo turned her full attention to me, one hand cupping the back of my head, the way a healer might have touched it, except she was so secular and powerless. "I just wanted to see you."

"I'm fine."

"How was the hospital?" I squinched my face with distaste, the way Daniel had about Minneapolis. "I've never even been in one, except to visit." It was Foo's turn to squinch, as if there was something obscene about this bald fact. Still that ache of injustice, that she should be home free while the castles of pain were full to bursting.

"At least I fell in love," I said—then bit my tongue, in case she thought I meant to one-up her century of spinsterhood.

But she countered instantly: "Indeed! And what about him? Fifty years he walks around with that moony look on him, like he's lost his best friend. Wasn't my place. All I'd say every now and then was, 'Don't you ever get sick of art?' " The last word came out sharp as the crack of a rifle, and we both laughed. "Now he walks on air and forgets to tie his sneakers. First time he's ever been a little boy."

She beamed at me, the palimpsest of her face aglow with vicarious pleasure. I looked away, suddenly embarrassed. "Yes but—it's not going to last."

"Let me tell you something, Tom. Lasting's the least of it. Lasting is all I've done for fifteen years." She puffed out her lips with contempt, making a sound like *pish*. She looked out at the water, whose shifting sapphire had been hers longer than anybody's. "Not that I don't have nice *days*, mind you," she added judiciously. And I realized it was just what I'd said to Daniel, the same provisional wisdom. Happy was for birthdays.

Her eyes were on the horizon, dancing on the peaks of Catalina. "I've seen too much," said Foo, which coming from her just then seemed the opposite of a cliché. Then she looked at me again, exquisitely calm in her lounging posture, ancient but not old. "So, if you can walk on air and be boys for a while . . . well, that's the secret, isn't it?"

"Come on, Auntie, let's go," called Gray, and we turned to see him and Merle striding down the hill from the sycamore grove. "I'll follow you guys to the ranch and make you a nice cup of bouillon."

"Bullshot," replied the lady succinctly, in a tone that brooked no contradiction.

He grinned at her defiance and turned to me. "Everything falls apart when Gray's away. Merle says the furnace is acting ornery, and two of the horses are missing. Besides, I need clean clothes and—" He gave a helpless shrug, too many bases to cover.

"I'll be fine." I kissed him square on the mouth, right in front of his closest kin, and he didn't bat an eye. Merle had already stooped and gathered Foo in his arms. Gray and I walked behind as far as the pergola, lingering a moment. I called good-bye to Foo, who waved gallantly over the Indian's shoulder.

Gray poked a finger at my chest, touching it right above the heart. "But I mean it, you go rest. I'll be back tonight."

"Yessir." I didn't mind being left alone. I was glad he felt free to go take care of his stuff, and distinctly didn't wish to be constantly watched, in case I fell over in my soup. He trotted after the others, frisky as a boy, just like she said. And I had to admit, for all that I loved him, a little frisson of relief. We didn't need every minute together, no matter how loud the clock ticked.

I ducked through the french doors into the parlor, eager to get back to the brawl of my brother's testimony. Right off I saw the dining room was empty, but figured they must be getting coffee. Then, coming up to the table itself, I saw it was stripped bare—tape equipment gone, as well as the ponyskin briefcase. I reeled for a second, horrified they'd already barreled him out of there. No, he never would've let them—unless they tricked him. Maybe the only way to exile a man was to rip him away with no good-byes.

I raced for the stairs, and my head went into another hammer-lock, doubling me over. I held my skull and counted ten, but the jolt of pain only made me more frantic. I stumbled up, a step at a time, cursing the spinal. When I reached the top, my cranium still shooting stars like a planetarium on acid, I staggered around the stairwell. Reached for the door to Cora's room, prepared to scream if my brother was gone. Then I turned my head sharp, for the very wail that was struggling to break from me was coming out of the tower.

I lurched that way, fingers pressed to my temples as if I were moving by telepathy, through the doorway arch and up into light. Brian was perched on the narrow bed, hands hanging heavy between his knees, a broken player benched for the season. The sound he made was more of a moan than tears, a sort of toneless keening. But the moment he saw me, that all changed. It was like he'd been waiting.

"Tommy," he pleaded, and though he was drowning in anguish, I could hear the same relief in him that I'd felt a moment since, when Gray left. I went and sat beside him, just as the flood broke. He seized me to him the way he seized Daniel the day of the rain. His torso shook with the sobbing, quaking like I did as I crawled up out of the grave of my stroke. I thought with a certain dark pride how much better he was at crying than the first time.

But that was my last objective thought, for then the mirror of his grief broke in me, a thousand pieces. I'd lied out there on the terrace, over and over: I wasn't fine at all. Until I came to this solitary room with Brian, I couldn't begin to let it out. And so we fell apart, clinging to each other in that sunstruck place, weeping our different sorrows, though the passion was equally matched. He was a wrestler, and I was a diver.

This outcry of ours—so much lost, so much yet to be taken—was something a man could only raise with his own blood. Beyond what the fathers couldn't tell us, beyond desire, we made a common noise at last, high above the blank indifferent sea. Brian would leave, and I would die—all of this would happen. This crying in each other's arms was something we'd won the right to, by reason of pain and fear of time. We wept to be men—my brother the same as I, and I the same as my brother.

N I N E

WE ARE SPRAWLED ON A PAIR OF LOUNGE CHAIRS ON
the terrace, Brian and I, soaking up the last gold
burnish of the sinking sun. The bluff is windless,
no trace of the storm except the swooning smell of
green rising off the lawn. I'm turned on my side
with drowsing eyes, my cheek cupped in the hollow of my hand.
I study my brother a few feet away. His shirtless torso glistens with
a fine film of sweat, like an athlete oiled for an ancient game in a
stadium. His red hair flames in the naked light. He's drinking a
green bottle of beer, three empties on the grass beside the chaise.

I can't be certain how drunk he is, if at all, but he stares
unblinking into the west, mesmerized by the phosphorous sheen of
the sun on the water. Anyone else would surely be blinded by
now. Brian endures the dazzle, a test of wills between him and the
powers of the air. Yet it's myself who's most in danger here. For
the sun knocks out my T-cells with withering precision, nuzzling
my checkered flesh with kisses of melanoma. Robison has long
insisted on a sunblock of SP-30 or better and shrouds of clothing
besides, so vulnerable am I to the glare of day. But here I lie
regardless, naked to the waist and aping my brother, caution flung
to the winds.

I don't know how long we wept, clinging in the tower, but it felt
like hours. First and last of course I cried about AIDS, and the
cheating of all our lives. Then for Daniel and his exile, this part
standing in for me and the childhood I never stop mourning. But
somewhere in there, my face buried against my brother's neck, I
sobbed for the lost promise of West Hill Road—the four of us
trapped without a clue, the prison of our common blood. Even a
tear for my father, his dead heart and his strangled fury, no
self-knowledge from cradle to grave. It wasn't the same as forgive-

ness, but for once I pitied him. And just to hate him a little less was like having a knife pulled out.

The tears were wordless start to finish, more exact than words. When at last it began to abate, the two of us gasping to breathe again, we pulled away from our brothers' embrace. Yet there was no fear or shame in our touching anymore. We lingered on Daniel's narrow bed, cross-legged like a pair of kids on a raft, and recovered our equilibrium, knees grazing. The last wall of our alienhood, men from opposite planets, had tumbled down with the knowledge that we were both equally robbed. As for being shit on by life, it was something of a draw.

Thus the whole long battle between us—gay against straight, the surly pride and xenophobic curses—yielded at last to a treaty. We might have been two old men who couldn't even remember the country below the waist, except for a dull ache in the prostate. Our dicks were the least of it now.

So it isn't with any desire that I gaze across at him sleepily, drinking his beer. It's this brotherly feeling, all the dots connected, and I'm basking in it. I understand that Gray has made it possible, by overturning the hitherto immutable law of my separateness. Part of my languid mood is being out of the hospital, the relief of we-can't-find-anything having caught up with me and left me in a heap. Yet I'm bound by a most peculiar secret at the moment, something I dare not share with Brian.

Being happy.

My blubbering grief in the tower was real enough, but it's over. Brian's isn't. Perhaps because I've been miserable so much longer than he has, and now with the other shoe of my sickness always waiting to drop—time enough for all of that again tomorrow. But if the rest of the day is what I've got with my brother, I'm damned if I'll throw it away wishing it were more. This is without a doubt the most half-full the cup has ever looked to me. Maybe it's the dementia starting, turning me maudlin as an Irish tenor. At this rate I may go out grinning like Donna Reed myself.

"She's not a real nun, is she?" Brian asks abruptly. Not a word has passed between us since the first beer.

"Ex," I reply succinctly.

"I thought she seemed too smart," he says with a grunt of satisfaction. Not drunk, but definitely a small buzz. As far as I know he has never taken after our father in that regard, but the drunk gene is in both of us, an incubus of riot. "Who still buys all that crap anyway?"

The question hangs rhetorical. It takes me several seconds before I realize he's talking about Catholics. "Your wife, for one," I answer carefully, eliciting from Brian an even harsher grunt. "And pardon me, but aren't you a Prince of the Church yourself?"

He laughs. "That's just good PR, Tommy. Worked with the brothers at Saint Augie's. Works just fine in Hartford—where you still got a lotta micks in the legislature."

I'm bolt awake now, the muzziness shocked out of me like a plunge in the winter surf. "You mean—you don't believe—" I can't even think how to ask it, the territory is so vast. The virgin birth? The miracles? The nuns in grammar school hammering at us day after day that all non-Catholics would burn in hell? What had been the last straw for him?

He turns to face me, his eyes unsullied as an Eagle Scout's. "I believe in God, Tommy. I just don't believe in churches."

I nod dumbly. "We thought you were going to become a priest," I observe. Meaning my mother, who used to browbeat me with the specter of Brian's purity. I think she'd decided my father wouldn't be beating me senseless all the time if I was as lily-white as my brother.

Brian's still laughing. "Soon as I discovered my dick, I knew the priests and I were playing different sports," he declares, this man who used to cop the piety Oscar at Saint Augustine's, year after year. "But hey, I'm a born con man. I knew how to push their buttons and win for Jesus."

My turn to crack up. "Oh, you have no idea. The Brothers would swoon with desire when you were in uniform." Brian lifts his eyebrows in mild surprise, and I wonder how naïve he can possibly be about all of this. "The monsignor must've needed a fan in the booth, for all those steamy confessions. Every Brother in the order burning to sit on Brian Shaheen's pole!"

"I doubt that," he scoffs dryly, tipping the bottle and draining the last of the beer. He lobs the bottle beside the others in the grass. "I swear, you think everyone's gay."

"Not you," I correct him swiftly, matter-of-fact and without a second thought. "But didn't you ever think you might be cockteasing those coaches of yours? Not consciously, but how could you miss the way they looked at you? All sweaty in their collars and chanting rosaries in the locker room." I'm starting to sound a little lawyerly, though I try to keep it light and teasing. I grip the arm of the lounge chair like a trapeze as I lean toward him expectantly.

Finally he shrugs, with a slight flush of something like embarrassment in his cheeks. "I guess a little," he drawls in reply.

Point won. I shiver with impatience, a thousand more questions to ask. The most intense discussion of high theology I've had since catechism class. "Brian, if I'd had your looks and your pitching arm, I would've whipped those priest queens up to a frenzy. But then I'm a shameless exhibitionist. And not one of 'em ever made a pass?"

Brian stretches an arm above his head, rolling the shoulder in the socket, always in training to pitch his lightning curve. His forehead crinkles with concentration. "Well, maybe a couple of times they'd massage a muscle a little too long. And Father Dan—JV hoop—was always wanting to check us for hernias. 'Not a job for the school nurse, men.' " The gelatinous brogue is pitch-perfect.

"Ick," I remark with distaste, imagining the bald and leering priest, round as a basketball himself, juggling the boys' gonads while they coughed. "No wonder straight guys get so creeped. Thank you once again, dear Lord, for the blessings of the closet."

"Mm," he murmurs, his mind somewhere else.

It's beyond ironic, to think I became such a bloody anti-Catholic, pugnacious to the point of unemployability, and all because my brother was an Irish saint. Now it turns out he's as damned as I am. I draw my knees up, hugging them with my arms, exhilarated by this whole exchange. Feel like a boy again, or perhaps for the first time, never having connected before to the give-and-take of buddies. No more hours in the hayloft reading.

Now that I have the opening, I want to know what it was like to grow up as a god. But before I can formulate the question, I hear him whisper beside me. I turn with a questioning look, and his eyes fall to the ground as he repeats himself. "What about us?"

I blink, smiling hopefully. "What *about* us?"

He pauses the length of a held breath, like a kid passing a graveyard. We lock eyes. "The fooling around."

I can feel the burn in my cheeks. Then I lift my shoulders in a deep shrug, except it comes across more like a squirm. My lips are pressed tightly together, not the easiest way to talk unless you're planning a career in ventriloquism.

Brian leans his torso forward off the chaise, his back making a sucking sound as it comes away from the plastic pad. "Tommy? You know what I'm talking about, don't you?" His voice is tense with apprehension, as if he fears to be left all alone with it, that my stroke has erased the memory.

"Sure," I mumble at last. But I have to swallow a snarl of petulant rage, furious that he's brought it up.

"I don't know if I made you do it, or if it was your idea."

My shoulders haven't dropped from the previous shrug. "Little of both," I say. "It doesn't matter." But his anxious eyes don't leave my face, searching for psychic scars, till it forces me to answer the question direct. "Don't worry, I wanted it."

The "it" we are trying to talk about is the spring of his junior year, after Janice Mulroney gave up Brian's dick for Lent and came back from an Easter retreat sporting Norman Spires's class ring. She was instantly branded a two-bit whore by Brian's crowd, but meanwhile the league's star pitcher was left high and dry at the top of the season. So many vast forces at work cannot help but lead to strange bedfellows.

"I knew that," Brian says gravely, hunched on the edge of the chaise, combing a nervous hand through his hair. "I knew I could use you. It was all because I was pissed at this girl . . ."

"Janice Mulroney," I pipe in helpfully, always a whiz at the tawdry details. "Look, Brian, it's no big deal. Please—it was practically the only action I had between twelve and twenty."

Brian stares at his hands. He's not in sync with my flippant tone, still groping his way in the dark. What are we talking about here? Maybe twenty-five blow jobs between March and June, figure twice a week, and always the Friday night before the league game. After lights out, though we could still hear the old man downstairs clinking among the Seagram's bottles. The first time admittedly had been a little rough, Brian pinning me, shoving my head and slamming in till I gagged. But after that—well, I thought I took to pleasuring with quickening expertise.

Yet it's true, the whole scene would always pass in utter wordless silence, only the barest grunt as he exploded in my throat. And never a hint the next day that anything whatsoever had transpired. Secret as a dream, like Cupid visiting Psyche as she slept.

"I'd be crazy for it," Brian says now, "and then afterward I'd hate myself. And then I'd hate you."

I cluck my tongue. "So Catholic."

"But don't you see," he continues earnestly. "It made us stop being brothers."

I guess. The whole thing ceased without warning, the night before the league playoffs. Next day Brian was carried off the field on the shoulders of his team, a roar of cheering that shook the whole Connecticut Valley. The party went on for two days, the rowdy micks of Chester setting fires in a thousand trash barrels. And Brian the hero ended up scoring with the next awestruck girl of his dreams, Ann Waits with the thirty-six knockers. End of Cupid and Psyche.

"Ace, it doesn't matter," I repeat gently, reaching to pat his arm. "I needed to go it alone after that. It wasn't just you I was different from. It was *everybody*." My beaming face brims with reassurance, but my brother's downcast eyes are full of fret and melancholy still, for he can't let go of the mess we left a millennium ago. "Besides, there's a whole lot worse initiations than sucking your brother's baseball bat. Take my word for it. We're not going to hell for *that*."

He looks down at my hand on his arm, then covers it with his own, prodding my fingers apart till we are intertwined. This is altogether more intimate than sucking his dick ever was—or anyone else's, come to think, till the last few days with Gray. When he lifts his eyes they are shot through with glints of a heartbroken tenderness. It's the aftermath of losing Daniel, though I'm more aware of this than he is. For Brian the guilt over me and his son is seamless, sins of pride, and he still believes in a God that punishes, church or no.

Yet even now he smiles, trying to catch my playful tone—always a natural, no matter what game. "Not even purgatory?"

"Piece o' cake," I scoff with a crooked grin. "Didn't you hear, they finally put in a golf course there? All those novenas have paid off. The Percodan flows like honey. It's the afterlife version of Orange County."

My brother, hardly hearing, is looking at me with an almost frightening intensity, as if he is trying to memorize my face. I can see the guilt leave his eyes like a pool clearing. Whatever he has been carrying all these years releases its grip on his heart. When he speaks there's a tremolo in his voice, an operatic whisper. "I was always afraid to love you," he says, then bends his head and tenderly kisses the back of my hand, gallant as an Arthurian knight.

I wait for him to cry again, but he doesn't. He squeezes my hand and turns his head and gazes out to sea. I'm not used to straight people's feelings, or the curious tableaux they strike when they've finished dancing. But I sit there holding hands with my brother, watching the sun as it narrows toward the horizon. Because it's his last window of quiet before he hits the road, I let him make all the choices how we spend the time. Doing nothing is fine by me.

As for the lurching revelations just concluded, I suspect that our having it out has settled the issue for good in Brian's head. It's the cleansing of confession, beyond Dear Abby and Dr. Toni, more like the old Catholic way than Brian would freely admit. He thinks he's an *ex*-Catholic, but it's a pretty soft lapse if you ask me.

In any case, if he's feeling released from his ancient violation of me, then I'm the one he should thank. He doesn't suspect that the whole exchange—my sunny absolution, putting the past to bed, as it were—has all been a sort of performance piece. That I've swallowed a mountain of phlegm in order to whistle this cheery air. Even a month ago, what Brian so shyly calls our "fooling around" had been the stuff of railing and mad revenge.

I was raped by my brother, I'd announce to anyone who'd listen—potential boyfriends who found me skittish, twelve-steppers from here to Santa Barbara. My life was my brother's fault. And the incest survivors in the folding chairs, the sexual compulsives gripping their styro coffee mugs to keep their hands out of their pants, would nod in lonely sympathy, cursed as much as I.

So Brian has no idea how lucky he is, to have brought it up now, a week to the day Gray and I fell in love. For I don't care anymore what a hypocrite he used to be, sneering fag jokes with Jerry Curran, and my spit barely dry on his knob. Or the raging denial later, once I showed a little *cojones* of my own and came out to the old man. Brian's strutting outrage, louder even than Dad's, always had for me a certain secret satisfaction. Because he could never look me quite in the eye, knowing I knew he'd had a little taste himself. Once I was all the way out, the small part of me unconsumed by self-pity clung to a sick superiority over Brian—as if I'd raped *him*. Wherever I went, pursued by his contempt, I always carried the trump card of our secret tryst, like a diamond sewn in a cuff. Oh yes, he's luckier than he knows.

"I think I'll go down for a swim," he says softly, gazing without a flinch into the sun's fire.

"I wouldn't, not after a storm like that. Too rough. And *cold.*"

He laughs at my auntie's caution, but squeezes my hand in a comradely way. "Sorry, pal, but they dropped a couple of hints today that my ass is gonna get parked in Oklahoma. Might be the last time I ever get this close to water again."

With that he releases my hand and rises, blocking the sun for a moment as he rolls his shoulders. Then he kicks off his Nikes, one after the other, and strides across the lawn in just his faded jeans, making for the beach stairs. Irrationally I feel abandoned, plus a goose of the old inadequacy, never once picked to be on the team. I can't help it: my brother's throbbing good health mocks me in my frailty, even though I love him now. Always, always the same blind projection—a picture of life in which I am a blur, endlessly turning away. The camera doesn't want me—just Brian.

Then he pivots on the top step and cocks his head. "Want to come?"

What spinal tap? I am up and trotting in one propulsive rush, keeping my eyes on the grass because the sun is directly in front of me, and I mustn't get dizzy. So casual is the moment for my brother that he's already clumping down the stairs. I'm glad to reach the railing, for it steadies me, and down is easy anyway. There actually isn't any pain right now, neither my head nor the base of my spine, though I do wonder with a certain detached perplexity how I will make it up again.

As we round the landings Brian is just at the next turn, a flash of him disappearing as I follow. Below us, nearer and nearer, I see the white seethe of the surf bordering the dark emerald of the ocean. The sound grows more particular, the susurrus of the churning gravel. Downhill isn't all easy, requiring a certain steadiness in motion to keep me from pitching headlong. I stop at the final, fresh-built landing and prop my elbows heavily on the banister. Brian darts out below me onto the sand.

He halts at the brink of the foam, a wave's last clawing reach along the strand. The next instant it withdraws again, the undertow rattling the bed of stones as the next wave crests and smashes. From my vantage I can see the clog of litter that the storm tide carries, the labyrinth of kelp below and a strew of driftwood bobbing the surface.

"Don't go in!" I shout down to him.

But he's as contrary as I am, and my warning is like a trigger. Already he's yanking his pants down, then hopping from foot to foot as he pulls his legs free. I can't stop him. He tosses the jeans behind him onto the sand, then prances butt-naked into the swirling shallows. He whoops at the sting of the cold and flashes a grin at me over his shoulder, pantomiming a chatter of teeth. Then he lunges forward and dives, pitching into the green wall of the next wave.

I clamber down the last flight, stumbling onto the sand as he breaches the surface twenty feet out. Behind him at the horizon, the sun has dipped its toe in the water, sheeting the whole ocean with hammered gold. Brian waves, another whoop, then pushes what looks like a timber out of his way. The sea is a shipwreck around him. Meanwhile my first wobbling steps on the beach send a stab sharp as an ice pick to the bottom of my spine, on account of the uneven ground. I wave back at my brother, beckoning him in.

He laughs and dives under again, and suddenly I'm pounding with fear. It's as if he's flung open that door in the dream and tumbled out into blackness. I call his name, uselessly, the words drowning in the roar of surf. I skitter to the water's edge, grimacing from the darts of pain between the vertebrae.

Once more Brian explodes to the surface, seeming to dive up into the ball of the sun, mercurial as a dolphin. Then he wrestles a loop of kelp from one arm, twisting free. He's facing the shore again, his features frozen in stunned delight. He knows he's in over his head, barely holding his own against the furies, and he loves it.

"Aren't you coming in?" he bawls at me, treading the current. "It's great!" He sucks in a mouthful of seawater and lifts his head and spouts it out.

I can't even look, the sun is so bright behind him. I imagine I am cowering, helplessly rubbing my hands together, enduring the panic and praying for it to be over, whatever praying is. It takes a few moments before I hear an unearthly wail, more piercing than any gull's cry—then another moment before I understand that the sound is coming from me. A scream without beginning or end, except I know it will empty me out, like a last gout of arterial blood.

I don't see the jolt of fear in Brian's face, as he realizes his brother has cracked. All I know is, he's suddenly pumping for shore, grappling through the wrack and the pitiless current, pounding home with a butterfly stroke. My siren scream dwindles to keening as I slump to my knees in the quicksand. Brian stops swimming and rises up, swaying as he takes his footing in the foaming tide. It's only up to his knees, but he has to tramp like a man on snowshoes, bucking the ferocity of the water's drag, pulling for firmer ground.

"It's okay, Tommy," he calls to me, gasping. "I'm okay."

I know. There's more relief than panic now in the wordless cry that spills from me. My open arms are pleading like a child as he splashes toward me, the next breaking wave churning about his ankles and rising up the sand till it drenches my pants. Brian looms and blocks the sun, water streaming off him and beading like pearls in his fur. Born like a sea god, he crouches to embrace me.

"I didn't mean to scare you," he murmurs, and I'm engulfed in the shocking coolness of his skin, tasting salt as my mouth grazes across his shoulder. The flat of his hand strokes up and down my spine, as if he's trying to banish a chill, and yet it's he who's shivering. I can feel the heat of my own skin absorbing the water from his. Over his shoulder I watch the sun speed up as it sinks, the optical trick that lets you watch its final throes, bleeding from yellow to red. We cling together rocking softly, and the sun goes under.

"I'm sorry—" I try to blurt out, foolish now, but Brian cuts me off abruptly by lifting me to my feet. I let out a groan, seizing my forehead, trying to deflect the hammer blow of the spinal migraine.

"Don't move," my brother commands me, taking charge.

So I stand there, fingers pressed to my temples and breathing gingerly, while he grabs his jeans from the sand and roughly pulls them on. There's a moment as he tucks his equipment in, sheathing his sword, that echoes from an ancient place, a ring of runic stones. Then he swiftly buttons the fly and hunkers before me, presenting the broad beam of his shoulders.

"Get on."

No point in protesting. Right now I don't even think I could reach the stairs on my own steam. So I swing my knee across his back and clamber on, locking my hands about his neck. He doesn't even grunt as he rises, tough as a camel. His arms clamp tight around my thighs. "You okay?"

"Fine," I assure him curtly, stopping myself from apologizing again. He moves in a lumbering crouch across the sand, somehow without any jostle, as if he knows how to use his powerful legs as shock absorbers. My face keeps nodding against his wet hair. I'm trying to be as light a burden as I can, my hands away from his throat so I won't choke him.

Slowly he mounts the first step, testing the balance and shifting the load more securely onto his hips. And then we seem to glide the ten steps up to the first landing, effortlessly, though that is how Brian always makes it look on any field. He pauses once again to adjust my weight, breathing heavier now. His body's too cool to break a sweat.

We ascend the next flight more slowly as Brian paces himself, though it's clear he's enjoying the physical challenge and would happily carry me all the way up Everest. I flash on him straining to bench press in the garage on West Hill Road, all through the heat of the summer, the barbell bowed by the masses of rusty weights at either end. What I wouldn't have given then to have my arms around him as he pushed his limit.

Even now, it's the closest I've ever been to him, and I don't know quite what to do with it. I'm unaccountably reticent. I ought to be making breezy jokes, or clucking that I'm too heavy. When he stops at the next landing, moving to the rail to gaze at the sunset sky, an acid clash of tangerine and lavender, I'm positioned to whisper absolutely anything into his ear. And I'm mute. But then, the very thing I'd been waiting twenty years to confront him with—the carnal spring of '70—has turned out to be a mirage. So why should I trust that I know my heart now well enough to speak it?

Perhaps he senses the strain of my silence, for he gives a sudden shrug to jog me. "How you doing?"

"Fine," I repeat with quick animation. "Do you feel like a poster for Boy's Town?"

"Nope." He glances down the beach, drinking it all in, memorizing it the way he did my face. I'm racing to double-play the Boy's Town joke, Spencer Tracy in leather, but Brian gets there first. He says: "How long do you think you've got?"

Scratch the comedy. The horse decides which way we ride. "A year," I reply uncertainly, following his gaze along the juts and runnels of the cliff face. After a moment I amend the prognosis: "Not two."

He nods almost imperceptibly, then moves to go up the next flight. How many times this winter have I been up and down these stairs, testing the strength I have left but never quite asking the question point-blank? A year is actually fairly optimistic, but not compared to saying nothing at all. I've been operating for some time now, at least since coming to the beach, in a zone of deliberate gray with regard to lifespan. Almost a sense of indelicacy, as if it would be bad luck and bad manners both to pin myself to a time frame. But having said it now, chiseling it in the sunset air, I feel a sudden rush of irrational merriment. As if I have dared the furies as deeply as my brother did, rollicking in the storm-tossed sea.

We don't stop at the landing but head on up, biting off another ten steps. I can hear the grit of my brother's teeth as he pushes against the envelope of his strength. He almost staggers as he gains the midway platform. I long to offer a break, dismounting so he can recover, but I know better. He wants it as tough as this—a small Olympic event in which he is the only player. In the space of forty steps he has raised it to a mythic test, half to do with the athlete he used to be and half to bear his losses.

Again he lingers at the railing, staring out over the cobalt blue. I feel the most extraordinary balance, that he should be carrying me and I embracing him. There's a kind of perfection in this, a meeting of powers like the confluence of rivers. It's my turn to say the hard thing. "I promise, I won't waste a minute of it," I declare in a low voice close to his ear. "But I don't think we'll be seeing each other again."

The same barely perceptible nod, to sundown as much as to me. "I know."

The coolness has left his skin. My chest against his back is hot, a slick of sweat beginning to gather between us. When I bend to kiss his neck, I still don't know if the salt is Brian or the sea. "But hey, what do I know?" I ask with a curve of self-mockery. "I never thought I'd love *anybody*—let alone three in the same week."

His laugh is a kind of triumphal cheer, as if I have pitched a shutout. He clearly likes the company I've put him in, the short list of Gray and Daniel. "Well then, what're you complaining about?" he teases. "You've still got one left." Meaning Gray, like an ace in my pocket.

I slip my arms closer around his neck, a hug that holds no fear of choking. "I'm not complaining."

Brian tilts his head and rubs his cheek against my arm. "Neither am I."

Above our heads a tern is wheeling, and he starts to crow insistently, as if we have usurped his dinner perch. To us it's like the blast of a starter's gun. Brian pivots around, unbelievably light on his feet, no consciousness of the load. He takes the next flight at a near gallop, and I am as tuned to him as a jockey now, more lift than ballast.

"Yes, ladies and gentlemen," I announce to the denizens of the cliff, the tunneling gophers and ghosts of the Malibu. "At the three-quarter mark it's Shaheen and Shaheen. Nobody else is even in sight. What form—what fucking grace!"

Not even a pause at the next turn. I can hear the heaving labor of Brian's breathing, the thump of his heartbeat under my locked hands. Two more flights to go. "You're watching it live, lentils and germs! A new world's record in the stair-carry!" My bellowing is all free-form, for what do I know about sportscasting? Lesson one: it's the bellow that counts. "Coming into the stretch! This crowd is going wild!"

Round the penultimate landing, and then just eight more steps. Brian wobbles and shakes his head, blinking the sweat from his eyes. "Go!" I command him, clenching my knees. There's a growl in his throat as he pitches ahead, every step an agony now, beyond his strength. It's the last mile of the marathon, when you don't know why anymore and your body has to will it.

I'm bellowing "Go!" over and over, driving him like a locomotive, the first time I've ever cheered my brother. For I'm the will he needs to finish, craning to watch his feet and counting down. "Three . . . two . . . Go for it, man! One more! One more!" A thousand games are over as Brian plants a foot at the top of Everest, hauling us up. We've made it.

Then I'm drumming my fists on his shoulders, shrieking, as he staggers through the cactus. At the edge of the lawn he stretches upright with a groan, releasing his grip around my thighs. I slide to the ground with an ache of regret, and Brian buckles to the grass. He's panting and laughing at once, splayed on all fours.

And I have no headache whatsoever. My brother's hetero mania for making life a contest has saved me a probable blackout. Beyond the water the sunset glow is absolutely painless, silvery pink at the rim of the world. I know it's only a matter of time before Brian recovers his breath and his equilibrium. In the meantime I take up the slack. I don't know what to give back to him for the ride, except the picture of me standing here erect, so at least he won't have to remember me sick.

After a minute he pitches over on his back with a groan of relief.

He grins up at me. Nothing further needs to be said—except good-bye, of course, but that will come later. For now it's enough that we found the time to play together, a game of our own devising. My answering grin is as giddy as his. We are home free. Here on the last day, we have finally managed this boys' thing of putting together a team.

The first time I woke up clean, without any dislocation. My eyes blinked open, and I knew right away that the rustle at the foot of the bed was Gray. I flicked a look at the clock—11:06. Gray was draping his pants over the ladderback chair, getting the creases right. That poignant WASP exactitude for keeping up appearances, pouring tea as the ship goes down—milk or lemon? My own clothes were flung in an angry heap, my enduring protest against the rules of parochial school, where a tidy desk promised a tidy life. I made no move to unbend from my fetal curl on the moonlight side of the bed, or otherwise let him know I was conscious. I wasn't sure why.

He drew back the covers with excruciating care, lowering himself beside me without a sound. Well, perhaps a small contented sigh. I could feel him just a few inches away, mimicking the S curve of my body but making no move to touch me lest he jar me awake. The first thought always for me. This man I'd been waiting to meet forever, who banished all the mismatched ghosts of my previous tilts at love. So what was I so pissed about, that I should suddenly shrink and feign slumber like a mauled bride?

Certainly not Gray's fault. If he'd known I wanted to be alone with my brother to say good-bye—if *I'd* known—he wouldn't have dreamed of intruding. In any case, it was only an hour ago that Brian checked in with Nigrelli from the Chevron and found out the agents would be by to fetch him at 7:00 A.M. We'd have to be up before the sun to fit in a glassy-eyed breakfast.

I'd been in bed myself since shortly after the sunset caper, having a proper crash. Brian had been in twice, once with a mug of soup and then to announce the revised hour of his departure. The soup was there on the nightstand, cold. But even half-comatose, I'd promised myself to be present and accounted for at dawn. I would section the grapefruit and griddle the hotcakes, returning the favor at last for those years of breakfast on West Hill Road. A private exchange between me and my brother, meaningless to an outsider.

But how was Gray to know? He came back tonight for one reason only, to make sure I was safe. Besides, all I would have to do in the morning was slip out of bed as stealthily as he slipped in. Once I'd got it choreographed in my head, I was seized with a rush of tender feeling. I rolled over into his arms, burrowing in. I could feel him grope to the surface, the fastest sleeper in the West.

"You all right?" he murmured thickly. I nodded against his chest. He was already tipping back over, his head filling with white noise. Then he snorted and cleared his throat, swiping at the cobwebs. "Don't forget," he rumbled. "Twenty-four hours. No excitement."

Yessir. Flat on my back with the drapes closed. No tap-dancing on the beach stairs. "Graham," I whispered, "you know what else? I love you."

He was more under than not by then. His assent was hardly audible. "Good," I think he said. I most assuredly didn't require a declaration in return. It went without saying now. But what he did instead was reach a hand between my legs and cup my balls. I don't even suppose it was conscious, certainly not erotic. The perfect combination, in fact, of capture and protection. *Not a job for the school nurse, men,* indeed! I was fast asleep in half a minute.

The second time I woke was quite, quite the opposite. I came roaring up out of a sea cave with my lungs on fire, pursued by something horrible. I thought I must've screamed as I broke the surface, jolting up onto my elbows, except Gray hardly stirred beside me. I was drenched, truly as if I'd been underwater. Though I couldn't recall the monster's shape, the fear had survived my breaking through the membrane of the dream. Instinctively I shrank from the sleeping figure beside me, not so much to keep him dry as to spare him the taint of my dread.

It was all very out-of-body, even for a night sweat. I knew it was Gray next to me, knew he was my lover, and yet I was nagged by a vague anxiety that I wasn't in the right room. Silently I slid out from under the covers, leaving my wet bodyprint on the sheets and pillow. I swayed in the moonlight, catching my spectral image in the mirror above the dresser. At least I wasn't a vampire. But otherwise I scarcely recognized myself: How did I get so *old?*

I took a step closer and peered at my haunted eyes. The night wind from the balcony sent a shiver up my spine, as the specter in the glass seemed to direct me by telepathy. *Go to your room.*

I thumped into the bathroom, groping a towel from behind the door. Methodically I rubbed myself dry, in the process making sure

I was all there, no fingers or toes lost to the beast. Grounding was what was required to reconnect the synapses, a sort of metaphysical version of name, rank, and serial number. PWA's who went to parochial school undoubtedly kept half-gallons of Gatorade in the medicine chest, to goose their electrolytes, but I was a lost cause in the preparedness department.

I turbaned the towel around my head and sat on the can to pee. *Like a girl*, sneered the censoring voices of Chester. No! It was only that I didn't trust my aim in the dark and didn't want to wake the rest of the house.

I looked up sharply at the door beyond the tub. A woozy grin slithered over my lips as my bladder emptied. Of course—the rest of the house. *Thomas Francis Shaheen*, said the voice in my head, *210 West Hill Road*. It surfaced now like a mantra, drummed into us by the nuns, what to say if we ever got lost. The door opposite glimmered, the crooked line of my life having come full circle at last. Right through there was my room.

I stood up from the toilet and pressed the flush. The clinging fear of the beast was gone as I padded across the tile toward the past. The mirage was total. Had I glanced in the mirror over the sink, I would surely have seen a ten-year-old. I turned the knob as carefully as the combination on a safe. Then felt a tilt of unutterable relief as the door swung wide.

For a moment I saw what I wanted to see: the jumble of baseball gear, the crossed pennants on the far wall, Notre Dame and the Yankees. The moonlight was the ally of my memory, heightening the feel of the otherworldly. In the far corner, my father's dun-green sea trunk from the Navy, used by us as a toybox now. Under the window a hamster's cage, complete with runwheel, previously home to a green snake from the Essex marsh, and before that a pair of salamanders who willfully refused to mate. Unquestionably the same place, down to the Mickey Mantle nightlight grinning from the baseboard.

I made a move toward the bed, and the dreamhouse began to falter. For obviously there should have been *two* beds, with a nightstand in between supporting a deadlocked chessboard, the game abandoned as soon as Brian realized he couldn't win. In its place Cora's oak four-poster stood its ground, mocking me. I grappled to reconfigure, blinking to change the channel back. But once you see better than you remember, the mirage is over. I wasn't home on West Hill Road at all. It was now and getting later by the second.

And Brian wasn't there.

I lunged for the bed, swirling my hands in the sheets to see if they were still warm. Barely. The agents had only just bundled him out. It was Brian's muffled cry that had rocketed me awake in Foo's room. I pitched for the door to the upstairs hall, frantic now, ready to run up Highway 1 till I caught them. No one was going to take from me my chance to say good-bye.

I grabbed the newel post and swung around the stairwell. Then I froze with a stab of relief at the sound of voices below. I was in time! Problem was, I was also stark naked. I squirmed a moment in confusion. From where I stood I couldn't tell which one of the agents was talking, or maybe it was Nigrelli. Biting the bullet, I yanked the towel from around my head and cinched it about my waist, locker-room style. The sight of me *half*-naked, scrawny and pocked with lesions, ought to rattle the agents nicely. Then they'd damn well wait in the car while Brian and I got off a final volley of brotherly feeling.

I clutched the banister with both hands and began a labored descent, working it like a performance, focused only on my shameless bid for sympathy. The surly voice of the agent stopped midsentence as I came into view. I fixed my doleful eyes on Brian, sitting in tank top and sweat pants on the sofa, barefoot. I had an instant's curiosity as to why he wasn't dressed to leave, but I was busy smiling bravely, trying to project the vast nobility of my dying wish. The footlights of the moment had me blinded.

"Well, well, well," declared the agent smugly. "If it ain't Tommy the Tattle."

I didn't react at first, except to brace myself against the banister, for the fugue state apparently wasn't finished after all. I was back in Chester, just as before, when Cora's room was the lost world. For "Tommy the Tattle" meant one thing only: the schoolyard at Saint Augustine's. A cruel misnomer, since I'd never told on anyone, but who said life wasn't cruel? I cast a puzzled frown at Brian, to see if the past had claimed him too, but his own face was oddly blanched.

I shifted my eyes to the agent standing on the hearth, his leering grin as wide as his bull neck. He made a beckoning gesture with his gun. "C'mon join us, kid," he said. "We was just talkin' old times."

"He doesn't know anything," Brian hissed.

But I hardly heard him, so loud was the ring in my ears. I floated the rest of the way down, spellbound by the beckoning gun in Jerry Curran's hand. Not afraid of him yet. Too stunned—too *fascinated*. For the tube and the *Hartford Courant* hadn't done him justice. He weighed two-fifty easy, the tire at his waist like an eighteen-wheeler, a pig Republican fatcat. The armpits of his white button-down shirt were bluish circles of sweat. Nothing remained of the brawny mick linebacker, except the sneer.

"That don't surprise me a bit," retorted Jerry with a dry laugh. "Tommy Shaheen never knew shit. Played fourth base—right, Tom?"

Question rhetorical, no reply necessary. He kept waving the gun to the left, nudging me from the foot of the stairs across to the sofa. I sidled that way till he motioned me to sit, in the opposite corner of the sofa from Brian. The gun was a sleek machine pistol, matte black.

Jerry clicked his teeth. "Brian and I was having a little disagreement about how we managed to misplace seven million bucks." On the "mis" his lips simpered with contempt, as he darted a black glare at my brother.

"I told you, Munson ate it," Brian growled in answer. Another name I hadn't heard in fifteen years. Scotty Munson: center in the fall, catcher in the spring. Sewer-mouth.

"Oh yeah, them pension funds." Jerry wedged his tongue between his teeth, and the laughter came spitting around it like an adder's venom. "I sure hope you're wrong, Bri, 'cause Munson's real dead. And he died real slow."

Brian snorted. "You were always a cheap hood, Jerry. Scum for brains."

This much hadn't changed in twenty years: it was like I wasn't there. Unless there had been some reason to tease or torture me, I was so far beneath their notice that I cast no shadow. Though I'd lately conquered my invisibility with Brian, to Jerry I was the same fag cipher I'd always been. It made for a strange detachment in me, even with the pistol in his hand, as if I was too insignificant to shoot. Stripped like this, I realized my insignificance was a kind of shield.

"This is my last stop, buddy boy," Jerry said, swagging his arms behind him along the rough-wood mantel. "Nobody knows where I am, and nobody's gonna. I'm history. And listen, it's not like I need the seven. I got a mint out there." He waved the pistol toward the ocean, as if he had a pirate ship moored in the bay, its gunwales to the water from the weight of gold. "I just don't want *you* to have it, Bri. 'Cause you tried to put me away. Your best buddy. Shit, I put your first rubber on you—with my own two hands."

He boomed with laughter at his own joke, lolling against the mantel, his outstretched arms making him look like Miss Jesus on the cross. He was ripped on some kind of downers. The thought of which finally made my blood run cold, to realize how very loose was the cannon in his hand.

"Fuck you, Jerry," snarled my brother. "So how come *my* name was on all your toilet paper? You set me up, jerk-o." He slammed a fist into the sofa arm, snapping Jerry to red-faced attention. The barrel of the pistol swung dead-on, trained on Brian's skull. My brother didn't so much as glance up, let alone stare it down. In his sullen disdain he seemed singularly unmoved by the presence of firepower. A twist of fear cramped my belly as I realized Brian would play this scene like a game of chicken.

Jerry gave an impatient shrug, and the hand with the pistol fell to his side. For the moment the score was even, as far as the hurling of accusations. Jerry flashed a gelid smile, a used car in every garage. "Gee, I was hopin' to say g'bye to Susan and Daniel." He swiveled the smile to me. "Ya know, I'm his godfather."

"How very comforting," I replied tightly.

"All right, Tommy," Brian declared, "I want you to go upstairs and stay in your room. This is between Jerry and me." The last bit was clearly a warning, as if there were still some rules of battle here, a kind of Geneva Convention that covered the blood feuds of bandits.

"Hold it, hold it," snapped the hulking grizzly in the white shirt, though I hadn't moved a muscle. "Tommy and me, we hardly had a chance to say hello."

I returned his pigface stare, not about to go anywhere. If I was moved by Brian's impulse to put me out of the line of fire, I was even more ready to stand this ground beside him. "You got fat," I offered without expression.

Jerry chortled. "I sure did, fella," he retorted with sneering merriment. "I didn't stay in training like your brother here. Mr. All-American." The hate was palpable now, a labyrinth of old grudges. "After my wife took off wit' my kids, I kinda let things go. But I guess you wouldn't know about that, bein' a fag."

"Oh, I know about letting things go." There was something wonderfully quickening, a sort of hormonal buzz, finding myself on the old field of hard feelings. Who needed electrolytes?

" 'Cept you got *skinny*," grinned my nemesis.

"Leave him alone," said Brian through his teeth.

"Hey, who's dumpin' on him? I think he looks real pretty, all skin and bones like this. Huh, Tommy?" I froze as the gun swung toward my face. I could feel my brother clench the pillows. Jerry stroked the point of the barrel under my chin. "Isn't this how they like 'em? The muscle boys fuck the girlie ones. Right, Tommy?"

"Jerry, don't—" Brian's voice was ashen, pleading in spite of himself.

"Whoa." Jerry pulled back surprised, the gun veering away. "You suddenly gettin' all soft on your baby brother? Fuck. 'Scuse me while I blow my nose."

"Let him go," whispered my brother, his windpipe choked with rage.

"I got a better idea," retorted Jerry, practically purring now. The pistol lifted again, and he held it against the center of my forehead. "I think you were just about to tell me where that money is. Am I right?"

Talk about chicken. I must've been on an adrenaline high. Plus, a gun at your head turns out to be a fabulous tool for gauging how little you've got to lose. "I'm dying anyway, it doesn't matter," I observed with impeccable sang-froid. "Just tell the Hemlock guys I caught an earlier flight."

I felt the pressure of the barrel lift as his eyes darted from Brian to me. He gave me a second's blank stare, then shifted to the pale violet bull's-eye on my cheek. The gun still pointed, ready to blow my brains out, but now his nervous eyes were everywhere. The lesion on my shoulder, the one by my left nipple, the double one on my thigh. I watched it dawn on Jerry the same as it dawned on Susan a week ago, a kind of claustrophobic terror. He swayed a step backward.

"Don't worry, I won't sneeze on you," I declared, but not even trying to conceal the exhilaration of having shocked him. "Though if you're planning to use that"—I nodded toward the gun, a foot away now and trembling slightly—"I can't swear I won't *bleed*. I don't suppose you brought a rubber suit."

His eyes still raked me, inch by horrible inch. I could've told him there were eight altogether, plus two lumps between my toes, as yet not showing any color. Blooming, Robison called it. But I wasn't feeling especially leprous, despite the appalled intensity of Jerry's gaze. No, the opposite: I was charged with a drunken thrill of power, because I had just upturned the chessboard.

Jerry's sluglike torso rippled with an involuntary shiver. He grunted and shook his head. "Tough break, Tommy," he mumbled, eyes on the floor, almost sheepish.

There followed a queer embarrassed silence, awkward as a baby's wake. Or any occasion where men took off their hats in the presence of great sorrow, a last vestigial link of Irish brotherhood. I strained to hold my stoop-shouldered pose of noble pathos, all the while willing my brother to make his move. Now, while the bully labored to process his revulsion, uncertain whether to breathe in my vicinity. Now, before he fell back into the wiseguy mode. *Now.*

But nothing happened. No brilliant black-belt leap off the sofa—no flash of diversion—no improvised weapon. Helplessly I watched as Jerry recovered his balance, the curl of the sneer returning. "Hey," he remarked with an arched brow and a one-note snicker, "I hope you had yourself some fun gettin' there."

With a bloodless shift of gears his cold glare fixed once more on Brian. I knew the moment of turning the tables had utterly dissipated. Stung with defeat I shot a bewildered glance at my brother, sullenly staring at the arm of the sofa, indignant and strangely aloof. Suddenly he wasn't my father at all but my mother, a shell rather than a time bomb, spent from so much bad luck and the wrongness of the world. *Don't hit his head. I have no sons.* The surrender of the will to escape. Here I was, the only one with enough rage to get us out of this, no fear for myself at all, and I'd lost my shot.

"So where is it?" Jerry crooned with near-lascivious delight, producing from my brother a desiccated laugh like an old man coughing. They'd reached the wall. If Brian was telling the truth and he had no seven mill to trade, then this was the deal right here. Nothing further to bargain with, and the gun just aching.

"What's happening?"

I was the only one who didn't turn, my back to the stairs and my heart stopped. Jerry spun about, more agile than he looked, and bawled at the figure on the landing: "And who the fuck are you?"

There was the faintest clearing of the throat, as if to censure the ill-mannered tone of the question. Then Gray announced: "This is my house."

"Izzatso?" mocked the fat man. I was staring straight at his belt buckle, a twenty-dollar gold piece. The gun swung lightly from his left hand at about hip level. "Well, I'm havin' a private talk here with a couple my old buddies. So why don't you go crawl back into bed, and maybe tomorrow morning you'll still be a fuckin' home-owner."

Gray sniffed, a blip of defiance worthy of his aunt. "Are you the one who blew up Brian's house?"

Jerry lurched to face him direct. "I said move," he barked, the pistol swinging up to punctuate the rabid threat.

A blinding rush in my head seethed like the sea in a shell. That instant of the gun pointing at my lover, I saw into the whitest fire of outrage. How I spoke at all I'll never know, except that acting was my only commando training. "Gray, it's all right," I tossed back over my shoulder, a truly ridiculous lie, and all the while staring at Jerry's hip, a foot from my ravenous fury.

A shuffle behind me on the stairs, as Gray reluctantly followed my command, too polite to disagree. Then Jerry's hand with the gun fell to his side again—and I lunged and clamped like a bulldog.

Right through the swell of flesh between his thumb and fingers. Blood gushed into my mouth, metallic, as if I'd bitten the gun instead. His shout was a horror of being infected, rather than rage, so he panicked and flailed when he should have gone for the kill. I don't know why the gun didn't go off, except my teeth were hooked on tendons, paralyzing the finger that kissed the trigger.

When he couldn't shake me he pounded my head with his other fist, but now Brian was on him from behind, wrenching his arm away. So that all I had to do was heave my shoulder like a tackle, jamming the barrel into his bulging gut. My hand squeezed over his, and then we were dancing.

An ocean of blood poured through the shreds of his banker's shirt. Somehow it seemed more terrible that he never cried out after that first shout. He gulped in a great heave of air, standing rigid in stunned surprise, holding his breath like he was swimming under-water. The gun clattered to the hearth, a sound as hollow as plastic, a toy after all.

Doused in red I rose upright, just in time to see him teeter. His hands were pressed to the sieve of his belly, the look in his bugged eyes already far at sea. Then he keeled and went down hard, with a sickening whump of his head against the base of one of the andirons. The blood pooled around him on the hearthstone, the stone drinking it in like a pig's altar. Then the breath came guttering out, a queer inhuman whine of incalculable regret.

I looked up into Brian's eyes, staring at me in blank astonishment. I think I tried to shrug, except I was so bone-weary I could hardly move. No triumph in that first moment, not even relief. If anything, a pang of protective guilt for my brother's sake, that he should've had to witness the letting of the monster's blood. If I'd had a hand not slick with death, I would've reached out to shield his eyes. He wasn't nearly godless enough for this.

Then Gray's arms were around me, gathering me to his chest. I gratefully collapsed against him, but struggled to keep my bloodied hands from touching the faded blue cotton of his robe. They flailed the air above him like a pair of clipped wings, the drying blood beginning to stiffen. "Thank God," he breathed in my ear. Thank *me*, I thought with stubborn pride, never flinching from a credit dispute with the infinite. Already I was only half there, racing ahead to the cops' arrival. Determined that I would bear the full responsibility, leaving these two out of it. I braced for the shriek of sirens.

"I better go call Nigrelli," Brian declared uncertainly.

"Wait." I struggled out of Gray's embrace, my arms still raised as if I was being robbed. "We have to get our story straight. You guys shouldn't even be here."

"What story? You saved my ass."

I laughed. "Who's gonna believe *that*? I'm just this frail little AIDS victim. I'm telling you, they'll think you did it."

"Look, I don't give a shit—"

"Well, I do," I retorted impatiently. " 'Cause I don't want anyone stopping you from getting out of here. Or else you'll *never* make it back to the kid." Why was it I had to remind him what his goal was? His eyes wouldn't leave the body, wincing in disbelief, unready to go anywhere. I turned to Gray, his robe smeared with Jerry's blood despite my excruciating care. "Listen, you take him down to the Chevron. Call the Gucci lawyer. The feds can pick up Brian there."

"And leave you with *him*?" protested Gray, pointing at the ritual slaughter on the hearth.

"So what? He's gonna bite me?" I made a rude Italian gesture toward the dead man, feeling the caked blood crack along my wrist. But I also realized why they were acting so confused and indecisive. Neither of them really liked my attitude—not enough hush in the face of death. It only made me feel ever more drunkenly cavalier, for death was the very last thing that awed me anymore. As to having killed the torturer of my youth, I felt nothing—no, less than nothing. Lady Macbeth in a gym towel.

"When you get back," I declared with some belligerence, "we can plant him in the yard somewhere. Up by the fishpond, maybe—"

"That's okay. We'll take care of it."

No sirens at all. Agent Evans stepped down from the dining room, sharp in a charcoal suit and rep tie. If it had been Potato-face I might've turned and bolted, but the black man had struck me as a fount of empathy by comparison. I could feel Gray and Brian stiffen on either side, turning over the wheel to me to navigate the whirlpool. Evans's smile was as tailored as his suit, not the flicker of a glance at the problematic object on the hearth. No bulge of a gun was visible either, though he surely had one.

It was some small comfort to know he'd decided to keep it holstered, that he felt no threat from any of us. Because it was dead obvious that he'd witnessed the whole of what had happened. I just couldn't tell whose side he was on. "This is Jerry Curran," I explained, not pointing or nodding. "I killed him."

Evans frowned, his tongue darting out to wet his lips. "Ah, let's just say he doesn't exist anymore."

Our side, one to nothing.

"Brian, you'd better get ready," he continued. "Agent Dana will follow us in Curran's car. We'll be going to Reno first, to ah . . ." He finally looked at the corpse. ". . . drop him off." He made an elaborate show of checking his watch. "It's three-eighteen now. We'll be leaving in five, as soon as we get him packed." Another curt nod at the walrus body on the hearth.

"Wait a minute," my brother demanded, bridling now. "What's Reno got to do with it? Yesterday you said Tulsa. Look, I have to talk to Nigrelli."

Evans smiled, enjoying himself. "Nigrelli doesn't work for you anymore, Brian. You just got blown away. In Reno." The three of us must've drawn the identical blank, like a row of dullards on "Jeopardy." Evans chuckled at our perplexity. "See, we got a fresh kill up there. Some local punk. And we're going to put your wallet in his pocket, and the tag on his toe's going to read Shaheen."

His padded shoulders gave a brief shrug, casual as Nat Cole. A piece of cake, as Daniel would say. "So then you can disappear for real," he went on, "without all that looking over your shoulder. Our little present to you."

Honestly, I could've saluted the flag. At last, my tax dollars at work. I grinned at Evans, eager to pump his hand in gratitude—but careful to make no sudden move, because he was a tricky fucker. I turned to share the moment with my brother, and the grin curdled on my face. For Brian was still bristling with suspicion. He jutted his chin defiantly.

"So my wife's gonna think I'm dead?"

"Don't worry, she knows it's a setup. She'll *act* like you're dead."

There was a rustle behind him as his partner came in from the kitchen, dragging what looked like a black tarp. Agent Dana was as underdressed as before, another bilious Hawaiian shirt, and the lack of sleep hadn't made his tuberous face any prettier. As he came abreast of Evans I saw that the tarp had a long zipper: a body bag. I guess they kept one in the trunk beside the spare. Preparedness to the max, I thought, even as I recalled Mike Manihan and Teddy Burr being hauled away, the rattlesnake finality of that zipper. It was the last sound I would never hear, the day they came for me.

I don't know what Gray saw in my face, but he glided up next to my elbow, ready to prop me. "I don't understand any of this," he protested, just short of a huff. "Why is *that* one going?" Meaning Jerry, as if the fat man had been so rude and vulgar as to have forfeited all free rides.

Evans watched as Dana laid out the bag on the floor next to the fireplace. "Listen, for months he's been saying the Mob's out to hit him. Well"—he held up the rosy palms of his hands—"they just caught up with him in Reno. Two hits for the price of one. Brian, you better be getting your stuff."

At last my brother roused himself, tearing his gaze from his dead partner. He moved past us without another word and headed upstairs. Meanwhile Dana had straddled the body and was rocking

Jerry's shoulder, getting ready to roll him, taking care not to step in the blood.

"You got it?" asked Evans, who made no move to assist, lest he sully the spit-shine on his own wingtips.

The body came away from the stone with a sucking sound, heeling over onto the bag. I tottered and bumped against Gray, who caught my elbow firmly. Dana dragged at the zipper. I hated to look so seasick all of a sudden, for the corpse was nothing, a hunk of meat. It was all in the memory, the sound of the zipper like nails on a blackboard.

"Go on up," murmured Gray, pushing me toward the stairs. "See if he needs any help."

Any excuse to get out of there, as Evans stepped gingerly forward to help with the actual stuffing of arms and legs in the bag, the loose ends. I bounded up to the first landing, Gray calling after me: "Easy—easy!"

Oh of course, that twenty-four hours without any excitement. I slowed for his sake, a step at a time, but laughing inside at the rules of convalescence. *And avoid all stress,* as Robison would always advise with a straight-faced flourish, patting my shoulder and sending me out to do a little more dying. I turned at the top of the stairs and smiled at Gray below. With a hula bump I flipped the corner of the towel, flashing the family jewels. His face flushed crimson, turning automatically to check if the agents had seen. My hopeless unreconstructed WASP.

I headed for Cora's room. The body bag notwithstanding, at the moment I was feeling pretty irrepressible. Had anyone done a study, I wondered, on radical convalescence. Instead of the blinds drawn and a cold cloth over the eyes, you evened an old score. The revenge cure. This was bravado mostly, a pagan taunt to the pieties of Chester. But I was also acutely aware, stepping into my brother's room, that something had changed because of the swoop of death in the parlor below. I wasn't afraid to say good-bye.

"Sorry about those pancakes," I said.

He hunkered at the foot of the bed, stuffing his sweat pants into a backpack, blue with white piping like Daniel's. He'd changed into jeans and his Fordham sweat shirt, no more chances to catch him naked. As he stood and turned to face me, slinging the pack to his shoulder, he looked remarkably unencumbered, nothing more complicated in the offing than a day's hike up the beach. And an unmistakable air of impatience, as if he couldn't wait to be on his way. I think it had finally sunk in, how free he would be once the bodies were found.

"You all right?" he asked tentatively. He was in the lamplight, I in the shadow of the door.

"Oh, very," I assured him, stepping forward with open arms. "I just need to give you a hug."

He laughed. "Time out," he said, and for an instant I felt the slap of rejection, a clang of disbelief, that all our coming together had been just another mirage. What if the past didn't die after all? Even when you killed it.

But now he was reaching to grab my hand and tugging me into the bathroom, laughing still as he flipped on the light. Side by side we blinked in the mirror. The blood was everywhere: matted in my hair and splashed in rusty gouts across my torso and arms, an expressionist fantasia. The white towel at my waist was livid, a serial killer's dropcloth. Not exactly dressed to kiss.

"Get over here," said Brian, slipping off the backpack and propping it on the sink. He nodded for me to stand in the tub, and as soon as I stepped in he tugged the towel free. I felt about six years old—not a bad feeling at all. Then he bent to open the ancient moss-green faucets, flipping the porcelain crank to engage the hand shower.

He lifted hose and nozzle off the curlicue hook and swept it toward me, spraying my belly. I looked down to see the blood flash red again as it washed away. The white hull of the tub swirled like the drain in *Psycho*. Brian widened the field of the spray to my chest, cold as well water. He slapped a hand across my breastbone, smearing me clean, while I shook like a seal.

"You think he would've killed us?"

Brian nodded, gesturing for me to duck so he could do my hair. I bowed toward him, clamping shut mouth and eyes. Brian rubbed my scalp as the water streamed down my face. "I figured if he could just shoot me and get out of there," he declared, shrugging his own death. "Then *you* come down. And I'm thinking, fuck"—he tilted my chin and ran the water full on my face till I gasped and sputtered—"I can't just die, I gotta save Tommy. But I don't have a clue. Lucky for me, my brother's a wild man."

Abruptly the drum of the spray left my face, as he bent to hose my legs. I gurgled, water running out of my nostrils, and managed to choke out one word: "Teamwork."

Brian swung around and wrenched the faucets shut, which produced a grinding shudder in the prewar pipes. He didn't protest the chivalry of my characterization. Indeed we had worked together to overpower the beast, but we both knew who'd been quarterback. I stood unmoving as he grabbed a towel from behind the door. He caped it about my shoulders and started rubbing my torso vigorously, no nonsense, as if he was my trainer. Though I'd never won a game before, I understood that this was the treatment a hero got.

"I'll write the address, it's simple," I said, ducking once more as he moved to dry my head. "Just care of Baldwin—Route One— Trancas." I stuttered each phrase like a telegraph, my head pummeled by the furious buff of the towel.

"Sure," said Brian, whipping it off my scalp. Then he girdled it around my waist and tucked in the end at the hipbone. Through all these ablutions he hadn't ever touched my privates or dried me below the navel. And yet, as I stood there squeaky clean, the whole ritual seemed an exquisite balance of intimacy and modesty. It reminded me of the way Gray made love.

"And how about if you call the phone at the Chevron?" I proposed in a rush of eagerness. "We could plan it like Tuesday nights at ten—I don't know what that is in Tulsa. But I could wait down there, and you could call. Not *every* Tuesday—"

"Sounds good to me," he replied softly. "You ready for that hug?"

Well, yes and no. He opened his arms and made the first move, engulfing me about the shoulders. Because I was still standing in the claw-footed tub I towered two inches above him for once. But the hug itself was no problem—easy, unforced, without any clutch of desperation. Nevertheless, in the middle of it I had to swallow hard, knowing my bid to stay in touch had just been vetoed.

Not in so many words, and for all I knew with a nod of good faith, meaning to follow through. But he wasn't the type, my brother, to write his letters in longhand, and especially not to stand in the dark by a phone booth. He was only saying yes so he could leave with less good-bye. And I didn't blame him a bit, or even try to prolong the embrace to compensate.

"Brian!" Evans's voice echoed through the stair hall, brooking no further delay.

We pulled apart, effortlessly, no lingering messy feelings, no

Camille. Brian turned and scooped his pack, slinging it over one arm as he strode out through Cora's room. I caught a glimpse of me bloodless in the mirror above the sink, and could've sworn I'd put on some muscle through the shoulders. Brian waited in the doorway into the hall, with that crease between his eyes that said there was one more thing. My face lifted expectantly, prepared to give him whatever he needed. *No* didn't exist.

"Make sure you write Daniel," he said with a fluster of urgency. "You got that address?" I nodded. " 'Cause he'll just be with his mother and he's gonna need . . ." One hand floundered the air, unable to think of the word.

"Piece o' cake," I retorted, smiling. What he couldn't quite say was *a man.*

"Brian!"

We were on our way. I walked behind my brother around the stairwell, feeling a new sort of mirror image—as if I were as burly as he, the same unconscious swagger. This was how straight boys learned to be men, mimicking and preening, stimulating the butch gene. As I trotted down in Brian's wake, I thought about Daniel following him and following me. Somewhere there had been a tradeoff, gentling my brother and toughening me. Brian stopped at the bottom of the stairs while I hovered a step above him, four inches taller now. And I prayed to the nothing I didn't believe in: *Let the kid have it both ways.*

The body was gone. Gray knelt on the hearth like an Irish housemaid, bucket of water beside him, scrubbing the stone with a stiff brush. The ratchet scrape of the brush filled the parlor. Dog's work, the sort of stain that would never come out.

"Gray," said Brian politely, and the brushing stopped as Gray looked around. "Thanks for putting us all up."

Gray blushed. "Don't be silly. You'll come in the summer sometime. Daniel can sail."

Brian nodded, another of those necessary fictions. Then he crooked a thumb over his shoulder. "And keep an eye on this guy, huh? He's a terror."

"Oh, don't worry. He's on a *very* short leash, that one."

We all laughed. Gray had to restrain himself mightily not to leap up and shake Brian's hand. But he understood his place exactly in this business of saying good-bye, and so contented himself with a nodding smile. My brother and I turned away in relief and made our way through the dining room. Almost there, and no thin ice in sight. The will to get on with it—he to his life, I to mine—superseded all.

The kitchen door stood wide, the rumble of idling engines echoing in from the yard. The counters were bare of food, no muffins to tuck in his backpack. Brian stepped outside, and I almost followed but pulled up short, deciding to leave it there. The two cars were waiting in caravan, a stone's throw off. Please—no last words in front of the agents.

I put both hands to the doorframe, leaning out. "So . . . some Tuesday, huh?"

He half turned, the light from the kitchen throwing a glint in his eye. "Yeah. And tell Miss Jesus I'll see her in church."

He winked. Then we made a gesture toward each other, something between a nod and a bow, both at the same time, but not another word. Brian strode through the grass to the lead car and climbed in front next to Evans. I stayed in the doorway—I even waved. It wasn't breaking the rules as long as it went unspoken. I waved in the dark where no one could see me, the two cars trundling away down the drive, till the red lights turned on the coast road. Waved at the blue night sky like a wild man, wishing my brother safe passage wherever it took him, as long as it brought him home.

T E N

I WONDER IF MY MOTHER EVER DREAMS OF WEST HILL ROAD. Though she lives in the house at 210 still, her waking life these days is a fog of untouched soup and too many pills and a grim cushion of geriatric diapers. Mostly she lives nowhere now, following the sharp commands of Mary Alice Lynch, probably thinking, if she thinks at all, that she's a boarder in the nurse/companion's house.

But when she dreams, does some corner of her lost self ever open the door of 210 as it was? My father brawling at the kitchen table on his umpteenth rye-and-ginger. Brian wolfing supper in his baseball whites, nine innings to play before dusk. For her sake I hope she dreams of us, a flash of old footage knifing the dark with memory. For the house is nothing without that dream.

I will not be dreaming it myself anymore. That much I know already, and my brother hardly gone a week. I'm too busy playing over and over the days of our reunion. Somewhere in there the old world of West Hill Road has died at last of irrelevance. Or perhaps the gunfire and the rain of blood have left me with a nice amnesia. In any case the final bit of evidence departed here in the gold-tooled box with Daniel. No one will ever connect that solitary drunken snapshot of my dad's with me and Brian, because we have finally outgrown it. Good-bye and good riddance.

Gray says it all happened too fast for him. He hardly got to know anyone, too polite to ask what any of it meant, by which time the cyclone had blown in and out. But then, he's never been in a rush to get over his own ancient history, mirrored as it is in the Merlin presence of Foo. Besides, he still lives quite comfortably, thank you, on the West Hill Road of his childhood. All it lacked was me. And he managed to move me in without shifting so much as an end table. Violent change was not required, the very drama I'd been waiting for all my life.

He's right about one thing, though. The whole upheaval has been and gone without a trace. Monday and Tuesday, the first days after, I felt a certain shiver—thrill—whenever I passed the fireplace. Despite Gray's elbow grease the hearthstone seemed to bear a scarlet sheen, the parlor air thick with the fetor of rust and rotten fruit. For me the lingering spoor of Jerry Curran's blood was like a tonic, a breath of purest ozone.

Yet even that had faded by midweek, and the house on the bluff was as before, playing out its own tattered dream of summer. The stair hall reverberated not with the racing feet of my nephew or his mother's carping self-defeat, but the faint strings of the old musicales, flimsy as the gauze curtains that billow at the upstairs windows.

Not that I didn't have to endure a certain amount of hovering, especially from Mona. Once we'd told her the whole bloody tale next evening over pizza, her solicitude was relentless. "Are you okay?" she'd ask me again and again, the first day or so with a certainty that I couldn't be. By Wednesday she told herself I was in shock, and the question grew more aggressive, like trying to slap a hysteric. Except I remained so stubbornly unhysterical, till by Friday it was Mona who was in shock, especially when I announced my benefit gig for Sister Kathleen would be the following Monday.

"Girl, listen," I declared with rigor, chaise to chaise in the twilight, nursing mugs of cocoa, "Jerry Curran is over. What we have to work with here is Tom happy and Tom dying. Can you do those two at the same time? Because I'm definitely not happy dying. Maybe alternate days would work. You solve this one, Donna, and I'll take my hot chocolate I.V."

Meanwhile Gray had stayed over every night since, but to be my lover, not my nurse. Though he did toss out one morning, very offhanded, "You miss your brother?"

We were cutting back the bougainvillea from the cloistered arch by the fountain, our arms clawed like lion tamers'. I thought for a moment and then said, "Not really." And that was the end of it, as far as Gray was concerned. I suppose he wanted me to have my brother all to myself, whatever the feelings were. Maybe he even understood that, having gotten it right with my brother, I'm not missing anything anymore.

Whatever else my brother's sojourn in my life has left me with, I find myself possessed with having a whole summer here. The last Alaska storm was the end of the rainy season. Everyone says so—especially Merle, who squints at the midday blue of the sky and knows in his Malibu bones that we will be cloudless till November.

And that means a thousand chores to get us ready. An actual list in Cora's birdy longhand, several numbered sheets of Baldwin notepaper sporting the family crest. *Second week of April*, it says at the top of the page. We read our instructions, already days behind because of the turmoil of Brian's visit.

Half-ton crushed shells for the drive. No clams.
Strip the eucalyptus.
New rat-traps in the attic.
Cut bougainvillea to the bone.

What the list did not make plain, Foo was there to elucidate. It wasn't that clam shells were vulgar, but the shards too sharp for bare feet. Husking the bark of the eucalyptus left the trunks white and sleek as marble, not an arboreal choice so much as an aesthetic one, giving the line of trees at the top of the hill the look of columns on a temple. Readiness for summer invoked a spectrum of details unique to the house on the bluff, and the chores had evolved over sixty years to a state approaching tribal law.

Who would've guessed there were slipcovers tissued in the attic, enough for every upholstered chair to wear a tight-fitting summer dress gaudy with pink and white peonies? No task was too obscure, though I was handed the thankless brush with which to repaint the rose trellises along the garage. A two-day piece of work made brutal by the challenge of getting no paint on the bushes themselves, which twisted in and out of the diamond-slatted wood.

I did a tremendous job, but don't go by me. Foo came down every other morning with Merle, to check on our progress and oversee the fine points. She assured me I had far outdone her sister Nonny in trellis-painting, who always ended up blotching the rosebuds cruelly. In the old days, says Foo, most of the heavy work was done by ranch hands from up the hill, dispatched by Gray's grandfather to take care of his curious sisters.

"A house at the beach is a losing battle," she declares from beneath a straw hat, so frayed it looks fit for a donkey. "Unless you have an army working, Cora used to say, three good rainy seasons'll bring it right to the ground."

She delivers this flinty proverb from a kitchen chair we've carted out onto the back lawn so she can watch me at the trellis. Meanwhile Gray and Merle are spidering over the roof, checking the mortar between the brick-red tiles. Foo's been given a cup of bouillon to sip, but she's let it cool and spiked it with a shot of airline vodka smuggled in in her purse.

"So you don't have to make it perfect," she pronounces with a wag of her crooked forefinger. "Just patch and freshen, you hear? What do we care if the whole cliff breaks off next winter? All we want is one more summer. Am I right, Tom?"

Exactly. And for this summer I'm preparing, I try to think what I want for Gray and what for me. Days, mostly, unencumbered end to end except by the business of living here. They say you make bargains as things get tighter—a birthday, one more Christmas. As for me and my summer, I find that I'm writing a sort of continuous living will in my head. I want to go quick but not too quick, as little demented as possible. Already it breaks my heart to think of Gray watching me shrivel and lose the thread, blank as my mother on West Hill Road. Just this summer, please, April to October. Already a second bargain there, since a proper California summer goes on way past Labor Day.

Merle joins us for lunch at the dining room table, all of us still in our work clothes, Foo in her donkey hat. The burly Native American has dropped me from the Custer rolls, silently accepting me into the circle of the Baldwin tribe. Perhaps he sees how inevitable is the connection between Gray and me, but I think it's more, a warrior's nod of honor for my late blood conquest. Gray swears he's breathed no word of the killing to Merle or Foo, but somehow the Indian senses, a bear's nose for the spill of blood. All unconscious, since his twelve-step program hardly gives him leave to glorify a killer. But a shaman's blessing is in the air as we break bread and pass cold cuts. I am an honorary something, Malibu/Chumash, just like Gray and Foo.

Mona arrives in time for dessert, laden with hothouse peaches and champagne grapes and melon, a goose to summer at four dollars a pound. She has also stopped to pick up the mail at the cubbyhole Trancas P.O. "Card from your brother," she announces casually, flipping it to me across the table. It goes without saying she's read it. "Oklahoma," she observes with a grimace to the table at large, as she doles out the fruit.

On the face is an oil well gushing, an old hand-tinted photograph. The prairie around it is flat and dead as a nuclear waste dump. On the reverse the printed legend proclaims: *We're rich!* Then in the message space below, a brief scribble: *Tommy—Reno went fine. Package delivered. Tulsa's the pits. Are you eating? Go for some overtime! XXX Ace.*

"What's overtime?" I ask the group.

"When's the last time *you* worked nine to five, bunkie?" Mona drawls, slurping a slice of peach. "It's what they pay you for working extra."

"No . . . in sports."

A general frown around the table. Not exactly a roomful of jocks. "I think you get more innings," Gray offers tentatively. "If there's a tie or something."

"Uh-uh." Merle shakes his barrel head. "It's like in football, they give you more time at the end. After the clock."

We all nod sagely, even Foo, though I fear the concept remains a philosophical mystery. Nevertheless I'm flushed with pleasure to have the card at all. No return address of course, but he *wrote* me. I feel terrifically indulged and thrilled to be overruled—that our fast good-bye that bloody night wasn't the final word.

"Field hockey," Foo announces, a beat after everyone else. She nibbles at a bunch of champagne grapes like a tiny, gaunt Bacchanalian. "The Catherine Downing Academy in San Marino," the name unfurling like a banner. "I got a goal in overtime once. But I don't remember how you play. Some damn fool stick." Her spindle arm makes a vague wave at the air.

"You're all set for Monday at seven," Mona confirms to me. "She's only bringing about twenty. Field trip for her I-and-A girls. Incest and abused," she explains to the others, as I run my fingertips over the ball-point script of my brother's card. Mona sees I'm half-distracted, so she slips in casually, practically yawning, "I hate to let eighty seats go empty."

"Don't even think it," I retort automatically, fanning myself with the postcard. If I can't write back and we're both phoneless, how exactly do I get through?

"*I'm* going to be there," Foo puts in, with a brief imperious glare that cuts off any incipient protest from Merle or her nephew, let alone me.

I snap my fingers. "Kid needs a CD player." I point to Mona. "Can you get to Adray's before they close?" She groans and checks her watch. On Saturday afternoon the traffic into Hollywood is a killer crawl. "If they Fed Ex it today, he'll get it Monday morning." Mona's eyes roll, gimme-a-break. It's not like I need a blood transfusion. I toss the carrot. "Do it, and you can have twenty more bodies on Monday night."

She grins, on her feet already. As she hustles after me up the stairs, I'm laying down the conditions. Only friends and angels of the theater to be invited. No press—no public at large—no Daphne. Mona agrees to everything before I finish. To her it's all a wedge and a start, prying open the shell of my stubbornness.

She waits while I count out three hundred and fifty from the drawer in the nightstand, tucked in the flyleaf of *Emma*. It's the whole of my winter savings from my state disability, unsquandered on the Colonel and Big Macs because I've been living on Baldwin groceries. From the mirror's frame I grab the square of paper on which Susan has printed their Minneapolis address. Then I shoo Mona out to her mission, kissing the air by her parrot earring.

Things have to be done like this, speedy and on the spur. I dance four bars of a jig in celebration, having solved the ache of getting back to Brian with a bank shot off my nephew. All week I've been wanting to send something off to Daniel, but not an empty letter. Instead I have this mad urge to send him presents: skis, a racing bike, a pair of golden pups. Only my terminal poverty reins me in.

Speeding things up. Racing to get the place in summer shape. Am I really at the end stage, or is it all just the work of a drama queen wired from the acceleration of the last two weeks?

Depends on the time of day. When we're out there scraping barnacles, bleaching the grout in the fountain tiles, or up in the Chinese garden hauling glop from the lily pond, I'm boundless and inexhaustible, never sick a day in my life. If it's denial, it's got the wollop of Popeye's spinach. The smallest win over dirt and dry-rot sets the summer more firmly in stone. I feel like I'm buying time with hard labor. Even the oceanic naps that lay me out at the end of the day are a mark of my well-being, sleep like a long drink of water.

Night is something else entirely, waking up in a sweat next to Gray, and no more beasts to kill. I towel the drench from my hair and switch to a dry pillow. But the busywork doesn't distract me from the broken dream of my dying body. My waterlogged knee is horribly stiff, so I limp like Long John Silver. I'm trembly and slightly frantic, my lesions twinging like rat bites. I know I'm as likely to die by morning as Gray is to wake. As he sleeps and I cling to the bedpost, I might as well be a ghoul already, haunting the ground of my too-brief joy.

I slip out onto the balcony, a blanket caped about my shoulders. We're between moons, so the dome of the sky is awash with stars and the ocean a black gleam of patent leather. The night breeze ripples over me with a near-tropical sweetness, ripe as Hawaii, a summer that never ends. But my ghostliness won't go away. From both ends of my body, last week's spells of blank and my gimp knee, the message is grimly the same: *Who am I kidding?*

Once it's hit the nervous system, the game is all in overtime.

Still, I mustn't be dead yet, or how would I have the wherewithal to stumble in and back to bed? It's the ghost who's somehow got to be put to sleep, or how will I ever make it through to daylight? I snuggle up close to the warmth of Gray, holding my breath, fearful he'll wake with a scream at the touch of my icy flesh. I try not to grip him too tight. This is what haunting is, to hover in the place of love. The dead never sleep for a minute.

And yet, almost despite myself, I can feel the easy rhythm of Gray's breathing—like catching a wave to bodysurf. I swoon under before I know it, and happy wins out over dying for one more night.

Sunday we do windows. I'm on the inside, Gray is out, and Merle floats above us on the ladder doing the upstairs. We go through a gallon of ammonia and a mile of paper towels, scrubbing a half inch of grime from the sills as we go. "I always thought the sea air was so clean," I observe with some dismay, eliciting from the shaman on the ladder a grunt that sounds like "Dirt's dirt."

As I ease open one of the dining room casements, I send a nest of red-cross spiders scurrying. I shudder involuntarily, a terrible sissy when it comes to crawling things. And Gray turns sharp from the next window over. I see the flash of emergency in his eyes, thinking the look on *my* face is a stroke.

An instant later he knows he's wrong, no explanation necessary beyond my squinch of buggy distaste. He laughs and leans in at my window, kissing me square on the mouth. He's so grateful the world didn't crack in half, but clearly expects it any minute. In that one small opening I see what he holds in for my sake.

By midafternoon we're finished fenestrating. As I buff the final pane, I'm swooning from the hothouse beat of the sun in the tower. Gray and Merle have already moved on to the awnings. Below on the grass the swags of faded blue canvas are spread out like sails, Gray hosing them down while Merle tightens the awning struts above the parlor doors. I call down that we're out of ammonia, and I'll make the run to the Chevron. Gray looks up with a grin and squirts the hose at me, but it stops short, drumming the side of the house.

I give a last glance round the lighthouse room, where no trace of Daniel remains, any more than Nonny who lived here fifty summers. It's just an attic again, no overnight guests expected, no reason at all in fact to have its windows clean. Except we do things top to bottom around here, no corners cut, or else who knows what door we might leave open to an early winter?

The green surfboard keychain glows on the kitchen counter, the last thing we'll ever lose. It puts me in mind of my nephew as I drive stop-and-go in Sunday madness. The inlanders blare their horns and cuss out their windows, hauling their freeway etiquette here to the water's edge. I am a fountain of Zen calm by comparison, fingers tapping the neon surfboard as it dangles from the ignition.

The parking lot at the Chevron is jammed with Valley teenmobiles. Beach trollops in postage-stamp bikinis slouch and jiggle by the phone booth, nuzzling Diet Cokes. I feel as old as Foo as I thread my way to the minimart. Inside there's a chill like tundra from the air-conditioning, but it's also nearly empty because bare feet and loiterers are vigorously discouraged.

I grab up an armload of cleaning supplies, various prepacked toxic wastes, including even a bunch of submarine devices that turn a toilet's water Mai-Tai blue. Ghastly to be sure, but we're talking Donna Reed clean here. On impulse as I pass the freezer I reach in for a chocolate death bar, the same as Daniel and I pigged out on.

Miss Kitty is at the register, a hard-bitten brassy blonde in a Zody's muumuu, of the type whose screen career never even reached the cutting-room floor. Yet there's a certain star presence about her, a tragic grandeur in the purple-lidded eyes, as if she has fallen from very high up. I plunk my groceries down with hardly a nod, since neither of us is the chatty type. What they call frontier reserve. I tear at the wrapper to bare my ice cream as she starts toting up. I'm midbite, teeth frozen, when she lobs it to me underhand.

"You're the kid up the Baldwin place," she says, statement not a question.

"Uh—yes I am." If I'm blushing, it's from being called *kid*. I scramble for something nice to pay her back—

"We got a message for you. Somewhere."

Miss Kitty rustles a pile of papers by the register, then squints at the bulletin board above. She's impatient but not irritable. Apparently I have enough standing in the neighborhood for this favor I never asked. Who would leave me a message here? Now she's plucked the pushpins out and laid the paper on the counter before me. She goes back to the ringing up.

"Brian," it says in a big scrawl. "4165552484 April 30 10 oclock *his* time." No punctuation at all. *Whose* time?

"I don't understand."

"Fella took it down the other night. He was just sittin' out there in his car, and the phone starts ringin' in the booth, so he picks it up." She taps the paper with a lilac fingernail. "This is your brother."

"Yes, of course," I reply with a ruffle of dignity. "He wants me to call him."

"Eleven oh four," she declares flatly, shaking open a paper sack and beginning to bag me up. I peel a ten and two ones from the anemic roll in my pocket, and Miss Kitty pops the cash drawer to make my change. My hand is sweaty as it clutches Brian's message, nothing compared to the turmoil in my heart. "And ninety-six cents," she announces, a pool of coins in the palm of her hand. "Your Dove Bar's dripping."

I look down in time to see a slab of chocolate slide onto my wrist, and the next several seconds are frantic as I slather my tongue around the disintegrating sweet, consuming it to the bare stick. Then I swipe the counter with a napkin to clean up the drips. All one-handed, Brian's message still clasped in the other, like a dispatch I have to deliver through enemy lines.

Miss Kitty is already busy with the next customer as I turn to go, but she breaks her concentration to call after me, "Hey—your groceries!"

I retrieve my sack and thank her profusely, floating out once more to the heat of the day and the nubile clan of beach delinquents. Yet it strikes me with a sudden force of gratitude that one of these very teens might have taken the precious call from Tulsa. Maybe the coffee-colored boy in the booth right now, bare as a Fiji islander and muscled like the jigsaw *David*. I silently bless his whole beach tribe as I climb back into the pickup and smooth out the coded message on the hub of the steering wheel.

An hour's time difference between here and Tulsa, which means I better be here at nine, in case the *his* refers to Brian. Doesn't say A.M. or P.M., but night is the way I first proposed it. The hard part of course is that there's no backup if something goes awry, no second date for safety's sake. And in any case it's seventeen days away, so the biggest challenge is to Shaheen's First Law of the rest of my life, only to live today. Wild horses etc. couldn't keep me from the rendezvous, but a stroke sure would. I have no choice, despite the leaping joy in my breast, but to fold up the message and pocket it, placing no bets on the outcome.

Gray and I don't sleep in Foo's room Sunday night, for the mattress is slumped on the balcony rail, hauled out by Merle for a night's airing. It's the same in Cora's room, a bare iron bedspring. So we're banished to the tower by default, which goes to show that its attic status is as fluid as everything else about summer. And those windows, which seemed so extraneous to wash, they're as diamond clear tonight as the lens of a telescope. We lie in each other's arms in sweet exhaustion, the night so wrapped around us we might as well be camping out. All our chores accomplished, for just at dusk we came to the bottom of Cora's list.

"So tomorrow's the first day of summer," Gray murmurs into my hair. "That's an official Baldwin proclamation."

"No, Tuesday," I correct him gently, knowing it will have to wait till after the performance tomorrow night, Miss Jesus being my last promise to anyone else but me.

We make love for a while, glancing and dreamy, nobody poking too hard. There's nothing to prove by getting off, no urgency—the whole summer lies before us, stretching its tawny body like a cat. So we hold back, the pulsing ache of a half measure more satisfying than going over the top. Gray's lingering good-night kiss is a stir of anticipation, and time is on its side.

In the next breath he's asleep, his lips still grazing mine. I feel not loss or separation but only a vivid sense of drawing us out like golden wire, so easy have all our transitions become. The night sky is suddenly mine, and for a minute I want to lie there bolt awake till morning, tracing the warrior constellations as I cradle my love in my arms. Nothing is perfect of course. Even as I hold him fast I can see the stricken look in his eyes when I flinched at the scatter of spiders. I can't make his fear go away because he needs it to learn about grief.

Poor Gray, I think as I brush my cheek across his forehead, just where the hair is beginning to retreat.

Fortunately I'm dog tired, so the melancholy can't get a grip. Then like a shooting star the scrap of Brian's message streaks across my vision, light out of dark, and the pang of hope releases me to sleep. AIDS-less sleep, without any night sweats or dreams with doors. Most perverse of all, such length and depth—for the tower catches the crack of dawn, its circle of windows offering nothing in the way of shade. It's like a lighthouse turned in on itself, blinding bright by seven.

No wonder Nonny was always the first one up, clanging the bell for breakfast. Yet I sleep straight through till eleven, the sun full on my face. I see the gold dazzle of summer before I even open my eyes.

Gray has already been down to the Chevron twice, to check in with Sister Kathleen and Mona. Nineteen I-and-A girls have signed up for the field trip. Mona's got calls out to twenty-five angels, but on such short notice she swears we'll be lucky to pull in half. I feel no spurt of jitters at news of the house count, nor any pregame wistfulness at the prospect of my last home run. I'm so far past it already, no need to top myself. Performance is for younger types than I. Time to rest on my laurels, to be wheeled out every now and then for roasts and tributes.

I wander my shipshape acreage in a pair of cutoffs, eating Mona's peaches. Gray leaves me to my own devices for most of the afternoon, running up to the ranch to putter. He thinks I need the solitude to prepare Miss Jesus, not realizing I'm going the other way, disengaging, deconstructing. I stand at the top of the beach stairs and suck the peach juice from my fingers, batting away the random bee who thinks I'm sweeter than the cactus flowers.

And I face the curious question of my borderline career. Would

I have clamped so hard on the church, my jaws locked like a pit bull, if I'd been this happy before? Was it all just a tantrum?

I don't know. I can't conceive my life anymore without Gray and Brian. As to the rage I'll feel at the end for how briefly I possessed them, I'd rather face that when I get there. Otherwise, if a happy man is a lousy comic, then I'll be a bust tonight. Oh well, they're all being comped, and you get what you pay for. Miss Jesus always had more fun with this thing than I did. Even at my most notorious, I never stopped feeling a loser. I needed the act more than it needed me, and now I don't.

I certainly don't owe anybody a piece of my sudden change of heart, as if to be happy now were a sort of deathbed conversion. My values are intact. I still hate the Hitler Pope and all his brocaded minions. I still believe in Nothing. Well, not quite: this life of the dawning summer is inexpressibly green and balanced, sufficient to engage a pagan's faith. The gods are Apollo and Dionysus, not Big G—enough higher power to qualify me for almost any twelve-step program, but also enough to consign me to the Catholic hell, where the party is.

At the bluff's edge I fling out my arms to embrace the whole ocean, dancing on the balls of my feet, and I crow. Loud and long. I startle a pair of terns on the ledge below, and they flap away northward, bound for a summer of their own. My holler is otherwise lost in the wind that blows offshore. It turns no ships away from foundering on the rocks, and it raises no shades of the Malibu chiefs. It's just my personal siren cry, for nobody else. A cheer whose echo will ring for months, till the last mote of summer. I'm here and I'm ready. Start the clock.

It's not quite dusk when we climb in the pickup to leave for AGORA, but Gray flips on the lights at Carbon Canyon, where the fog is eddying in. We don't talk much—no reason. He hasn't said a word about my imminent swan song, even to wish me luck. I have a feeling he doesn't need it any more than I, not like he did the last time, the journey home from which sealed our fate.

Even as I recall it my hand reaches over to graze his thigh. Then we are coming through the narrows by the Colony, and the traffic slows to a waltz of pulsing taillights. As if on cue I tip over slowly, slumping prone on the seat so my head pillows on Gray's thigh. The milky green of the dashboard glows with dials and gauges, comfortingly nonmedical. I feel the same muscle playing under my head as

Gray's foot shifts from brake to gas. The difference is how far we've traveled in between, till his slightest movement feels like one of my own.

I'm about to reach up and click the radio on, feeling the need for a little country, when he says in a soft voice, "We got a sliver of a moon tonight. Oughta be full by the thirtieth."

That's how I know he's seen the message tucked in the corner of the mirror. I grin in silent pleasure, my cheek swelling against his thigh, for the secret was no fun till there were two of us in it. I snap the radio dial. Instantly Dolly and Linda and Emmylou are singing in perfect sync, lush as a Methodist choir. *Farther along we'll know all about it*, they croon in their First Communion whites, not a hairline doubt among them. God is at least a hit single.

> *Cheer up my brother, live in the sunshine,*
> *We'll understand it all by and by.*

My sentiments precisely, brother and sunshine both. I'm feeling positively ecumenical as the harmony enfolds us. Before the final chorus I'm dozing, hardly the mark of a one-man show getting juiced, let alone one whose star is the Antichrist. At some point Gray takes a hand from the wheel and strokes my head in his lap, setting me to purring. Later I feel the pull to the left as he takes the turn one-handed up Chatauqua. I don't even have to think about where we're going. He'll get us there.

If I have any conscious thought at all, it's that I'd gladly die right now, the moment is so complete. Only another way of saying I'd like it to go on forever, just like this. The contradiction seems entirely apt, and thus not contradictory at all.

The reason I know I've fallen asleep is the sound that wakes me: "Uh-oh."

Even as he utters it he pumps the brake to stop us short. I sit up sharp, shaking the grog, and see in our headlights the dusty stand of royal palms in the parking square. Cars are all around us, for once outnumbering the dumpsters in the industrial barrens of Ocean Park. I peer across at the theater entrance, the squiggle of sputtering blue neon tracing the rim of the awning—our postmod marquee. Beneath it a mob of people is swarming around the doors, some with placards waving.

"Oh Jesus, who told *them?*" I groan, picking out the heft of Mrs. Beaudry, her bovine goose-step unmistakable at fifty feet, leading her picketing troops.

"You didn't think you'd get away with it twice, did you?" Gray noses the pickup into a free space by the loading dock. "Family Values has a special SWAT team, just keeping track of you and Miss J."

I can read the placards now. BLASPHEMY IS CRUCIFIXION, red on white, a professional print job, several of those. SAVE JESUS, proclaims another, this one scrawled in longhand. My favorite is DEATH TO THE CHRIST KILLERS, waved aloft by an Aryan thug in a clerical collar. Many of the protesters are younger than I, some barely out of their teens. They all have a Disney polyester sheen, and are easily distinguishable from the wincing patrons who make their hunched way through the gauntlet into the theater.

The protesters are seasoned enough to know not to block the entrance completely, or else we can have them arrested. They content themselves with snarling and spewing hate in the theater-goers' faces, as if AGORA were an abortion clinic.

Gray gives my hand a squeeze as we move to get out on either side of the pickup. The melee is only twenty feet away, but nobody recognizes me out of costume. Gray steps in front of me heading up the ramp, parting the waters of the crowd with a low WASP murmur of courtesy: " 'Scuse me. Coming through." I follow tight behind him, reeling from the memory of the previous skirmish two years ago—when I was young and strong.

We get to within ten feet of the door. I can see Mona checking tickets, a Latino security guard beside her armed with only a nightstick, and looking vaguely frightened himself. Gray waves a finger to try to catch Mona's attention, and then Mrs. Beaudry pounces from the right. "Here he is," she revels, pushing her blazing face into mine. Donna Reed on crack.

I grin, pulling my tits together. "Mrs. Beaudry, how've you been?" I greet the lady cheerily. "Hon, you've cut your hair. The bangs are heaven." All around me I can feel the troops gather in a circle, grim as witches at Stonehenge. Gray's shoulder brushes mine. "Honest, you look ten years younger," I continue giddily, hyperaware of the silence as the protesters defer to Mrs. B. "Is it just clean living, or did you get yourself a lift? Isn't that a little tuck up there?"

I raise a hand to gesture at her temple, and she recoils with a hiss. "Don't touch me with your disease!"

And the spell of silence breaks. The troops erupt in catcalls, rattling their placards. "Blasphemer" is the nicest thing they call me, quaint as *The Scarlet Letter*, though I happen to stare point-blank at a young man waving a sign that says PORNOGRAPHERS TO HELL! He's as blond and finely chiseled as my Fiji surfer, and he barks directly at me: "You fuckin' dirtbag."

I raise two fingers above my head, very popish. "Bless you all for coming," I call out over the din. Gray is tugging my arm now. "I know how busy you are, fellating your sons and ravishing your daughters."

Funny, I never used to provoke. I'd march through, shoulders back and haughty as Garbo. The din becomes a roar as I let myself be pulled along by Gray. The guard has meanwhile stepped into the fray, opening us a channel. I bat my eyes at Mrs. Beaudry and point to Gray.

"Hey, did you meet my husband?" I hold my hands a foot apart and give her a bawdy wink. "The human kielbasa."

Somebody spits in my face. And though I flinch I feel exultant. I raise no sleeve to wipe my cheek but wear it like a badge. The Aryan priest appears to be the spitter, bellowing next to my ear that I'm a godless communist. I swear, these fundies are all over the board with their agenda, nailing me for a thousand crimes, and the only curious thing tonight is that nobody calls me a fag. Mona beckons impatiently from the door, sweeping Gray past her into the vestibule. The Latino guard is beside me, arms raised to deflect any further abuse. Mona grips my hand.

But I hesitate crossing the threshold, perverse as ever, reluctant to leave the field. "Juiced" doesn't even begin to describe it. *Here's* where I want to perform. I toss my head back leering, to give them a parting shot. And there in the midst, being buffeted, a terrified look on her face, is a woman of indeterminate years, blue-haired and sporting a navy suit. Very uptown.

"Please—I'm on the press list," she protests, struggling to get past the mad-dog priest.

"Let her through!" The boom in my voice is Old Testament, shaking the very ground. The protesters balk, realizing they're out of line. The impeccable woman walks gratefully toward me. I fling out an arm to gather her in. "Welcome to the theater of the damned," I toss off with a gallant nod, ushering Nancy Marlowe in before me.

For it is unmistakably she, the white-glove critic from the *Times*, previously known to me only in theater-party group shots in the paper. She expels a wilted sigh and declares, "Thanks—I thought I was going to be trampled."

Outside, the noise of Mrs. Beaudry's goons has dimmed considerably, deflated now that I've gotten past them. Mona whips over to cluck a hasty apology, eager to steer Ms. Marlowe to her seat, while I reflect on what a spiffy review I'm likely to get after saving the critic of record from the jaws of a mob.

I go straight to the office, cutting behind the bleachers, and don't need a head count to know that Mona's got us nearly full to capacity. I was promised forty-five, fifty max, but the body heat and the bleachers' squeaking tell me we're double that. In addition to which, the Marlowe reference to a "press list" makes it clear what a busy girl Mona's been.

In the office Sister Kathleen perches on an orange crate by the water cooler, the latter a bone-dry relic of the pen factory. Gray's behind the desk, the mountain of grant applications before him no closer to being filed. The two of them eye me warily, trying to leave me some room to react. The sideshow has left them both deeply unamused, but mostly anxious for me.

"Was that a Polish wedding or an Irish wake?" I wonder aloud. They shake their heads grimly, ready to declare martial law on Disney World. I reach to the desk for a tissue and gamely wipe my cheek. "Has anyone got some peroxide? I think I just got exposed to rabies."

"You don't have to do this," Kathleen declares emphatically. "We can all go home."

"What—not perform? Because of them?" I hook a thumb over my shoulder, insolent with disdain. "Please. Think of Noël Coward at the Savoy, singing through the blackouts. Bombs exploding on every side." I cross to the closet and lift out my caftan, holding it close against me as I tilt my head and give them a noble profile. "We play for England."

Then I make a shooing motion at Kathleen. "Go tell Mona five minutes. If she wants to pitch the angels, she should keep the telethon short."

Kathleen rises from the orange crate, throws her arms about me, and plants a kiss on either cheek. "Tom of Arc," she whispers proudly into my ear, then turns and hurries out to do my bidding. My very own nun.

As I fling off my sweat shirt and peel my jeans, Gray is fetching the sandals, wig, and crown from the closet shelf. It's as if we've been playing the provinces for years, him dressing me, a combination manager and front-man. "You can do ten minutes if you like," he says, fluffing the Dynel curls. "No one expects the whole show."

"How come? They think I'm half-dead or something? Of *course* they get the whole show." I'm rooting around in the top drawer of the file cabinet, where the chaos of dusty makeup tubes and broken pancake suggests a mortician's palette. I pull out a red grease crayon and toss it to Gray. "Okay, Daddy, whip me please."

He looks confused, till I turn and hunch before him, offering my back. He draws a tentative stripe along my spine. "More—more," I urge him on. "Think Jackson Pollock." He gets a little more enthusiastic, slashing and doodling. "We'll have to make do with these," I declare ruefully, checking out my Jockey shorts for stains. "My loincloth is long gone. In a reliquary, no doubt, somewhere in Orange County."

"Okay, you're a bloody mess," he laughs, dropping the crayon back in the file drawer.

I duck into my caftan, letting it fall to my ankles. As I turn to face Gray, curtseying slightly so he can tug my wig into place, I can tell he understands now the paradox of my drunken mood, that I am playing tonight for keeps. The fracas outside has merely given the final goose. I'm Merman on the last night of *Gypsy*. Prospero giving his powers away, to be a mortal man again. *Ariel, I free thee.*

"Ouch," says Gray, pricking his finger on my crown. Carefully he places it on my head. "You're a vision," he pronounces wryly, sucking his punctured finger. Then he kneels to do up my sandals.

In the theater Mona has called for attention. Her sob story and plea for funds are second nature by now, but tonight there's the added weight of the First Amendment to defend. Mrs. Beaudry and her Coalition are always a boon to our bank account. Mona lays it on extremely thick, what price freedom and all. They came for the blasphemer and I stood silent and then they came for me. Go, partner.

I gaze down tenderly at the top of my lover's head as he fastens the straps. His beautiful vanishing hair. It all seems unbearably blessed right now. No dying for miles around.

"There—you're all shod." He's up off his knees, an effortless grin, as eager as I to get on with this.

We step from the lamplit office into the theater's shadowed dusk. It's a six-step grope to the corner of the bleachers—I can do it blindfolded. What I *don't* expect is Merle, standing mute as a cigar-store Indian, holding my cross erect. Close up he doesn't look so comfortable, clasping the central implement of the Passion, though I'm sure he's done an ace job on the toggle bolts. Gravely he hands me my toolbox. I've never had a crew before, and I like the feeling. A star's retinue at last.

"Our special guests tonight are from Salva House in Venice," announces Mona McMahon, shamelessly calling the press's attention to our good works. She introduces Sister Kathleen to a scatter of polite applause. "And as for our performer, he needs no further introduction than the reception you got coming in."

They laugh at her droll delivery, but under the laughter there's tension, a collective brace for a pipe bomb through the door.

"But let me add that he's done more for *my* family values than anyone I've ever known. My first real brother." She swallows thickly. Mona honey, please, it's not my memorial service yet. "Ladies and gentlemen, the best of the breed. Won't you welcome the Second Coming. *Miss* Jesus to you."

The plain-chant tape hisses on over the clapping. Gray shifts the cross from Merle onto my shoulder, bending close to murmur in my ear, "When you're done, I'll be right here. You can't miss me. I'll be the one ready for summer."

I can't even turn to blow him a kiss, now that I'm yoked to the cross. Besides, I'm already moving out into the light, on automatic pilot. The applause is enthusiastic from the start, no loxes in evidence. They get the Jeffrey Hunter joke and guffaw when I call my first incarnation a wet dream. They're right in the palm of my hand, almost too easy. I drag my burden upstage and prop it against the platform. They continue to hoot appreciatively as I run through my flouncing warmup. Then I strip off my caftan, and the quiet is swift and palpable.

Not because of the whip marks. It's an extratheatrical response, like Liz Taylor sporting one of her rocks onstage, except in my case it's AIDS. Guiltily, maybe unconsciously, they're scanning my body for lesions. Yet their scrutiny neither bothers nor inhibits me tonight, as I climb on the cross and begin the crucifixion. I use their squeamish sympathy the same way I use Mrs. Beaudry's shocked disgust—to up the ante. And so I proceed to hammer the nails in my hands, groaning with pleasure. This is the part that makes even the liberal Westside vicars cry uncle.

Yet I'm only half-there. Not exactly detached, and certainly giving no less than 100 percent to the show. My carnal writhe on the cross pulls out all the stops. By the time I hit them with "I bet you never realized I liked it," I can hear the strain in their laughter.

But all the while I'm breaking the first rule of acting, drummed into us back at UConn: no picking out friends in the crowd. Foo's in the front row, far left, chin on her owl-headed cane. Kathleen's three rows up in the middle, surrounded by her girls. Gray and Mona stand at either end of the bleachers like sentries. I feel an irresistible desire to break the fourth wall and wave, like a kid in a Christmas pageant.

As the Mormon Choir hallelujahs in the background, I climb from the cross and head downstage for a stand-up riff. Miss Jesus the revisionist, explaining how the whole idea was gay from the start. I reel off the Apostles, enumerating their kinks. Now I'm watching the I-and-A contingent, clustered about the grinning figure of Kathleen. The battered ladies are riveted by my irreverence, too startled to laugh but clearly delighted. I'd still prefer a few ringers from Mrs. Beaudry's flock. There's not enough potential here for outrage. Given my own abstractedness right now, I suppose I'm better off without the rotten tomatoes. It's just that it feels so tame.

"Have you noticed that Catholic men prefer to fuck their daughters rather than their sons?" The I-and-A's are at the edge of their seats. Yes, they've noticed. "Whereas your average *priest* is much more into diddling boys than girls. This is what's called the separation of church and state."

Then I'm off to set the table for the Last Supper, rattling off the particulars of my on-and-off with Judas. It's all there, graphic as ever, down to the smegma on Judas's uncut knob, but the shock's gone. Oh, not for the audience. They're laughing and gasping in all the right places, as I tick off the proper etiquette for serving blood at dinner.

"Fingerbowls are a must. And lemon wedges, to cut that gamma globulin aftertaste."

It's myself I can't shock anymore. The naughty boy has lost the thrill of flashing his dick in church. Though I feel no special overwhelm of regret, I'm glad it didn't happen any sooner, or else there might never have been a Miss Jesus at all. Besides, I didn't require a whole life of being happy. I like it this way, dancing behind the end credits. And it doesn't surprise me that I'm giving a splendid performance tonight, because I'm really acting. It's not life-and-death anymore, the way it used to be.

"God shouldn't date," I declare with a wagging finger I learned from Foo. "Unless it's the Pope, in which case it's infallible. Hail Mary full of dick."

What's next? The Jesus game show. I'm floating from bit to bit, totally painless. I can already see the first barbecue of the summer, out under the pergola. And then suddenly I'm feeling rather chilled. Without skipping a beat about partying at the Vatican, I sidle upstage and scoop my caftan off the floor. I don't usually put it on again because it's so tricky getting my head through the neckhole, my crown like a bristle of antlers. Tonight I have no choice. I'm shivering now.

"We usually do it in the Sistine Chapel." I slip my arms in the sleeves and gape the neck. "All those musclemen on the ceiling. The first Colt video."

My head disappears in the folds of the garment as I ease it over the thorns. I don't know what it is that hits me, but I realize with a jolt that I've forgotten Brian—I mean Aaron. My upper body is shaking with the cold, and the wool is snagged on a thorn. I can't imagine what I look like squirming headless under my tent, but the crowd ripples with laughter anyway, since everything's part of the act. Aaron my brother—where did he go? And what was the bit exactly?

The fabric slips free of the thorn, and my head pops out as the caftan settles on my shoulders. I stare at the tide of faces, no one-liners ready. Am I still freezing? Yes, but the shroud of the caftan hides the shakes.

"If you ever need a carpenter, by the way, you should call my brother Aaron. He's the best in Nazareth."

Do they care that I dropped the Pope story cold? They don't seem to, but then I'm trying *not* to look at my friends now, for fear they might be frowning, as if something's not quite right with me.

"Aaron never believed in me *that* way. I mean, if I'm such a miracle worker, then how come I can't hit a baseball?" I laugh, and it sounds like I'm the only one, a hollow reverberation in the rafters of a pen factory. "I wish he'd come back like I did, so we could go into real estate together. See, I don't have to pay taxes. All you have to do is put a steeple on it, and bingo, you got a money machine."

The last time I did this I saw him so clearly, down to the scruff of the beard and the laborer's massive forearms. Now I have no picture of him at all—except for Brian, who doesn't fit in this story anymore. I'm aware of the silence around me and wonder how many seconds have passed since I dropped the ball. I take a deep breath and try to jump-start.

"He used to say he was an only child, 'cause he couldn't stand all the publicity. I can't say I blame him. Everyone out there wants to be cured of something, and they think the God juice runs in the family."

It's not a chill now. It's a wave of unutterable fatigue. I've been working too hard for days to get everything ready, and now I'm paying. Just at that moment my random gaze happens to fall on Foo. Her goggle eyes behind her glasses are shimmering with tears. It's as if she wants to reach out her cane like a branch to a drowning man. And I feel a flail of longing to take care of them all and reassure them.

"*His* son's the only child," I say, trying to push through the last mile. "Nice kid. Didn't get much from *my* side of the family, except maybe his gorgeous looks. No, seriously—I'm glad he doesn't have all this transcendental baggage. He's just himself. His name is . . . uh . . ."

When do you know you can't do it anymore? When you can't think of one more alias. I flash on Daniel—studying his jigsaw, thrown by the swerve of the pickup, staring at me in terror as I fought the stroke. Even half a continent away, he's more real than anything I can say here. Or else I've come to love reality too much to be making it up.

So I'm standing there unblinking, gaping for all I know. The stillness is unnerving, the hush that follows a head-on crash. They're going to think I've had another stroke. Which makes me look over at Gray, so he won't be scared. But no, his smile is as wide as his shoulders. It seems he's followed my train of thought better than I. The fourth wall shatters soundlessly when he speaks.

"Let's go home."

I almost stagger with relief, nodding like a puppet till I find my voice. "Okay," I reply in a whisper. Then I look at them, sitting so quietly in their rows, hardly daring to breathe. I shrug and lift my brows expectantly, as if to ask is it all right. In a burst they begin to applaud, a paper audience if I ever heard one. But that doesn't mean I don't enjoy the fuss.

I respond with a low bow, as deep as Gielgud, and the tilt causes my crown to tumble to the floor at my feet. A surge of laughter swells their applause, as if the fallen crown is a master stroke of slapstick. Entirely too easy, but of course they mean well. I'm still feeling dead on my feet. I fling out my arms like I did on the bluff, embracing the sea, only this time I'm beckoning Gray and Mona from their sentry posts at the corners. Both of them balk, reluctant to steal my thunder. I make a face at Gray, lolling my tongue as if I'm about to fall over. In two long strides he's beside me, an arm around my shoulders. Mona's quick to buttress the other side.

The audience, loving a theater tableau, gives us a fine extended burst. My arms are draped about their necks, allowing me to sag nicely. Sweat pours down my face, so my sudden fever must have broken. I can see Kathleen beaming as she claps her hands. Foo's stick drums the floor. I raise a limpid hand from Mona's shoulder to call for quiet. They stop applauding instantly, as well behaved as the middle school at Saint Augustine's.

"Now listen carefully," I instruct them in a low voice. They all lean forward, creaking the bleachers. "We're going to slip out that way, me and my boyfriend." I point stage right, to the darkness by the loading dock. "You guys stay right where you are for about five minutes. Keep the laughs going, so they think I'm still out here blaspheming." I hook a thumb at the front entrance, where Mrs. Beaudry's minions wait for the exit crunch. "You got that?"

Dutifully they laugh as one, following orders to the letter, especially the I-and-A girls. For them my leaving is pregnant with drama, like the Trapp Family waltzing off, over the pass to Switzerland. I feel a tug of regret, thinking I've somehow failed them by collapsing in the middle. Did I make any dent at all in the brute scar tissue of their lives? They appear completely satisfied with half a show, as they pick up the ragged end of applause to send me on my way.

"Thanks, baby," says Mona, smearing my cheek with a cherry-red smooch as she stands aside to let us pass.

Gray steers me by the elbow, heading off right, and I feel the old

perversity kick in. Drained as I am and wafted by applause, I'm not
sure I want to go off now. I forgot to tell them never to give up hope.
Would they figure it out on their own, seeing me leave on Gray's
arm? That if I could find it, right in the middle of dying, without
Miss Jesus or even a car, then anyone could.

We're just at the edge of the arc of stage light, by the corner of the
bleachers. If Gray notices any friction of resistance in my exit, he
doesn't show it. I turn and shoot up my hand in a last wave. They
retort with a laugh to cover my tracks. Then we're groping across the
pitch-dark wastes of the loading bay, skirting dusty cartons of novelty
pens. Just ahead, there's a clunk as the back door opens, held by the
mute and stalwart Merle. We slip past him without a word, and the
night air enfolds us, sharp with the tang of ocean.

We step across the platform to the rim of tires. Instinctively we
both look over to the entrance ramp, where a straggle of the
Coalition waits in the blue neon glare, placards propped by the
door. We're in shadow and draw no notice. Gray climbs over
the tires, silent as a Chumash, and eases himself to the pavement.
Then he holds up his hands to lift me down.

I fall toward him and feel him grip my sides, as he sets me down
lightly on earth. At the moment I'm too exhilarated to remember
what my symptoms are. The pickup's only a few cars away, and we
more or less skulk toward it, ducking in on either side. I stay low,
and as soon as Gray's got the engine running, I tuck into my first
position, head on his thigh. I'm still in my Jesus wig, the swirl of
hair in my face coy as Veronica Lake.

As he pulls us in reverse, I look up through the windshield and
see the sliver of moon. Then as he turns in a half circle, the shaggy
tops of the royal palms come into frame. Gray checks the rearview
mirror to make sure no one's following.

"You ready for a little summer?" he asks.

I laugh, rocking in his lap as he hangs a sharp left and makes for
the beach. "Oh yes indeed," I tell him. Home is the place you get
to, not the place you came from. "Haven't I told you? Summer's my
middle name."